Twisted fate

A Twisted Fairy Tale: Book One

by Ace Gray

Cover Design by Bex Harper Designs
Editing by Love N. Books
Formatting by Dee Ellis

For Boner Breath 69. You know what you did.
For Ashley Vigoren. You remind me I'm a badass.
For Denae and Dyllan. You guys inspired me to start writing
again.

Thank you.

ACKNOWLEDGEMENTS

Where to even start with this little set of acknowledgements? I can tell you, not my husband because he doesn't read my books. Fucker. But because he's such a good little fucker, I'll keep him anyway. Dammit! Here I ended up thanking him anyways…for being good in bed no less…shit. I suppose I should thank him for always being there for me, for being a cheerleader, and being tolerant A.F. You rock lover.

Before I got so ridiculously sidetracked, I'd decided to thank my readers first. I mean, I'd be nowhere and nothing without ALL of you guys. And the fact that any of you are taking a chance on this book is, well, humbling. That you guys dealt with my stuffy domineering suit, my sexy soccer stud, my bumbling FBI agent and still want to take a chance on my soulful savage means EVERYTHING to me. You're all my Ladyfaces, and once you read this book (assuming you finish it) you'll know how much those two sentences mean to me.

A few very special readers deserve thanks all their own.

Amanda Owens for being the first person to call me her favorite author. I called her a liar, I still call her a liar, but that someone has said that ever about me, means the world to me.

Morgan Pomphrey…I still can't believe there was a time you carried my books around with you. I hope your back/shoulders are okay. I couldn't hurt someone as special as you.

Sahara Jones please tell your daughter you can stalk me all the time. It's more gratifying and special to me then it is to you. Swearsies.

Cassandra Magnussen for the email blow by blows. I swear that they're the best emails I get all year. I reread them ya know? Any time I want to give up, you save me.

I could keep going—I swear. You guys are all incredible and I consider each of you friends. Legit friends.

Emma. There are no words. I love you. I'm grateful for your patience and cheerleading, your swear words and GIFs, and of course, when you voice message me because it's sexy as hell. Will you read me the Starbucks menu next time?

Bex for always having my back. Your artwork elevates my book. Your friendship elevates my life.

My little Cole club, Mel and Mix, for knowing this book and these characteristics for so long, for being so supportive...I can't even. Would this series even exist without you? I don't think so. I don't even want to think about it. Writing it with you guys there, step by step, made it the best writing experience of my life. You guys kick so much ass it hurts, even across the country.

AM Johnson for being my penguin. 'Nough said.

AllieKat for taking a chance on my book and me time after time.

Denae for loving the characters as much as I do, if not more. And for helping me find my fingertips again.

Dyllan for reminding me of the beauty of fresh eyes and a full heart.

Ellie because I'm afraid not to thank her. And because she's awesome.

Dee Ellis for becoming a great friend. Her talent and willingness to help are beyond imagination.

A Wilding Wells, Stella James, Christine Besze, and M Andrews for being constant inspiration and soul sisters.

Lisa, Mg Herrera, Taylor, Kate, Cheryl, Brenda, Liz, Sallie, MyMy, Abdulia, Ira, Kellie, Jen, Dita, Ginger, Kcee, Teresa, Sanella, Alice, Yvette, Martha, Mell, Shannon, Rennery, Jenny, Ashley, Kamber, Mackenzie, Lozzie, Simmy, Tiffany and Trashy for being the baddest ass ARC team ever. Thank you for taking a chance.

My whole family for always loving unconditionally and teaching me to shoot for the stars.

My "other" friends—aka the ones that don't read my books—you guys are always amazing and while you may never read a page, you always call me an author. You also don't unfriend me on social media for constantly posting porn. THANK YOU!

Last but not least, fucking BB Easton. You're an inspiration. Your books, your words, your unending help, and shit...just the way you live your life. NEVER have I been able to talk to someone I admire so much and feel such genuine care and love reflected back. The spirit animal may have started out as a joke but it is incredibly real now. It would be an honor to follow in your footsteps in any small way. Thank you for taking the time to befriend crazy humans. Thank you for writing beautiful and touching words. Thank you for being light where there's a lot of dark. The tattoo was worth every drop of ink. And of course the blood…

On that note, enjoy…???

Elle

"That's it!" I shrieked, slamming down my iPad, unconcerned with what it did to the seat in front of me. But it wasn't just that particular passenger whose head swiveled to stare at me. With a captive audience, I had to commit despite how out of character making a scene was. "As soon as we're off this godforsaken plane I want a divorce." I bit the inside of my lip to force tears to well in my eyes.

"But what about counseling? We talked about counseling?" Cole tried to calm me, reaching out for my shoulder with his big bear-like hand as I flew up from my seat.

"She's your mother, Cole. Us going to counseling isn't going to fix *your* mother." I made my voice soar a few octaves as I turned toward the bathroom.

I caught the momentary furrow of his brow at the mention of his mother but he fell back into character the moment I stomped off.

"Elle," he called and I *humphed* as I beelined for the bathroom. "Ladyface, wait. Stop. She's a doctor, you know that's the only reason she feels like she needs to know your ovulation schedule."

That bastard.

The telltale sound of seatbacks creaking as he shoved down the aisle after me was the only thing interrupting the normal hum of the airplane. Every set of eyes fell away from us at the airing of our intimate dirty laundry. Even the flight attendants were clearing out of our way with a simple *ma'am* or *sir*.

"It's not because she's a doctor, it's because she wishes you were still attached to her teet," I shouted as I whirled into the bathroom, slamming the door with a flourish. I jumped at the noise I made, surprising myself.

"That's low. You know she suffered from postpartum depression." The barrier did little to muffle his thick honey voice.

"You're twenty-nine Cole!" I kicked the rickety door for emphasis.

The soft tones of flight attendants politely trying to diffuse the situation mingled with Cole's grunts and groans.

"Ladyface." He mellowed a little, cooing as he wrapped his knuckles on the bathroom door. "Ladyface, please. At least talk to me."

"No." I stomped again.

"Elle, let me in there now. We are talking this through, and we're talking this through now. You can't run from me on a motherfucking plane." The moment he swore, he apologized to the people nearest the bathroom I'd locked myself in.

I tried to remember their faces and couldn't. But I could perfectly map the sharp angles of his along with the way tattoos threatened to envelop each ridge. I hadn't been able to think of anything else all day.

"Elle, open this door." Cole's voice had changed again, this time it was a rough, snarly, commanding thing.

My fingers trembled a little as they reached for the lock. I popped it to find Cole waiting with an attendant behind him, peeking in curiously. I thanked my lucky stars anxiety had kept my teeth firmly latched to my cheek.

"Talk to me," he pleaded a little too loudly for the sentiment.

"Fine," I sighed and pulled open the door. It may have been my imagination but the flight attendant standing over Cole's shoulder seemed to nod in encouragement.

2

And why wouldn't she? Cole was a breathtaking man complete with tattooed muscular forearms, and darkly golden hair fashioned into a cut David Beckham probably paid serious money for. He was wearing dark, fitted jeans and a short-sleeve button-up that was a classy accent to the dangerous and drool-worthy ink. Any red-blooded woman would scream *he's a keeper, if only to climb like a jungle gym!*

"You can't leave me," he snarled as he stepped in, latching the door.

"Think they bought it?" I murmured before whining, "I can't stay either. Not like this," at an unnecessary decibel.

"Hook, line and fucking sinker." His whisper was laced with a husky chuckle. "And added benefit, fighting with you has me harder than the stroking before."

I purred and reached across the minuscule distance to his erection, which was in fact, straining almost painfully against the trouser trap of denim.

"Cole, I just can't be married to both of you anymore. She's a succubus."

His hulking frame was made all the larger by the confines of an airplane bathroom. Big, strong hands wrapped around my thighs and rucked my knee up to his hip. He'd helped me dispose of my thong from under my skirt ages ago—*thanks scratchy blue felt blanket*—and he unceremoniously slid into me.

"Fuck, babe." His words were a very real reaction to being inside me and I had to dig my fingers in where I clutched at his biceps to remind him *we're acting you, asshat.* He caught the drift. "How do you want me to respond?" he strangled out as he started thrusting shallow and slow, letting the tip of his delicious dick tease my sex.

"I want you to pick me." My voice wavered at the same time everything in my belly clenched at the idea of him actually picking me.

Cole gasped when he felt it then shoved in fully. I leaned in and bit into his chest to hold in the haggard sounds of pleasure I wanted to let loose.

"I did. I will." His voice was almost agonized.

3

I prayed his voice read tortured in love rather than holding back cum.

"You say that, Cole."

On second thought, I prayed no one was listening anymore at all. Our acting was getting weaker than my quivering knees as he started hammering into me. My ass hit the counter a few times before he fully gripped and lifted me. The way he curled his fingers had one of his tattooed digits pressing against the pucker of my ass.

"I mean it." His barely remembered line reminded me of cheap daytime soap operas.

His finger pushing into me then against his hammering dick reminded me I didn't care. Cole plunged and thrust, alternating his digit with the almost belligerent force of his cock.

"I'm at my wit's end," I yell-moaned.

Fingers crossed more yell than moan.

Cole arched back and looked directly into my eyes; bright, blazing green meeting lucid, icy blue.

"Me too," he strangled out.

His eyes confirmed what we were both implying. He pushed a second finger the tiniest way into my ass and I exploded. When I clenched down on him, his fingers split into a V and he rubbed himself through me. I bit into his shoulder again rather than moan as wild and wanton as I wanted. I felt his orgasm hit inside me, my body jerked with each little assault. I bit harder into his flesh.

The moment he could manage he added loudly, "I guess that's it then."

"Yeah, I guess so," I gasped a little more wildly than him.

Cole smirked as he set me back down gently to the floor, a deep and delicious dimple carving into his cheek. "That was fucking unbelievable," he whispered as he pulled out. The heat of his cum dripped down onto my inner thigh. As best as he could, he folded in the small space, bending down and grabbing a paper towel.

"Don't." I batted at his hand. "It's a souvenir."

"God, I think I may be in love with you." Desire shot through his beaming eyes and made his shoulders shudder.

"Good. People need to think as much for the next thirty to forty-five minutes. They think we're married remember?" I arched an eyebrow as I splashed some water on my face, purposely making tear tracks I could wipe off in the aisle.

A knock at the door made me jump but Cole was calm and collected as he swept his eyes over me. As soon as my dress dropped down to my ankles, he popped open the door.

"Sir, Miss, everything okay in here?" The flight attendant's stern face faltered when she took us in.

"No. She's fucking leaving me," Cole snarled and whipped past her.

"I...I thought...it sounded like...I'm so sorry," she stammered.

Clearly, we'd been as loud as I feared and only recovered at the last minute by miraculously looking like we'd ruined something deep inside each other rather than just wrecking everything between my thighs.

"It's been a long time coming." I bit my lip, pretending a quiver hung on it rather than a Cheshire Cat grin. "I'm just sorry that it came to a head here." I added volume to the second part, hoping it sufficed as an apology to the cabin.

"We're a completely full flight, I can't reassign your seat, but perhaps I can coordinate a swap," she added kindly.

"No. That won't be necessary. The damage is done. The drama has passed. Thank you though."

I pushed past her to my vacant seat next to a huffing Cole. He snuck me a devastating wink before I plopped next to him. As soon as I did, he grazed his knuckle along my thigh. The one that had a cat on it. I remembered the animal vividly from when he drummed his hand on the folding tray—I'd pictured his pussy deep inside mine. The finger along with the newly minted memory made me smile, and once again, I found myself biting too hard on the inside of my cheek.

Perfectly timed tears welled in the corner of my eyes as the flight attendant took it upon herself to bring me a tiny bottle of

Jameson. I nodded, doing my best to look choked up rather than fantasizing about choking on Cole's cock. She handed him a similar bottle then turned.

"Ice?" he questioned under his breath.

I shook my head and tipped my bottle to stealthily cheers his, unscrewing it and putting it back with a simple unhinge of the throat. I swallowed hard and made the sour face that always accompanied a shot but then let out a deep and satisfied sigh. I turned to Cole, hoping to sneak a small smile in his direction. Instead, I found him watching me wide-eyed as if he'd never seen a woman shoot whiskey before.

"Should see me with cum," I mouthed the words more than anything but he caught my drift, his whole face changing.

Heat radiated back at me, his eyes like the blistering ripples that wave up from the pavement, his muscles taut like he might pounce. I crossed my legs trying to suppress the arousal quickly spreading between my thighs and Cole's eyes darted down to watch. His gaze was the sun filtered through a magnifying glass, and at any moment I might explode into flame. When I pressed harder and both the sticky and scratchy patches of Cole spread across my thighs, my blush bloomed across my cheeks, a fire all its own.

He cleared his throat, pulling my eyes back to his. When we locked on each other again, he unscrewed his lid, shoved his tongue out and made a clover looking shape. He poured part of the tiny bottle into the well he'd created, pulled his tongue in and swallowed. The rose colored heat spread down my neck and wove like vines along my collarbone. He stuck his tongue back out, making a simple circular tube. Without another flourish, he poured the rest of the bottle down the makeshift straw.

Cole let a smug smile spread across his lips when he'd gulped the whiskey down. He didn't need to mouth, *no, you should see me with your clit.*

"Ladies and gentlemen, this is your captain speaking. We have begun our final descent to the Chicago area. Please make sure your tray tables are locked and your seatback is in the full upright

6

position..." The captain continued his automated spiel, breaking the spell that had held Cole and me captive.

I looked away first and kept my eyes downcast for the rest of the flight.

When we shuffled out, the flight attendants each gripped my shoulder, undoubtedly hoping to show support. Only a small part of me felt bad for deceiving everyone. The rest of me wanted a pat on the back for having my way with a gorgeous stranger in the bathroom.

And yes, big, beautiful, art-covered, five o'clock shadowed Cole was still a stranger to me. I'd approached him on a whim in the terminal then we'd spent a flight rubbing on each other, teasing and tormenting each other. I hadn't even seen underneath his shirt. He was *supposed* to stay that way.

So I kept walking. Up the gangway, out through the gate, down the terminal then toward the exit. Each step created delicious friction below my waist and reminded me there was still signs of what we'd done coating my skin. It made my internal temperature sky rocket.

And become desperate for an orgasm.

I tucked into the bathroom, fully intending to rub one out while I pictured his cat tattoo inside me all over again when I noticed a cocktail napkin shoved into my purse. As I smoothed the crinkles, big bold letters bled across the flimsy white paper.

Send me a souvenir
-Cole
970-215-5586

I swallowed hard as I stared at his request. Of course I knew what he was asking. I'd used the word after all.

For a moment, I considered balling up the napkin and chalking the whole thing up to a one-time sex checklist item. I mean, a man like that was absolutely zero good in real life. Right? But then I pictured him gulping whiskey out of an impossible to make with your tongue shape and decided good things come in bad and beastly packages and slipped into a stall with my phone at the ready.

When I pulled up my skirt, little crystalline patches ran like the Nile Delta across my skin. The moment he came flashed vividly back to mind. My finger was reaching toward the slick folds of my sex before I even gave it full thought. The second I laid the pad of my finger to the tiny nub of nerves my body twitched and jerked. An orgasm was waiting just around the corner for me courtesy of Cole No-Last-Name-But-Hulking-Shoulders.

I flipped the camera to video and positioned myself so the screen was filled with cum covered flesh, hiked up skirt and a glistening, slick sex. One finger pressed the big red circle on my phone while the other pressed on a *very* different button.

My hips bucked up into my hand and I had to keep my feet from sliding out into another stall. I couldn't help but watch as my most intimate bits tightened, twitched and trembled. Two of my fingers dipped inside me, following their far too familiar path and crooked up into my G-spot.

Cole wouldn't be able to see but my head rolled back against the wall and shook side to side. When my eyes fluttered shut it was all him, my fingers weren't mine anymore. He stroked me. He teased me, circled me, caressed me and swirled around in the arousal thick between my legs.

It took me almost no time to come, though I almost bit off my tongue trying not to shriek, and even less time to send the video via message along with the text:

you did this to me.

Almost immediately the telltale three dots appeared in response. But then just as quickly, they vanished. I gulped hard on the lump in my throat, feeling regret seep into my pores. A stranger had a video of me orgasming and he didn't even appreciate it. Or worse, didn't want it. There could even be a girl threading her hand into his that still had me all over them.

Fuck, fuck, fuck.

What had I done? Not only sending the video but on the plane. I'd spread my legs like it was some pervy game of Getting

8

To Know You. Like it was no big deal. Like I did that, did guys casually, on the regular. Where was my dignity? Where were my walls? Why hadn't they contained me? My skin flushed to rosy pink.

But then the dots picked back up.

```
I'm turning the car around. meet me in arrivals.
I haven't kissed you yet. this isn't remotely
over…
```

Cole

I'd almost wrecked my fucking car when that message popped up.
Good Christ.

I was going to send that smug smile emoji in response to Elle's perfect pussy shot but then the pic started moving. She'd gone and sent me a video. It took me all of ten seconds to turn around after watching, cutting in front of cars and listening to blaring horns as I made sure I could circle back. Wherever Elle was, her pussy was still coated with *me*. I needed that wherever she inhabited to be significantly closer to my face. I wanted to bury myself underneath that skirt.

The first time I'd said her name, it tasted good on my tongue. And now I couldn't stop imagining tasting her. Every goddamned inch of her. With any luck, she'd have that hint of sweetness.

All the best pussies reminded me of French fries dunked in milkshakes; sharp salt assaulting the tongue first, then a perfect hint of sweetness weaving underneath to drip down my throat. I lived for the moment I found out if a woman was vanilla or chocolate, strawberry or peach.

I caught my reflection in the rearview mirror and a bolt of inspiration struck. Elle had propositioned me for sex shortly after I sat next to her in the Seattle terminal. I'd gravitated toward her small figure topped with beautiful breasts and sunshine locks, then she'd just asked, *wanna join the mile high club?* If that was her

10

game, why couldn't I play a little too? My smile grew and my dimple deepened where it showed in the mirror.

Elle was easy to spot on the curb despite the thick rope of cars between us. My eyes found the spot of glowing gold as if they already knew where to look. She couldn't stand still and her eyes darted from side to side searching, but they never settled. Her knees knocked together, then shimmied, drawing her thighs even closer together.

Her cum covered thighs.

From my vantage point, I watched as she bit her lip, threw her head back and shuddered. She was hypnotic.

I couldn't help but rev my engine, letting the loud, throaty snarl of my vintage Dodge Charger startle the people lined along the curb. Almost all of them jumped, including Elle, and my smile tugged all the wider on my cheek.

Even after the other eyes fell away, Elle's raked over the car. My tint was dark enough she couldn't see me, but she was still appreciating the machine. A girl devouring my car was almost as tempting as a girl devouring me. The things I wanted to do to her…

I shook my head and maneuvered my hot-rod to the curb, smoothly pulling up in front of her. When I glanced over, I swore I saw the lines of her fuck-hot body through the slightly transparent white cotton dress I'd shoved up around her hips just an hour or two ago. She was small with dangerous curves, delicate but the way she'd knocked against the bathroom sink while I fucked her told me she was strong, too. I blew out a deep breath as I pushed the button to lower the window.

"Wanna ride?" I asked as I leaned over and quirked my eyebrow up.

Elle's eyes lit up, twinkling in the same way they'd done when I told her we got away with it. She bit that full bottom lip of hers and I inwardly kicked my ass for not sucking on it earlier. My dick agreed, twitching against my fly.

"I don't bite…hard." I intentionally loaded sex into the sound of my voice.

11

Her head rolled back and her body automatically arched toward me. The graceful curves of her neck lengthened, accentuating the hollows above her collarbones. I couldn't help but picture the ink coating the back of my hand wrapped around the pale creamy skin of her throat. My hands flexed inadvertently at the fantasy of choking her just enough that she gasped for air while I climaxed.

Before I came from daydreaming alone, I popped the trunk. Her breathing hitched up at the sound but she otherwise stayed frozen. I was half tempted to get out of the car and kidnap her like a savage caveman when she snapped to, swiftly grabbing her suitcase and easily hauling it into the trunk. I watched as her chest jiggled in the mirror when she slammed the door.

Fuck. Yes.

The moment she whipped open the passenger door, I shoved my hand across the seat to keep her from sliding in.

"Elle, see that lever there on the side, near the bottom?" I gestured as I asked.

"Yeah…"

Goddamn her voice was like caramel, warm, sweet, rich and sultry as hell. I shifted in my seat, hoping to alleviate a little of the pressure on my now raging hard-on.

"Flip it."

She followed my command without hesitating and the seat jutted forward. I reached across and pulled, helping to slide it forward.

"What the…?" Her voice had a sexy rasp as she trailed off, her eyes shifting from me to the backseat.

"You gave me an idea. Get in before I get in trouble for idling." I jerked my chin toward the backseat.

Her beautiful brow furrowed but she squared her shoulders and slid in. I shoved the seat into place, locking her in, and revved the engine as I pulled away. She gasped when the car snarled and vibrated beneath us. I couldn't help my husky chuckle or that I revved the engine all over again.

"I liked the video, Elle. A lot." I caught her eye in the rearview mirror.

12

"Oh yeah?" She arched her eyebrow and a small but proud smile crept across her face.

"I want to watch in person this time."

She shivered and my balls tightened automatically. How I was going to deal with my near painful erection, I had no idea, but if she said yes, I'd figure it the fuck out.

She blew out a deep breath. "Like now?"

I reached up, grabbed the rearview mirror and angled it down. The fold of her hips was perfectly framed by the thin black line circling the mirror. I gunned the car for the third time and watched a little too enrapt as she pressed her knees together in response.

"Now would be fantastic," I practically growled at her.

Elle didn't need more convincing. She bent down as best she could in the tiny space, her long locks brushing my forearm, and making it my turn to shudder. Thank God only a heartbeat passed before she sat up, bringing her skirt with her.

I should have been prepared for the sight but I wasn't. At all. The car swerved and horns wailed in the next lane when her dripping slit appeared in my mirror. I stared unabashedly at my jizz where it mixed with her wetness and only blindly tried to right the car.

"You've been inside it, Cole. If you wanna get near it again, I'd suggest not wrecking the car." Elle gracefully rounded down to meet my gaze in the downcast mirror.

I nodded quickly, my eyes still wide and my mouth still slack, as she sat back up. She artfully draped herself across the upholstery of the bench seat and her head rolled back, putting her throat on display again. The same filthy vision of choking her flew through my mind and my hand clenched the wheel so hard my tattoos speckled.

But then her gentle gyrations started and I was instantly snapped back to the action in my backseat. Her fingers danced on her clit and any thoughts besides *watch* and *don't die* left my mind. My eyes flitted more frequently between the road and her reflection as she circled herself. She was tracing her slit, stopping only to rub smaller circles at the apex of her thighs. Her hips

13

themselves started rocking in tiny circles in time with her hand. If I'd thought she was hypnotic before, watching her tease herself was absolutely bewitching.

I didn't know if she was watching me watch or surrendering fully to her long, dainty fingers. Honestly, I didn't fucking care. When I looked away for a split second to check the dotted lines of the Kennedy Expressway, she groaned.

If her voice was caramel then her groan was the rest of the sundae—ice cream, chocolate, whipped cream, jimmies—and damn did she have my nuts in a twist. It was guttural and unashamed while still being her sticky sweet tone. My gaze automatically snapped back to her.

Elle had pushed her finger inside, slick skin now swallowed it almost whole.

My breathing hitched up when she left it there and let it swirl. A horn blared beside us and I barely looked to see if it was directed at me. She started thrusting, swiveling her hips to meet her hand as she slowly dragged her finger out then curved it back up in. In and out, in and out, in and out. Over and over and over.

Shallow, ragged breaths pulled far too much air into my throat and my lips started to crack. I tried to wet them but my tongue wasn't much better. Elle had me panting like I was a dog in heat.

She groaned again, this time her voice was strangled, breathy, like she was already close to orgasm. I took a good look at the cars surrounding us and the lane in front of me. There was space. I let the Charger snarl and as I shot off, my eyes fixed on the mirror.

Just as I hoped Elle reacted to the car. Wildly. She planted her feet on the floor, the backseat so small she was probably wedged under the seats, and shoved her hips up to full on grind her hand. Her groans shifted into nonsensical whimpers.

Even when I slowed the car, she kept her hips up. I could tell she was crooking her fingers up to stroke her G-spot.

"Good God, Ladyface. I'm so hard it hurts." My voice was a reflection of her pained whining.

"Do you want me to come?"

14

"You're asking?"

She was giving me the chance to deny her. Or make her wait. My dick twitched painfully hard at the idea. I'd been oh-so-right when I said we weren't remotely finished. She'd let me control her the way I wanted, she'd let me take from her in all the ways I pleased.

"Cole." Elle made the O of my name so long and agonized, every single muscle in my stomach tightened.

"Yes, Ladyface. Come. Come hard and fast. But for the love of God come now."

Her hips were still up off the seat. One or both of us should have been worried about someone else seeing but in reality, we were both too fixated on the crashing wave of orgasm about to splash over and consume Elle. Her legs bunched, highlighting toned thighs and hinting at a plump little ass. Every inch of her started to quiver.

I barely remembered to check traffic and looked out just in time to see stopped cars in front of us. I swerved as I slammed on the brakes, but it wasn't enough. I pulled the steering wheel and headed for the off ramp I was lucky enough to be near, all to the sound of furious horns.

None of it fazed Elle. Her shoulders slid across the seat making her look even more frantic, but she just continued fondling in, out, and around her sex. The way she worked her body reminded me of an artist laying paint to canvas in wide strokes, small detail, large splatters, beautiful and wild.

After I was done, she'd be some sexual Jackson Polluck.

I slowed at a stoplight letting the car rumble beneath us. I felt each and every shake in my bones, and double in my now-throbbing cock; it threatened to unhinge me. If the vibrations were this painful to me, I completely understood why Elle had shoved herself up off the leather and into a makeshift bridge. My hips shuffled, instinctually drawn to hers. I hit the steering wheel instead and howled when I did. My sounds mixed in with hers, so animalistic, so hot, that I didn't care if I'd bruised my dick.

My eyes snapped to the mirror in time to catch Elle's quivering spread like wildfire and envelope her body head to toe.

Every muscle trembled, her hips raised and lowered with no rhyme or reason. A small foggy patch appeared on the glass above her lips.

A horn blared, another chimed in, then two more followed from further back, all in rapid succession. The sound tangled up with Elle's mewling cries. I didn't give a fuck. I sat at the green light, relishing the gift of sight as I watched every inch between her thighs start to clench and release.

Her orgasm was infinitely better in person.

I could get the finger from every driver on the ramp, a ticket for obstructing traffic, even a massive dent in my fender, but nothing was going to stop me from watching the way her pussy grabbed onto her fingers and pulled them in deep. Or from imagining that magic little slit was milking on my dick rather than her fingers.

Elle came crashing back to earth and my upholstery right when the light flipped red. Her hand fell away from her body leaving an unobstructed view of her perfect pussy that had gotten even prettier. It was now a lovely shade of dark pink glistening in the last bit of daylight and swollen where it was framed by the untamed folds of her skirt. Every inch of her frame shook with labored breathing and her hair was a tangled nest of just-fucked waves.

And it was that panting, wrecked woman in the backseat that did me in.

The second the light turned green again, I slammed the car into gear and spun out around the corner. I found a space on the side of the road and all but drifted my car into it, letting the machine screech and squeal as it pleased. I slammed the stick shift into neutral and yanked on the emergency brake. My fingers fumbled with the seatbelt but only for the briefest moment. The second it was off, I turned and lunged at her. My body barely fit between the seats but I managed. I would have torn the interior to pieces if it meant getting to her at that point anyway.

My hands wrapped around her thighs, my tattoos stark against her pale skin just as I'd imagined. I dug my fingers in and yanked her down the seat toward me.

16

Every bit of me was shouting *taste her*. My tongue wanted to play all its tricks to make her drip. I licked my lips at the thought. Elle's hooded, fuzzy gaze was locked on my mouth and my smile crooked up automatically in response, my dimple hollowed my cheek. She tried to press her legs together but I kept them wide.

"I told you I wanted to kiss you," I rasped and Elle squirmed beneath me. "And I know you fucking want me to."

She tried to arch her neck up to meet me, sneaking a squeeze of her thighs inward as she went. My smirk broke into a full-blown smile as I eagerly moved to meet her. At the last minute, though, I redirected and planted my lips on her overly sensitive clit.

A pained cry filled my ears as my tongue wove in all its best ways against her. I made a point to make out with her pussy before my slow and steady thrusting. And when she dripped, I couldn't pay attention to the sound anymore, my other senses were far too enrapt.

Elle tasted like cherries. Fucking perfect cherries.

Elle

"Cole, Cole, ColeColeColeCole..." I screeched in time with the devilish laps of his tongue.

My body shuddered like I was living through the shifting of continents. The fact that the godforsaken engine was still rumbling beneath me made my teeth chatter. Or was that the orgasm I was about to have?

Because I was headed for the most spectacular orgasm of my life. I couldn't decide if each touch was a firework, a bright and beautiful star or the swirling insides of a comet itself.

I blindly patted around to find his hands where they dug into my thighs. My fingers curled into his and encouraged him to dig in even harder. Warm puffs of air from a barely-there laugh tickled between my thighs and my hips twerked all on their own. Cole laughed louder.

"Cole, please. Please let me come," I begged.

He wrapped his tongue around my clit and by some miracle of mouth muscles rolled it along the tiny bud of nerves.

"Fuck. Please!" I dug my nails into his hands where I held them.

"That makes me so hard it hurts, Elle." Cole sat back as he said it, that painfully attractive smirk pulling across his face. In the dying afternoon light, his face glistened with my arousal.

I groaned then added a ragged whisper, "Please."

Wordlessly he shook my hand free of his big palm. My arm crashed gracelessly back into the leather of the backseat.

"I got you, Ladyface."

He balled his hand except for one finger. The cat tattoo on his middle finger was left on full display. His mischievous dimple hollowed out his cheek just before he pressed his finger into his mouth. Just a second later, he pulled it out, every bit as shiny as his cheeks. Cole disappeared back between my thighs and his wet finger slid into me just a moment before his mouth was back on my clit.

His pussy danced inside mine, teasing me, tormenting me as he petted every inch inside. I digressed into nonsensical whimpers when his tongue folded on me. His finger found my G-spot and roughly pressed.

In less than a minute, my world shattered. I screamed a guttural, banshee sound that I didn't recognize as my own. Waves rolled through my body and broke along his finger. His tongue didn't stop its stupid, wonderful, insane, heavenly dance. I couldn't help but watch him, slack-jawed.

Bright green eyes bored into mine, leaving me exposed even when I tried to shutter myself up. The quiet slurping and delightful lapping between my legs slowed on the heels of the most spectacular orgasm I'd ever had. The intense engine threatened to unhinge my bones and scatter me across Cole's backseat.

"Elle," he growled, "do you like milkshakes?"

I couldn't help but crinkle my nose at the unexpected question. "Yeah, but only cherry. Why?" I managed between deep, haggard breaths.

Cole burst out laughing. His real laugh was brash and boomed through the car, equal parts joyous and sinful. I wanted to squeeze my legs together at the sound but his fingers were still clawing into my skin.

"Cherry?" His answering smile threatened to split his face, and if it were possible, I would have fallen into the deep well his left cheek was sporting.

"Yeah. Why?" I wiggled against his grip, hoping to sit up a little straighter and salvage what may be left of my dignity.

Cole just laughed all the louder as he let go of me and twisted to slide back into the driver's seat. He took a moment to adjust the rearview mirror before answering. "You taste like a cherry milkshake." He leaned across the seat and popped the front seat forward before looking up at me from under long eyelashes. "And cherry is my favorite."

Was every sentence out of his mouth sexier than the last?

"Get up here." He jerked his chin toward the front and I couldn't help but press my legs together again.

I shoved my skirt down then slid over to the door. As soon as I popped out, Cole shoved the seat back into place and patted the leather waiting for me. I sat and pulled the door shut, leaving only the rumble of the car to fill the small space between us.

The Chicago skyline pierced the faded blue hombre of Cole's windshield, I blew out a deep breath that rustled the golden waves hanging in my face. Out of habit, I shoved my hands through my hair then sagged back into the seat. Chicago always meant trouble.

"You all right, Ladyface?" Cole slid his hand behind my neck and started massaging with the same strong fingers that had their way with me moments later. I groaned and let my eyes flutter shut.

"The orgasms make things better." I let out a giant sigh. I couldn't help it. His fingers skated up and down, alternating gentle touches and strong, soothing strokes.

"You wanna talk about it?"

"Cole, you don't even know my last name. You definitely don't want to know the darker things." I shrugged off the gray cloud and twisted to look at the gorgeous man filling up the driver's seat.

"You're right. But I know every single fold of your pussy, so that's gotta count for something."

I couldn't help but smile, and smiles were pretty rare as of late. Cole's rough touch made it so the world didn't seem so dark. With another deep breath, I let my eyes flutter shut as I gathered the strength to say the words I hadn't been able to muster yet. The words that had sent me into his arms for the most reckless sex of my life in the first place. Then the three orgasms after that, too.

"I'm in Chicago for my mother's funeral."

I wanted to reel the words back in as soon as I spit them out. Most people had looked at me with pity when I managed to relay that my mother passed away. Their hollow faces and bleary eyes had twisted me up. Particularly because they made those innocent bystanders seem more upset than I was. Pity was slowly gutting me. Pity for a woman that didn't deserve it and a daughter that didn't love her anyway.

But, Cole? *He* was the last person I wanted to look at me like that. I wanted him to continue to look at me like he might eat me. I didn't want to see how sympathy hung on his face.

His fingers clutched into my neck every bit as hard as he'd held my thighs. For a moment I thought he was trying to coax my eyes open but just a heartbeat later, he pulled on me and smashed his lips to mine. A spark jolted me the moment his perfect pout found mine. I gasped but I didn't get to pull away. Cole held me too tightly. So tightly that his fingertips almost hurt the back of my neck. Almost.

My lips tingled and they threatened to lose all feeling. I was disoriented. I only managed to keep my lips moving by a slight miracle or magic.

Cole used his grip to keep me pinned while his mouth proceeded to consume mine. If he'd been tenacious in his assault on my clit, then the way he kissed me qualified as unrelenting. Lips that were soft but firm, warm and just the slightest bit rough worked against me. Cole tasted like me, a little salty and a little sweet but it mixed with his flavor. Ink, fresh spice and sex hung on his skin and danced on my tongue.

The devilish tongue I'd been so drawn to on the plane had its way caressing my lips then plunged into my mouth and tangled every bit as skillfully with mine. He swallowed my breaths every time I tried to gasp for air. Every single one of my moves was matched then answered tenfold. Cole kissed the way he fucked, aggressively and as if he might actually want to break me. For good.

My hands shot to his hair and started grabbing, pulling, all of their own accord. He snarled against my lips and his grip on my neck shifted. His other hand wrapped around my throat and the harder he kissed me, the harder he squeezed. As if his kisses themselves hadn't left me breathless enough, now he was actually choking me.

I gasped but I couldn't force much air into my lungs. My heart started thundering, my lips went dry. Cole kept right on kissing me, devouring me. Every single inch of me throbbed, begging for air, begging for release. My hands dropped from his body and landed limply at my sides. I whimpered into his ravenous mouth but it turned into an unladylike gag. The edges of my vision blurred.

Then Cole's hands abruptly fell away and he sat back.

My vision came barreling back and I caught him panting raggedly as he fell back into the driver's seat. The rush of air into my lungs set a euphoric honeyed feeling shooting through my veins, almost like I'd orgasmed all over again. My heart pumped all the harder, shaking my chest, and I wasn't sure it would beat right ever again. My fingers trembled ever so slightly.

"You choked me," I managed between haggard breaths.

"Yeah, I did." He closed his eyes and smiled brightly as he leaned back against the headrest. "Usually I ask first. Glad you loved it."

"Did not."

"Elle, are you thinking about anything but me? Anything besides sex, orgasms or how your pussy is dripping onto my upholstery?"

My mouth flopped open, ready to argue, ready to scold— he'd cut off my air after all—but the truth was he *was* all I could think of. Since he'd chosen to sit next to me in the terminal, I hadn't been able to think of anything else. And if I were being honest, I was eternally grateful I'd followed through.

I scoffed, mostly at myself and how I'd been thinking with my clit and nothing else for the past eight hours.

"I'll take that as a *no, Cole. I can't think of anything but your dick.*" He mocked me but it was such an exaggerated goofy tone, I simply reached out to smack his shoulder.

At that, he burst out laughing and I couldn't help but follow suit.

22

"For the record, I just wanted to make things better." He reached over and squeezed my thigh. "I wanted that frown that turned your lips to go away."

"You don't even know me."

"Is that a big thing for you, Ladyface? You said that before, like you expected me to be a dick with a giant cock and nothing more."

"Giant cock, eh?"

"Tell me you weren't impressed." He smirked but it wasn't as mischievous as before. He was being soft with me but somehow knew I didn't need sympathy.

"Eh," I laughed breathily, "we'll see if I choke on you or not before I answer."

"Deal."

We both sat for a minute, the car was silent besides the rumble of the engine. I was lost in my thoughts. These past few hours with Cole were good. I felt *normal*. No, better than normal. I felt free.

"I'm sorry about your mom." Cole's voice was simple and soft rather than sorrowful.

"Don't be," I said far too quietly as my eyes fell to my hands. He could judge me for that all he wanted but if he knew everything, if he could even fathom, he'd understand. "And thank you."

"For choking you? You're more than welcome." He laughed a gentle, charming laugh.

"God, it makes me sound like a freak but yeah, thanks for choking me. And the orgasms. For letting me drip all over your car." I rolled my eyes but I meant it.

"Believe me when I say it was my pleasure."

He reached over and notched a single knuckle beneath my chin. Gently he coaxed me over to kiss him. This time he was so tender it was like he was afraid I'd turn to glass and break.

"So where can I take you?" He all but whispered against my lips.

His green eyes bore into me the same way they had when they'd been framed by my thighs. The way that took my breath away.

"Hotel…" I finally managed the solitary word. "I have one. My stepfather and I aren't speaking. We haven't been for years. He's… Well we're…" All the shit that followed my mom and that dirtbag started piling up inside me, crushing my words in my chest.

His thumb came up and trapped my lips. As soon as I stopped speaking, he let the pad of his finger explore my pout.

"So you're free to have dinner at my place," he said matter of fact, like he'd known all along.

"Yeah, I guess I am. What are we having?" I smiled and all my tension melted as I pictured staying seated next to him. Then writhing underneath.

"I'm thinking ramen for me." His wicked smirk and the adorable dimple were back. My lips parted and a small little gasp slipped free as I inadvertently imagined licking it.

"And for me?" My words were breathy and I had a feeling I already knew what he was going to say.

"You'll have cock, of course."

Cole

I stared up at the ceiling but I didn't see the plaster. I saw Elle. Or remembered Elle and the way she had sucked my cock like a pornstar an hour ago. On the plane she'd joked about what she could do with cum but now I knew this girl could put blow jobs on a resume.

I'd gotten takeout at the place around the corner while Elle made sure I didn't get a ticket for loitering. As a thank you for sweet talking the cop who came by, I picked up special champagne and red velvet cake from the bakery across the street. I had every intention of eating when we got in but Elle had taken it upon herself to strip.

My jaw almost hit the floor when she stood in nothing but woven wedges and a white lacy bra. Her skin was even creamier than I imagined. Her golden locks hung to frame her tits. I couldn't help but slowly look her up and down. Twice.

"Fuck," I swore under my breath.

She bit her lip and her hands fluttered to cover up.

"No." I jogged across my loft to her. "Fuck no. You're gorgeous, Ladyface. You make me hard." I took the hand that was trying to shield her pussy from me and pressed it roughly to my dick.

The corners of her smile pulled up even though she was still biting her lip. She flexed her fingers into me and damn it if I didn't shove my hips to meet her. Her hand folded around me as if it was built to cocoon me. The little bird used her grip to pull me to my bed. I was gladly going to follow her down but she stopped me with a single finger.

I would play the memory of Elle lying out before me like a buffet over and over in my head until I died. She spread her legs then dug her heels into my mattress just before she laid back and let her head hang off the edge closest to me. Her hands worked, perfectly talented, at my belt and she yanked my pants far enough down that my thigh tattoos framed her slight face. She didn't even give me a minute to process the view before she pulled my dick into her mouth.

And groaned.

Her throat vibrated around me and my whole body trembled, my teeth even chattered against themselves. Elle steadied me by wrapping her hands up and around then digging her fingers into my ass. She drove me into her throat repeatedly and unrelentingly.

"Fucking shit." I couldn't close my eyes, I couldn't take my eyes off her throat.

God that throat...

Once or twice I almost took over, my fingers itched to, but Elle sucked me so perfectly I made myself stand back and enjoy the ride. She was fucking her own throat and mercifully using my cock to do it. Her body rolled up with a rhythm all it's own. Her legs jolted and twisted every time she gagged. I might have gotten off watching that.

But then she held me in deep. And rippled along my shaft. She was choking but she wasn't fighting to get free. The outline of my dick was obvious in her throat. Her legs clamored and her heels were tangling in my sheets. Gagging, quaking tits, wheeling legs were hypnotic. The sensation of her mouth was incredible. Her puffs of breath on my balls made them tighten. But then *she* came, arousal splashing across her thighs and onto my sheets.

I'd been lucky I hadn't lost my mind.

Now soft sounds of her breathing next to me, and warm skin wrapped around me, only enriched the memory.

I could vividly remember taking over by ripping off my shirt and brutally fucking her mouth. I'd even brought my hand

26

down on her throat and squeezed. She'd almost bucked right off the bed. But she'd kept clinging to my hips, pulling me in over and over and over and over…

My dick twitched against the sheets at the memory.

Then a slight finger matched the whisper touch of the fabric across my chest. Elle's small pastel pink nail traced the dark lines of my chest tattoo. Warmth spread from where she outlined the flowers covering my pec. Her feather light touch was something new, nothing like cum covered thighs, choking or dick outlines but with her I *liked* it. Really liked it. And I didn't want her to stop.

She was barely touching me but I could feel it deep in my bones. It was an intimacy I never felt, I wouldn't let anyone close enough to.

I tilted my head so I could watch her and she sensed the purposeful flex of my muscles. She sucked in an audible breath and her finger froze, hovering just above my skin.

"I didn't mean to wake you," she whispered.

"I was awake. There's no reason to stop. I liked it." I was equally quiet as I grabbed a fistful of her hair and pulled so she'd look up at me. "Why aren't you sleeping, Ladyface?"

"Haven't lately." There was something swirling behind her big blue doe eyes but I couldn't tell what. It seemed to sit somewhere between regret and fury. I loosened my hold and her finger found its way back to my body to skate across the panther on my abdomen.

I used the arm that had been wrapped around her to tuck her closer to me. I twisted to kiss her forehead, hoping it would melt some of her pent up emotion. She sighed a warm, breathy sigh that pulled on my heartstrings every bit as badly as it made my dick twitch.

"Never been much of a sleeper myself," I said as I watched her finger, transfixed.

"Busy rattling headboards?"

I couldn't help but laugh. Elle said it so differently than other women. She wasn't accusatory or digging for dirt, she was just asking. Her finger didn't waver, nor did she pull away from me.

27

So I was honest. "Lately? A little." I couldn't help but chuckle at some of my more idiotic exploits. One of which was definitely Elle. But I couldn't regret any of them, particularly her. Nor could I shut my mouth; my secrets just spilled out. "But that's not what I meant. I grew up on the streets. I've always had one eye open."

The shadow of my past flew into the room on soft wings and rustled up my insides. Elle noticed the change and her head snapped up as her hand flattened on my stomach. My muscles hollowed out and I automatically arched to meet her gaze.

"Is this the part where you tell me your deep dark secrets?" She was staring up at me, worry plain on her face as her fingertips dug into me.

"No, Ladyface. They're buried deep for a reason." I tangled my feet into hers. "But my past? That's easy. My parents sucked, and I left. I started stealing cars and getting ink. I liked the tattoos, I loved art. I apprenticed while I paid my dues to the mean streets of this city. It took a while but I have my own shop now."

Her fingers started back in on the outlines of the designs. This time, four dainty fingers all followed along, sweeping across my skin.

"That's what you do? You're a tattoo artist?" She leaned up on her elbow to look at my artwork, her hair cascaded around her shoulders and danced on my abs. They flexed involuntarily beneath the whisper touch.

"Yeah, but those aren't my work." I nodded toward the tracks she was still making.

"Oh, right." Her warm little giggle tightened everything below my belly button and I reached out for her. Elle folded onto my chest, her chin resting right on the nose of my panther and her bright eyes studying me. "Did you ever practice on yourself?"

I held my hand up and showed her the back of my palm. "A lot of these." I couldn't help but shake my head at myself.

"Like the cat?" She giggled at me and I didn't blame her.

"Yeah, Felix is mine." I laughed and she wiggled on my torso in the faint moonlight.

28

"He has a name?" Elle folded her hands under her chin, still just watching me as we spoke. Her eyes danced and had the faintest twinkle. If it was possible, she was even more irresistible than she'd been before.

"Course. All good pussies have a name. Yours has to be something about cherries."

Her cheeks flushed and she twisted away from me but didn't stray from my side. Something inside me clenched, but this time it wasn't below my belt. Who knew a night lying in bed with Elle was a bigger treat than her sexual exploits?

"What do you do, Elle?"

Deep, stunning eyes twisted back to meet my gaze and she smiled again. "I'm an artist too. I work mostly with metals, etchings, prints and such. I have a few large installations in more modern buildings in Seattle."

"Damn." I knew the type of equipment that required. Elle played with fire, literally. Her almost shy smile split her face but then her stomach rumbled. "Shit, I never fed you."

"Well technically you only promised cock so…"

Her full, bright and unashamed smile spread across her face and for the first time in years, I felt myself falling. I'd maybe been in love once. Maybe. Even then, that relationship was…*different.* And long. Even more complicated. I'd known Elle for all of twelve hours. It couldn't be love, but that didn't stop it from being oddly intense.

She interrupted my thoughts by pushing up off me and walking toward my kitchen. In the loft I could follow her silky, smooth silhouette as she snaked toward the pile of takeout still on the counter. A goofy grin split my face when she lifted up onto her tiptoes to survey the boxes.

Elle snatched something and turned, still on tiptoes. She was holding a singular pink box, the one that held the cake. She sauntered back to bed, letting me appreciate the sway of her hips, then effortlessly sat cross-legged next to me. I shifted up, letting the sheet fall from me as I hugged my knees, more interested in watching her than sharing.

"Silverware, Ladyface?" I asked when she popped the lid, no utensil in sight.

"Nah." She settled further into her seat, gently rocking side to side, then snatched a piece of cake.

Elle wrangled the crumbles as best she could and lifted it up to her lips. She arched her head back to catch what she could of the cake and frosting and I couldn't help but think about my hand around her throat again.

But this time I could act on it. I rose up onto my knees, dragging a finger through frosting as I went. Elle's big eyes watched me and I stretched over her. Just like I imagined, I grabbed her throat and squeezed. Her eyes widened but they didn't threaten to bug out this time. Whether she said it or not, she trusted me with her body.

I squeezed harder as I bent to kiss her. I roughly took her lips, kissing her until she gasped raggedly against my skin. Only then did I pull back. I barely lightened my grip on her throat. But I took the moment to shove my frosting coated finger into her mouth. Every muscle in her neck rippled beneath my hand as she closed her plump lips around and sucked. My dick perked up.

When I pulled my finger from Elle's lips she gasped. I grabbed another piece of cake and pushed it into her mouth. She chewed a little on the luscious cake and the flex of her neck got me nice and hard.

She used the frosting on her fingers in defense, dragging it down her front and circling one of her nipples. A primal snarl ripped through my chest without me meaning to make a sound. I used my grip on her to push her down to the bed and pin her there.

Her breaths were short, small gasps but she didn't stop me—she didn't even make a move to lighten my grip. My mouth moved down the trail of frosting with licks and kisses, even nips. Her hips rolled an easy rhythm, her eyes fluttered shut and her hands simply balled at the covers beneath her.

Elle *loved* it.

I captured her nipple and pulled. A mangled cry left her throat as best it could. I reached for more cake and fed her, lightening my grip so she could swallow. She groaned again but this time it was that loud, lusty groan of hers that tightened my balls. I couldn't help but laugh against her soft skin, never letting her nipple leave the trap of my teeth.

I scooped more frosting and painted her stomach in it. Still holding her throat, I let my tongue travel across her body. She tasted every bit as good where there wasn't frosting. My lips made it to her clit and for a second I thought about biting down and mercilessly pleasuring her the way I had in the car. If her skin tasted good than her pussy tasted downright magical.

But I stopped short.

The urge to kiss a very different set of lips overwhelmed me. I wanted to be close to Elle, close to the woman that had me tumbling.

I changed directions and captured her lips. I kissed her wildly as my grip fell away. I didn't need to squeeze her throat to take her breath away this time. Besides, I needed that hand to scramble and pat around for the condoms I hid beneath the mattress.

When I couldn't find one, I looked away. When I turned back she shoved a small bit of stolen cake in my face. Her laugh was pure gold.

"Lick it off," I challenged.

She didn't even hesitate. Her mouth was on mine, her tongue at my cheeks, sucking, licking the frosting and crumbs from me. A shiver ran down my spine. My dick begged to burrow inside her.

I roughly shoved my hand into the cake and smothered her lips to tits before I pushed into her. I'd been inside her before but not like this. Not naked skin to naked skin. Not in my bed. Not with her shy smiles and epic blow jobs and confused eyes. Not when I felt...*something.*

I couldn't help but cry out, something ragged, pained and about four octaves higher than I would have liked. She just felt so damn good.

Elle let me hammer into her, her hands raked over me trying to find somewhere to hold. I kept moving though, into her, to taste her, to suck on the cake that was squishing between us. And then I found her throat again. I couldn't help but squeeze.

She screamed but it cut off in a gargle. I picked up my pace, hitting the end of her each time. Every inch of Elle trembled beneath me. Her legs started scrambling again and her breasts shook and swayed with every single thrust. Her face was turning a shade of red to match the cake. I let up just enough that she could gasp for air then slammed into her again. And clamped down on her throat again.

This time she shoved at me but it wasn't at my hands. She railed against my shoulder and after a few decent thumps I knew what she wanted. I grabbed the crook of her knee and flipped us so she was on top. Her slight hand came to mine and encouraged me to squeeze even harder on her neck.

My eyes went wide. A flooringly gorgeous woman sat on top of me, balanced on my dick. Her hair was matted down around her chin and breasts, tears pooled at the corner of her eyes, her skin was a dark shade of red and her lips had dried from desperate breaths but I'd never been so enamored by raw beauty before.

Then she started to ride me, setting a rhythm all her own.

Her eyes rolled back as her fingers dug into me, clawing at the flowers she'd been tracing earlier. She never arched too far, content to keep her throat in my clutches. It didn't stop her hips from waving expertly up and down the length of my dick. Without moving her neck she could roll her body up so high that I almost fell out, then shove it back down and sit flat on my hips.

Elle was a goddess. And I was going to come far too fast.

I dropped my hand, hoping that it would cool things the slightest bit for me. She took it as an invitation to lay down along me. Her nipples pressed against my chest and I could feel them grow harder. Soft breaths became desperate moans against my skin. Then I remembered what she'd let me do to her backdoor on the plane.

Without hesitating, I wrapped around her ass and shoved my finger in.

Her whole body clenched down around me and I swore. Heat shot through my body and collected where I was busy pounding into her. I couldn't remember my own name in that moment.

I came hard and fast into her. Everything below my bellybutton clenched and waved painfully hard, almost like a jackhammer was being taken to my body. But there was no pain from the assault, only pleasure, releasing like hot butter on a skillet as it skated across my body.

An otherworldly shriek brought me halfway back to the apartment, just in time to watch Elle as she convulsed on top of me then collapsed the last inch onto my chest. I was barely aware as she nuzzled, still whimpering, into the crook of my neck.

"Oh Ladyface," I breathed.

There were a million ways to finish that sentence but I was too far gone to figure them out. *You do something special to me* seemed appropriate but far too intimate. So, I simply turned and kissed the corner of her mouth.

Elle

I nestled into the navy sheets and breathed in the smell of Cole. There was something raw and husky underneath the fresh spice of his deodorant that lingered behind him. I breathed it in deeply as I lay alone in his bed. Just like his insanely tattooed skin, and his haunting green eyes, something about his musky, manly, delicious scent, made the outside world melt away. I could get lost in Cole and for that I was grateful. I wanted to be anywhere but my life right now.

The beautiful loft was a perfect hideaway. Three walls were weathered, exposed brick, each peppered with massive windows that sunlight flooded in. Raw reclaimed wood ran the length of the place, except for the subway tile in the bathroom. A small couch and TV were in between, easy to maneuver around if you walked diagonally to the kitchen. His dresser and a benchpress were the only things between the closet and bathroom doors. Everything about it screamed bachelor but the stunning art on the walls made it homey.

"Morning, Ladyface." Cole bent over me like he was going to kiss me. At the last moment, he zigged and caught my pert nipple in his teeth and bit down.

"Fuck," I swore as my hands flew to his shoulders.

Every muscle flexed beneath my hands as he lowered himself to my body. His tongue rolled around my nipple, miraculously touching every inch. He was so painfully talented, he made my whole body tremble. His teeth closed to replace his tongue and he gently rolled them side to side, spinning my sensitive skin left to right then back again. My fingers clenched into his skin and I groaned.

"Are you going to fuck me sideways today?" I managed to gasp.

He kept my breast in his mouth as he rolled his head side to side like he was contemplating whether he wanted to. My skin pulled and my back jerked off the bed. Some incredibly breathy, awkward sound shot out of my lips when he changed directions.

"Am I allowed to?" His voice was muffled since he hadn't bothered letting go of my nipple.

"Sideways? Sure." I couldn't help but gasp as I pulled him up toward my lips.

Cole didn't let go, stretching me to the max; I cried out with the lightning that shot straight to my clit. But I didn't stop pulling him upwards. My body was bowing wildly off the bed when Cole shoved my hips down. My breast fell from his teeth and jiggled slightly, sending aftershocks through me.

"A Saturday of playing with your body? Yes, please." He sounded like a kid in the candy store and I had to press my thighs together.

But then *Saturday* hit me like a ton of bricks and the world was back, hanging heavy on my neck. I let loose a heavy sigh before I thought about it.

"Something about that sound bad to you?" He sat back and my hands fell away when he looked at me—really looked at me.

Cole's eyes were evaluating my every motion, piercing straight into me and laying me bare. I was ready to surrender all over again to the man that made me feel so...*much,* but it was the whole reason I'd come.

"The funeral."

"Ladyface," Cole only breathed the word before he launched himself at me. His lips devoured mine, his tongue roughly pressed into my mouth and his body blanketed mine. "I didn't expect it to be today. I thought there'd be things for you to do." He kissed me. "Or family for you to see." He traced his nose along my jaw. "I mean, you got here yesterday and came home with me."

"My family didn't plan the service. We hadn't spoken in years. I honestly don't know why I'm here." I spat the words out, thinking about which family actually coordinated everything, which family my mother had chosen over me, and let the anger and fury I felt spill over.

"I've been to services like that, and known a family or two just like yours. " He kissed big, open mouth kisses down my neck and then across my chest. "I'm sorry," he breathed the words across my skin.

He snatched up the same nipple he'd had before and once again latched on. This time he held softly with both his teeth and lips. Cole used the tip of his tongue to flick back and forth on my sensitive nub.

The pounding notes of *Notorious* by Notorious B.I.G. started to blare from my phone somewhere over by my discarded clothes.

"Ugh," I whined as I wiggled away from his wanting lips. He held my nipple as long as he could but then let me go with a smirk.

"That's your alarm?"

"My stepdad's ringtone." I slid out from under him and tiptoed over to where my phone was buried in my bag.

With a click, I silenced it and turned around to find Cole in nothing but soft boxer briefs laying across his bed like an inked Adonis. I inwardly sighed and let my eyes wander the artwork I'd gladly traced last night.

"Elle?" The question was inherent in Cole's voice and I bit my lip waiting for the rest of it. "Why are you single?"

I blushed a color that would put a rose to shame. I hated that question. I mean why was anyone single? Why did guys in bars or bros with Tinder profiles find it particularly odd that I was unattached? Why did Cole?

The answer was so complex. It was knotted up with everything ugly, inky black and overly sticky about today. Everything I'd be damned to hell for bringing anyone into.

36

Particularly someone like Cole who looked at me with *those* eyes. He deserved better.

"I should've said that I'm grateful, whatever the reason. I'm just curious because so far, you're fucking everything as far as I'm concerned."

His few right words, the simple and straightforward way he said them, made the darkness of my family fade away. I needed to get ready and get going—I still needed to scrub the cum off my thighs—but I couldn't make myself.

As sexy as I could manage, I walked toward him then slithered across the bed. I pressed against his hip, wanting to roll him onto his back. He didn't budge.

"No way." He arched an eyebrow as he smirked. "I was promised a sideways fuck."

Cole grabbed my shoulders and pulled. His perfectly sculpted arms were that way for a reason, pure strength could pin me any way he wanted. And now it had me plastered against his skin, my back to his front, and his arms wove around me like restraints. One crawled up toward my throat while the other plunged between my thighs.

His deliciously perfect erection pressed firmly against me and he rocked his hips slow and steady just to make sure I felt it. Every single inch of it. I gasped and my hand shot back to wind around him and grab onto his ass.

"I like the way your body fits with mine, Elle. Perfectly fuckable at every angle." His breath was warm against my shoulder as his fingertips pushed my chin up, opening my throat up and giving me a view of the headboard. A small horse figurine sat at the top and started to sway with the slow movement of us lining up together.

His other hand shoved at his boxer briefs and my body jolted with each slow steady shove. When the fabric was free of his legs, he wound them into mine. His dick twitched against my backside and I purposely shimmied against it.

"You don't need to encourage me, Elle. I got hard when I first saw you in the terminal." Cole's fingers squeezed into my throat, his others brushed against my ass.

37

"I was a little turned on myself. That's why I propositioned you." My voice was already fading, words barely weaving through the tight space he'd left me.

"Thank God for small miracles." He bit down on my shoulder at the same time he pushed his cock into me.

"There's nothing small about you," I groaned the words then let them become something else entirely.

"Glad you like it." His words puffed against my cheek as he wrapped around me so completely that his body almost swallowed mine whole.

Cole stretched me just like he had each time before but that wasn't what threatened to split me in two. It was him. It was him wrapped around me, kissing me, biting me—choking me—and the absolutely odd things that stirred in me. It wasn't until he picked up the pace that it became a very real fear that he could break me. Thank God he held me together.

His hand moved down my hip, my leg. He wrapped around my thigh and slid up and down. Two fingers even worked their way to my clit. He made sure to rub every bit as leisurely as the way his fingers wandered. The slow and soft mixed with the fast and furious epitomized Cole and everything I was becoming ravenous for.

Hip bones hit my backside over and over and I could picture the leaves and panther inked across those bones. I could picture the equally intricate tattoos covering his hands as they explored me. Well not so much explore as dominate. Cole's grip was getting tighter. I gasped but it choked off partway when his nails dug into the side of my neck. His pussy wasn't playing with mine this morning but it made me drip all the same.

We rolled together in perfect unison and I melted into his hands. Cole had complete control of me and my body and I wouldn't have had it any other way. His dick was at the perfect angle and his head was hitting my G-spot every time he pushed in. I couldn't catch my breath, not even to screech or moan.

"Can I?" Cole asked as his hand drifted back to the flesh of my ass cheek. His hand played at my backside, teasing ever so slightly.

My gasping picked up pace. I couldn't answer him, I couldn't even moan or gasp. All I could really do was burn brightly for him. The only sensation I had left was in my fingertips. Those I put them to work, reaching for him. I grabbed his rock hard shaft and pulled him from my sex. He groaned a wholly pained sound into my ear, and he was so close, it reverberated through my bones. When I pushed his shaft toward my ass he groaned again, letting himself nestle between my cheeks.

He started to nudge against me. My face throbbed, my heartbeat thumped against his hand and my breathing was almost nonexistent.

"Relax." His word tickled my ear.

I couldn't. The gasping for breath was making it far too hard. My hand flew to his, still wrapped around my neck, and I pulled. He didn't let me pry his fingers from my flesh but he did loosen his grip the slightest bit. It was enough for my body to mellow and breath to filter into my lungs again.

Cole took advantage. His hand that was on my hip fell away and a moment later the watery slickness of lube slid along the curve of my ass cheek. Then further down, hitting its mark. Cole barely hesitated before the tip of his dick pushed into me.

I screamed, I couldn't help it. Cole clamped down effectively cutting off my air again, and ending my shriek prematurely. I tried anyway as he nudged further and further into me. The blood rushed in two very different directions, bringing a fevered heat and a ragged beat to both my face and between my thighs.

It took a few rocks of his hips but he finally pressed in fully to sit flush with my backside. I gasped shallow, wild, haggard breaths. His hand moved back between my thighs to flick my clit. My body short-circuited and I bucked against him.

His hand splayed across my stomach to still me. My body had a mind of its own, writhing wildly despite his desire to pin me. He wouldn't let me move.

When I finally stilled, Cole started hammering into me at a merciless pace. His hands finally moved from my throat to find other real estate. His fingers found my nipple and pulled. Hard.

This time I could cry out. My voice echoed off every corner of his loft. He groaned into my ear.

We flowed against each other, perfectly timed and body fitting to body exquisitely. I cried out each time he thrust up into me and he groaned in reply to almost every one. It was my symphony of pleasure; with him providing accompaniment.

Cole threw his leg up and over mine, pulling me back into his body even further. We were a twisted mesh of limbs on the bed. His cock was hellbent on acquainting itself with every inch of my ass. Over and over and over.

I lost myself to the perfect feeling and let tingling spread throughout my body. It wasn't long before the wave of a perfect orgasm crashed down around me and the world went fuzzy then turned a blinding shade of white.

"Ladyface," Cole breathed into my hair.

"Umhum?" I questioned back, unable to make sentences with his semi-hard cock still inside me.

"When do you have to get going?" He leaned in a kissed my shoulder. Despite his touch, I felt the suffocating black reaching for me.

"Shhhhh," I whispered as I closed my eyes, willing the bright light to come back.

As if on cue my phone started ringing. *Notorious* was back, echoing through the room the way my shrieks had earlier. A giant boulder dropped into my stomach. Jimmy wasn't giving up today.

Darkness took my heart back swiftly and squeezed. I sat still for a moment, hoping Cole would start his hypnotic roll again. When he didn't, I shimmied against him, desperate to provoke round two. He just laughed then blew out a low whistle.

My phone started ringing again.

I sighed and pressed away from Cole, letting him unceremoniously fall from me. I grabbed the phone in one swift movement and headed to the bathroom. Gently, I pushed the door shut and leaned against it without a word of explanation to Cole.

"What?" I answered sharply.

"Why didn't you check in?" My stepdad's oily voice rolled across the line.

"What do you mean why didn't I check in? Are you having me watched?" I shouted far too loudly.

"No," he snapped at me the way he used to snap at my mom and it made my blood boil. "But *they* are. They wanna know where you are."

My legs gave out and just barely managed to find a perch on the ledge of the tub. Everything in me was bottoming out, completely erasing my orgasm. Hell, completely erasing Cole. There was only one *they* in my family's life. They'd been there since my stepfather came into the picture. I was sure they'd be involved today but I didn't think they'd be interested in me. I'd kept my distance from day one. I'd run across the country at sixteen when they stole my mom from me the first time. They were nothing but bringers of doom and death.

Mom's death.

The thought popped into my head automatically. The truth of it resonated in my bones.

"What have you done? What did they do?" My voice went low, raspy, barely able to sneak out.

But I couldn't listen to my stepdad's answer. A perfectly sculpted Cole stood in the doorframe, his semi swinging squarely between artfully etched tattoos and even more skillfully sculpted muscles. His head was cocked as he watched me, his eyes cutting through me once again.

I tried to swallow the lump of glass in my throat. Part of me wanted to believe the anxiety was from my stepdad, or even *them* but I knew deep down it was because right here, right now, I was going to have to answer for it.

Sure enough, just a weak heartbeat later, clear, concise and sharp over the jibber in my ear on the phone, Cole asked, "Ladyface, what the hell is going on?"

41

Cole

I'd made her cry. Tears pooled so quickly in the corners of Elle's eyes that they spilled over her plump cheeks and danced on her cherry lips.

Of all the filthy, nasty things I'd seen and done on this earth, Elle crying was the one that gutted me. I hadn't had the heart to question her after that. Matter of fact, I hadn't been able to do anything but kiss her until I swallowed all her tears and replaced them with the warm water of a shower.

And the sight of water dripping down the perfect curves of her pale body was the reason I agreed to come. Well, begged to stay by her side was more like it.

Now here I was, shutting off my Charger in the parking lot of a church. A Catholic church I knew all too well. I would have done anything for the teary Elle of this morning—more than just attraction had tethered me to her—but in hindsight, I don't know that I would have willingly agreed come here.

Years ago when my life had been *different,* I'd been here too many times to count. During the thick of the turf war, almost every week. The stones of this building reminded me that my foundation was built on death and destruction. The Reaper himself would have found this place too thickly coated with blood to come in.

Of all the churches in Chicago, why were we here?

"You really didn't have to come, Cole." Elle's voice was small from the passenger's seat.

When I swept my eyes over her, my response came easy. "Yeah, I did."

The confident temptress from the plane had disappeared. The woman beside me seemed thinner, small somehow. Her skin was waxy rather than peaches and cream. Mischief didn't light a single one of her features. I wanted to protect this woman every bit as much as I wanted to fuck the other side of Elle.

Without hesitating, I grabbed the back of her neck and pulled her violently to my lips. I kissed her as if it would breathe the missing life back into her. My fingers squeezed her flesh, my tongue lapped every inch of hers, I even felt myself shoving over the console and stick shift to get at her. If I didn't stop…

I dropped my hold and plopped back against my seat, blowing out a deep breath as I went. If I was honest, I didn't care that I was here. I cared that I was with her. She'd become heroin in my veins in a matter of minutes, and I was making bad decisions all over again because of drugs.

The black Range Rover that pulled into the lot and sat in the back row of cars said just how piss poor this decision actually was. For the first time in years, fear, real guttural fear, socked my insides. I knew that driver. I knew who he drove. And I knew why we were at this particular chapel.

"Cole," Elle's voice pulled me from my spiral, "that's my stepdad. He's… not a good man." She leveled her finger at a tall but slightly tubby man with greased back black hair pacing behind the church—a man better known as Jimmy Ponies—and the havoc churning through me broke loose into full chaos. "I need to talk to him alone."

Before I had a chance to respond, she pushed out of the car door and was gone.

I couldn't appreciate the way the black fabric of her skirt danced across her legs, or that she reminded me of a beautiful black swan. Three years as a law-abiding citizen, a business and an honest living had been thrown out the window for electric attraction. For fate.

Maloneys and the fucked up family business surrounded me.

I'd clawed my way out. The price I paid still felt sticky on my skin some days. I scrubbed too hard in the shower too many mornings to count. It had taken too long to look myself in the mirror again, too long to feel like I had a future. A future I might share. With someone like Elle.

Fuck.

My blood was boiling, my bones vibrating as I shoved out of the car and stalked toward Elle. Fury and fear had awakened the primal beast in me. The monster fed on Elle's shrieks and whimpers, both broken terrified, as they drifted on the wind.

The closer I got the tighter my fists balled.

"What did you do? Tell me! What kind of trouble are you in?" Elle was blubbering through tears.

"Nothing your mother didn't know about. Nothing she wasn't riding shotgun for."

"You ruined everything." Elle's voice was as sharp as nails on a blackboard.

The body I'd become intimately acquainted with told me what it was doing a split-second before Elle launched herself at her stepdad. I caught her mid-pounce and hauled her into my chest. My internal chaos made me squeeze a little too tight. She didn't seem to mind when she slumped into my chest, a snarling wildcat and a mewling kitten all at once. Her tears were warm through the fabric of my button up shirt.

"Well look who the cat dragged in." Jimmy was coolly detached as he met my gaze head on. "Cole." He nodded with a bastard-ass smirk playing on his lips.

"You two know each other?" Elle questioned me, her voice muffled in my suit.

"I could say the same for you, Ponies, though I pity the cat that had to drag your ass anywhere." My fingers dug into Elle as I glowered at him over her golden hair.

"You shouldn't be here." Jimmy shook his head side to side as he spoke.

"I wasn't gonna let her come alone. And that was long before I knew she was walking into the killing fields."

"She's not innocent. This family as a whole is in as deep. Six feet under whether we like it or not."

The very thought of Elle six feet under had fury unhinging me. I was seeing red when I let go of Elle and swung at Jimmy. I caught his shoulder but he ducked before I could land another blow.

"Cole!" Elle was right behind me, her slight but determined hands yanking at my shoulders but she couldn't move me. Not with Jimmy and his threats square in my sights.

I lunged at him, balling my hands into his lapels and pulled the slimy rat inches from my nose. "Don't you dare threaten her. Ever." I shook him with each word, unconcerned that speckles of spit were flying into his face. Honestly, I wanted something far more disgusting, maybe even something deadly to fly in his face.

"Cole, you know how I feel about people touching my things." A new but all too familiar voice complete with Irish accent crawled up my spine and made me shiver.

"He's yours Mick? I had no idea." My voice was icy as I turned toward Mickey, Jimmy still in my clutches.

When I laid eyes on Mickey Maloney, I wished it were Elle beneath my fingers. Why I'd let her go, I had no idea. Her skin would soothe me, her heartbeat would reassure me, her cherry smell would ground me; she'd keep me anchored in the sea of terrifying memories.

Mickey was a little more salt and pepper then the last time I saw him and the creases around his pale green eyes had gotten deeper. His five o'clock shadow was a little closer to six and his lips were thinner than I remembered. The only thing that didn't look older was his body, which despite his age, was honed tight enough to perfectly fill out the suit her wore. He was still a formidable wall.

"Let him go, Cole. He's valuable." Mickey sneered when he said valuable and my back bristled. "You're lucky I let you touch Elle."

My switch flipped. I dropped Jimmy and wheeled on Mickey despite the reputation, despite the people I'd seen him murder, despite the things he'd made me do. I would have taken on

45

him and the whole of his hierarchy if it meant getting Elle's name off his lips.

"What did you say?" I snarled, my nails digging into my fists.

"Jimmy has forty-eight hours to come up with one of my prized possessions. I'm guessing we'll need to make alternative arrangements. And since he's worn out his usefulness and his collateral up and died…" Mickey jerked his head toward the church. "He's gonna have to get creative this time around."

My stomach rolled then I heaved.

I knew why Elle's mom laid in a coffin just behind me in Satan's chapel. The story was as familiar as my nightmares. I'd lived it. No, this story was worse. It was very, very real and revolved around my Elle.

"What do you mean?" I asked even though I knew. And Mickey knew that I knew. His eyebrow twitch said everything. He took a step toward Elle and gave her the once over.

God love Elle for pulling her shoulders back and narrowing her eyes at him. She may not have understood the severity of what was happening but she sensed a fight and was rising to it.

It was the worst time imaginable to get semi-hard.

But that's what she did to me. Her gorgeous dress and golden hair rustled in the wind. Her long legs disappeared beneath that deceptively innocent skirt. Those plump lips she was trying to thin into a straight line. She was everything. And everything worth fighting for.

"Jimmy's a worthless, gutless fish. He's worth nothing but the cash he can scrape up. But the lasses he keeps 'round? We'll see how this one does at fulfilling his debts." The corner of his smile cricked up.

I swung at Mickey before I thought about it. The sound of shoes scuffing on the pavement and the grunts of a few men were punctuated by Elle's shout then the crunch of a crushing hand wrapping around my fist. It stopped me faster than a brick wall.

"Wouldn't do that if I were you, Cole." Another familiar, though far softer and friendlier voice accompanied the sickening splinter of my bones.

I turned to find the dark brown eyes of my best friend staring back at me. Or former best friend. Or my fuck if I knew. Horse and I gotten caught stealing cars and started doing Mickey's dirty work to cover our asses and pay our debts. Somehow the debts never went away and the list of sins just got longer. His hulking hand was wrapped around my trembling fist.

"It's all right, Horse. Let the lad go. We're all having an emotional day," Mickey said without taking his eyes off Elle.

The Hulk that was Horse pushed my hand down by my hip then smoothed my jacket.

"How you doing, Cupcake?"

I couldn't answer. I couldn't make my jaw unclench. When he slapped me on the shoulder, I made a point to stay rooted and glare past Mickey. Siobhan stood behind him with her familiar wry and evil smirk hanging below her freckles. Her copper red hair swirled in the wind around her emerald green eyes and danced on her ample cleavage. When she winked at me then licked her dark lips, I shifted my eyes back to Mickey only to find him measuring me up.

"Cole always was a hot head. Let's go pay our respects and give him a minute."

Mickey held my gaze, waiting for my eyes to fall away, to show my deference. For years I'd nodded and let Mickey walk out of the room with my eyes downcast, but for Elle, he was getting a big fuck off.

To my surprise, he laughed. Loud.

"You always were my most rebellious. I think it's why I considered you a son. I *know* it's why you're still alive." The crunch of the gravel beneath his feet echoed deep inside my soul. "It's probably best you try and stay that way," Mickey added the last bit under his breath and in a tone only a handful of people had lived to recall. "Jimmy, are ya coming?"

I watched the men walk away until they disappeared into the church. Horse led the way, glancing back once or twice to check on me, Jimmy slunk a few feet behind. Mickey adjusted his suit, he nodded to the people filtering in, he hugged a few of the wives that walked up. At the last minute, he turned back toward us

47

and a wicked smile split his face, a smile that was meant for me, one that threatened to split the earth beneath me if I let it.

"Cole?" Elle's voice was still a wreck, a perfect mirror of my insides. Her hand tentatively found my shoulders and pulled.

My body reacted immediately to her touch. I turned abruptly and grabbed her. We were a tangle of limbs and legs as I shoved her up against the stone wall closest to us. I leaned in and bit on her bottom lip.

Cherry.

My tongue traced along what my teeth were violating. My hands gripped tighter on her wrists and thumped them against the wall once or twice. I shoved my knee between hers, forcing her to hitch her leg around my hip.

"We can't here," she said breathlessly into my mouth.

I didn't hesitate, I simply took her wrists and pinned them over her head. I shifted my grip so I could hold her slight bones in one hand. My free fingertips brushed down her cheek, along her jaw, pressed firmly across her neck for a few leisured kisses, then worked lower.

My hand was under her skirt and I was tracing the legs I suddenly adored. I tried to find the spots on her inner thighs that had been slathered with me but one shower had erased my mark.

I growled into her mouth and kept exploring. Eventually I brushed her pussy only to find her slick and waiting. I thumped her against the wall again and did what I could to devour her.

Elle kissed me back just as urgently. Her hands tugged at my grip and her thighs shuffled against my hand and wrist.

She made it all fade away. My past wasn't on the other side of that stone wall, my nightmares weren't living, breathing ghosts. For the moment, only she was real. For the moment, I was home.

I couldn't stop kissing her—I wouldn't.

My fingers were slick from exploring between her legs. I pulled away from her and watched as her lips followed mine, searching just for a split second. Her eyes fluttered open as she flopped back against the wall. I took advantage and shoved my Elle-flavored fingers in her mouth.

48

She gasped and her big doe eyes snapped to mine. I couldn't smile for her but I let my guard down completely, I let her see everything happening inside of me. Something about it encouraged her to bite down, close her lips around me, and suck. Hard.

It was my turn to groan as I let my hand twist in her mouth. My nose skated along her jaw and neck for a split second before I pulled her mouth open and latched my fingers around her throat. I dropped her wrists from above and grabbed her hips instead, yanking her flat against my body. My grip on her neck tightened as I found any space of free skin to suck along her neck.

Ragged sounds slipped from Elle's lips over and over. My lips wandered over her skin, relishing the taste. I was sucking too hard, biting too hard but I couldn't stop. When life got hard again—and it would get hard again—this is what I'd close my eyes and remember. Her and the way her body bent beneath mine.

I pulled back to look at her, her red face desperate for air, her knees knocking together, her golden hair still blowing in the slight breeze. The small tears pooling in the corner of her eyes got to me. I wouldn't see her cry real ones again. I swore an oath to myself right then.

My fate was sealed.

My lips crashed back to her collarbone as my hand fell from her back to fumble at my belt. As soon as I got the fabric out of the way, my cock was searching for Elle's sweet folds beneath the wispy fabric of her skirt. When I found a tiny scrap of lace fabric in my way, I yanked. She whimpered and shoved her hips toward me. When the fabric finally split across her thighs, she screamed into the parking lot.

I tucked the lace into my pocket just before I guided myself into her.

It was my turn to moan into the open air as I started thrusting. Her face was getting darker, her breathing shallower, both of which somehow made her lips far plumper. She was gorgeous. And for the moment, she was mine. I needed her kiss. I dropped my hand from her throat only to steal her breath all over

49

again. The faintest taste of her pussy hung on her lips. I kissed her all the harder with no intention of ever stopping.

My thrusts picked up speed and I gripped her standing leg, lifting her easily off the ground. We crashed back against the stone of the church as Elle's arms wound around my neck. As soon as she had a good hold, I wound my hand underneath her skirt and found her clit. She was soaked and slippery as I circled on her. There was a gentle rock of her hips against my thrusts that had me gritting my teeth. I pulled away just enough to brush her lips as I spoke.

"Fuck, Ladyface, I'm gonna come. I can't…"

Elle's wild moans cut me off. Her eyes had slammed shut and her mouth made a perfect O. Her breasts trembled above the neckline of her dress as she forced her hips to keep bucking against me.

I let myself go when her orgasm rolled along my dick. Little muscles waved along me as I shot into her. For a minute the world melted away. Heaven was within reach rather than hell.

Heavy breathing replaced the moans from earlier, then church bells rang over top.

"Cole?" Elle's voice quivered "What just happened?"

"Ladyface, if I have to explain sex to you, I think we have some problems." I tried to smile down at her but couldn't quite manage.

"Cole." She playfully smacked my chest but couldn't get her face to match the gesture.

I blew out a deep breath as I set her back to her feet. I snatched her torn underwear from my pocket and used it to clean up as best I could when I pulled out.

"You don't want your cum all over me?" She squeezed on my biceps as I tended first to her, then tucked myself away.

"Course I do." I kissed her forehead as I buckled my belt. "Just thought we were pushing our luck enough with a church parking lot."

She managed a wry smile. "Explain Cole. I went from ranting at my stepdad to being a pawn in a game I don't understand. Don't let me walk in there blind."

50

"You won't be a pawn, Elle. I promise." I'd made up my mind about that before I fucked her.

"Don't do this. Jimmy does this evasive, sit down, shut up because you're a woman thing. Give it to me straight."

I sighed loudly again and turned to rest flat against the wall next to her. Her fingertips brushed against mine and I wove my fingers into hers.

"I take it you've heard of the Maloney Family if your stepdad is Jimmy Ponies?"

"Yeah. They cast a long shadow that's made my family pretty dark for a pretty long time." Her voice got quiet and thick.

"Dark's an understatement. Death is more apt." I squeezed her hand. "I don't know the story, Elle but if they're here. And I mean here, this church. Your mom's death was Maloney related. If I had to guess, Maloney caused."

"I knew it!" She shot off the wall and was barging toward the entrance without a second thought. Luckily, I had her hand.

"Elle." I yanked her back in. "That's what happens when you get tangled up with them. Jimmy has been fixing races, letting them use the back barn for shakedowns, and hiding bodies for years. Something went south, way south if he owes Mick something other than money. Your mom already paid for it, and it wasn't enough. Now they want you too."

A tear trickled down her cheek and I curled her into the crook of my shoulder.

"Don't worry, Ladyface. Okay? Promise me you won't worry. I know how to handle this. When I told you about being on the streets, about deep, dark secrets…Just trust me, okay?" The organ started reverberating through the walls but otherwise we sat in silence, taking turns rubbing the back of each other's hands. "We should get in there," I finally murmured.

I leaned in and slowly kissed a trail from her shoulder up to the corner of her jaw, only to nip at her ear. That seemed to bring her back to life the smallest bit. She squeezed my hand harder as she gracelessly wiped away her tears with the back of her hand.

The crunch of our shoes seemed to get louder as we got closer to the door. Each footstep was heavier too. Perhaps it was because of my own personal memory lane. Perhaps it was the death march I knew I was walking.

We stepped inside and a weight crashed onto my shoulders. It came in the form of the red candles flickering on each side of the entryway that I'd lit too many times. They still cast a sullen light on the already morbid resurrection scenes depicted in stained glass. The burgundy carpet was still well worn between the darkly, polished pews that led to a site that was just as familiar as the small details of the church.

A dark black polished casket sat front and center, closed and coated with lilies to hide the fact that the body wasn't in a state to be seen. I'd had to put a few of those bodies in those coffins. Once or twice I'd had to arrange the lilies on top myself. And now...

"Elle, go take a seat. I'll be right there."

She shot me a look.

"Just go, okay? I'll have to punish you later if you don't." I managed a smirk and turned her down the aisle toward the pew she'd share with Jimmy and whoever had actually killed her mom. Mickey always liked to remind the living they were that way because he allowed it.

I turned toward the back right corner of the church. Mickey sat alone in the back row, with Horse and Siobhan just in front of him, his other enforcers across the aisle.

I shook my head, trying to clear the memory of the many times I'd sat in front of him, right next to Horse. I didn't know if they were better or worse than the times I sat at the end of that front pew next to a grieving family. Without making up my mind, I slid across the polished wood of the pew. At least four thugs stood up.

"He's fine." Mickey held up his hand. "How have you been, Cole?"

"Good, Mick. Real good." I sighed and let my head fall into my hands, my every move a contradiction to my words. "But we both know you don't give a fuck."

"But I do, laddy. I mean look at who you walked in with. She's something, isn't she? Jimmy didn't do her justice."

I knew without looking up he was staring hungrily at Elle.

"You can't have her, Mick."

"Sure, I can. Jimmy owes me. She'll choose to play along once I lay her options out for her."

His sentence made my stomach turn. I knew she'd play along too. Anyone who wanted to keep breathing did.

"What if I have a different option for you?" The words were heavy in my mouth. Thick and jagged and sour all at once, but I forced them out.

"I'm listening." The smile was obvious in his voice.

This was the last chance to back out. To chalk Elle up to hot airplane sex or a perfect weekend and wash my hands of her. I could turn my eye and let Mickey keep doing what he always did. I was sure he'd done it a million times since I'd gotten free. Once more wouldn't bother him. It shouldn't bother me.

But Elle…

So, I did the only thing I'd been able to think of. My fingers dug into my temples and I had to clear my throat before I said it but I managed.

"Mick, take me instead."

Elle

Something had shifted inside Cole at the church. The moment Mr. Maloney walked up, maybe even the moment Cole saw my stepdad his world shifted. We might have buried my mom minutes ago, but it was him that needed consoling, not me.

"Cole?"

He jumped at my whisper even though we were alone in his loft. Then like he'd done a few times today, gathered me into his arms and pinned me to his chest. Each time he'd folded me in closer, tucking me into his shoulder and resting his chin on the top of my head. This time he lightly kissed my forehead.

Something was *way* off.

"What happened back there, Cole? What did I miss?"

I was pretty sure whatever it was had happened when he slid onto the back pew, but the massive man they'd called Horse had blocked my view.

"Nothing, Ladyface. Nothing important. Guess just now that the funeral is over, you'll be leaving. I'm not real fond of our expiration date."

"Liar." My word was muffled by his chest.

"So you're staying?" His voice was equal parts excited and...*scared?*

"No. I can't. But that's not what I was saying. This morning you were choking me, now you can't stop holding me. Something changed."

"You want me to choke you?" He nudged his cock against me and I reached down to grab it.

I cradled his shaft through the fine fabric of his suit.

"All I have to do is squeeze."

His hand appeared at my throat. "Me too."

"Cole, come on." I rested my hand into his loose grip and let my other one fall away.

He sighed and our hands dropped, only for his to wrap back around me.

"What do you know about Mickey?" he finally asked, his grip getting closer to the way he held me during sex.

"Mr. Maloney?"

He nodded.

"Not much I guess. I know Jimmy got money from him and that he burned down one of my mom's houses when he didn't get paid back on time. I know he and my mom…" I trailed off. I couldn't say Mickey forced her, she'd certainly been a willing participant, as had Jimmy, but I still couldn't formulate the words to tell Cole what I'd walked in on. What forced me to leave the city at sixteen.

It had never crossed my mind to share the family secrets hidden behind my dark black fortress walls but with Cole, they just fell out. I wanted to reel them back in the second they were out. No one deserved to be mixed up in that shit.

"He does that." Somehow, he'd read my mind and I arched back to look at him. "Have his way with anybody that owes him…*anything.* I've seen him do it plenty of times."

"You've seen it?" I gasped, unable to wrap my head around a perfect stranger sharing a thread that fate had woven for me.

Cole shivered and I nestled into him this time.

"Yeah. I used to be part of the family, Elle. I got out but the things I saw…" Cole, the tattooed hunk of chiseled stone, swallowed a giant lump in his throat and his voice went weak. "He likes it when people watch. He likes to watch. He'll command a scene to remind people of their place in his world—beneath him and as pawns."

55

Cole pushed away from me and bolted for the kitchen. Before I could even move he wretched into the sink. I scampered over to rub his back while every one of his gorgeous muscles tensed and heaved with him. When he finally stopped, he bent to drink from the faucet and swished water around in his mouth. He scooped a handful and let it wash down the back of his neck before shutting off the water. He stayed gracefully arched over the sink while he started talking.

"Are you okay?"

"I can see it all sometimes, the things we did. The things I did. It's like they're happening all over again. Mick's watched me before." Cole's body heaved beneath my hand again. "I wish that was the worst thing he's made me do."

My hand wavered against his back. This gorgeous man who tenderly held me had a reason he liked choking. Deep down he was a savage brute who'd done horrific things. And to innocent people. But it made him sick. Truly, physically sick.

"Is that what he meant about me fulfilling Jimmy's debts?" I was afraid of the answer, but I had to know.

Cole's whole body responded again, this time all the more violently. I rubbed along his spine, tracing the contours of his muscles as he dry heaved into the sink. I was desperate to hold him but he bunched and coiled far too wildly.

Inwardly, I blew out a deep breath. Whatever he'd done, whoever he'd been, this was the man he was now. A man in pain at the thought of what might happen to me. Something inside me jolted awake. Something about a foot north of where Cole usually sent shockwaves through me.

When his body calmed beneath my hand and he started swishing water through his mouth again, I grabbed a washcloth. I wet it and patted the damp towel to the back of his neck. A few beads of water dripped down to his collar and turned the white of his button-up sheer.

Tanned, tattooed skin poked out through the fabric. I squeezed the towel all the harder, sending rivers of water down his neck to wet the fabric. My lips were drawn to the see-through spots and I was kissing over top of them before I even realized it. They moved along the wings of the eagle on his back adding nips as I went.

He shuddered beneath my mouth, letting me explore the way he had last night with my finger on his torso. I moved squarely behind him, wrapped my arms around his chest as I kept up my tracks through the soaked fabric across his back. It wasn't until my lips were scratchy from the cotton that he turned.

Cole's lips found mine as if they were always meant to land there. His hands came to my cheeks and skated along my jaw to cradle my face. His shoulders crept up as he kissed me with everything he had. I could barely come up for air, his intensity was fully focused on the way we kissed. My fingertips found his forearms and dug in.

We were frozen like that for a while, only lips and tongues moving besides thundering hearts. Cole was the first to move. His hands went to my zipper, mine simply slipped up his arm in response.

"When do you leave Elle?" His breath was warm against my ear just before my nose traced up along it.

"Tomorrow," I barely whispered back.

He didn't answer, he just started in on the zipper as he kissed along my neck. When the zipper was all the way down he stepped back and let it fall to the floor. I reached for his belt, only for him to grab my hands and kiss my fingertips before pushing them back to my sides.

"One last time, Ladyface."

Those words made me want to puke.

"Don't say that," I murmured.

I couldn't stay with him, but I couldn't walk away either. Maybe in the future, maybe every once in a while, some sliver of hope had to exist.

Cole didn't answer. Instead his hands were at my bra, gently unhooking it and tossing it to the side. I stood naked in front of him and he sucked in a deep breath. I wanted him back against my skin, I wanted to feel him take me. Whether it was the gentleman or the beast, I didn't much mind as long as it was Cole.

I bit my lip and looked him directly in the shimmering green eyes. They shifted from worried to hungry in a matter of moments and when they bored into me, I couldn't meet them anymore. My blood boiled too hot.

As my gaze wandered down him, I drank in the wet shirt clinging to his insanely sculpted muscles and the artwork that was fuzzy behind it. Until the end of time, I would dream of that body and the things it did to me. I choked on the past tense.

But then Cole's hand moved to his belt and I snapped back to the present, determined to enjoy him while I had him. He undid his belt but didn't pull it off, didn't work on his fly. His long fingers undid a few buttons then yanked the shirttails out of the waist of his pants. As soon as it was free, he peeled it off over his head. Every single muscle, every single art piece danced.

His eyes didn't move from me as he finally pulled his belt free. Neither of us flinched when fabric hit the floor but my breathing was picking up pace. Arousal was already spreading down my thighs.

For the first time, I felt like someone was really looking at me. Someone knew the underbelly, or at least part of it, and still wanted to dive in. And knowing that, seeing that reflected back was kind of awesome.

Cole stepped toward me and in a simple movement had his belt behind my neck. He used it to pull me to his lips. My hands crashed into his washboard abs, then curled. He kissed me hard and his knuckles brushed along my collarbone but he didn't grab me. I nestled against him, my hands flat against his skin, just before he slipped the buckle back on and pulled the leather tight.

I gagged when Cole kept pulling. He lifted the tail up over my head and I rose on tiptoe to follow him. My hands automatically scrambled to pull at the belt where it crossed my throat. Green eyes swept over me and flames danced behind them. An inkling of fear smoldered in the pit of my stomach now that I knew what laid in his past.

Before I got swept up in either lust or fear, he used his grip to spin me and shove me down to the kitchen island countertop. I yelped before he tightened the belt enough that I couldn't squeak.

58

He kept a tight grasp as he dragged his lips down my back then over the curve of my ass. When he settled in between my cheeks, he pulled the belt tight enough that I arched off the countertop. The throb in my face was amplifying but not nearly as quickly as the throb between my thighs. That was the throb his tongue quickly tended to.

Cole licked fully across me then set his tongue to work on my clit. He flicked it side to side until my body tremored in front of him. I tried to gasp his name over and over as I stood on the precipice of a massive orgasm. Just when I thought I'd explode from pleasure or lack of oxygen—maybe both—his tongue fell away and he dropped the belt unceremoniously across my back.

I sucked in a huge breath that somehow still sounded like his name. I wheezed and rolled my head to press my check to the granite counter that was still cool. My hands came to the countertop and pressed against it hard. The moment Cole pressed into me, they scrambled back to shove at his thighs.

He thrust into me over and over and I couldn't reach far enough to keep him from hollowing out my insides. Our bodies moved against each other the way they always did: perfectly. Whether it was biological, crazy chemistry, or the magic of all great fairy tales, Cole knew me. He knew he could grab the belt again and pull. It tightened on my throat just before he hooked his finger in my ass. I cried out, feeling my throat ripple against the leather. Then his cock nudged against his finger and my body jerked against the countertop with pure pleasure.

Cole thundered into me. His finger crooked with each move, the leather shifted too. My hands automatically dug at my throat or batted at his thighs but I wouldn't have really stopped him. I couldn't.

He rolled against me over and over. My breathing was going shallow and my head thudded all over again. The edges of my vision went fuzzy. Electric tingles replaced any real feeling in my fingertips. I tried to moan over and over but my throat just constricted on itself.

His thumb cricked back, pressing into his erection and pulling tight all at once. I came spectacularly. Lightning shot through me, spreading tingles everywhere like the ones in my fingers. I was screeching against the pull of the belt but no noise was coming out. When the waves finished wracking my body I slumped into the counter and let my legs turn to Jell-O.

Cole wasn't done though. His hand slipped out of me and shoved under my ribs. He easily lifted my limp body and turned me. I folded to my knees partially because of his look and partially because I couldn't support myself. When I sagged to my calves, he pulled on the belt to perk me up.

Automatically I lifted myself to hip height. He kept it tight and pressed his thumb into my mouth. I weakly sucked at it, still at the mercy of my melted body.

"Suck, Elle." He yanked on the leather to reinforce his point.

And I did, even though it made breathing all the harder. When he was happy with my hollowed cheeks, he used his thumb to pull my mouth open and shove his cock in.

I took it all.

Numbness was taking over as he thrust over and over. Every single fiber in my body should have been protesting this fucking, protesting him, but I couldn't. I left my hands at my sides. Even if I'd been able to feel them, I wouldn't have tried to stop him.

Being savagely taken made every inch between my thighs clench. The more I surrendered, the more likely a second orgasm was. Cole's ragged moans barely reached my underwater ears but they were amplifying my arousal all the same. The belt still snug around my throat was spurring me on too.

Cole shoved to the back of my throat and sat there. That was all it took. My body jerked, wanting air and release all at once. He pulled tighter on the leather. Waves of an orgasm pummeled my body and crashed against his pull. I shook violently then felt myself drip with pure pleasure.

"Fuck!" Cole bellowed a moment before he shot into my mouth. He tightened his hold as tension gripped every inch of the chiseled man before me.

I couldn't swallow and the cum spilled down my lips and onto my breasts. Cole whimpered something wholly devastated then fell to his knees in front of me. The belt loosened completely and I gulped in air like I'd been underwater for a lifetime. The sharp intake made me woozy and stars studded my field of vision. The salty strands of Cole that slipped down made my throat even more scratchy.

My body weighed a thousand pounds and I teetered on my knees. I crumpled into Cole's lap unable to control my limbs any longer.

"Oh, my God, Ladyface. Oh, my God." His dick twitched against my face as his finger traced the hot sticky coating on my chest. I laughed a breathy, shotgun laugh but managed little else.

He didn't say anything as we sat in a heap on the floor, he just kept tracing the marks he'd left covering me. I shifted the smallest bit to see his face. His eyes were pointed at me, but the vacancy behind them said he was somewhere else entirely.

"Cole, it's going to be okay." My hand drifted up, still not fully-functioning, to graze his cheek.

He managed a wry smile but it didn't reach his eyes. They were still dark and distant, equal parts terrified and manic. For the very first time since meeting Cole, the outside world wasn't falling away. It was a living breathing monster and I had a feeling it was close enough to hide under his bed.

Cole

The inky stain of memory wove into my mind and grabbed hold. Darkness sat heavy on my chest, having tea with the devil himself. I was a monster and I felt the claws sharpen beneath my knuckles and my heart start to harden to stone.

Elle breathed softly beside me in bed with bright and angry marks from the belt worn like a collar on her throat. She hadn't questioned me about the choking, the dominance or the bruises, which jumbled up my insides all the more. She hadn't wondered if I was a monster—or at least she hadn't asked—and I hadn't had to explain it was just a way to prove to myself I could be me without leaving death lilies in my wake.

I wove her golden hair around my fingers, braiding it, twirling it and using the ends to trace the cum she still wore on her chest. That pulled a smile across my face. The plump lips and perfect tits of my angel were as dirty as me. She actually fit me, my soul, like a puzzle piece I'd never known I was missing.

I sighed loudly into the dark of my apartment as I studied the shadows city lights cast across my place. The only thing I could be grateful for was that the soft, steadying breathing of my puzzle piece, my Ladyface, wasn't mixed up in this *thing*.

This...*monstrosity*. Because that's what life with the Maloneys was. A snarling, dragon from the depths of hell, determined to pull people down further than death. But I would put her on a plane tomorrow and keep her from its jaws. That was something I could hold on to, something to help me sleep at night.

I pulled her toward me and breathed in her scent. That smell, cherry, vanilla and sex, would soothe me when the going got tough. Wrapped up in her, I started to doze off.

Until a booming knock echoed through the apartment, ping-ponging off the wall and chattering my teeth. Elle murmured next to me and her soft body rolled gently against me but she didn't wake up. Not even when the knock pounded again. I slid out from under her then shot over to the door, whipping it open without a second thought.

"What in the hell are you doing here?" I spit the words out at the brick wall that was Horse.

"Came to join in." He smiled his big, dumb, face splitting smile as he reached out and drug his fingertips down my stomach before letting it fall away.

I lunged, swinging first for his kidneys then for his jaw before yanking up my foot to crash down on the inside of his knee. He didn't even flinch when I hit him but when my foot came up, he swiftly wrapped his arm around my neck and curled me under his armpit in a headlock. Since I had a foot in motion, it was easy for him to send me off balance and own me.

"You hurt your hand?" Horse asked still holding my boxer-brief-clad ass in my hallway.

"What are you doing here, Horse?" I asked, muffle against his ribs.

"You know what I'm doing here, Cupcake."

"Don't call me Cupcake." I jabbed at his kidney again.

"Fine." He untwisted me with enough force that I stumbled back and flattened up against the wall. "Stop punching me?"

"Fine." I sighed and shoved my hands through my hair. "What does Mick want? Jimmy still has forty-eight hours to find...*whatever.*"

"You and I both know Jimmy isn't gonna find it." Horse rolled his eyes at me. "Get your clothes, we're going for a drive."

I sat, plastered to the wall, staring at the man whose body had gotten harder but whose heart stayed soft in the past three years.

"Come on, don't make me make you, Cole. You know I can and that's without waking up the girl."

At the mention of Elle, my temper flared again. I bent and ran at Horse, knowing hitting his balls or his throat were the only ways I could beat him. It had been that way since we were about fourteen. He knew what was coming but couldn't stop me as my flat fingers darted into the meat of his throat. He gagged and grabbed at his throat and doubled over.

I was almost in my apartment, a heartbeat away from slamming my door when Horse's giant Hulk hand crushed down on my throat.

Horse wheezed. "Not cool, Cupcake. Not cool." I couldn't breathe, my hands dug into his. "Unless you want Elle waking up with my dick up her ass you're going to go in there, put on something respectable and get your ass in my car." He squeezed a little and used his grip to draw me close. "I know how much you like this sort of shit. The offer to join in still stands," he whispered into my ear.

I elbowed him but it wasn't aggressive. Horse let me go and quirked an eyebrow.

"I don't do that anymore," I said as I rubbed on my throat.

"You *didn't*. For a while. You also weren't part of the family. You know what's coming, though." He sighed and leaned back against the hall railing. "Besides, together we weren't all bad."

"Horse, this was never about you."

He sighed. "This isn't about you, either. Just come on. I'll get you back before she wakes up." His voice was quiet, defeated almost.

I knew the feeling.

With another heavy sigh, I turned and walked into my apartment. Elle was still tangled up in my sheets, fast asleep but a hand reached out for where my body had been. Everything inside me twinged. I kept my eyes on her as I dug for a pair of jeans and a shirt in my dresser.

When I was dressed, I walked over and bent down to kiss her. I pressed my lips to the thin bruise forming around her neck.

She let out the softest, sweetest sigh and her hand curled into the sheets where I should be. Everything below my belly button clenched, my dick twitched.

"Cole." Horse's deep voice and dark eyes urged me from the other side of my still open door.

I scribbled a *'be right back'* for Elle then turned to follow Horse to the street. Once or twice he sucked in a deep breath to start a conversation but the permanent pinch of my face was enough to stop him in the tracks.

The 1971 Hemy-Cuda parked on the street was familiar, with its custom rims and pristine leather interior. It was as familiar as Horse and every bit the dip in the memory pool as he or Mick was. It was the first car we'd stolen for Mick. Horse had been obsessed with it, sometimes he talked about it more than the girls Mick paraded around. When Horse became a man in Mickey's eyes, it had shown up in our driveway, keys and all because no one would take from Mick Maloney.

I'd fucked in that car. *We'd* fucked in that car. There were countless late nights aimlessly driving, singing as loud as we could to the White Stripes, drinking out of paper bags. I'd killed in that car.

My insides balled up and the bile rose in my throat. Horse watched from the driver's seat, his features illuminated every block or so by the streetlights. His heavy stare had been able to cut through me since we met in fourth grade.

But he didn't say anything as we pulled up to a curb and he shut the rumbling engine off. I didn't need to look out my window, I knew what hell-hole stood beside me. Fury welled in my chest and a belligerent scream threatened to shriek out. A part of me wanted to cry and still another wanted to grab the gun inevitably tucked beneath Horse's seat and go ape shit. It was that urge that upset me most.

I breathed in the smell of leather polish and the piney scent that had always hung in this car and wished it was warm cherry mixed with dirty sex. I pictured naked Elle and my cum covering her body, she was enough to make me unclench my fist.

"Why'd you do it?" Horse's voice cut through my fantasy. His soft, gentle tone kept me from snapping at him. "I can tell being here makes your skin crawl so...*why?*"

I folded forward and let my head sag into my hands.

"Will *I don't know* work?"

"For getting mixed back up with Mick? No. Not even remotely."

We let the silence hang between us the car. Besides our breathing, all there was to keep us company was the usual hum of the city outside, a siren in the distance, a train rattling, a car alarm, something knocking into trashcans. We'd sat like this so many times it was almost comfortable.

"Come on, Cole. Talk to me." Horse sighed and his giant paw came to rest on my shoulder. "You never stopped being my best friend. I was happy you got out. I checked on you from time to time and I was always proud of you. I never minded that you left me behind."

I twisted in my seat to look over at him. In that moment, he wasn't the Hulk, he was the same gentle, scared kid crashing on my floor after his folks came home belligerent.

"I have nightmares about leaving you," I admitted with a heavy sigh.

"Well now we just sound gay," Horse snarked.

I couldn't help but laugh. "You're the one that likes dick."

"And pussy. Don't forget pussy." He joined in with a soft chuckle. I sat up and sagged back into the seat before the car went silent again.

"It was her. Elle. I couldn't let this happen to her." I shoved my finger at Mickey's brownstone.

"I can't believe we didn't know you guys were a thing. Mick's had his eye on her for a while what with Jimmy being Jimmy."

"We haven't. I've known her maybe seventy-two hours." I closed my eyes and shoved my hands through my hair.

"Fucking cats, Cole." He banged his hands on the steering wheel and the whole car shook. "You did this for a fucktart? I

66

oughtta kill you right now because if you've gotten that goddamned stupid you're not going to last long."

"Give me more credit than that. I mean no complaints about her *fucktart*, like at all…" I let my mind wander over her body, the things she let me do to it and couldn't help but smirk. "But it's way more than that."

"She better be the goddamn moon for what you just gave her."

"If I weren't a black hole, she could be the whole universe Horse." I realized how stupid I sounded. She was a girl I'd fucked. Hard. And there had been little else between us besides moments.

But those moments were everything.

Her sweet talking the cops about my loading zone parking, her tracing my tattoos in the dead of night, her blaring Notorious BIG ring tone, were just tiny little things but they added up to something explosive. And if that hadn't been enough, she'd looked right at my demons and didn't flinch.

"Well let's get this over and get you back to her."

Horse stepped out of the car and the whole thing shook. I sighed into the empty front seat but couldn't quite talk myself into moving yet. Horse leaned against the hood just in front of me, once again jostling every inch of the substantial car. It was a not so subtle reminder that he could make me if he wanted to, but also that he really didn't want to.

He jerked his head, signaling for me to get out of the car. I looked over at the dingy brick beside me, the steps I'd run up a million times. The brownstone was large and had ornate finishes on the wrought iron of the railings and bars that covered the windows. Besides being the biggest house on a rundown street, it was unassuming. Graffiti covered Mick's trashcans just like everyone else on the street.

"Cupcake," Horse taunted and I finally shoved out of the passenger seat.

I jogged up the stairs the way I always had, my muscles accepting their fate far easier than my mind. When I went to knock, I couldn't force myself.

67

"I've got your back. Always." Horse had managed to creep up the stairs without making a sound before he said it low and earnest behind me.

His hand extended around me to knock on the door and I automatically blew out a deep breath. Both my mind and my body were on board with trusting Horse. I always could and certain things never changed.

Horse shuffled beside me and pushed on the door when the buzzer clicked. I glowered at the camera I knew was watching as I stepped into Satan's lair.

Inside everything was different than the street outside. Everything was deep, dark wood, dark lighting and spots of candlelight. Both accentuated the black velvet furniture and twisted paintings. Downstairs was a traditional layout, used as more of a waiting room than anything else. The smattering of handguns, blades and brass knuckles on the coffee table were the only hints the decor didn't mean different, it meant sinister.

My skin crawled all the same.

I'd sat on the couch in the living room gathering my nerves to follow through on Mickey's orders. I'd sat on that couch, wishing I were in the shower, scrubbing off the filth I'd been a part of.

"Take a seat, Cole." Horse interrupted my memories and gestured toward the seats.

The springs squeaked and bounced beneath me just as they always had and it was as close to homey as this walk down memory lane would get. I scanned the room as Horse started up the grand staircase, noticing more artwork than the last time I'd been here. Most of the walls were covered in framed canvases or photographs and a few morbid pieces leaned against the walls on the floor. They'd gotten progressively more haunting in recent years.

One seemed to be a river of dead bodies that I couldn't pull my eyes from. The longer I looked, the more I convinced myself I recognized the faces. I stood before I thought too much about it, drawn to the picture like a moth to a very black flame.

68

Up close, I *did* recognize some of the faces. I remembered what they looked liked scared, bloody and knowing they were going to die. I'd always turned away after that. But here were the dead faces of men I'd killed, staring back at me with their death masks on. Before I knew it, I was choking back bile.

"You like Mick's own personal River Styx?" Some new kid called from the bottom of the stairs.

If the bile hadn't been choking me, I would have shot a snarl at him. Telling him just how many bodies I'd put in that river instead of Mick. But I couldn't quite swallow what I was doing here, let alone the vomit it put in my throat.

"Leave your weapons." He jerked his head toward the pile on the coffee table then toward the stairs. "Mickey will see you now."

I walked toward him without hesitating at the table.

"I said leave your weapons." He puffed up his chest and narrowed his gaze.

A dark laugh bubbled up in my throat. "Kid, I've been out for a while. I don't carry." I walked toward his perch on the staircase, toward Mick and my future. I paused to whisper in his ear, "But even now, I wouldn't need them if I wanted to take you out."

Without waiting for an answer, I climbed the rest of the stairs and pushed the massive single door open into the den of vice.

Spread legs and a quivering pussy greeted me. Mick sat behind the woman he had offered up on a tray in a king-like throne. The same dark lighting cast shadows across both her skin and his. Mickey's eyes and the girl's sex were accentuated in the little bit of brightness.

"The prodigal son returns." Mick spoke with Siobhan to his right and Horse to his left. "I got you a present," Mick added with a jerk of his chin towards the girl trembling on the table, tied down and spread for me.

"I'm good, thanks Mick. I'm here on business, not pleasure, remember?"

Horse cringed when I said it, Siobhan's eyes glinted. I was undoubtedly playing with fire but I couldn't bring myself to care.

"Fine. Business it is." Mick's voice was dark, darker than normal, as he rose from his chair and circled the girl. He dragged his hand across her skin as he walked toward me. She trembled, and it wasn't at the tender touch of intimacy either, it was fear, plain and simple. Her whole body jumped when he smacked her hard on the hip just before stepping nose to nose with me.

"Just what business do you think we're in, Cole?" He enunciated his every icy word.

"Murder, Mick." I met his gaze unflinching. "Sometimes money laundering, grand theft auto, drug running, prostitution…"

"*You're* in the business of shutting the hell up and following orders, Cole. *My* orders." He cut me off, hissing in my face. "And I said take her."

"No, Mick." I softened but I didn't flinch. "Please."

"Did you think you could take Elle's place to simply placate me? That it wouldn't mean anything? That just hearing the words would be enough?" His volume was rising.

"That's not what I mean…"

"Because now I fucking own you, Cole!" He screamed in my face, his breath assaulted my skin. "And I want to see you lick this." Mick shoved his finger toward the girl's open legs.

"I have Elle." It was the only defense I had.

"You don't have her," he sneered. "We've been watching her for a while and you're just a dick she jumped on. She's just a cunny you're enjoying. So stop feeding me lines and prove your loyalty."

My eyes fell from Mickey's and he let out one breathy laugh. I looked over to Horse and tension wracked his body, his fingers were digging into the chair, white visible even from over here. His eyes were pleading with me. Siobhan was cackling across from him, pleased to see me bend.

"Lick it, Cole," Mickey snarled in my ear, pressing his barreled chest against mine.

I had to beg for Elle, I'd go home to her and she deserved that much in our last few hours. I couldn't live with myself if I caved, despite the face I'd save.

"Please, Mick."

70

His arm swung up and around my neck and wrestled me to his hip. I automatically tensed but forced myself not to fight him. His knee snapped up hard and fast to my gut and I groaned. His grip tightened on my neck, making it hard to breathe. I still didn't fight him but I felt the fury throbbing in my face.

"You'll lick that cunny if I say. You'll fuck it if I say. You'll kill her with one word, you understand me, laddy?" He kneed me harder this time and I made a downright pathetic sound, barely able to breathe.

Mick squeezed tighter with the arm around my neck and my hands finally reacted on instinct to pull him away. As soon as I started to struggle, he slapped me full across my face. I fought harder against him only getting myself two more hard knees into my stomach and a punch to my kidneys that brought me to my knees.

The second I hit the hardwood floor, Mick let go and I slumped down, gasping. I was completely defenseless sitting like that, and anywhere else I would have let the monster I tried to keep at bay run free, but with Mick, I knew to stay submissive if I was going to get a favor.

A small telltale click made me wish I'd fought back. The cock of a gun preceded the press of cold metal against my temple by a single heartbeat. Mick pushed hard against me, grinding the barrel left to right. I closed my eyes and took a deep breath, wanting to see Elle, smell her, remember her taste if I was really lucky.

I did catch the scent of a turned-on woman but it wasn't Elle. It made me heave but I couldn't stop sucking in deep, haggard breaths. When he didn't pull the trigger, I opened my eyes to find myself staring between the legs of Mick's waiting woman.

Once more, he pressed hard against my head, jostling me enough to press my cheek against the girl's trembling thigh.

"Lick it," he commanded, and this time, with my life on the line, I did.

Elle

It was the deep pounding that woke me rather than the cascade of the shower, or even the vacancy Cole left beside me. I squinted a few times, barely able to believe the night was just starting to fade from black then rubbed my eyes and stretched.

Each of my bones creaked but it was the ache of my throat when my muscles tensed that stood out, but I didn't mind. All I had to do was imagine Cole's intensely burning eyes when he yanked on the belt to turn myself on all over again. I pushed out of bed without giving it a second thought, magnetically attracted to Cole more than anything.

I pushed open the bathroom door and was enveloped in steam. My blurry eyes took a minute to adjust to the skewed brightness but when I did, Cole was hunched behind the glass door of the shower. He had one forearm resting on the tile supporting the graceful curve of his perfectly muscled and inked body. Only after watching for a little while did I realize he was brushing his teeth almost violently. His body shook under the ferocity of it. Each time he spit, he pounded his fist against the wall where it rested.

"Fuck," he swore then tilted his head up for a mouthful of shower water and spat it out. He banged his hand a few times in quick succession and swore even louder.

"Cole?"

He turned at my voice and the steam he'd created in the bathroom swirled around his god-like body.

72

"Ladyface? Did I wake you?" It took a minute for him to find his voice and even then it was shaky.

"Yeah, but that's okay." I walked over and pushed the clear glass aside. I stepped in only to screech when the water scalded my shin.

"Shit, sorry." He scrambled for the dial and turned the water down. His hand reached for me the next moment and pulled me into the waterfall.

I wrapped myself around him only to discover angry welts from the heat he'd been showering in.

"Good Christ, Cole." My fingers traced up his arms, across his shoulders then up his neck. Beneath my fingers, the muscles twitched as Cole jerked away from me. "Are you okay?"

Green eyes zigzagged up and down my body as his mouth opened once or twice to say something. When he didn't manage anything, I let my fingertips trace the side of his panther, relishing the dips and grooves of his abs. When I got lower on his body, he cried out.

My eyes bugged. I couldn't help it.

"What did I do?"

"Oh, Ladyface." His whole face contorted, every bit as pained as when I touched the sensitive spot on his abs. "You didn't do anything."

"I can do something to cheer you up." I reached for his cock and went to stroke but he grabbed my wrist mid-pump.

"Can I hold you?" His voice still wasn't his. In some ways, it was darker but in others, it was broken.

"Yeah, of course." I wove myself into him without hesitating and let my fingers brush across his back.

Cole twisted himself around me like roots desperate to hold a massive tree steady. I pulled his face down to me and gently kissed each of his eyelids then leaned my forehead against his. He breathed in deeply as I played with the edges of his hair.

The man that cuddled into me like a kitten in a warm blanket was such a sharp contrast to the one that had needed control earlier. Only one explanation made sense, and whether it pulled him from me or not, I needed to ask.

73

"Did you leave me tonight, Cole?"

"When's your flight, Elle?"

"So that's a yes." I arched my eyebrow at him even though he pulled me tighter so he had no way of knowing. "Was it because of Mr. Maloney?"

His whole body convulsed underneath me at the mention.

"Cole, you have to fill me in. Please," I begged still holding tight to him.

"There's nothing to fill in, okay?" He nuzzled his nose into the wet strands of my hair.

"You're a liar." I would have shoved away from him but I didn't want to hurt him. Cole was fragile to the point of breaking, to the point of recklessness, something I recognized intimately. It was something my mom and Jimmy had shoved on my shoulders so many times. It was part of my ugly that Cole had wordlessly accepted yesterday whether he knew it or not. Perhaps today he didn't want it, perhaps he'd learned…

The water ran cool and Cole reached around me to crank it. His hands came back to me and skated along my curves.

"You gonna answer me about that flight?" he purred.

"If you answer me one thing."

"I'll sure try."

"You really want me gone, don't you?" I buried my head in the crook of his shoulder, unable to meet his eyes when he answered.

He didn't speak. Instead he pulled my chin so his lips could find mine in the cascade of the dying water. He kissed me with everything he had, pulling, pushing, caressing. His hands found their way into my hair and yanked, tilting my chin up to the ceiling. He nipped and licked along my jaw then started down my neck.

He kissed the sensitive spot where the belt had been then his lips hesitated against my skin.

"Yes," he finally breathed the word. "I'm a monster." His finger traced along the mark I wore from last night. "And you need to be as far away from my marked soul as possible."

Our last moments haunted me as I sat in the terminal of O'Hare.

"You're everything, Elle. Absolutely everything."

"You don't have to placate me, Cole. I don't think I mean much to you."

"Ladyface, I pray to God you never know how much you mean to me."

As soon as he'd finished speaking, he kissed me. Hard. His hand shoved up my skirt and clutched my ass to yank me onto his lap in the driver's seat. He wrapped around me so every inch of my chest pressed against his. His hand came to the back of my neck and squeezed; his thumb and forefinger dug into the faint bruise I wore hard enough to bring back the feeling of ownership.

I kissed him all the harder.

When cars started honking behind us in the drop off lane, Cole's tongue wormed its way into my mouth and danced its intimate dance against mine. He explored leisurely as if we were still in his bed and I was more than happy to match him move for move. It wasn't until TSA knocked on the passenger window that he stopped and slid me back to my seat. Security banged again and I started collecting my things.

Cole didn't say a word. Hell, I don't think he breathed as I climbed out of the rumbling car. But at the last minute, right before I was going to shut the door, he lunged across the seat and grabbed my hand. He yanked roughly on me, toppling me back to the seat.

"Everything."

His whisper barely preceded the sweetest kiss to the tip of my nose.

The whole thing had left me thoroughly upset. Not because there was anything wrong with it—the goodbye was actually painfully perfect— but because there was so much left unsaid. He'd stayed hidden and I'd swallowed three very important words.

I grabbed my bag and darted to a quiet corner of a different gate area that was bathed in sunlight. I dug for my phone as I went, almost colliding into a few different people as I all but shoved my head in the bag. Phone in hand, I barreled toward the windows and flipped the video on. I hit the icon to turn the screen then held the phone at full length and hit play.

Without saying a word I waved at the camera then smiled as wide as I could. I kept the goofy grin on my face while I pointed at my eye, then right to my heart and last but not least at the screen where Cole would be. The moment I stopped recording, I sent my *eye heart you* message and turned off my phone to board.

The plane ride was torture. Every single thing reminded me of Cole and I half expected him to file in and sit next to me. When I went to the bathroom mid-flight, I let my fingers wander over the dingy plastic casing and took note of how much larger it seemed without Cole in it.

I sighed. Over and over and over again. Throughout the entire flight back to Seattle. I missed him and in a far deeper way than I should. I knew it didn't make sense, I met him Friday morning, and here I was flying home on Sunday, but my mind wandered through the steps it would take to move to Chicago all the same.

It was still meandering down that path as I walked through the Seattle airport. Cole's manly scent and piercing eyes filled any part of my brain that wasn't required for walking.

"Elle Belle, earth to Elle Belle."

I snapped toward my nickname, so dazed that I didn't recognize Conrad. My perfectly coiffed best friend looked like a golden god of a Southern California surfer even though he refused to touch the ocean. Fish were "gross." And now he sat with his head cocked, arms crossed, and his usual glowing halo as he watched me walk through the airport like a zombie.

"Hey. Sorry." I tried to shake the image of tattoos flexing over top of me as I turned to walk toward him.

"Did it go that bad in Chicago?" He threw his arm around my shoulder.

"It went…*different*." I scrunched up my nose.

"So Jimmy was decent? Your skin didn't crawl? You cried?" he asked with sass thick in his voice. "Give me details, girl." He used his grip to start us walking toward short-term parking.

"Jimmy was Jimmy and he was definitely responsible for Mom." I sighed loudly.

"Good. Tears dry out your skin."

"I may have cried a little. She was my mom after all. But come on, the shit that they did, that they got mixed up in?" I couldn't soften the little bit of disgust in my voice.

Conrad curled me into his chest and I wove my hands around his waist. For the first time in ages, his toned chest and narrow hips didn't feel like home. I readjusted.

"Elle Belle?" He stopped walking and I looked up to find his eyebrow quirked up.

"What?"

"What's up? Something else is going on."

I sighed as I buried my face into his ribs. "There's this guy."

"What?!" he shrieked and shoved me to arm's length. "You go to a funeral for the weekend and you meet someone, I'm on the market for months and not one guy! Ugh, life is not fair." He stomped his foot then seamlessly started pulling me out of the airport again.

"Dead mom, remember?"

"Heaven above can have my mother if it means I get a big ole dick." He sighed then crossed himself. I couldn't help but giggle. "Girl, spill already!"

"I met him at the gate. He was flying back to Chicago too."

"Love in the air. So Hollywood. Perfect. Continue."

"I talked him into joining the mile high club with me." Heat raced into my chest and cheeks even though Conrad and I had shared the most devilish details with each other over the years.

"Shut up!" He pulled me up short and shoved me to arm's length again. "You had sex on the plane?"

"Yeah and why don't you yell about it a little louder while we're in the airport." I rolled my eyes at him.

"Girl, you look like a Swiss milk maid, TSA wouldn't dream of arresting you, you look too innocent." Conrad rolled his eyes right back. "Now tell me more."

"He's gorgeous and really strong. He has these intense green eyes and tattoos *everywhere*."

"And his dick?"

"Was fabulous. Just like his hands and his mouth." I smiled genuinely as my mind flashed to his lips on mine, his lips on my skin, his dick… Well, just his dick period.

"He went down on you in an airplane bathroom? What I wouldn't do for a blowie from a hot stranger somewhere public. You're living every gay man's fantasy." He sighed dramatically and we started walking again.

"I went home with him. That's where he went down on me." I nudged his ribs. "Wait, that was actually the car. I went down on him at his place, then he choked me. A few times."

Conrad made a screechy sound laced thick with jealousy then abruptly fell away from me. I turned to watch him finish his completely dramatic, completely staged fall straight to the ground. I tried not to giggle as I stood over him with my hands on my hips.

"Rhett? Rhett?" He did his best Southern Belle voice and let his hand drift limply toward me as he decided to come-to.

"Is he okay?" Someone asked from beside Conrad. I noticed a few of the people trying to exit baggage claim had stopped when he hit the floor. We were garnering stares from the rest.

"Besides general idiocy and being dropped as a child, he's just fine." I shook my head.

"Rhett? Is that you?" Conrad was committed to his act and I knew I had to play along.

"Come on Scarlett O'Whora. You've attracted more than the usual amount of attention." I reached down for his one hand still wheeling in the imaginary wind but he wouldn't let me catch it.

When I finally snatched it, Conrad grabbed me and yanked me to my knees beside him. He didn't say anything for a minute while he fanned himself.

"He's fine. He's fine." I reassured the new wave of people walking by.

"He sure is," a deep, manly voice from the crowd answered.

Conrad shot up to sitting then scrambled after the random voice, leaving me kneeling on the floor.

"I should've just gotten a puppy," I mumbled to myself as I rose and hauled my bag onto my shoulder.

"A puppy wouldn't want to hear all about your orgasms." Conrad was already back and kissed my temple.

"But a puppy may be interested that I fell in love."

I didn't even flinch when Conrad's hand fell away and I heard the gasp and telltale thump all over again.

Cole

I pressed play on the video for what was probably the hundredth time today. If I counted the whole week, it had to be close to ten thousand. Elle's goofy wave made me smile each time but her signed *eye heart you* did different things to my insides.

Every emotion had come up while watching her and this time anger snarled in my chest. Pure fury that I couldn't go after her, that I couldn't have her, that Mickey had erased the taste and feel of her.

I replayed the night he'd made me prove my loyalty again. When Jimmy hadn't delivered, Horse had shown up, his head hanging low. I didn't fight him this time, the only consolation I had was that I got my friend back. But that night he'd been a silent, stoic friend.

He hadn't needed to say anything.

The Maloney family was no family at all. It was a collection of depraved villains searching for ways to rain down destruction and make cash while doing it. Mayhem, cocaine and pussy had sounded great at fourteen, but now I knew better. Horse did too.

Mick gave two choices when it came to swearing in: murder or sexual deviancy. I'd watched both far too many times in that darkly lit room that doubled as the Devil's playground. And for my second swearing in, I was given the choice of killing an Italian kid who'd stolen from Mickey or fucking Siobhan. For a good ten minutes, I thought about killing the kid. Pulling the trigger would be instantaneous, the guilt would hang like a thick chain on my neck far longer, but he wouldn't be the last.

In the end, I couldn't do it. He was maybe thirteen and balling where he was chained in front of Mickey's throne. They'd beaten him into submission, blood dripped onto the denim of his jeans. I was a monster but that seemed like a new low.

I trudged over to Siobhan and reached for her dress.

"It's not going to be that easy," she said seductively just before she slapped me and lunged.

I wasn't prepared and she clawed down my cheek and chest, making me stumble backward. A roar rumbled in my chest as I grounded myself. Siobhan and I stood across the small space, both breathing a little heavily. Her smirk matched Mickey's and red started to edge my vision.

A drop of blood from where she'd broken skin with her talons dripped onto my lip just before I bolted for her. I trapped her and squeezed tightly but she fought like the wildcat she was. She bucked against me, letting her knees fly into my thighs. Her claws dug at any part of my body she could reach.

When she landed her knee straight to my groin, I automatically cried out and dropped her. I crumpled to my knees holding my crotch and groaned like a little kid. While I was down Siobhan walked over and brought the point of her fancy leather stiletto to my chin and lifted it.

"You went soft. Thank God Mick has me." She spit on me, her venom landing across the cheek she'd drawn blood from, and I was grateful. It reminded me I wasn't fighting a woman, I was fighting a poisonous rat. And I was going to have to fight dirty.

She kicked against my chest and I let it topple me back. As soon as she pressed her heel to my throat, I grabbed her and twisted her leg with all my might. She screamed loud as pops and cracks moved up her leg and she crashed to the floor.

It was my turn to smirk.

She tried to crawl away from me but I'd actually done damage. I watched her try and crawl away from me for a moment, only to reach out and grab her wounded ankle. I dragged her back across the floor to where I was still kneeling. She shrieked the whole time.

I flipped her on her front then straddled her, notching each of her wrists beneath my knees then reached for her hair. She flopped like a fish, still trying to fight, as I yanked hard on my fistful. She moaned loud and lustful into the dark room as I leaned forward so I could growl through gritted teeth in her ear.

"Mick and you deserve each other but don't for one second think you're better than me."

She whimpered again, more sexual than pained.

I shoved her head down to the floor with far more force than was necessary, hearing another crunch of her slight bones beneath me, then leaned back. Her body finally stopped fighting beneath me and I shoved her skirt up. With a single, swift movement, I ripped her tiny lace panties away. She barely made a sound.

Even when I undid my belt and shoved myself unceremoniously into her, she stayed fairly quiet, dazed and defeated. She was so wet she was slippery and something about that made me all the more furious. I let my hands find her neck as I started hammering into her and I squeezed all the way around. She gurgled beneath me and I felt bile rise in my throat.

"More skin, Cole," Mick yelled from his throne and everything inside me boiled.

But I listened. One hand left her neck and ripped off my shirt then shoved my pants down as far as I could reach. I likewise ripped on her dress.

"Good. Very good." His cackle cut through the room before he started clapping a sinister slow clap.

I knew how it went. I finished or Siobhan fought me off. Those were always the rules. Considering she was barely breathing beneath me, I had to come to get this over with. As I thrust harder and harder, I pictured Elle. Her curves beneath that white cotton dress the first day I'd seen her. Cherry milkshakes and cream cheese frosting. Those delicate little fingers across my ink and wrapped around my dick.

82

She was everywhere I could fit her. In every sense, in every memory. She filled the room, not Mickey Maloney's underlings, not Horse, not his motherfucking laugh. Just Elle.

My balls tightened, my thighs bunched and that feeling she gave me in the pit of my stomach told me a second before I was going to fill Siobhan. I pulled out, dropped a hand from her neck and stroked myself a few times before calling Elle's name as cum squirted all over Siobhan's stomach.

The laugh that Mickey let loose had haunted my dreams for the past week. The fact that I couldn't remember how Elle felt around my dick, but could feel Siobhan, had left my walls with a few holes in them. They were nothing compared to the gaping one left in my heart.

Neither video Elle had sent me could bring her back. Nor could they bring me back to her. I was drifting.

Horse's knock echoed through my apartment, more a threat to break down the door than a request to let him in. I tried to shake off the filth of the memories covering me as I got up to answer the door.

"Hey," I said gruffly.

"You're still up here? Thought you'd be tattooing by now." Horse cocked his head as he studied me.

"I canceled some appointments this week." I walked away from him and crash landed back into bed with a bounce.

"This still about Elle?"

I grunted rather than answered.

"I could kiss it and make it all better." Horse wiggled his eyebrows from where he leaned against my kitchen island.

"You're disgusting, you know that?" I rolled my eyes whether he could see or not.

"What can I say? I got a taste watching the other night, and now I'm just hungry."

"Don't fucking talk about that night!" I shouted as I sprung off the bed and sprinted across the room. I balled my fist into his shirt and cocked my fist back ready to take him down for reminding me of what I'd done.

83

Horse barely moved, simply reaching up and wrapping his hand around mine.

"Sorry, man. Really I am." His whole face shifted, sincerity taking over completely. I dropped my fist to my side but didn't let go of his shirt. Fury still pumped through my veins but I knew it was directed at myself, not Horse.

"Have you talked to her?" he asked quietly, and I knew he was trying to calm me down with the mention of Elle.

"No." I dropped his shirt with a little shove and circled the island to grab a beer from the fridge. I popped the bottle top with the switchblade laying on the counter and relished the first swig of crisp bubbles dancing on my tongue. "She's called a few times but I can't bring myself to answer. She can't be tangled up with me, with *him*. She needs to forget I exist."

We sat in silence for a few minutes and I knew that meant Horse understood. Maybe even agreed. He helped himself to a beer but otherwise didn't interrupt my brooding.

"You ever think what it would be like for both of us to have her?" He sucked in a deep breath, no doubt worried I was going to fly off the handle again. And I was possessive enough that I didn't blame him. But I'd gotten a taste of something the other night with Siobhan, something I didn't entirely loathe—our old and utterly savage ways.

"Yeah, Horse. Just every other fucking fantasy or so."

He blew out a deep breath that turned into a soft chuckle.

"Good. For a second I felt bad about it."

"In an alternate universe she'd be mine and I'd share her from time to time." I chugged my beer to help erase the fact that would never happen.

"Cheers to alternate universes then." Horse audibly glugged his beer then all but slammed his bottle to the countertop. "All right, Cupcake, we've got business to attend to."

"Figured," I mumbled and went over to put on shoes. I tried to push the image of an Elle sandwich from my mind by cleaning the scuffs off my Chuck Taylors.

I grabbed my jacket and wordlessly followed Horse out of the apartment. We walked in sync down to the car and I slid in so naturally, it was like we'd been apart for just a few hours, not a few years. Horse fired up the engine and brought the car to life, the familiarity of it all was oddly soothing.

After all, I was in now. Deep. As deep as I'd been in Siobhan. Whether I liked it or not, whether I wanted to forget it or not, my reality was the Maloney family. I was alive, Elle was safe and Horse was back. Those things couldn't be considered all bad.

"So where are we going?" I asked when we idled at a red light.

"There's Italian rumblings. I think they're trying to edge in again."

"Are you serious?" I couldn't mask my shock.

"As a fucking heart attack, man." For the first time in ages, fear trickled into Horse's voice.

The death and destruction that had blanketed every facet of our life last time this happened descended in darkness. It had almost cost Horse his life and it had forced me to find a way to get mine back. Almost everyone attached to either the Maloneys or the Giancomos had been left hanging to life or freedom by the thinnest nail.

"I thought we'd come to an understanding?"

"So did Mick."

Those words were like a boulder. If Mick hadn't seen this coming, heads were going to roll and blood would spatter the walls in no time. The street around us seemed to run red with it.

"So today's surveillance?" It was wishful thinking but I asked anyway.

"We're questioning a guy." Horse's knuckles turned white when he adjusted his grip on the steering wheel.

I didn't have an answer. Questioning was as good as saying a beat down in the Maloney book. The idea of fists, bruises and broken bones made my stomach lurch, but why it made an enforcer like Horse a little squeamish was beyond me.

We pulled up to a nondescript bakery with cannoli's in the window. Horse blew out a heavy sigh after the engine went silent.

"You have my back right?" he asked, his eyes unable to meet mine.

"Of course. Why wouldn't I?" My brows knit together as I looked over.

"I know you have *my* back but…how do I put this…in there? Do you have my back when things go sideways? When we have to do what Mick wants?" He was the most serious he'd been since tromping back into my life.

"Fuck Mick," I grumbled.

"Yeah, we get it, Cole. He's horrible and terrible and a goddamned monster. But he owns you. He owns me. And unless you wanna go to war, you've gotta accept it."

A minute ago I had, I'd looked at the positive and let this sort of shit slide off my back. I had to keep that up. I had no other choice.

"I said fuck Mick, not fuck you. I have your back and I'll do what we gotta do."

"Good. In that case, reach under the seat," Horse commanded as he slid out of the driver's seat.

I didn't need to pat around to guess what was down there. I reached, my muscle memory guiding me more than anything, and my hand found cold steel. The hash-marked grip of the gun was as familiar as the motion. Without looking, I knew this was the Glock I'd slid across that disgusting wood floor the day I'd walked out.

In one swift movement, I pushed out of the car and shoved it in the back of my waistband. I fell into step behind Horse as we walked into the bakery. The man behind the counter was helping a little old lady but his voice faltered when Horse filled the doorway. He picked back up with his description of desserts as we settled into the back of the room.

The moment the Italian grandma shuffled out, the tension amplified.

"I think you're closed," Horse said gruffly and the man wordlessly slithered from behind the counter and flipped the open sign then clicked the lock.

He hung his head as he came to stand in front of us and I had to check my empathy. I shoved it deep in the space that Elle and everything else that used to be light in my life occupied.

"What do you know about the Giancomos buying up warehouses right on the fringe of Maloney territory? How do they know which buildings they can buy without an immediate hit," Horse growled matching his imposing stature rather than his gooey insides.

His tone told me everything. The man whose chin trembled in front of me was going to die.

"Don't lie to us either. We know you know," Horse continued.

And like clockwork that's when the scrambling began. The *I don't knows* and the *I'm not mixed up in that,* sometimes even the *not sure what you're talking abouts.* This guy did it well, spinning wheels and tales as quickly as his motormouth would allow.

Reading Horse as well as I always had, I knew what was coming a split second before it did. His fist crunched into the man's face with all the force of a Mack truck. His jaw crunched and twisted as blood shot from his lips. One punch from Horse was enough to level him to his knees.

Horse jerked his chin toward the puddle of a human and I knew what he wanted me to do. I stepped behind the man and grabbed his collar, extending his torso so it was a wide open target. He barely waited for me to stretch the whimpering baker out before two Hulk fists pummeled into his stomach. He wheezed and tried to curl onto himself and out of my hands. I adjusted my grip so I had him by the throat.

Following the usual pattern, this was when the story changed a little. Suddenly the baker knew things, vague and hypotheticals, but things nonetheless. Horse peppered him with blows, even a few kicks, hoping to draw the whole story out.

After a particularly hard toe to the ribs, Horse stepped back and met my cold gaze. "What do you think, Cole?"

"I think he knows more than he's saying." That was always the truth after all.

"Mickey would appreciate it if you get it from him."

The mention of Mickey automatically had me wanting to rebel, but Horse glowered at me, reading my thoughts perfectly. So

I shot him a look and squeezed the man's throat. Hard. All the muscles of the baker's neck tensed and wiggled beneath my hand.

"How do they know?" I kept my voice low and icy in his ear.

His hands came to mine and scrambled to break my grip. I tightened it.

"Tell us."

He sputtered, still clawing at me. His neck was a thick block of wood, so hard, so tense, I was trying to crush it rather than just choke him. Even the skin on the back of his neck was turning a purplish hue. He wheezed a few syllables again.

"I think he's trying to tell you something, Cole."

I dropped my grip and let him collapse to the floor. He took two deep breaths before I nudged his shoulder with my Chucks. He flopped flat on his back. It took his eyes a split second to focus on us but then they shifted between both Horse and I where we leaned over him.

"It's Jimmy Ponies. He's playing both sides."

Fury roared inside of me as violent as Mickey himself. Without thinking about my actions, the repercussions—without thinking of absolutely anything—my mind cleared, my breathing slowed and operating on instinct alone, I grabbed my gun from my back, pointed it at the beet red baker and pulled the trigger.

Elle

"The modern medical system doesn't account for the underlying causes. They want to slap on a Band-Aid or prescribe a pill because it's a one-time cost, not an ongoing treatment plan to actually fix the problem. Biomechanics are the root of almost all chronic pain and if they'd just let us take the time to fix biomechanics, we'd solve so much."

"Wow." I said it more because I couldn't believe my date was still carrying on, not because I found his rant on physical therapy entertaining.

"Right?" He totally misinterpreted me and launched into more details.

I had to bite my lip to keep from saying something stupid, or something about strangling Conrad when I got home.

After I told him the full story, about Jimmy and Mr. Maloney and how Cole knew them, about what I felt for Cole, Conrad immediately stopped faux-fainting and went completely serious.

Was meeting you a coincidence?

Conrad had asked like the obvious answer was no. He reasoned that if Jimmy was in deep, and Cole was connected to the people he was in deep with, couldn't he be spying on me? Couldn't he be ensuring payment? The thought had never crossed my mind. But now as Dr. Know-It-All babbled on about the United States health care system, my mind wandered back.

I'd called and texted Cole for a solid two weeks and heard absolutely nothing. I had sent one last text before agreeing to this date.

> Just tell me if you were watching me because of Jimmy or if it was real. I mean, it felt real to me but...

I sounded like an idiot and I knew it. I couldn't even finish the text for Christ's sake but it nagged at me. More than Cole not answering, the seed of doubt that Conrad had planted was far worse. I could live with not talking but I couldn't deal with our moments together being an act.

"See you've got to have decent shoulder tension or maybe even tension headaches but I can fix that by the release of the upper traps and retraining of the lower traps, lats, rotator cuff." Dr. Know-It-All reached across the table to rest his hand on my shoulders.

They melted and I hadn't even realized they'd crept up to my ears.

"I'm fine. Thank you." I gently reached for his hand and pushed it down to the table. The thought of him caressing my neck made my skin crawl.

Apparently my body only responded to brutish strangers choking me.

"You're fine now but give it a couple of years and..."
Blah blah blah.

The date was as blah as the guy, both paling in comparison to the bone shaker that Cole had been. To pass the time I imagined Cole's tattoos on the doctor's skin, it was the only way to keep my eyes attentive and my smile polite. The ink didn't fit beneath his khaki blazer but it passed the time.

Before I knew it I was dodging his kiss as I all but shot into the back of an Uber. I grabbed my phone, ready to screech at Conrad for what he'd done, but it opened to my texts. My empty texts. Cole hadn't taken the opportunity to explain himself.

90

I should have taken a video of a far too aggressive middle finger but I just couldn't. The distress he'd worn the last time I'd saw him stopped me short. That wasn't the response of a man on a literal mission. That was honest and pure, and it made me miss him all the more.

I scrolled up through the messages to find the one message I had from him. I couldn't help but trace the letters of his text with my finger.

"On a date?" My Uber driver tried to strike up a conversation, I grunted and bent over my phone.

My finger caught the edge of the video I'd first sent him. The one of me masturbating with him coated on my thighs. Cum on camera was all I had left of Cole. It wasn't a lot, it certainly wasn't those bewitching green eyes, deliciously roped body or the bruises he left me with, but it was him.

When I glanced up, my driver was finding anywhere to look but the backseat, so I pressed play. I admitted it was slightly twisted to watch myself touching *myself* but it was for Cole. And it was him speckling my thighs after all.

I surrendered to it. And when I did, the video was hot. Like good porn hot. Arousal was spreading between my thighs at the sight of, well, arousal between my thighs. Watching, my body remembered how I'd trembled beneath my fingers, then beneath his. How warm I'd been when he was coming on me, and it wasn't the heat of his jizz but a fire far deeper.

I looked up and checked the Uber driver's line of sight again in the rearview mirror. The memory of Cole watching me in his mirror pounced on me. The need to get off built and broke inside me in a matter of moments.

My teeth bit down on my lip far too hard as I shuffled my bag onto my lap to shield me further from the driver's eyes. I worked the fly down on my jeans and pressed my fingers between my thighs. I adjusted my phone so I could watch again and pressed play. Synchronized with my videoed movements, I started to rub one out in the back of a 2013 silver Prius.

I wasn't there anymore. I was in a vintage Charger, an airplane bathroom, a leather belt latched across my throat. My

91

fingers rubbed and dipped around my clit, sliding easily everywhere it went.

My teeth were going to break right through my lip. In hindsight, a silent orgasm inspired by Cole was a horrible idea but I was too turned on now to stop. My finger skated around and around, in and out, just as I'd done in the video. My hips bucked up but after just a moment I shoved myself down remembering I was in an Uber, not Cole's bed.

I peeked up at the mirror and it only fueled my fire. The video playing out did too. I was building, courtesy of my hidden finger, and fast. I pictured Cole, what he would say, what he would do if he were here now and I felt the build up.

Remembering him vulnerable and scared in the shower the last few moments we'd been together pushed me over. Waves of an orgasm crashed into me and I couldn't help but close my eyes and drown in it. When the palpitations stopped, I was left gasping but still kept hold of my bottom lip to do what I could to disguise it.

Cole. Cole. Cole.

My body trembled at a rhythm that was all his.

"Miss, we're here." The Uber driver was glancing back in the rearview mirror and even just the movement renewed the trembling in my body.

I didn't try to hide it this time. I couldn't. My lip sprung free and a whimper ghosted across my lips. His eyes bugged, and I flushed from head to toe. But I couldn't make myself feel bad. The delicious orgasm alone wouldn't let me. The very real memory of Cole's hands on my body was a second and very enticing reason not to give a single fuck.

His gaze shifted down to my take in my heavy breathing and then further to where my bag sat piled on my lap. Beyond a shadow of a doubt, I knew he knew what I'd just done. It colored his face a darker shade than mine had to be.

Cole would laugh. Hard. And then he'd rub his hand overtop of mine where it still lingered inside my fly as he kissed me in that completely soul shaking kind of way. With his smirk in the back of my mind, I pulled my hand out, unseating my bag from my lap and exposing my open fly. I zipped it and the sound spliced through the dead silence of the car. My driver's eyes went even wider.

"So, um, yeah. Thanks." I shot a hand gesture that was a lot like a gun in his direction and slid out.

The tires of the Prius squealed on the pavement as much as Prius wheels could and the second he was back in traffic, I doubled over laughing. It took me a while to let go of my knees and stand up straight. It took me even longer to catch my breath. But the giggles didn't fade as I walked up the stairs to my apartment.

"What's so funny?" Conrad asked from the couch when a second wave of giggles overtook me with the door firmly closed behind me.

"Nothing," I answered, waving him off as I chucked my bag on the table.

"It's not nothing." He stood up and walked over to lean against the wall, crossing his arms to study me as he went. "You orgasmed."

"What?" I tried to sound more shocked than guilty.

"Don't you dare what me. That wrinkle," he stepped toward me and pressed his pointer finger to the middle of my forehead, "disappears when you come. Was the doctor that good?"

"The doctor blew." I didn't even bother to check myself as I wove around Conrad and yanked open the fridge. I popped open the wine and poured it into the nearest coffee mug before turning back to him. "You ever set me up with a piece of cardboard like that again and you're going to find yourself on the streets."

"Just because you sell a few of your art pieces for serious money doesn't mean you own me. Just the condo. It takes way more than a lease to boss me around." He quirked his eyebrow.

"Yeah, a big dick and low standards."

"True." He smirked. "Now spill."

I sighed as I studied my best friend. He had that thin-lipped and pinched brow look that he got when he was focused. When he was writing that face show up when the words were flowing past his brain and directly to his fingertips. It was the epitome of determination.

93

"Fine." I grabbed my phone, flipped to the video of me doing me, "I was thinking of Cole and watching this. I got myself off in the backseat of my Uber."

My phone clattered against the tabletop and Conrad reached over for the moving screen.

"Oh holy fuck. That's a vagina." He dropped it like I'd handed him a hot coal.

"That's my vagina." I arched my eyebrow.

"You got off watching yourself? What kind of monster are you?"

My giggles were back in full force.

"I mean is that an Oedipus complex? Should I worry about having to save you when you fall in? Or have you become a lesbian without telling me? Because maybe then we could get married." He looked over at my phone once or twice and pretended to vomit.

"I was thinking of Cole. Of how he made me feel." A contented smile spread across my face.

"Girl, you have got to get off that mob train or whatever it is. Nothing good will come from that." He sounded like my mother. Or like my mother would have if she gave a damn, if she hadn't been wrapped up in that *mob shit* herself.

"Except orgasms," I countered.

"Except orgasms," he agreed. "But that's not enough Elle Belle. Not even remotely. Apparently great orgasms come at the touch of a button these days." He pointed toward my phone.

"They've always come at the touch of a button." I pointed down at the apex of my thighs.

"Touché." He blew out a deep breath. "Just remember that, okay?"

My eyes roved over Conrad as I debated just what to say to him. Or whether to say anything at all.

"What?" His eyes narrowed as if he could read my thoughts.

"Nothing, I didn't say anything." I held up my hands in surrender.

94

"You didn't need to. I could see it. But now I wanna hear you say it. I want you to hear you say it." He shoved his hands on his hips.

"Fine. Here you go." I sucked in a deep breath. "You know that Greek myth? The one where Zeus split four armed, four legged humans in half?"

Conrad rolled his eyes but he nodded all the same.

"What if he's that person for me? What if the reason he's etched inside me is because he was always meant to be there?"

"That's horseshit and you know it," he scoffed.

"No. I don't actually. And neither do you." I walked over and poked him in the chest. "You believe in big love, Cinderella, you just don't know what it feels like to lose your balance and fall face first into it."

With that I shoved past him and into the spare bedroom we'd converted into a studio space. His side was scattered with newspaper and magazine clippings of his various articles, his silent computer and the loose pages of his never-ending manuscript. I scowled at it the way I would have at him.

I slipped over to my side and grabbed my headphones, pulling them on quickly and pressing play on the first playlist that popped up. My pencil found paper and lines started materializing. I wasn't thinking about shapes or shading, I just let it flow.

Cole still filled my senses. A part of me wondered if he'd ever leave. An even bigger part worried that somehow he would.

I pray to God you never know how much you mean to me.

Those words, those beautiful bastard words were proof it wasn't a setup. Right? He'd felt that magnetic pull of myth, hadn't he? I asked myself the questions over and over, tracing the words as they materialized in my mind the same way I had his tattoos. My hand scrolled against the paper and I bobbed in time with the music but I was a woman consumed.

It was probably an hour or so later when the speaker of my headphone pulled away from my ear.

"Are we fighting?" Conrad asked quietly.

95

I sighed dramatically as I put down my pencil and looked up at him. He stuck his bottom lip out and held his hands up like a begging puppy.

"No." I drug out the word so it had ten syllables. "I just..." I didn't know where to start. "You can't..." How could I make him understand? How did I for that matter? Forty-eight hours of sex shouldn't feel like a lifetime of right.

"Stop with the don't, stop with the can't, okay? You can't stop thinking about his dick. You don't want a smaller, weaker one. End of story, Belles. It's literally not healthy to feel more than that."

"It's okay to need him," I mumbled.

"It's okay to want him," he snarked back.

My eyes fell from his and found what I'd been doodling on my page. It was abstract, nothing I could ever carve but it was familiar all the same. The panther with glowing eyes looked back at me from the paper the same way it did from skin. Cole's skin.

It was a snap decision, every bit as instinctual as every other interaction with Cole but the words were tumbling out of my mouth before I realized it.

"No. *Need.* I'm going back. I need to see him."

Cole

"Fuck. Fuckfuckfuckfuck, Cole!" Horse bellowed over the corpse on the floor. "This wasn't a hit, it was a shakedown. Mick's gonna be pissed. He doesn't want to provoke the Giancomos but that's what we just did."

"He's not part of the family or he wouldn't have caved," I grunted back. "No one in that family actually caves."

"Why'd you do it? I mean you're a fucking talented monster once you make up your mind, but we used to have to sit in the car and talk about all the reasons you needed to kill someone. It's never been easy, you've never been reckless."

That was the million-dollar question wasn't it. The answer was Elle, but why Elle was an answer in the first place was beyond me. That she'd altered everything inside me in so short of time was stupid. But it was true.

"It's her." I finally tucked my gun away still staring down at my headfirst dive back into the made life.

Horse scoffed, making some noise that was exactly Horse-like before pulling out his phone and dialing. After just a few quipped sentences he slid the phone back into his pocket. Just like that, the family cleaner was on the way.

"What did this chick do to you?" he asked as the sun started to cast deep shadows in through the windows.

"Fuck if I know. Haven't a clue how to explain it." I rubbed the back of my neck. "It's like she tore up everything inside me

97

with a look, then smoothed it back over with a kiss. She saw *everything* about me, even this," I gestured at the dead baker, "and didn't flinch."

"She saw you kill someone?" His brow creased, then his whole face crinkled.

"No but she knows about the Maloneys, she knows what her mom did, she knew what it meant when I said I'd been in with them."

"I got news for you, Cupcake, she has no idea what monster's lying in her bed. Until she stands like this, like us right now, she won't." He clapped me on the shoulder and started to pull me toward the backdoor. We didn't speak until we'd walked a few blocks in the wrong way then circled back to the car from a different direction.

"We have to tell Mickey," Horse said as he slid into the front seat.

Shivers rolled up and down my spine. Mick was going to have my head for making waves and leaving bodies. I'd have to toughen up and quick to deal with that. It was his other reaction that had me worried. If Jimmy Ponies was the one giving info to the Italians, if he'd given them Mickey's lost possession, he was as good as dead. And if he was dead, this mystery item unrecovered, Elle was fair game. To deal with that, I'd have to get smarter even faster. The roar of my protective fury had pulled the trigger but I was in desperate need of finding level footing. And staying there.

"Yeah," I mumbled, pressed up against my window watching the slight fog from my breath disappear beneath the glow starting to come from streetlights.

"Are you ready for that?" Horse's voice was tentative, something it only ever was when he worried about me. I guessed he'd come to the same conclusion about Mickey as I had—Elle and I were fucked.

"I have to be."

Neither of us spoke again as we drove away from the bakery. Horse was lost in thought, staring out at the road barely blinking. My mind raced the car to Mickey's place. I had to have my words straight before I walked in there. If Mick fueled my temper, something I'd regret was bound to happen. Our past two meetings were proof.

We pulled up to the house and I all but jumped out. I was ready for Mick, ready for anything he could throw at me. Pulling the trigger had rooted me back in this life I'd been trying to float above. It only took one bullet to remember the game and how to play it. And as long as it meant keeping Elle out, I was going to win.

I barged in, letting the door bang against the wall as I did. The same kid that had taunted me the first night I'd been back jumped up from his perch, sending the chair flying and a clatter echoing through the room. He was scrambling to draw his gun but I was faster. I had mine pointed at his head in a single breath.

"Don't give me any fucking trouble. Where's Mick?"

"He's uhhh…" The kid's eyes crossed at the barrel of my gun. He stammered a few more weird sounds.

"Jesus, kid." I bent down and placed the gun on the coffee table. "How about now? Can you tell me if he's upstairs now?"

Horse chuckled behind me a little bit and I knew he'd wanted to put this pup in his place ages ago.

"Yeah but…"

Oh God, I knew what that but meant. It meant he was in the middle of something, likely something I didn't want to see. But want and need were two different things in my world now. I started up the stairs and felt Horse quick on my heels.

"Kill one guy and you're back? Completely back?" he whispered in my ear.

"I kind of have to be now, don't I?"

I clenched my fist by my side just before I shoved into the den, bracing myself for whatever was going to meet me. My stomach turned all the same when I took in Mick, balls deep in Siobhan and two barely legal girls sucking on her tits.

The spectacle was center stage in front of a whole group of thugs and underlings. All eyes were fixed on the sway of Siobhan's body in time with Mick's thrusts. The girls beneath her both sat on their hands, using their mouths to capture and suck on any inch of flesh they could find.

"Horse, Cole, so good of you to join us. Want in?"

Siobhan threw her head back, letting her flaming ginger locks cascade down around her face. She still wore the fading remnants of a bruise on her temple and a healing gash above her eyebrow, both of which I'd given her. They added a downright menacing shadow to her wicked features.

Her emerald eyes bore into mine as a downright evil smile spread across her face. Her talons sharpened into the girls' shoulders beneath her. They both faltered underneath when she drew blood before she encouraged, "Lap my little kittens. Make him desperate to join us."

"I'll kill you before I fuck you again, Siobhan," I spit the words out at her as she took the railing Mick was handing down.

"Awe, Cole I love it when you talk dirty to me."

I walked right up to her and grabbed around her throat. I used my grip to pull her up to standing. Mick laughed when she was eye to eye with me and he thrust into her all the harder. I squeezed on the curve of her throat and glowered at her.

"You're done here ladies." I didn't even look down at them. "Go."

They didn't hesitate, both scrambling on hands and knees out the door.

Mick laughed harder. "Choke her, Cole," he managed between gasping thrusts and breathy laughs.

"Gladly." I squeezed hard, as hard as when I'd thumped her head against the floorboards to leave her limp, forcing her onto tiptoe.

A downright sinister laugh came from Mick. Siobhan's gargle mingled with it and her hands came to mine. She didn't pull though, instead she ran her fingers across mine, caressing where they pressed against her skin. She mouthed *I missed you* at me and disgust welled inside me.

Without thinking, I used my grip to pull her the slightest bit higher. Her toes scrambled for the floor but Mick just adjusted his grip to allow me to pull on her. When she was completely at my mercy, I threw her.

Mick faltered the tiniest bit and snarled but it was nothing compared to the sound of her bones thumping into the floor. She screeched, which only brought back Mick's diabolical laughter. He started jerking off on her piled flesh.

"I killed him, Mick. I killed that baker." My shoulders heaved as I spoke.

"Oh yeah?" He continued stroking himself. "Tell me. Tell me how he begged. Tell me if you choked him. Tell me what his blood looked like on the floor."

"He looked dead, Mick. Like a dead fucking Giancomo informant. He kind of looked like Siobhan down there."

"MMMMmmm Laddy, did you stand over him and shoot him in cold blood like you would me if given the chance?" Siobhan purred from the floor, her hands finding her nipples and gently flicking at them.

I didn't give either of them the satisfaction of an answer. Horse grabbed my shoulder and pulled me a little bit back from their filth as we waited for them to finish. Both had fingers flying against themselves, stroking however they saw fit while the rest of us simply watched. When Siobhan finally came, she was loud and her body shook against the hardwood. Mickey groaned, pained, and plead with me once more.

"Was there blood everywhere, Cole?" His voice was haggard and rough, his tugs and pulls on his dick getting more furious.

"It was more of a puddle, Mick," I answered and Horse's fingers curled into me.

He came with a groan and his spunk dribbled down onto Siobhan. She twisted to make sure it landed on her chest and I curled my lip up at the whole scene. The room was thick with heavy breathing but no one spoke as a purring Siobhan and a downwardly spiraling Mickey came to.

"Why'd you kill him?" Micky asked as he tucked himself away. "And get up, put some clothes on." He nudged Siobhan with his toe.

101

"He deserved to die," I answered simply while I watched Siobhan pick herself up and stomp over to a discarded scrap of fabric.

"I appreciate the attitude, it's like I have my boy back, but let me rephrase. Why the fuck did you kill someone with motherfucking Italian ties?" Mick turned to snarl in my face.

"He spilled," Horse spoke up behind me.

Mick jerked his head toward the throne he loved to sit on. I followed to stand in front of him as Horse settled into the familiar chair to his left. Siobhan checked my shoulder with hers as she sidled up to sit on Mick's right hand side.

"Cole's going to tell me a story, lass. You can sit elsewhere." He brushed her off with the flick of his wrist, his gaze not wavering from me.

She stomped away and fire blazed in her eyes like the devil himself lit the inferno. Horse shot me a worried look, speaking volumes about the meaning and danger of me replacing Siobhan at his right hand.

"So?" Mick asked as he pulled a large knife from somewhere and started to dig dirty, or maybe flesh, out from under his nails.

"He gave us a name," I said as Horse's worried face came back, he even chewed on his big ole bottom lip.

"And?"

Horse and I locked eyes for a moment and I took a breath. If things went sideways, a guy who gave me *that* look had my back. I swallowed the breath I wanted to blow out.

"I'm not sure if he's just informing or actually working for them but…" I looked around the room, just now wondering if he'd die tonight on the floor in front of me. There was no trace of inky, greased back hair. "It's Jimmy Ponies."

Mick started laughing, wilder and more crazed than before. Siobhan joined in too. Horse just hung his head.

"What's so fucking funny?"

After his devious laugh had run its course, Mick calmed and looked me dead in the eye. "Of course, it was Jimmy Ponies. The fucking rat has been giving them any kind of information he can to save his worthless hide." His lips curled up in a wicked smile. "I needed to see where your loyalty really was. Whether it was with that little lassy or with me. I also needed to see if you'd gone soft."

He clapped his arm around my shoulders, his knife tapping my shoulder, and my skin crawled. My temper bubbled up too. In a swift move, I got out from under his grip and shoved my forearm to his throat. I slammed him back against the wood of his throne. The blade clattered to the ground.

"Don't you ever fuck with me again, Mick."

His eyes flashed whether with hunger or pride I couldn't tell. I dropped my arm a moment later and rolled back into my seat. The second I relaxed, he lunged at me. His hand came to my throat. I went to block him—I'd always been faster than Mick—but my hands fell away.

Mick's fingertips were digging into my skin. He used his grip to bang my head twice as hard as I had his.

"I'll fuck with you, hell, I'll plain fuck you. You're mine, Cole. And I do what I want with what's mine."

He leaned in and I had to fight the urge to fight back with every fiber of my being.

"Good boy," Mick purred and the corner of his smile turned up.

But he didn't let go.

"Siobhan, come here," he commanded.

She appeared over the top of his shoulder and her eyes glinted with the same unholy gleam as Mick's. Her fingers tentatively reached out toward my throat like she wanted to replace his hand. I couldn't help but tense away from her.

"What can I do for you, Mickey?" She nuzzled down into his back like the twisted fucking cat she was.

"You're going to Seattle," Mick said, twisting the slightest back toward her.

"No," I wheezed out from behind Mick's hand.

"Yes, Cole." He squeezed and thumped my head again.

This time I didn't care if I was supposed to show my acceptance, or let Mick dominate me, I fought back. My hands came to his and pulled. When he only squeezed tighter, I made a fist and crushed it down on Mick's arm. He automatically let go and I lunged for him. We toppled to the floor in a pile of bodies but I landed on top.

I cocked back to let my fist fly at his face when once again a crushing Hulk hand wrapped around it. Then around me.

"Let go of me, Horse," I barked as I fought against his grip. As strong as I was, I couldn't budge against the boulder that was my best friend.

"Calm the fuck down," he whispered in my ear and accented his words with a squeeze where he bear hugged my body.

"You're lucky Horse stopped you when he did." Mick stood and swiftly let loose a punch to my gut. "You're lucky that I'm impressed with you murdering that informant in cold-blood." He punched the other side of my stomach. "You're lucky I'm glad you're back."

This time his fist crunched into my jaw.

"Get your mind fucking right, Cole. That pretty little blonde is going to be mine. Just like you." Mick eyed me without the slightest hint of humor in his eyes. "Siobhan, go get Elle Leroux and bring her here."

Mick circled away from me and seated himself in his chair. He found his knife again and started picking at his fingernails. He dismissed Siobhan with a wave of his hand and she turned on her heel. At the last moment, he called after her, a chuckle thick in his voice.

"Lassy, do try and keep her in one piece."

Elle

I blew out a deep breath as I threw my backpack over my shoulder in the terminal. Now that I was thinking through my actions, this part presented some problems. I mean, I didn't really know where Cole lived. Nor was he answering my calls. I hadn't left a message saying I was in Chicago, I didn't want to scare him, but now I needed an address. Or even a direction.

The drive to his place was a little vague considering the orgasms and whatnot. The giant buildings of downtown had come into view but little else was memorable. There was that bakery we'd stopped at but the name wasn't coming to me. Likewise, the route from his place to the church had been a whirling blur of emotion.

I should have paid more attention.

Because now I was in O'Hare after dodging Conrad's lectures and sneaking out of the apartment to catch a red-eye decidedly alone. The idea of Cole was enough to keep me going down to the train and venturing into the city.

We rattled into the Clark stop at the heart of downtown and I stepped off the train with no better idea of where to start. The station was the epitome of a big city. The noise of the trains blurred with the din of the crowd shuffling from train to train, complete with a violinist playing for tips between the dingy tiled pillars.

I rode the escalators up to the city street only to add blaring horns to the cacophony of noise and sensation. Equal parts trash and coffee drifted into my nose on the wind. Tall buildings enveloped me and another train line made a rough rooftop to my city cocoon. I filled my lungs with the city and smiled.

Cole was somewhere close and come hell or high water I was going to find him. Even if he told me to fuck off, or that he had been sent to find me, at least I would know. And there was a certain freedom in knowing.

I started to wander, finding dilapidated bookstores, a croissant to die for and a vintage store that I'd have to check out when it opened. It was still early but the city breathed a calm electricity that suited me. Adventure coursed through my veins.

Well, adventure and Cole.

Wind blew down the building corridors and made my hair dance around my face. My natural reaction was to turn around and walk with the wind at my back. It blew off the lake and carried me into a totally different neighborhood. This one had smaller buildings, all of which seemed converted warehouses and housed trendy restaurants and bars.

It all felt vaguely familiar.

Deliriously good smelling burgers grabbed me by the stomach and pulled. I followed my nose into a small diner that had been upgraded to look sleek but still featured a long-countered bar. They seated me right away and as I slid onto my stool, the two bartenders started talking about tattoos.

My eyes flicked up and I traced the ink they were discussing with my eyes the way they did with their hands. Something about the lines and detailing seemed familiar.

"Yeah, Cole down the street is the shit."

The name was enough for me to drop the menu.

"Did you say Cole? Where are you guys talking about?"

One of the bartenders looked over and his eyes lit up.

"Well, hey there. How are you today?"

"Good. Great. Fine. What were you saying about tattoos?"

"There's a shop here in the Fulton Market District that's awesome. A guy named Cole owns it. Maybe four blocks down, three blocks up near The Aviary. Sick work." His eyes hooded a little and his smile quirked up. "You got any tattoos you wanna show me?"

"Nope." I popped my P and jumped off my stool.

I swiftly grabbed my bag and bolted out the door. As I ran the blocks, the streets seemed a bit more familiar. When I rounded the corner, I noticed the familiar tattoo shop sign a split second before recognizing a far more welcoming sight. His stairwell.

I took the stairs two at a time, remembering the steel steps and the sound they sent echoing out into the corridor. His door was familiar too and my fingers itched to knock. But now that I was here, my insides churned.

What if he didn't want to see me? What if it was all a trap?

What if he was my missing half?

The last thought had me pounding on the door before I thought twice. I banged harder than was necessary but God…the man on the other side was worth it.

After just a heartbeat the door swung open. Before I could even process that Cole stood before me, the barrel of a gun was pointed at my forehead. My breath caught but fear didn't filter through my body. Mainly because I recognized the tattoo covered fingers wrapped around the trigger.

"Cole?" I leaned out from behind the barrel to meet his eyes.

The green burning intensity that met me sent butterflies ricocheting through my insides, despite the fading bruise that colored his left cheek and eye. Electricity threatened to short circuit my whole body until his face fell, crumbling piece by piece as he whispered a ghostly, "No."

I inwardly disintegrated right along with him.

"Look I know this is weird but…"

He shoved the gun in the back of his pants and I almost drooled at the way it made his shirtless torso dance. The delight was short lived though because a single second later he snapped up keys from somewhere beside the door, snatched my arm and started yanking me down the steel stairs.

Cole hadn't bothered with a shirt and when he swore and started hopping, I noticed he hadn't grabbed shoes either.

"Cole. Hey!" I shouted, my voice adding to the sound reverberating through the hallway. "Talk to me." When he just kept pulling me out onto the street and toward his Charger, panic set in. "I'm sorry. Cole, I'm so sorry. I just wanted to see you."

"Gotta get you on a plane but not home. God, where do I send you…?" he muttered to himself as he rounded the hood of his car with me in tow.

He shoved his key into the lock and opened the passenger door before shoving me in. The second the door slammed in my face, he bolted behind the car and I watched his body coil and flex in the rearview mirror. The sculpture was almost enough to make me forget the whirlwind of rejection he was putting me through.

Cole slid into the car next to me and I noticed he was gasping for air. "You can't be here. You just can't." His voice broke.

"I can't be there either," I whispered before capturing my bottom lip, refusing to let go.

"Hey," he said softly as he turned and grabbed my face between his rough hands. The eyes of a crazed man studied my face. "I have to keep you safe." His thumbs traced along my cheekbones, his other fingers tangled in my hair.

He pulled away from me and jammed the key into the ignition. The Charger roared to life with its snarly, panty dropping rumble and I couldn't help but purr. Cole looked over and a hint of a smile pulled on his lip.

"I never thought I'd see you again, Ladyface. I can't decide if it's a good or a bad thing that I'm wrong."

"What does that—"

A massive thump on the hood cut my sentence short. I was sure we'd hit someone despite never pulling away from the curb. My head snapped toward the hood to find a giant man leaning over the hood of the car, glowering at Cole.

After a minute, I remembered where I'd seen him before. My mom's funeral. He'd been with Mr. Maloney. He'd stopped Cole from taking a swing at the pig.

"Fuck," I murmured and Cole nodded slowly in agreement but otherwise no one moved.

The man's shoulders rose and fell a little too quickly and the dips and grooves of arms flexed in time with his haggard breathing where they peeked out of his gym tank. His deep chocolate eyes were every bit as intense as Cole's but they appeared to be equal parts warm and furious. His jaw tensed, forcing his big pouty lips to thin to a frown as his fingers tried to dig into the metal of the machine.

"What do you think you're doing?" the man roared over the engine.

"You know as well as I do," Cole yelled back.

"Signing your death warrant?" When the man crooked his eyebrow underneath his baseball hat, his features lightened and he became truly handsome. His words had me balling my fists into the seat all the same. Cole and death didn't belong in the same sentence, of that much my very soul was sure of.

"Don't you dare get yourself hurt," I said as sternly as I could manage under the circumstances.

Both men looked at me, Cole from beside me and the brute from the hood, they both smiled. Big, charming and oddly matching smiles.

"Cole, whatever's going on, please, please, please promise me you won't put yourself in danger," I begged as we stayed locked in the stand off.

He turned the key and the engine fell silent.

"Good choice, Cupcake."

The man left the hood and came to my window. He knocked and smiled the widest, most charming smile I'd ever seen. The kind that would send Conrad into full-blown hysterics. He gestured for me to roll down my window and with his goofy face egging me on, I did just that.

"Hi, Elle." He reached into the car to shake my hand. When I threaded mine into his, he didn't shake it, instead he turned it with a crushing grip then kissed the back of my hand. "I'm Horse. It's good to meet you." His chocolate eyes danced where my knuckles and his hat brim framed them.

"Hi, Horse. Mind telling me how you know who I am?" I cocked my head to the side when I asked.

109

"You're a popular lady around these parts," he started.

"Horse, don't," Cole warned from over my shoulder.

"Cole can't talk about anything but you, either. Made for boring conversation until I saw you just now." Horse bit his lip in a way that made something flutter inside me.

"Knock it off, Horse..." Cole was forceful beside me. "And let us leave."

He let my hand go so he could fold his forearms along the window ledge as he crouched down to level with us. Horse was a perfectly apt nickname because even balling in on himself he filled the open window.

"I can't Cole, and you know it. You can't, and you know it. Letting you guys go is a surefire way for all three of us to end up dead." He wasn't threatening Cole this time, it was more like he was simply stating facts.

"Making her stay is a surefire way she ends up worse than dead."

My mouth dropped. I didn't quite understand what was happening but it was bad. Bad and *serious*. They kept up their conversation as if the world wasn't falling out from underneath me.

"There's nothing worse than dead, Cupcake."

"You haven't tasted heaven," Cole answered quickly and his hand came to the back of my neck, squeezing in a way that was possessive and dug into the side of my neck the slightest bit.

"But I've lived in hell," he said with a sharp edge. "Perhaps you should share?" Horse's voice turned up at the end obviously asking a question.

"Horse..." Cole wavered for the first time, tensing against my flesh again.

"You said you fantasized about it." His voice was still softly questioning rather than challenging Cole. "Give me a reason to put my life on the line. Let me taste heaven."

"You know I like it, you know I wanna share, but Elle is her own woman. Hell, she's her own universe. It's not my call."

I looked over at him when he called me a universe and for the first time since I'd shown up on his doorstep, his face was lit up as he let his eyes rove down my body.

"You're right, technically it's Mick's," Horse's voice went low and severe again.

"You wouldn't dare," Cole roared and slammed his palm into the steering wheel.

"Give me a reason not to," he challenged unaffected by Cole's outburst. "Give her a reason to give me a reason not to."

Cole's heavy breathing and anxiety filled the car. His fingers were digging into me but I wouldn't break his hold. Instead, I turned and cuddled into his hard chest. His grip responded, holding me tight to the crook of his shoulder. He twisted, bringing his lips to my forehead and he breathed in deeply.

We sat like that for a few minutes before the softest whisper of a touch skated down the back of my arm. I jumped away from Cole and toward the hand that had taken the liberty of touching me.

"What are you doing?" I asked Horse sharply.

He made a face at Cole that I couldn't possibly decipher. It was almost expectant, like he wanted Cole to answer the question I'd asked. Cole blew out a deep breath, forceful enough to rustle the wavy strands of hair hanging in my face. He pulled me back into the crook of his shoulder.

"Ladyface?" he questioned with his mouth right against my ear.

"Yeah?" I nuzzled against his warm skin and breathed in deep, relishing the scent that hung on his skin.

"You got a half hour to spare?" His lips brushed against my skin.

"Of course. Why?"

"I need to tell you a story." His grip got uncomfortably tight.

"What about?" I asked, almost breathless.

He blew out another one of those world-weary breaths and curled around me the way he had that morning not too long ago in the shower. Cole cleared his throat but his voice wavered all the

111

same as he answered, "The murderer you're about to have a threesome with."

Cole

Elle lurched away from me, shoving at my chest then at the handle. Horse stood and stepped back, letting her storm out of the car with the door left bouncing on the hinges. I shot out of the car and rounded the hood after her. She made it two steps before Horse's Hulk hands found their way back to her arm. This time he gripped rather than stroked her bare skin.

"Get your hands off me," she squeaked and my heart thumped.

I wanted to slug Horse hard enough that he'd let her go. I wanted to hear her scream profanities at me as she walked, no *ran*, away. I wanted her free. But none of those things were going to happen now, except maybe the screaming. Horse materializing from nowhere had left me with almost no options. Almost.

"Cole!" she screamed and it tightened everything inside me. I thought I might liquefy when she added, "Never mind you monster."

"Oh my little Fucktart, he's the farthest thing from a monster. You of all people should know that." Horse's hands were moving a little too low and her body responded to their movements whether she, or I, wanted to acknowledge it.

"What's that supposed to mean?" She bucked against his grip and my dick twitched as she struggled.

"Can we just talk, Ladyface? You and I?" I eyed Horse when I asked, wordlessly telling him to stand down and give me a minute.

"You'll tell me what he's talking about?" She stilled slightly in his arms.

"I'll tell you absolutely anything." I held my hands out wide to her. "First things first, how about I start with telling you it was real. Every single second of it. I was on my way home from a tattoo expo in Seattle when I crashed head first into you." It was the answer to the text messages she'd sent that I tried to ignore.

"Let go of me." Her voice was smaller now and far less furious.

I nodded at Horse and he studied me for a split second before dropping his hold. Elle collided into me. I gladly caught her and wrapped my arms around her, hoping it wouldn't be the last time.

"Tell me. Tell me everything," Elle's voice was muffled by my skin and I liked the way it vibrated my skin.

"I think it's best we get out of the street," Horse interrupted and I automatically looked up to scan the area. He did the same. "And her phone. I mean…it's Siobhan."

"Shit," I swore under my breath. "Ladyface, give me your phone."

She didn't question me this time, quickly digging into her bag and pulling it out. After she glanced at it, I snatched it and threw it to Horse.

"You'll do the honors?" I showed him my bare feet to explain why I wasn't.

He nodded and dropped it, only for it to crunch under the heel of his boot a second later. Glass and plastic confetti littered the street.

"Hey!" Elle shoved out of my arms again and pride flashed in my chest as she wheeled on Horse.

I wrangled her and her back landed against my front, even furious, I liked the way she fit against me. She fought my hold half-heartedly, so I squeezed a bit.

"Second," I murmured into her ear, "everything I've done since I met you has been *for* you. Including smashing your phone, as delusional as that sounds."

Her body melted into mine.

114

"Guys, you're real lucky Mick trusted me enough to watch Cole. It could have been anyone across the street. There still could be anyone across the street. Let's not push it." Horse jerked his head toward Cole's stairs.

Elle didn't say a word but she didn't fight either. I let go and reached down for her hand. My fingers wove as naturally into hers as my body did around her. Hers wrapped back. It made me shiver for all the right reasons as I started stroking her thumb with mine. Horse followed behind us as I gently pulled her back to my apartment.

As soon as we were inside, I sat her down on the corner of my bed and Horse made himself scarce. I pulled on her knees to twist her completely away from any view of him. I needed her focus solely on me.

"Where do you want me to start?" I asked as I crouched in front of her and found a spot to trace on her knee.

"The murderer part is probably a good place." She swallowed the word murder, her body rejecting the dark.

"Yeah, I should have softened that," I rubbed the back of my neck in time with the spot of skin she kept letting me touch. She didn't answer, she just waited. Her silence was more nerve-wracking than her angry spew. I sighed loudly.

"You remember I said I grew up rough? Well it was with the Maloney family. Horse and I got into some trouble when we were younger, running around like we owned this city. We stole the wrong car..." My voice faded out. "Turns out, one mistake and Mickey Maloney owns you." I looked up into her eyes but I didn't recognize the emotion, just that the blue was a calming sea for me. "He told us we had a debt to pay, then had me do a lot of things I'm not proud of as payment. Things that keep me up at night even now."

She sat perfectly still above me.

"Things got really bad during a turf war that started about five years ago. The blood rained down in droplets. A lot of my friends died in those days. I put a lot of men in their graves too." I shivered and flinched, looking away, not wanting to see what she was reflecting back at me. "I lived in that world of death for two

115

years before it became too much. I had a card I could play that would get me out, and I threw it on the table. When I was free, I didn't look back." I focused on the spot of skin I was still touching on her knee. "Until you."

"Me?" Elle's voice was warm but I still couldn't meet her gaze.

I was lost in the story anyway. That card I'd played still swallowed me whole some days. I didn't talk about it—I wouldn't. And even touching on it made my insides swim. Hell, it had a hold on me and just the mention of it had the flames of Hades lapping at my ankles.

"Cole what do you mean 'until me?'" Her delicate fingertips came to my chin and lifted, forcing me to meet her gaze. It was the tranquil sea that kept me afloat and I couldn't help but smile.

"He was going to take you too if Jimmy couldn't deliver. I couldn't let him." I whispered. "I have to live with the horrible things I've done every day. That I can handle. But the idea of you getting sucked into that…" I was still unsure how exactly to phrase it. "Well, let's just say I just couldn't live with that. I traded places with you."

She lunged at me and the sheer momentum of it toppled me back to the floor. Her lips found mine and kissed me hard. Her breath was hot against my lips as our tongues tangled and it was like she was breathing light and life back into me. Her knee hitched up against my hip and her hand moved down to stroke my dick.

My whole body responded to her movements. I groaned and shoved my hips up into her hand. She rubbed up and down on my erection working with friction to drive me fucking insane. The taste of cherry milkshake dancing on my lips didn't hurt either.

I shoved my hand up her skirt and grabbed her ass. I used my grip to start a gentle rock of her hips against mine. She dragged her baby blue nails down my chest and I moaned, her open mouth somehow both amplifying and muffling my sounds of pleasure.

Horse clearing his throat stopped me short. My eyes shot open and my free arm went protectively around her shoulders,

116

pinning her to me. I stared up into Horse's eyes for a minute willing him to stay silent if not disappear completely.

Elle adjusted her body against mine and her soft lips brushed against my earlobe.

"What's the story with the linebacker?"

"Horse is my best friend. I lost him when I walked away but some things never change." I smiled weakly up at him where he stood over us.

"Have you shared women before?" Her voice trembled a little but I got the sense it wasn't with fear.

"We've been together with women before," I corrected.

"What?" She tried to sit up and as much as I wanted to keep her pinned, I let her go. "Like guy on guy?" Her head whipped from one of us to the other. "Are you gay?"

"You can ask me that with a straight face?" I smiled at her and reached up to grab her breast. She gasped when I squeezed.

"Well, I don't know. I mean you don't hear about that kind of threesome often." Her voice faded off and I could tell she was deep in thought. "Could I watch the two of you together?" Something danced behind my little bird's eyes.

"I wouldn't mind," Horse piped up.

"I'm sure you wouldn't." I rolled my eyes. "Horse is bi. He's just as happy with good pussy as he is with good dick."

"And I'm sure I don't need to tell you Cole has a really good dick." He winked at Elle with his biggest smile in place. She couldn't hold her answering one in check. "Secret is he's got an even bigger heart. When I kissed him the very first time, when Mickey had us fuck a girl together, he only punched me once." He laughed shyly and a lot of the emotion he held for me leaked out.

"It became natural after that. It's not that I like guys or that I like dick, it's that I like Horse. And him on one end, me on the other never felt quite right." I reached up to push some of her beautiful blonde locks behind her ear.

"And now you guys want me in on it too?" she asked quietly.

117

"I want you any way you'll let me have you, Elle. You're fucking heroin to me, alive and addictive in my veins," I matched her timid tone.

"Not gonna lie, I kinda want to know what all the fuss is about." Horse stepped closer to us, and bent down, pressing his thigh up against hers where it straddled mine. He blew out a deep breath before speaking. "And if I'm going to lay my life on the line for you, for both of you, I guess I want some sort moment to hold on to. Some sort of bond we can all share."

"You're going to help me hide her?" A giant weight lifted from my chest and for a moment I thought about blowing Horse like he'd always wanted.

"Yeah. Turns out I'm a big ole softy and I can't let anything you look at like that get shredded by Mick."

I smiled the biggest smile I could at Horse as I coaxed Elle's hips to pick back up their slow rock.

"Mickey Maloney wants me still? Even after you…" Her eyes went wide as saucers as she looked down at me.

"Shhhhhh." I swiftly twisted so that Elle was on her back between Horse and I. "I won't let him get to you. With or without Horse." I grabbed his thigh and squeezed hoping he wouldn't go ape shit at the admission. "Though it's a lot easier with Horse." I smiled up at him now almost nose to nose.

"Kiss him, Cole," Elle purred from beneath us. "Kiss him then kiss me."

I looked down at her and her eyes had gone a little hooded, her hands were finding spots on both Horse and I. My fingers wandered up her thigh and pushed her thong out of the way before pressing slowly into her. She gasped loudly as I started leisurely stroking inside her. Horse hummed as he watched.

When he looked back up at me, I flipped his baseball hat off with the flick of my finger. His dark hair was short but had slight waves that were tousled in every which way until I grabbed a fistful and yanked him toward me.

Horse's lips found mine the way they always had. They would have swallowed me whole if I ever let him. It was that passion that convinced me to keep up with it even when Mick

118

wasn't watching. For so long, the nameless or faceless women between us meant nothing, but him, and us together was a real and intimate connection that I craved when everything else was going to shit. The way he kissed me now, biting on my bottom lip and reacquainting himself with the shape of my mouth, felt almost as right as being with Elle.

Almost.

"Shit," she swore and I broke away to look down at her. "Kiss me like that," she barely breathed the words.

I bent down capturing her pout between my teeth and biting before taking her lips in a kiss fueled by every ounce of pure attraction I had for her. I pressed my body down to hers, still stroking her pussy as I added a slow rub of my torso against her chest. As our tongues danced with one another, I felt the warmth of Horse's hand against mine between her thighs.

He pressed into Elle without a word and she cried out into my mouth. I laughed lightly and breathily as I turned to find Horse again. He was waiting and kissed me hard, twisting his finger around mine where they were deep inside of Elle.

She bucked her hips up and started to grind on our fingers. I broke away to look down on my Ladyface and smiled. She was so turned on she was lost to anything but sensation.

"Unwrap her for me," I commanded Horse as I started to rub my cock.

He was a little rough with her, yanking on her Jell-O body to bend her in any way he pleased. She made graceful arcs as he stripped her down to a simple black thong. He dove down to snatch her perky little nipple in his mouth and I leaned up on my elbow to watch, still stroking myself.

Horse tongued her, flicking fast and furious across her tiny little cherry buds. Across my tiny little cherry. I rolled over to work on the same breast as Horse, letting our tongues tangle with each other as they explored her body. His hand started to wander up my back and cupped my head. He pushed me harder onto her breast, filling my mouth with Elle. She screamed in response.

Big plump lips kissed down across my shoulder as I sucked on Elle. I shifted the slightest bit so I could watch Horse kiss down

119

Elle when he slid off my tricep and onto the hollow of her stomach. He kissed her several times before he ran into the simple black fabric of her thong. He balled his hand into it and yanked. The scrap fell free of her body with almost no effort and I moaned even with a mouth full of breast.

"Oh my God," she whined beneath us.

I switched breasts just as Horse latched onto her clit. Her hand flew to my shoulder and dug in. With just the shift of my gaze, I found her other hand clawed into Horse's hair. He lapped her hard enough that her body rose and fell with his mouth. I rolled with the waves of Elle to trail kisses down her trembling body to meet him.

As soon as my nose brushed against him, one of his hands came to my throat while the other plunged inside Elle. He kissed me, dragging his lips across mine, letting me taste her mixed with him. I rubbed my dick up against his thigh, her shin, wishing it was free to feel their skin warm against mine.

When I pulled away from Horse to undo my fly, he squeezed my throat.

"Fuck no," I chastised him with a devilish purr and pulled his hand from my throat. "That's not how this goes."

I reached over Elle and grabbed his throat, squeezing just the way I liked. Horse submitted beneath me and rolled onto his back. I kept squeezing tighter, turning him that perfect shade of red. When he sputtered the slightest bit, I bent to kiss him. When I came up for air, I let go of his throat and he gasped into my open mouth.

"Strip down," I murmured softly to him as I returned to Elle's lips.

Horse jostled the bed next to us and when his hand fell away from Elle, I replaced him, flicking her clit side to side. Her body went rigid and jerked against me. Her arousal spread wildly across her thighs and I wanted nothing more than to taste it.

In the smoothest move I could manage I wrapped an arm around her waist and pushed her up to her knees.

"Straddle me, Ladyface. Straddle me and sit on my face," I growled a purely sexual sound at her.

Her legs were wobbly and she slid her thighs onto either side of me, facing down my body. I wrapped my hands up and around her legs, helping her seat herself and clawing into her ass cheeks in the process.

I smothered myself in her. Her taste, her smell, her extravagant wetness. The cherry milkshake taste hadn't changed, and I swear to God it made me harder like this than it had before. I could explore every inch between her thighs in this position. I twirled on the nerves of her clit, circled the lips of her pussy and then shoved my tongue right up into it.

Her hands came down to my chest and I expected her to claw into me but she didn't. Instead she started to trace my ink like she had in the moonlight and I shivered.

As if I needed more proof that Elle was mine on a primal level.

For the slightest minute, I was lost to her. The very fact that I had her again at all was a miracle. That it was like this, with no boundaries, would have left me speechless if my tongue wasn't otherwise occupied.

I lifted her off my face just a little bit. Enough that the tip of my tongue could trace her while I watched a naked, seriously sculpted Horse devouring the sight from our feet. His eyes raked up the near painful push of my dick on my fly, across my abs, then up Elle's perfect body, before heading back down again. He was a starving man watching us eat at the most delicious buffet and all because I'd put him in his place.

Elle started to move, lowering down to my body. I pulled my tongue away completely and arched back to bite into the fleshy curve of her ass. She shrieked and dug her nails into my chest in response.

I hoped Horse saw my smirk before I spoke against the warm, sweet flesh of Elle's thighs, "But Ladyface, if you suck my dick, what does that leave Horse?"

Elle

"Oh my God. Oh my fucking God," I moaned almost nonsensically now. It was partially Cole's insane tongue that could fold and undulate all over me in ways no other man's ever had. But it was also because I was watching Horse, a truly ripped and rippled animal, unzip Cole's fly.

The story Cole had told me was enough to send chills to my very soul. But what he'd done for me warmed everything—and I mean *everything*—up inside me. I would have ripped his clothes off and let Horse watch without anyone asking.

Watching Horse's giant biceps flex as he shimmied Cole's tight, dark jeans down was far, far better. The V of Cole's hips and the flowers that covered his hipbones slowly being revealed was better than Christmas. The fact that Cole kept teasing and exploring me with his tongue, his hands a vise grip on my ass, was just icing on a really delicious cake.

Cole's perfect rock hard dick finally sprang out from behind a denim cage and Horse trembled as he reached for it. My breath caught for no other reason than I had a front row seat to watch. The hands at my backside pulled and Cole blatantly licked up from my sex to my backside in perfect unison with Horse grabbing his cock and licking up the underside of his shaft.

"Oh my God," my voice broke.

Horse's long pointed tongue ran along Cole, up and down tracing a track that had him shuddering beneath my fingertips. Cole's tongue worked similarly up and down on me, dipping into my sex then licking back to swirl around my backside. When he pushed his tongue into my ass, my eyes slammed shut, relishing the feel of him as deep inside as he could go.

When Cole moaned loud against my skin, I managed to pry my eyes open. Horse had wrapped his big lips around Cole's shaft and was working up and down on him. His cheeks hollowed out beneath his sharp cheekbones, highlighting his tightly trimmed facial hair. Horse took him all and my jaw dropped.

Watching a man blow another man was fascinating. Big beefy man shoulders lay across thick sculpted man thighs, a pile of muscles and because of Cole, ink. Cole was splayed out, spread wide. It was the only way to make room for Horse. He held Cole more possessively than anyone I'd ever seen, his fingers digging in the way Cole's did to me.

He deep-throated Cole and when he gagged on his cock, his whole body rippled, muscles bunching and flexing. Cole moaned into me, his warm breath puffing against my backside. A similar groan left my lips that was every bit from what Cole was doing to me as it was for the sight in front of me.

Horse stayed down on Cole, and the tip of his tongue shot out to tease Cole's balls. Cole jerked beneath me, and shoved his hips up to meet Horse's lips. He never forgot about licking or tongue thrusting me but he wavered when Horse added the flicks to his balls. Slowly, Horse pulled off Cole, revealing his shiny, slick cock inch by inch.

I wanted nothing more than to dive at it. To show the love to Cole that Horse had so expertly doled out. Horse shifted down to suck on Cole's balls and I lunged at his dick. His tongue fell from my backside and he snarled at me before it digressed into a breathy shotgun sound no doubt in response to the way Horse unabashedly sucked on his boys. I took the opportunity to capture his cock and slide down as far as I could.

Horse stopped me before my gag reflex, smiling and winking up at me before he let Cole's balls drop only to shower kisses on my hollowed out cheeks. After he'd fluttered across my face he moved back to servicing Cole.

Cole called out a few times before his mouth found its way back to me. He kissed along my upper thighs and across my ass, a similar sweet pattern to the one Horse had made across my face. They were perfectly matched for each other, the same but so very different. But it was Cole that was in control of both of us, coaxing us to compete as we doled out affection.

We found a rhythm, Cole, licking me in time with my swallows on him. Horse sucked hard on Cole and tickled my face with his scruff as his hand wandered across any of my skin he could reach. The sounds coming from Cole's lips and vibrating against my clit were that of a man on the brink; desperate, delirious and relishing every single slurp. They gave me goosebumps.

"Stop," Cole begged when I deep throated him and Horse gently slapped his cock through my cheek. I started to pull up but Horse held me down as I swallowed. He guided me up and down on Cole once or twice before Cole lurched up.

He unseated me as he lunged at Horse. I scrambled up after them as they crashed backward with Cole on top, his jeans down mid-thigh as he straddled Horse. "I said stop," he repeated roughly before he bent down to kiss him. Horse's hands explored the ridges and dips of Cole's body.

It was god on god action.

I crept up to the edge of the bed for a better view and perched on my knees. My hands curled into the edge of the mattress as I shamelessly watched. There were muscles everywhere and they twitched and flexed both in time with and in response to each other. Two perfect and rock hard dicks rubbed against each other and my hands twitched to reach out for them.

Horse trembled beneath Cole. Each of his kisses seemed like he was trying to breathe Cole in. His hands skated down towards his ass and when they got there, Horse grabbed hard. The perfect muscular curve of Cole's ass was bunched up in big rough hands.

"Holy shit," I said softly, more in awe of how hot it was than anything else.

Cole turned away from Horse and his eyes danced when they met mine.

124

"You like to watch as much as you like being watched huh, Ladyface?"

I bit my lip and nodded. He didn't take his eyes from mine as he rolled his hips against Horse. Their dicks slid past one another and Horse pulled Cole to bring their bodies closer together. I reached out for Cole, letting my fingers push through his long hair on top then down along the buzzed sides before following his jaw to his lips. He ground against Horse as he turned and kissed along my wrist where he could reach.

When he couldn't reach my skin anymore, Cole moved swiftly off Horse and back toward me. He stepped out of the jeans that finally fell to his ankles and snatched me up. As soon as my toes touched the floor Cole wrapped around me. His arms and legs tangled in with mine and his tongue did too.

He tasted faintly like Horse and I purred at the combination. I wrapped my arms around his neck and pulled him harder to me. He answered by moving to the back of my neck and squeezing. He used that grip to turn me around so my back was to his front. His hand slid around my neck and squeezed. I leaned back against him and surrendered.

Cole's free fingers found their way to my nipple and flicked. Electricity shot straight to my thighs. My knees knocked together and shuffled side to side, moving in time with Cole's hand on my throat or nipple, until big hands came to my knees and pushed them apart. It automatically tightened Cole's hold on my neck but it made room for Horse between my legs. His tongue started tracing me but it was different than Cole's. More exploratory than dominating.

He flicked on my clit then took it between his lips and rolled it side to side. Teeth came to the incredibly sensitive skin and he nibbled the tiniest bit. I tried to cry out but couldn't with the grip Cole had on me. I was getting lightheaded and I couldn't tell if it was from getting choked or from the way Horse played with the nub of nerves between my legs.

I was building. Cole playing at my nipples was making sure that I couldn't calm myself. When he yanked one straight down and Horse nibbled on me again, I came. I gasped wildly and my hands developed a life of their own. One flying to Horse's hair and pulling him up to his feet and the other going behind Cole's neck, shoving my chest deeper into his hand and pressing my back flat against his body.

Horse's lips came to mine as the waves of orgasm shook me. The arousal spreading between my thighs was just like the slickness coating his lips and cheeks. I licked where I could see myself speckling his cheeks then kissed him as best as my gummy limbs would let me.

As his tongue tangled with mine, Cole coaxed, "Get inside her."

Horse didn't hesitate. He fumbled for a minute between my thighs then pushed into me. I screamed again, a soundless writhe against Cole's grip. Horse was named Horse for a reason. If I hadn't been so turned on he would hurt. As it was, it was so tight I didn't think he'd be able to thrust too much inside me.

"He's big huh, Ladyface?" Cole asked as he kissed up my cheek and pulled on my earlobe. "Good girl for taking him all."

Horse pulled on the back of my knees and I naturally hooked my leg up around his hip. He clutched my ass and pulled me up off my feet. I wrapped fully around him, finding myself notched into the muscles of his hips. My arms clawed against him like I was climbing a mountain, which in a sense I was.

His big hands lifted and lowered me at his will. Cole still held me by the throat and kissed along my back. His hand ran down my body and studied the curve of my ass. I gasped in deep breaths and rolled my head back onto Cole's shoulder.

He kissed along my neck then across my cheek to my lips before biting down. Hard. Horse kept moving me up and down in a movement so delicious that I almost forgot I was arched against Cole. Almost.

But in reality, he was consuming me. Cole had claimed my senses on day one and my mind held a road map to his sharp body. Even when he barely touched me, I couldn't forget about the way he possessed me.

126

Horse and I rolled against each other as Cole's hand traveled along my curves. His lips crossed my shoulders side to side and back again.

"I'm gonna get inside you. I'm going to feel every inch of you."

Instead of leaning back and shaking my head for him, I curled forward and nodded into Horse's shoulder. The warmth of Cole behind me disappeared for a moment only to be replaced by a cool stream of lube that trickled down my backside a moment later. I bucked all the harder against Horse and he groaned into the loose strands of my hair.

I pressed my body against Horse, relishing his grip on me. Relishing the way he thrust into me. But after only a moment, Cole took advantage. His finger unceremoniously pushed into me and skated against Horse. My body involuntarily jumped against the ripped man in front of me, still a slave to the one behind me.

Cole's strokes had me dazed, confused, time stood still until he pressed the tip of his cock to my ass. I moaned loudly before biting into Horse's chest. A pleased sound dripped from his lips. I bit harder and Horse shoved me down roughly on his firm cock.

Cole didn't hesitate this time, he swiftly shoved his dick up into my ass. I cried out loudly until his hand came to my mouth and covered it. I could keep crying out but his flat, firm palm muffled the sound.

They took turns shoving into me, alternating their deep soul shaking thrusts. I cried out with each of them but my sounds crashed against the unrelenting cap of Cole's palm. They each hit the end of me every time and rubbed against each other. They took turns making sweet and savory sounds that filled up the air around us. I may not have been able to join them but I tried.

Cole pressed harder against me, his well-defined muscles undulated against me and I could feel the ridges of his abs and pecs. I let myself soften into him. He pulled my head back to rest on his shoulder, his palm staying across my mouth. I rolled toward his neck, wanting to see his face. His intense eyes were looking down my body as beads of sweat rolled down his forehead.

He twisted to kiss my forehead and my breath stuttered against his hand. He doubled the intensity of his thrusts and I could do little more than nuzzle my forehead into his neck and take it.

"Ladyface," he groaned out raggedly and let his lips drag across my nose and his hand as if he'd kiss my lips if they were available.

His other hand came up to Horse's neck and he pulled him closer to the both of us. He adjusted his grip on me but it jostled me enough that I came without warning. I screamed into Cole's hand and my limbs went rigid. My sex waved up and down on Horse and my knees dug into his sides where he held me. I clenched down hard on Cole.

"Fuck, I'm gonna come," he swore low and breathy against my skin.

"No," Horse cried out, pained. "Please, Cole. Please."

Cole's thrusts slowed and he used the grip he had on Horse's neck to pull him in close. They rested their foreheads against each other's with me, little more than a rubber body, between them.

"Okay," he breathed. "Take care of my girl though."

"Always." Horse bent to kiss my neck where it was open to him with tender trembling lips.

Cole let go of my mouth and I sucked in a deep breath before whimpering with the aftershocks of my orgasm. He shifted my body so I was draped across Horse. One of his big hands came from my hips to my shoulders as Cole disappeared from behind me. Horse gently set me down on the bed before he pulled out of me.

I gasped wildly, missing him the second he was gone and feeling wide open without him filling me. My hand flew to cover myself, never feeling more exposed than I did right then. Horse grabbed my hand and wove his fingers between mine before he twisted them up and pinned them to the bed near my shoulders. He dipped between my thighs and tentatively lapped at my sex.

My whole body trembled at the soft touch, my muscles tensed and melted in a split second. Then he did it again, shuffling his knees onto the bed and pushing my body up as I jerked again. I leaned up to see a massive coil of muscle bent between my legs. His ass was in the air putting a full, broad and insanely sculpted back on display.

"Fuck." The word was a whisper just before I moaned because of Horse's body shaking tongue.

Cole watched me beneath Horse for a few moments. I tried to hold his eye contact but every time Horse licked me, my eyes would flutter shut. When they'd open, they'd find Cole, still watching, breathing hard and coated in sweat. I smiled widely and curled my fingers into the back of Horse's hands.

When Horse latched on instead of letting go, my head rolled to the side and I started breathing heavy again. I felt his every lick, his every flick against me and I bucked my hips up to his face.

He cried out and the sound was filled with so much pleasure it was mangled and haggard. Horse's lips didn't come back to me for a moment and I turned to see what had him breathing roughly against my inner thighs.

Cole stood squarely behind him, pulling at his ass the same way he had mine. His fingers were digging into Horse's flesh as he thrust slowly against his backdoor. Horse hung his head between my thighs, moaning in time with each of Cole's nudges.

If watching them before was hot, this was the inferno. I propped myself up on my elbows to get a better view. What played out between my legs threatened to get me off all over again and without Horse's mouth coming back to me.

Cole's abs flexed each time he thrust, his forearms were taut, highlighting every single muscle up his arms to his defined chest. His mouth hung open but he was silent as he watched his dick move in and out of Horse.

Horse had submitted completely, his hands went limp in mine as he melted completely beneath Cole. A sheen of sweat coated every inch of his Adonis body and the most passionate sounds I'd ever heard slipped from his lips over and over. They sent shivers up my spine and spread goosebumps across my skin all on their own.

Cole dropped one of his hands only to land a firm, loud slap where he'd been holding. Horse cried out just before he was spanked again, and harder this time.

"I told you to take care of my girl," Cole said roughly as his eyes swept over my reclining body.

He fisted into the spot he'd turned dark red on Horse's ass cheek as Horse's tongue came back to me, this time pushing inside and licking as far along the front side of me as he could. Cole started to thrust harder and it shook the both of us. The way it pushed Horse's tongue deeper into me had me collapsing back to the mattress.

When I managed to look back up at Cole, he was back to watching me with a smile playing at the corner of his lip. He shoved into Horse hard and it shook me, making both Horse and I moan. Cole stilled completely only to do it all the more dramatically again. I groaned but made myself meet his gaze.

"You're everything, Ladyface," he purred just before he picked back up to a furious pace.

He didn't thrust for too much longer when his ragged, "I'm coming and you aren't stopping me, Horse," cut through the sounds of sex flying free from Horse and I.

"Yes," Horse moaned, "God yes. Come in me."

Cole slammed his hips against him a few more times before he stilled and threw his head back. Cole cried out loud toward the ceiling making all the muscles of his neck flex in time with his beautiful, passionate bellow. The way his low abs tensed and released where Horse's ass framed them told me he was coming hard and fast, just the way Horse had wanted.

I was fascinated by it. By how goddamned sexy it was. I could have watched the muscle on muscle action all afternoon, but Horse released my hands, grabbed my hips and yanked me down the bed. I landed squarely beneath his perfectly tanned and toned torso, my hands naturally reaching up towards his shoulders.

One flexed beneath my touch and I looked down to find him stroking himself the split second before he shot cum across my stomach and up onto my breasts. His sounds were choppy, breathy and almost pained before he collapsed onto me.

130

The weight of Horse was crushing. He was too much muscle to blanket me and my breath automatically went shallow. Before I could say anything, Cole knelt beside us and shoved at his shoulder.

"You'll smash her if you're not careful."

Horse gracelessly flopped off and bounced on the bed beside me. Cole collected me into his arms and slid back on the bed to lean against the headboard behind the mattress. The small horse figurine above me had a whole new meaning.

Cole cradled me against his chest as both our breathing slowed. His finger slid in the cum coating my stomach as he opened and closed his mouth like he had something to say. I leaned up to kiss the corner of his mouth and held the kiss for as long as my fatigued body would let me. Horse was still draped across the foot of the bed where he'd landed, staring up at the ceiling with a blissed out smile.

When I collapsed back into his arms, a matching wasted glaze to my face, Cole looked over with his dimpled smile on.

"You're okay, right?" he asked, concern coloring his tone.

"Better than," I answered and nuzzled into his sticky skin.

"That all happened a little fast, any questions about…well…about any of it?"

I knew he was asking me about seeing him balls deep in Horse. It wasn't the way it usually went according to books or movies, hell, even porn. Guys didn't usually play with each other, just with their toy. But the way Cole had looked at Horse said it all. It was almost as electric as the way he looked at me. I understood them the same weird way I understood him.

I smiled as warmly as I could manage, the pleasure still heavily coating me, making motor skills difficult then asked, "Only question I have is, what do we do now?"

Cole

I blew out a deep breath as I brought the crook of my finger to Elle's chin. I tilted her lips up to meet mine and bent to kiss her. Despite what we'd just done, my dick twitched beneath her, tempted to dive in all over again.

Telling Elle she was everything would never be enough. It would never fully explain what I felt for her or how I saw her. There was no reason for it either. Not besides simple biology or chemistry. My body needed hers to survive the way it needed air or water, I was magnetically drawn to her on an elemental level.

When I finally broke our kiss, her bright blue eyes were waiting, unwavering from mine. I shoved my hand up into her golden hair and cradled her.

"Now we shower." I kissed the tip of her nose, which pulled a giggle from her.

That sound alone was worth living and dying for.

"Cole, you know what I mean." She shook her head at me and let her fingers aimlessly travel along the edges of my ink.

"Yeah, course I do, but I'm stealing twenty more minutes from the shit storm outside my door and spending them lost with you." I rubbed my nose across her temple then pressed my lips gently to her skin.

"Is Horse joining us?" she asked and I couldn't tell if she was hopeful or not. I couldn't tell if that bothered me or not.

"No," Horse groaned from the foot of the bed. "I'm never showering again. I wanna smell like that until I die." He leisurely rubbed up and down his stomach then lifted to sniff the palm of his hand. "Goddamn did I miss you, Cole. In every single way someone can miss someone else." He smiled wide. "And Elle, it's a fucking pleasure to meet you."

She laughed again. "It's a pleasure fucking you too, Horse," she said so easily that it made me laugh right along with her.

I swung my legs off the bed and stood, keeping her tight to my chest. I rounded the bed and playfully kicked Horse's leg. "You're disgusting."

"So much," he reached between his legs and grabbed his junk before letting his arm flop back to bed.

I rolled my eyes as I walked around him to the bathroom. I set Elle down in the tub and cranked on the water. She squeaked when she was blasted with cold water and I dove into the stream to block her little body.

"Holy fuck, that's cold," I gasped and spun to slam the dial even further to the left as water shot everywhere.

When it warmed up the slightest bit I turned back to her, water still spraying off my body in every direction. I pulled the door shut then wrapped my arms around her in one simple movement. She tried to burrow further into my body, somehow finding an even closer spot to settle. I thought about the time I'd called her my missing puzzle piece. After what she'd just let us do, it was safe to say she was the whole damned puzzle.

I brought us deeper into the waterfall and collected her hair into a lose ponytail, relishing the touches every bit as much as the warmth of her breath against my skin.

"He loves you, ya know?" She let her hands wander around my low back.

"Oh yeah? I love him too." My fingers tangled in her hair as I kept aimlessly playing with it.

"No. I mean he *loves* you. Like he'd marry you and have your intense little babies."

I felt the corners of her lips turn up in a giant smile at whatever played in her head.

133

"On second thought, there'd be nothing little about either of your babies." She let her hand slip from my back and reach between my thighs. I shamelessly pushed my dick into her hand, liking how big I looked in her tiny little hands.

"You wanna go again?"

"I don't know if I can." She blew out a deep breath but didn't stop stroking me.

"Then you're gonna have to knock that shit off." I captured her fingers and brought them up to my mouth, sucking the tips then setting her hand between our chests. "I'll have to make Horse finish me off, and honestly, I prefer you."

"Does he know that?" Her fingers found a way to wander on me the way they always seemed to.

"Yeah. Always has." I reached over for the scrubber and loaded it with body wash before bringing it to her stomach to scrub. "He's always known it wouldn't go that way for me. I'm only with him from time to time for fun or maybe because I'm missing intimacy. I mean, two options rather than one *is* fun and who do you know more intimately than your best friend of nineteen years." I started scrubbing down her shoulder and she held her arm out for me, watching me intently. "I like women. Always have, always will. I like *you*. End of story."

"And you like sharing me." She didn't ask, she said it like it was a simple fact.

"I like watching what your body does every bit as much as I like feeling it. I like tasting you, and hearing you and smelling you. Sharing you is just a different way for you to fill my senses."

Elle bit her lip as she took the scrubber from hand. She started down my body, washing me gently before she soaped up her hand and reached for my balls. Her hand massaged me like she was still washing me, but this was foreplay pure and simple.

I groaned loudly as she pushed on my shoulder. I let her roll me so I was pinned to the cool tile behind my back.

"If you like me so much why didn't you call me back?" she asked coyly.

Two minutes of hearing her voice had been too much to ask. Two minutes was a risk I wasn't willing to take.

134

"I couldn't knowingly bring you into this. I wouldn't." I stayed pinned to the wall exactly as she held me, feeling every bit as helpless to the world around us as I was to her.

"But now it's okay?" She dropped her hands from my body and it was the first sign that she wasn't as all-in on this whole thing as she'd seemed. I couldn't blame her one bit.

"Now you're in it whether I like it or not." I sighed. "So I might as well get what I want."

"And what's that?" She leveled her gaze at me.

"You. Every fucking inch of you. For as long as I'm allowed to have you." I yanked her toward me with one hand at the small of her back and the other crept up her body and I traced along her throat. "I meant it when I said this was real. As real as it fucking gets."

"And here I thought fairytales didn't exist." She barely breathed the words as she lifted her chin, making her neck even more available to me.

"This is no fairytale, Ladyface, and I'm no Prince Charming. This is one of those stories about a villain trudging straight through hell and hoping there's still something worth living for on the other side."

"I'm not waiting on the other side, Cole." She looked up at me, trembling but not from fear. "I'm trudging through hell right next to you."

Something shattered inside me. Elle had officially broken me and I was pieces left piled in her little hands. I wouldn't have it any other way.

I snatched her throat, squeezed, and dragged her lips to mine. She kissed me back as hard as she could. I answered her move for move, squeezing as the intensity between us ratcheted up. When she couldn't kiss me back furiously, I dropped her throat then dropped to my knees.

A small gasp came from above me and that sound meant everything to me. It was shocking for sure but it was heavy, like she knew why I'd crumbled beneath her. I looked up through the veil of beating water to find her looking down on me. Her hands

135

came to the side of my face and gently held me until I leaned in to rest against her thigh.

"I hate to interrupt this, but we have to go," Horse's voice was quiet but deathly serious behind me and my stomach dropped.

I turned to find him leaning casually against the wall, watching us.

"Why?"

"Mick knows she's not in Seattle." Horse jerked his chin toward Elle where she stood over me.

I shot up, panic coursing through my veins. I grabbed her automatically and pulled her in tight, shielding her without any real cause beyond desperate need.

"He doesn't know that she's here. At least not that I know of." Horse was still naked and twisted to lean his forehead against the wall. "He does think you had something to do with it though."

I let go of Elle and turned to face him.

"I can handle him."

"Cole." Elle's voice shook behind me.

"It's okay, Elle. Whatever he throws at me I can catch. I swear."

Horse's face crumpled against the wall. "What if it's a chick, Cole. What if it's Siobhan?"

Fury bubbled up in me at the suggestion of either. My shoulders started to heave until little fingers started to trace the eagle along my back. She was trying to soothe me for *Siobhan*. That was a fresh hell I couldn't face, and since I'd told her everything else…

"Give me one minute, Horse. Just one."

He nodded and sauntered out of the bathroom.

"Elle." I turned and let my hand rest on her shoulder, my thumb stroked across the meat of her neck. I couldn't find a way to tell her what I'd done. What I might have to do. Words wouldn't form.

"He's gonna make you…" her voice wavered, "*be* with someone isn't he?" She shivered and I prayed it was the water, not whatever image in her head.

136

"Maybe." I barely breathed. "He did while you were gone." Those words were even harder for me to get out.

She wordlessly pushed past me and out of the shower. For a second she stood on the mat without grabbing a towel, water dripping off her and adding to the massive puddle on the floor. Her tiny hands came around her body and she held her sides.

"I didn't think I'd ever see you again." I shut off the water and followed her. I grabbed a towel and wrapped it around her shoulders. She flinched. "I *knew* I wasn't worthy either way."

She tightened the towel around her shoulders and walked out.

"Elle?" Horse's voice echoed in from the other room. "Elle, you okay? You're white as a sheet."

She didn't answer him, or at least not that I could hear. My shoulders sagged under the weight of her anger. Or was it disappointment? That hung even heavier, somewhere a little closer to my heart.

"What just happened in here?" Horse consumed the doorway when he came back and leaned against the frame on his forearms.

"Would you put some clothes on so we can go?" I snarled at him.

He straightened up and walked directly to me. "What did you just do to Elle?" he asked just as gruff, shoving his face into mine.

"I told her the truth, okay. Are you happy?" I shoved past Horse and out into my loft.

Seeing her wrapped in that towel, balled on the couch gutted me. I couldn't keep my temper. I couldn't even keep my train of thought. After less than a heartbeat I was back kneeling at her feet.

"Ladyface, I'm sorry. Please forgive me. Please," I whispered.

She didn't respond, just turned further away from me.

"Remember." I tried to move in front of her face, she twisted away from me again. "You. Are. Everything." I enunciated each word and spit them out with all the sincerity I could muster.

137

She didn't flinch.

I shoved away from the couch and stalked over to my discarded jeans. I yanked them on battling with the water still fresh on my skin. When I got them up and buttoned I grabbed a drawer so hard it slid out of the dresser completely and banged on my shin.

"Fucking shit!" My voice boomed off the bricks as I threw the drawer onto the floor. It splintered into pieces when it hit.

"Calm down." Horse's hand came to my shoulder as soon as he'd pulled on his shirt.

"Don't tell me to fucking calm down." I swatted his hand away as I picked up a shirt from the scrap pile of wood and cotton now sitting at my feet.

"Fine. Get your ass, along with your temper, out the goddamned door." He pinched his face, knitting his brows together and thinning his lips into a straight line as he pointed toward the front door.

I slid into my hightops without tying them and grabbed my Glock from where I'd abandoned it by my keys. I threw open my front door and wheeled out without looking back. The look that Elle would give me, or rather wouldn't give me, wasn't something I could face.

Elle

"Whatever you do. Do not leave this apartment. Not even to grab food or smokes from the corner store. Do not answer this door. Even if it's the ghost of your recently departed mother." Horse's big chocolate eyes were level with mine begging me to understand. "Whatever happened in that bathroom, I don't care. You stay here. And you stay quiet. He's going to save you the only way he knows how." He swallowed a giant lump in his throat then leaned in and kissed my forehead.

He stood and turned on his heel to follow Cole out of the apartment. The keys he grabbed scraped against the table and grated against my nerves but then the door shut behind him and I was left in silence.

The cold slap of being alone started tears trickling down my cheeks without warning. I tried to wipe them away at first with the edges of the towel but they came too furiously for me to stop them.

In a matter of hours, I'd searched for Cole, found him and lost him all over again. He'd been with somebody else. Whether Mr. Maloney had made him or not, the idea didn't sit well with me. Matter of fact, it damn near crushed my insides.

If Mr. Maloney was as bad as they said, I couldn't blame Cole.

But I also couldn't quite swallow it.

I started to replay the day since I'd arrived in Chicago. There was the gun in my face, but in hindsight, the man behind it, unafraid to die was far more unsettling. There was Horse pounding on the hood of Cole's car, but Cole's very real terror had been hidden behind my thundering heart. Of course there was the threesome, but we had only started kissing on each other once Horse had said he'd help Cole hide me. That was when the levy had broke and Cole became *my* Cole again.

Then there was just now. He'd thrown a tantrum for sure, but once again it was the emotion behind it that was what I'd missed. He was trying to prepare me for what might come, he was trying to be honest with me about how dark things really were. I'd cast that aside based on wounded pride and storybook notions.

This is no fairytale, Ladyface, and I'm no Prince Charming.

He got the first part right but not the last. He was charging at the dragon all right, determined to keep me free, using the only weapon he had.

And I'd sent him off to die without so much as a goodbye.

The tears started pouring down my cheeks again and this time, I didn't even try to slow them. I wept for my own stupidity every bit as much as the things that I may never get to say to Cole.

I shoved off the couch and started pacing through the loft. A million jumbled thoughts whipped through my head, none of them really making sense but all of them screaming Cole at me. I ran for my jeans where Horse had discarded them, searching for my phone. When it wasn't in the pocket, I scrambled around on all fours looking for my bag.

Another memory crashed into me. The one of Horse splintering my phone like it was fragile glass beneath his boot.

I couldn't call Cole to tell him all the things I wanted to now. Things like *I'm sorry* and *I do understand* and above all *please come back in one piece.* After all, this was real life, and people ended up dead. I knew that first hand.

My teeth dug into my bottom lip and my fingernails into my palms. It was the only way to keep from tearing my own hair out. Well, that or call Conrad.

"Fuck," I swore into the empty apartment realizing I'd never called him. He'd be in a tizzy wondering where I'd gone off to. If he figured out I'd flown to Chicago, he'd probably explode.

I'd let two of the three men in my life down without even thinking about it.

"I'll be damned sure I don't let down Horse, too." I murmured to no one in particular.

I blew out a deep breath, hoping it would steady my churning insides. It did jack shit, so I started to get ready instead. I tucked the towel in on itself and walked back to the bathroom. I swallowed hard, wishing that our last interaction had gone vastly different.

I opened the drawers beneath the sink and found a tortoise shell comb. It was the sleek, expensive kind that reminded me of the 1950s and James Dean. Picturing Cole bent in front of the mirror, styling his hair into the perfect and painfully trendy cut he wore the first time I saw him, pulled a smile across my face.

My hair was tangled but taking the time to pick one knot out at a time was keeping me distracted. When I finally got it smoothed, I found a pencil that I used to twist my hair up into a bun. I grabbed Cole's toothbrush and helped myself, brushing my teeth made me feel a tiny bit more human. And a tiny bit more sane.

I stripped out of my towel and used it to start sopping up the massive amount of water coating the linoleum floor. Between our playful moment and my melt down, it was a lake. I made myself think about the light moments, or when he'd fallen to my feet rather than that *other* stuff. I wiped up the footprints as they trailed out of the bathroom and into the loft.

They eventually led over to where the dresser drawer laid obliterated. I sat back on my heels as the image of a devastated Cole washed over me. If I hadn't been on the floor, it would have leveled me. As it was, I crumpled further. I aimlessly shuffled the splinters into a pile but I was lost in a sea of *what if.*

What if he hadn't done what Mickey said? What if they'd gotten to me? What if he thought I wouldn't forgive him? Or worse, what if the last moments in the apartment were our last moments, period?

It would be because of me. *ALL* because of me.

I was desperate for Cole. Not because I was magically over it and totally fine with what he'd done but because I understood why he'd done it. I needed to say that. I needed to explain. And tell him that my heart had inexplicably split wide for him.

The faint smell of Cole, sex mixed with fresh spice mixed and warm wood, lingered on his t-shirts where they sat amongst the splinters. I grabbed one of them and pulled it on, holding the collar up to my nose to breathe in as deeply as I could, hoping to fill more than my lungs with that smell.

This time it wasn't tears that overtook me. It was sheer and utter panic. The words left unspoken threatened to be my undoing.

My lungs wouldn't expand. A grip every bit as intense as Cole's had my throat but there was no comfort of blazing green eyes or perfect warm flesh. It was just a ghost dedicated to my demise. Blackness edged in on my vision and the horns honking in the distance faded even further away.

I wasn't losing it over a guy. I was losing it over the life I saw slipping away. He'd looked at all the inky, ugly black in my life and still seen a blonde haired, blue eyed girl rather than a vortex. He'd seen a kindred spirit. I'd recognized another half.

And I'd let him run head first at the jaws of death, livid with me.

My shallow, haggard breaths seemed like boulders in my head, clanging into each other and echoing through the void. I prayed I'd pass out. Maybe when I woke up, Cole would be back and I could breathe *I'm sorries* into our kisses.

But no such luck.

I was left hyperventilating in a ball as I suffered an irregular heart jackknife alone on the cold and empty floor of Cole's loft.

142

Cole

"You need to get your shit together," Horse said sharply from the passenger seat.

"I know what walking into that room means. Especially tonight," I growled back.

"That's great. And not at all what I'm talking about." He looked over at me and I could tell he'd arched his eyebrow even though twilight played tricks sometimes. "I'm talking about Elle and you know it."

"Tread carefully, Horse."

"Same goes for you, Cupcake. Don't destroy her. Because you can, ya know." He turned and looked out at the street. "It's only the people we'd die for that can truly kill us," he said quietly, almost so quietly I wasn't sure I was meant to hear.

I wanted to fight back, to tell him that she could do the same to me, that I hung by the tiniest thread and Elle held it. Tonight, Mick could cut it, Siobhan would relish snipping it, fate may even have a go, but it was her just letting go that was terrifying. And that was what she seemed to be contemplating back in the apartment, cutting loose and walking away. Spelling that out for Horse, was a wholly terrifying thing.

I pulled up to the Maloney house and turned the key in the ignition. My Charger slowly faded to silent but neither of us moved.

"I'll treat her better, I swear." I reached up and patted his shoulder before letting my hand slide over and rub his neck. "I'll treat you both better."

He turned and rolled his eyes at me but he couldn't quite hide the smile tugging at his lips.

"I mean it. You laying down your life for her means everything to me. I'll spend my life repaying you."

"If it really means so much, you should blow me." His full smile broke across his face and his eyes lit up.

"You have my cum covering your ass, let's call that good for now." I shook my head as I got out of the car.

"Oh yeah." He acted like he hadn't remembered and scratched his ass as he walked toward the front door ahead of me.

We both laughed a little as we took the steps two at a time. The guttural cry that wafted downstairs along with the smell of blood and death when we walked in the door made us swallow our laughter and quick. Horse looked over at me and we shared a look before he nodded for me to head upstairs, him falling into step right behind.

My hand tingled as I turned the handle, opening the massive door into the den. The lights were lower than normal, highlighting a bright white spotlight. A lumpy figure of a man, covered with bruises and wearing tattered clothing sat heaped on his knees, bathed in light and spattered in crimson. There was a fresh trail of the blood oozing from a limp hand, bent in a decidedly wrong direction.

"Where the fuck is Jimmy Ponies?!" Mick roared at the figure before rushing into the light and shoving what seemed to be a bloodied fingernail into his mouth. Mick smothered the man's mouth with his hand then pinched his nose up. "Swallow it, then answer me."

Mick's shoulders heaved and his eyes betrayed the wildness brewing inside him. The man mumbled beneath his hand and Mick pulled his hand away.

"Do tell," he purred.

"I meant it when I said, I don't know," he trembled and it made his voice warble.

144

Mick crashed his elbow across the already battered face and the man crunched to the floor. Then his eyes locked on mine.

"And you." He lunged at me, landing his fist across my face.

Only when the crunch was so painful I thought my teeth might shatter beneath the sheer force did I realize Mick was wearing brass knuckles. They glinted in the faint light a minute before he hit me hard in the stomach then redirected to crunch upward into my jaw.

My instincts were screaming to fight back but something even deeper was reminding me of the sole reason to keep my cool—Elle.

"Where is she?" he screamed before jabbing up into my diaphragm and making me double over. "Where did you send her?" His elbow crushed down into my kidneys and I dropped to my knees next to the clobbered almost-corpse.

"Who the fuck are you talking about, Mick?" I managed between wheezes.

He raised his shiny pointy toe loafer and nailed me in my side. I did what I could not to react but I winced as I grabbed my side and held it.

"Mick," Horse tried to calm him down.

"Don't you dare take his side." Mick's shoes shuffled against the ground and I pictured him toe to toe with Horse. I prayed Horse backed down.

"She's not in Seattle, Cole." He grabbed my hair and wrenched my head back.

"Elle?" I walked the fine line of playing dumb but not too dumb.

"Yes, Elle. It seems this family has a knack for disappearing." He shoved my head back forward and stalked around the front of us.

"I didn't tip her off, Mick." I was forceful even though I stayed on my knees. "I'm not that fucking stupid."

"Are you saying that Siobhan is covering for her? Or maybe that she can't do her job?" He shoved his face right up into mine.

145

"I'm saying that she's been gone for maybe twelve hours. Did Elle not come to the front door when Siobhan knocked?"

"Or perhaps a bleeding heart called the one it beats for?" Mick was deadly serious, icy even, as he leveled a gun at my chest.

My heart jackknifed against the steel.

"Check my phone, Mick." I shoved my chest into the barrel, praying I was calling his bluff. "I know you own me."

Mick moved swiftly, pulling his gun from my chest and pointing it at the broken man on the floor. Without hesitating, he pulled the trigger. The sound was almost deafening in my ears, an explosion followed by intense ringing. Something warm spattered across my face but I was so consumed with the intense throb in my head that I didn't care.

I covered the ear closest to where the gun had gone off, hoping that would ease the pounding. It didn't do anything except distract me from Mick circling back to me. He used the barrel of the gun to pull my face up to his.

It was hot against the sensitive skin beneath my chin but I didn't dare move. Instead I met his eyes as directly as I possibly could.

"If I *ever* find out you're lying to me…" He sounded like he was underwater but the severity of his voice wasn't lost on me. Nor was the click of the gun when he pulled the trigger.

Mick's maniacal laugh cut through the ringing in my ears when the empty gun clicked, still pointed at me.

"Didn't even flinch. Atta boy, Laddy." He whirled away from me, pointing the gun and pulling the trigger at a few other people in quick succession.

When he plopped onto his throne, he leveled the gun back at me and pulled the trigger once more, making a big boom crackle through the room with his voice. I stared directly at the mad man but he just reclined in the chair, tossing a leg over the armrest and waving the gun wildly in the air while his laugh bubbled back up from the depths of hell.

"Horse, help him up. Cole, come sit at my right hand."

Horse's hands came gently to my shoulders and hooked underneath to help me. I shook out from his help then batted his

146

hand away. He wordlessly dropped his grip and walked away, his eyes locked on me the second he sat to Mickey's left. The worry that creased his brow was deep, changing the whole appearance of his usually light features.

I moved to stand and everything in me protested. Mick had hit hard and in all the right places. I collapsed back to my knees with a sound too pitiful for this room. It had Horse back on his feet in a split second.

"No. He didn't want help." Mick held out his arm, blocking Horse's path.

I shot a look at Horse that said the very same thing. I knew damn well that I had to get up on my own and walk over there. Weakness was the last thing that I could show with Elle on the line.

This time when I bent to push up to standing I expected the thunderclap of pain that roared through me. Knowing it was coming didn't make it any better but it was enough that I could push past it. I was shaky when I made it to my feet, still doubled over at the number he'd done on my organs but my feet were rooted.

I pictured Elle's tiny fingers tracing the panther covering my stomach and made myself stand up and stretch that ink for her. Horse watched me like a hawk as I took unsteady steps to the seat beside Mick. When I gracelessly flopped into the chair, it took everything in me not to cry out.

Mick clapped his hand around the back of my neck a moment later. He patted and grabbed like a proud father, each jostle sending shockwaves through my body that I could only grit my teeth and take.

"I missed you," Mick purred, his lips less than an inch away from my ear.

Everything in me simmered. I wanted to let loose and punch him. Preferably with brass knuckles. I would break his jaw if I hit him the way he'd hit me, and that was something I'd relish.

I pictured standing over Mickey Maloney's dead body. In my mind blood barely poured from his body—a man with no heart surely wouldn't bleed that much. But that hellfire that always danced behind his eyes would be extinguished. I could kick his corpse, bash the skull of Satan repeatedly into the wood floors, unload a clip into the soulless form. What I wouldn't give to be the one responsible for sending that demon back to the depths of hell.

But for now, I took it. I let him shake me and whisper in my ear. I kept my temper and my gun in my waistband.

"Now for you two, you're both getting tasks."

"I'll help Siobhan," I spat out even though the words made my jaw ache.

"You'll help her right off a cliff is how you'll help her." He laughed as he said it.

"Well…" I growled. Picturing Siobhan plummet to her death was every bit as easy as picturing putting Mickey in his grave.

"I know you want to prove that you didn't squawk to your little lass but I don't know that I believe you yet." He used his grip on my neck to pull me back toward him, pressing the gun to my temple this time.

"I'm not dead, which means you believe me." I turned in his grip and pressed my forehead to the empty barrel.

I didn't pull away as I dug for my phone. When I fished it from my back pocket, I threw it on Mick's lap.

"Check it. The code is forty-forty."

He pulled the gun from my forehead and dropped his hold on me. Mercifully the metal clank and scrape against the armrest covered the whimper that escaped my lips when I slumped back into my chair.

"There are messages from her on here."

"From her. Not me." I added through gritted teeth still trying to find a semi-comfortable position.

"There's one. Right up here by this video."

Shit!

The video of Elle smiling at me was enough to get me off, so I'd forgotten about scrolling up to the one that had originally hooked me. I could spring across the chair—well, as much as my rickety body would let me—and keep that piece of her secret or I could sit still and keep *her* secret.

148

"Oh this is good, Cole. No wonder she's so far under your skin. She has a lovely little cunny."

I bit down on my cheek so hard, the metallic salt of blood pooled into my mouth.

"Little Elle Leroux and her perfect French kitten," he murmured as he rewound the video.

Bile rose in my throat as it had every single time I thought of Mickey getting his hands on her. I choked down the burning acid mixed with the warm salt of my blood and rooted my hands in clenched fists at my side.

"Is that cum on her thighs?" he asked, excitement coloring his words.

I was too busy playing rigid statue to answer. If I moved, spoke—hell, if I breathed—I was going to snap.

"Cole, answer me." He flung a hand into my side, jabbing the hot poker already digging into me and pushing it further.

I cried out for a brief second then snapped my mouth shut. Horse's eyes were molten behind Mick when I turned in their direction.

"Yeah," I grunted.

"Tell me. Tell me about being inside her." He was replaying the video again.

Horse swallowed a lump as big, if not bigger, than the one blocking my throat. When I hesitated, he jerked his chin, urging me to start talking. When my lips thinned further his face changed, I recognized it from bed this afternoon, he was begging me. And with every fiber of his being.

God in heaven, forgive me. Not for my sins, but for what I'm about to do Elle.

"She's tight." I managed, my throat constricted to the size of a pin. "But she's warm and velvety. Her hips buck wildly." I tried to swallow again but couldn't. "She tastes like cherries and smells like expensive vanilla. The only thing she swallows better than dick is cum."

"Have you had her ass?" Mick had started leisurely stroking himself over top of his jeans.

149

"Yeah. She screams when you push in." I tried to detach myself from the memories, telling myself this was a story about a chick and nothing more. I had to pretend it wasn't the most intimate details of the woman I needed more than air.

"I don't know if I want her or to watch you with her more." He unzipped his fly and started stroking himself in time with Elle's tiny flicks on the screen.

I couldn't find words. And it wasn't just because I was busy swallowing the vomit in my mouth. No matter what Mick did or said, I couldn't put her up on a platter any more than I already had.

I should have let him kill me.

Mick was too busy to make me continue, transfixed on the screen and the way he'd lined up his erection with her folds. He murmured *cherries* and *cum* from time to time, but otherwise, the room was silent while Mick masturbated to my girl on a throne above a dead body.

I turned and wretched on the floor, unable to choke it back anymore. In the smallest miracle the darkest corner of the globe ever saw, it was blood red. Whether it was the chunk I'd taken out of my cheek or the severity of my injuries, blood was acceptable. It wasn't a sign that Mick was dissolving my soul with the acid of his actions.

"Horse, get Cole home. I think he's had enough for one night." Mick didn't even falter with his strong, choking strokes on his cock. "I'll keep this for now. I'll give it back when you two find Jimmy Ponies." His voice was getting husky, breathy and I wanted to vomit all over again.

Before I could decide whether or not to add to the blood on the floor, Horse was in front of me.

"Get up," he whispered as low as possible.

I tried but almost instantly wobbled back into the chair.

"Cole, get the fuck up now." Horse was sharper and a little louder but his plea was covered by the sexual moans pouring from Mickey's lips.

My stomach revolted again, knowing that he was still jerking off to her, still mumbling words about *her*.

150

Horse didn't wait for me to pull it together, or for me to push up on my own. He yanked on my shoulder and pulled me up from the chair. I cried out in agony.

"Ah yes!" Mickey called out too, no doubt egged on by the blatant pain in my voice.

Horse pulled hard on me, harder than I wanted, but my feet weren't really working anymore. When my body almost slipped from his grip, he threw my arm over his shoulder and wrapped his around me. There was nothing gentle about his grip, there was nothing subtle about my painful cries.

He dragged me around the corpse and my limp toes tracked blood from the puddle. I watched the track up until I made the mistake of looking up. Mick was mid-orgasm, cum shooting from the tip of a red, angry dick and onto my phone. Onto my Elle.

Elle

Cole's apartment was home to four classic movies, two architectural posters and a nightlight that looked like a butt plug. He had three pairs of high top Chuck Taylors, a pair of Doc Martins and two sets of Adidas soccer cleats. His sheets were a high thread count cotton and his Thai leftovers were two weeks old.

Absolutely none of my snooping made me feel better about Hurricane Cole decimating my insides. Thinking about Horse, giant, King Kong Horse full of unyielding love, having Cole's back was the only reason I'd been able to get off the floor at all.

I debated curling back up in a ball while I tried to catch my breath every few minutes or so. They'd just been gone so long. Nothing good could come from that much distance, the deafening silence. Just as I was about to surrender to my panic a rough knock pounded against the door.

"Fucktart," the voice boomed from the hallway. "Elle, let us in." The begging was familiar but desperate, I couldn't quite place it.

"Ladyface, please." That voice I knew and it had my springing up from the couch so fast I crashed into the coffee table and swore.

"Ya all right, Fucktart?" The protectiveness in that voice made it instantly recognizable.

"Horse?" I asked quietly, still hesitant on the other side of the door after the warning he'd issued.

"It's me, Elle, and I've got my hands full. I can't get the keys."

"It's okay, Ladyface," Cole said softly, trying to soothe me but something was off in his voice.

I whipped open the door only to find exactly what Horse's hands were full of—Cole.

"Oh my God. What happened?" I stepped out of the way to make room for them as Horse dragged a limp and bloodied body into the loft.

"Mick knows you're not in Seattle," Horse said simply as he gently laid Cole down in bed. It took all of thirty seconds for Cole to pass out.

"He already knows I'm here?" My insides bottomed out.

"If he knew you were in this apartment, Cole would be a corpse."

My breath caught in my throat. Sure I got the idea that Mickey Maloney was dangerous. I knew he was a killer first hand. But I'd never seen it. Seeing it, seeing Cole wearing it was gonna make me puke.

"Is he…" I couldn't finish the sentence.

"The vet couldn't find any internal bleeding, but we have to keep an eye on him. If that bruise on his back goes bluish rather than red or purple, we have to get him to the ER." He blew out a deep breath and his brow creased as his gaze swept over Cole where he breathed soft, shallow breaths on the bed.

"Is the vet some mob doctor or something?" I asked, equally transfixed by Cole's labored breaths.

"No, he's a vet that owes me a favor." Horse bent down and started unlacing Cole's hightops.

"You took him to a vet?" I screeched and Cole stirred, weakly reaching out for me.

"Yes. Doctors ask too many questions and the guy could ultrasound the area, see some of what's up. He has pain meds."

Horse let Cole's shoes fall to the ground before starting in on his pants. Cole hadn't put on boxers before leaving the house and his tattoos peeked out as Horse's big hands pulled down the denim.

153

"What can I do?" I asked, stomaching some of the shock.

"Grab some ice from the freezer. If he's got enough to make two packs that would be great."

I inched away from the bed, hesitant to walk away from Cole, worried the light may snuff out of those green eyes at any moment. But the direction Horse had given me was good. The fact that I'd rifled through drawers this afternoon was better. I filled a Ziploc bag with ice and grabbed the edamame sitting next to the trays.

When I turned back toward the bed, Horse was sitting with his back to me as he tucked the edges of the comforter around Cole. His hand moved up Cole's body and hovered above his face, poised to cradle it, but he didn't. Instead his hand trembled the slightest bit before he balled it and let it flop down to the mattress.

"Is it hard for you?" I asked quietly as I handed the ice over.

"To watch him get pummeled? Fuck yeah," he said roughly, letting loose a little bit of the anger that he'd likely swallowed.

"That's not what I meant." I managed a weak smile for him as I rounded the bed to sit opposite him.

"You mean being on this side of the comforter?" Any hint of anger faded and his fingertips inched toward where Cole's were hidden under the soft blanket. I nodded as I captured my lip between my teeth. "You make it easier," he sighed and his hand inched back.

"How so?"

"Hope, Fucktart." Horse looked up at me with a forlorn smile. "The way he looks at you is hope personified. Like maybe he's found something worth living for. Gives me hope I still might."

My heart whomped in my chest and my throat went dry. I wanted to lie down and press my body to Cole's, to feel the dips and grooves lock into place with mine as if they were always meant to match. I wanted to whisper that he was my hope, too.

154

"Why do you call me Fucktart?" I scrunched up my nose and made a funny face, hoping it would lighten the mood between us.

I was rewarded with Horse's warm laugh, rich and thick like caramel.

"Because Poptarts are tasty enough to fuck. Just like you."

"What?" I squeaked before digressing into giggles.

"Oh yeah." His big smile overtook his entire face. "The cherry kind, with their bright pink frosting and little red sprinkles." He licked his lips, letting his eyes roll back in his head as he did.

"I taste like a fucking toaster pastry?" Laughter shook my shoulders, I just couldn't stop it.

"You fuck like the first time you taste a toaster pastry too."

I busted up, slapping my knee and everything. I couldn't help it. Horse laughed along for a minute then reached over top of Cole. He righted me by grabbing behind my neck then pulled my lips towards his.

"You brought him back to me, Fucktart. You and sick, twisted fate." He was so close, his pout brushed against mine. "Thank you."

He barely finished the words before he kissed me. It was gentler than I expected, and more passionate too. His lips tumbled over mine, making sure every inch was well loved. He only tentatively poked his tongue into my mouth, grazing rather than tangling with mine.

Cole groaned between us and I automatically pulled away. I expected Horse to do the same but he used his grip to guide my lips back to his.

"Thank you." He kissed the corner of my mouth. "Thank you." Then the other. "Thank you." And finished with a soft, sweet kiss on my lips.

When he pulled back he looked down at Cole, his eyes sweeping down his body then back up to his face.

"One of these packs stays on his jaw. The other down above his hip but below his ribs, okay?"

155

I nodded as my fingers came up to my lips where they were haunted by the ghost of Horse's. His big, beautiful charming smile spread like wildfire again.

"Keep a sheet or a thin towel between the ice and his skin and do twenty minutes on, twenty minutes off."

"Are you leaving?"

His absence felt a little like the sun was slipping behind the clouds.

"Somebody's gotta feed you. I haven't looked but I guarantee this motherfucker has nothing besides gross leftovers."

I shook my head with a small smile.

"Some things never change." He rolled his eyes as he stood. "Anything you're in the mood for?"

"I feel like we should eat Poptarts." I couldn't hold in a light chuckle.

This one stirred Cole again, his hand shoving against the blanket towards me. When he whimpered in frustration, I caught it and stilled it against the mattress.

"Take care of him," Horse said softly, his gaze falling to where my hands cupped Cole's.

The tone and the hint of wetness dancing in the corners of his eye gave me the feeling that he was talking about more than just tonight.

"Don't you fucking touch her, Mick." Cole's voice was sleep laced but it made my blood run cold. "I'll rip your fingers off myself."

I was curious what he'd tell me in his sleep but when he started trashing against the covers, I shoved a bookmark into the book I'd picked up and ran over to him.

"Cole," I said softly, hoping to wake him but not startle him. "Cole," I coaxed as I folded onto the bed next to him. Whatever had happened, wasn't good.

"She's mine," he snarled and it sent shivers up and down my spine both for how possessive *and* how furious he was. He was every bit as terrified as Horse had been and I could guess why. I tried to swallow and couldn't as I went to wake him.

156

"Cole," I said sharply, not wanting to have to shake his damaged body.

"Ladyface?" he asked, more groggy than anything.

"Hi there." I couldn't help but smile down at him.

"Hi." He let out a deep breath then his smile spread to match mine. "How did I get here? I remember Horse getting me out, a few blocks in the car then nothing."

"So you don't remember your trip to the vet?" I cocked my head and my eyebrow.

Cole started to laugh only to digress into a haggard moan. My hands shot out for him before I realized I had no idea where to grab to comfort him. They fell back to my lap.

"Some things never change," Cole wheezed.

"I've heard that before."

Horse's voice was easy to hear saying the same words even though he'd been gone for an hour.

"He's always been afraid of the doctor. Dr. Baker has been stitching him up since we were kids."

I couldn't hold back the smile at the thought of hulking Horse afraid of the doctor. For some reason, I pictured him with a lollipop, shoved into the tiny chairs of a vet's waiting room and started laughing all over again.

"God is that the best sound on earth or what?" He closed his eyes with a wide contented smile across his face.

"You breathing is better," I said shyly; his smile grew.

"It takes more than this to get me down, Ladyface."

He shifted and winced then started to sit up only to cry out.

"Cole, what are you doing?" Panic laced my voice as my hands shot out to his shoulders.

"Getting up," he groaned again and pressed against the palm of my hands.

"Like hell!" My voice was almost as distraught as his. "Whatever you need, I'll get it. I'll do it for you."

"I have to take a piss. And, Ladyface, there's a hell of a lot of things you can do *to* my dick, and *with* my dick, and even *for* my dick, but that's not one of them." He chuckled but it was breathy and laced with pain.

"Fine. At least let me help you up."

"Elle." He rolled his eyes but relaxed against my hands.

"I thought so." I raised both my eyebrows then cupped my hands over the top of his shoulders. "Count to three."

He did as I asked and on three he pushed up while I pulled as best I could. The whimpers that crossed his lips tugged at my heart and my fingers curled into him far harder than I intended. Not even the covers falling away from his naked body distracted my hold.

"I knew you were a little kinky…" he gasped. "But taking advantage of me while I'm out cold is a bit much." He smiled as he looked down his bare flesh then up at me from under his golden lashes.

"Dream on. Horse stripped you down."

"Any excuse that man can get to check me out." He burst out laughing again, only to damn near crumple in my arms. I did what I could to catch him and keep him upright. I couldn't help but yelp at the idea of him hitting the floor.

"Knock it off, love." I wedged myself under his shoulder and gently wrapped around his torso, mindful of the spot Horse had shown me that was a decidedly angry swollen bruise. We managed a few wobbly steps when he stopped.

"Did you just call me love?" His arms wrapped tighter around me.

"It was that or punching bag." I almost choked on my embarrassment.

"Call me either as long as you're close enough to call me something." He smiled and bent down, bringing his lips down toward mine. Halfway there, he cried out but he didn't straighten. Instead he sucked in deep, jagged breaths inches above me. "Kiss me. Please, God, kiss me. I've been awake five minutes and I haven't tasted you."

The amount of need in his voice had me pushing up onto my tiptoes to kiss him. He grunted against my gentle kiss and I couldn't tell if his sounds were lust laced or full of angst. When I broke away, he stayed bent, his lips still searching for mine. When he tried to reach me, pain shot like lightning across his face.

158

"I thought you had to pee," I whispered.

He tried to hold a smile while he twisted in my arms and his semi hit my leg.

"About that…"

Cole

My jaw pulsed with pain and it felt like I was being stabbed with a hot poker near my kidney but Elle… Elle in my arms was the ice to my jaw and the salve to my side. Then there was what she did to my insides. And my dick.

"You know you lose steam and can't cum if you've gotta pee?" She quirked her eyebrow up and it pulled on the corner of her lip, making her seem mischievous; I had another type of ache all together.

"Well then help me in there." I jerked my chin toward the bathroom and immediately regretted it.

She notched her shoulder underneath mine and straightened her back. Of course I noticed how perfectly she fit but I also noticed how strong she was. I was no slouch and she shouldered my pathetic ass seamlessly on her little bird bones.

I couldn't help but look down at her as she gingerly helped me. The adorable wrinkles on her forehead and the way she tugged on her lip in determination were almost enough to make the pain worth it. She dragged me almost as effectively as Horse, or I was too distracted by the way her tits looked beneath the cotton of my t-shirt to care.

"So…" She drug out the word as she flipped up the toilet seat. "When you're done, just yell."

"I thought you were going to help me with anything," I smirked.

"I thought me and piss were keeping our distance."

160

"You're one of those girls that always shuts the door, aren't you?" I knew she wasn't, a girl that prude wouldn't do half the things Elle had, but it was fun to tease her.

"Fine." She huffed. "I'll hold you up. You want me to shake for you, too?"

"Yup," I said, just to challenge her.

She adjusted herself under my arm and her little hands wandered down tentatively toward my dick. I was growing harder and twitched away from her grip in anticipation. Her little hand caught me and wrapped around my shaft, making me look huge in her palm.

Elle hadn't done anything sexual but she was going to make me cum. Her bright blue eyes when I woke from a nightmare, her tender touch, the snark and sweetness oozing from every pore—I was a goner.

"Okay, okay, okay." I took my cock from her, sucking in a few deep breaths as I moved. "Turns out you get me too excited." I cringed when I pushed my growing boner down toward the toilet. The twist and flex on my abused ab muscles was enough to make me cry out.

"Cole?" She had a way of setting my skin on fire with the way she said my name.

"Here." I shuffled her behind me with only moderate effort. I grabbed her hand and pulled it over the top of the ink on my uninjured hip. "Just help keep me steady."

She buried her face into the dip of my spine and breathed in deeply. I sighed at the feeling that shot through me and closed my eyes, praying to God that when I opened them, I was still here and she was still there. If I was dead, Elle wouldn't be helping me take a piss.

I blew out the deep breath and opened my eyes. It was the happiest I'd ever been to see the damned backsplash I'd worked forever to install last summer. And to feel another human pressed against me.

"Anytime," she taunted me but her lips brushed against my back and my balls tightened up. At this point, I was worried the whole thing was futile.

But I managed. Barely. Her breathy giggles against my back didn't help me in the least.

"All right, Ladyface."

She slid back around my body and used her pointed toes to flush my toilet. Her creamy thigh was on display, a magnet drawing my touch. It didn't take much for my fingers to skate up her thigh to find her perfect little pussy, wet for me, even bruised and helpless in the bathroom.

Part of me wanted to be well enough to turn and fuck her beautiful brains out against the wall. The other part of me kind of liked being vulnerable with her, at the mercy to whatever she would give.

Elle straightened up underneath my shoulder and my own little crutch helped me hobble back. She had to lean to counter my weight when I gingerly lowered to the bed. Before I could lay back completely she reached to fluff the pillows behind my head. My eyes fixed on the way it made her tits bounce.

I had to have her. Beat-down be damned.

When she turned away from me and walked into the kitchen, I almost cried out in need. But she simply fished in the freezer then turned back. She had ice, and the thought of the cool soothe against my skin was almost as enticing as her.

Almost.

"Are you playing nurse?"

"Horse gave me strict instructions." She shot me a look.

"More vet wisdom put to human use."

She cracked a smile but the way she tried to wrangle it was what was really charming.

"Ice massage is more effective than twenty on, twenty off. Gets deeper into the muscle with less time," I said it with a sultry purr so she'd know there were other benefits as well.

Just like I hoped, she grabbed an ice cube and adjusted her grip on it to massage along my hip.

"Oh God, yes." My desperate cry was every bit as much for the ice as it was for her hands welding it.

She circled on the skin and I tensed and flexed away from it. The ice was chilling but it was Elle that gave me goosebumps.

162

When I was good and numb, I reached up and pointed to where my jaw had been cracked. She seamlessly started massaging that bruise.

Water droplets trickled down my neck and I felt them stream down my throat to pool on the bed behind me.

"You're getting me all wet, Ladyface," I purred.

"Likewise." She ever so carefully slipped her knee over mine and bent down to kiss the droplets that had pooled on my skin.

My breath caught loud enough that she stopped and sat up, studying my face.

"That's all you," I said softly.

She caught my meaning and that mischievous smile played back on her lips. My cock twitched up and hit between her thighs. All I wanted to do was bury myself there, but I was at her mercy. Her lips started down my chest. Each and every breath twinged my abs and back but I wouldn't have stopped her if my life depended on it.

"You'll tell me if I hurt you, right?" she asked from where she was pressed down along my chest, her big blue eyes peering up at me.

"The only thing that would hurt me is if you stopped," I murmured as I let my hands shove into her hair and pull her head back.

God, I wanted to reach down and squeeze her neck. I wanted control back after a tailspin of a day, but my body wouldn't let me. I doubted my sexy, sultry little nurse would either.

"Take off your shirt, let me see your skin. Let me imagine what it tastes like." My voice was barely more than a gravelly whisper as I dropped my hold on her.

Elle sat up and peeled off my shirt then balled it and threw it to the side of the bed. Her body flexed with the toss and her hair waved in front of her pert nipples. I started salivating like a dog hoping to get treats. Her gaze met mine and swept to where my eyes stayed fixed.

163

"You want a taste?" She didn't even wait for my response before carefully shimmying up my body and pushing her breast in my face.

I groaned loudly.

So loudly I didn't hear the door unlock.

"I leave you guys alone for a little more than an hour." I didn't need to look away from Elle's flesh to see that it was Horse. Or that his eyes had lit up. "You're hurt Cole," he scolded halfheartedly.

"Blue balls would be worse," I shot back as I switched to Elle's other side.

She moaned when I latched on like I'd hit some sort of magical button and I forgot about Horse and his chastising completely. The arm that didn't pull too hard on my sore spots slid up to her back and pressed her flesh further into my mouth.

Her hips gently rolled across my chest and the wetness I'd put between her legs slid up and down my skin.

"Don't stop moving, okay?" I looked up and met her eyes, she nodded unblinking down at me.

Her body rolling had her nipple stretching away from my teeth then falling back to them. She arched her back to get a rougher pull and my body tensed.

"Mmmm, quite the show, Fucktart." Horse pulled a chair up to the side of the bed and reached his hand out to skate along Elle's body.

When he got to her ass he shoved her. She cried out until I released the nipple that was between my teeth. Horse lifted her until her perfect pussy was right in front of my nose. My one good hand—well, less painful one—balled into the flesh of her ass cheek and pulled her level with my lips.

"Eat her, Cole." Horse was turned on. I could tell even though the pale skin of Elle's thighs was effectively blinding me. "Eat her like she's your last fucking meal."

I didn't need his encouragement. The very smell of Elle in front of me was enough of a treat to latch on and suck. When her clit was in my mouth I rolled it around then folded my tongue around it in a clover shape.

164

She gasped the way she had every time since I'd showed her the shape on the plane. Her hands flew forward, one grabbing the headboard and the other curling into my hair. She pulled on my head, sometimes jerking too forcefully but most of the time just the right amount for me to bury into every single space inside her. Her hips started a slow rock and my lips, my nose, my tongue moved against her in a rhythm as natural as breathing.

"Let me turn around. Let me return the favor." She gasped the last words as I hit a new spot inside her.

"No." It was Horse who laid down the decree. "Explore every inch, Cole. Memorize her thighs, her lips, her clit. What does she feel like? What does she taste like? Remember every single thing about her."

I did as I was told even though Horse never ordered me around in bed. Maybe it was *because* Horse never ordered me around in bed. As my tongue and lips danced across her, I leaned back the slightest bit so that I could look up at her.

My nose notched against her responsive clit. Her stomach was flat besides dips and planes over her bones that made her seem more overwhelming then her small frame should. Her muscles moved in time with the grinding of her hips on my face. The most perfect tits on the planet bounced the slightest bit in time with her movements and her hair was a golden cascading curtain around her face.

"Fuck," I murmured and she moaned at the way the word vibrated against her.

I turned and kissed the spot on her thighs that I'd coated when we'd first met.

"That's right," Horse encouraged. "Breathe her in. Lap every inch."

Hearing him beside me was making me harder; together they were my sexual kryptonite.

The bed flexed underneath of me and Horse's warm breath puffed against my cheek where he peeked around Elle's thigh.

"Tell me about it." He brushed his nose along my temple and I clutched my hand into Elle even harder. More arousal spread down around my cheeks.

165

"Her skin is so soft," I mumbled into the apex of her thighs and Horse hummed in pleasure and let his hand skate along her body. "Look at how she trembles." I took her little nubbin of nerves back in my mouth and folded neatly around her. Sure enough her whole body jerked. Horse palmed his hand into her ass to match mine.

"She hasn't touched me and I'm going to come."

It was the truth and when they both groaned loudly in unison, my whole body tensed. Elle flopped forward, surrendering to her own orgasm and spread slick arousal all over my face while gasping and screeching. Her, lost and writhing on my face overrode the pain still radiating through my body and I shot my orgasm, hands-free, onto my stomach.

The heat of cum was in sharp contrast to the cool where she'd iced me and the wildfire on my face. The sensation was enough to make me forget anything but the wicked sex we had together.

After a few minutes and many rough breaths, Horse lifted her from my face, easily cradling her as he lowered her beside me. He rubbed his fingers across her slit and watched her jerk a few times at his mercy. His big smile spread across his face, and I knew he was pleased with himself and the effect he had on her. On us.

When his hand dropped away from Elle, he bent down to me and his lips met mine. He kissed me gently at first, but then I reached up and grabbed behind him, deepening our kiss to something rough and wild.

He was just as responsible for that orgasm as she was. And he'd saved me tonight every bit as much as Elle. I slipped him tongue until it made my jaw ache and the pain overtook me again.

I pulled back and reached for the partially melted ice, placing it to my cheek. Horse's warm chocolate eyes were watching me intently, lust burning brightly behind them.

"She tastes like cherries," I added as if I was still under Horse's sexual orders.

He smiled so big I thought his face might split as he looked over at Elle. Her breathy laugh punctuated my thundering heartbeat. Horse's hand came to my thigh and rubbed.

"This I know, Cupcake. This I know."

Elle

Waking up in the morning next to Cole seared something inside of me. I couldn't tell if it was the way the light fell across his body, or the way his ink softly rose or fell, or perhaps it was just some response I had to him.

My fingers itched to reach out to him but the pain he'd been in last night stopped me short. I settled for following the outlines of his tattoos with the tiniest breath of space between us.

"You can touch me, Ladyface. I'm not gonna break." His voice was warm, rich honey.

I let my fingertips press gently against him. His muscles pulled, quivering beneath my touch and I curled into the pillow beneath me to hide my beaming smile.

"Well I might if you hide that sunshine smile of yours away." He moved his hand away from his side and slowly but surely came up to cup my face.

He only winced twice along the way.

As soon as he rested his big hand against my cheek, he brushed along my skin with the pad of his thumb. The smile that broke across his face threatened to kill me.

"I think you're the one with the sunshine smile," I said softly as I let my fingers wander down across his washboard.

"Agree to disagree." His hand left my face and captured my fingertips before they could go too low. "As much as I'd like to, I'm out of hard-and-fast-fuck commission and I have things to do today."

"Oh." My hands fell away from him. "Right. I should've thought of that."

I turned over and burrowed into the bed, choking back the emotion that came along with the idea of a day without him.

"You're coming with me, ya know?" His arm wove around me and pulled me toward him. He cried out but he flattened my back to his side all the same. "I'm not letting you out of my sight." He kissed along the ridge of my shoulder then up into my hair.

"I thought I couldn't leave. That it wasn't safe."

Horse's warning hung around my neck, weighed down by Cole's dark bruises.

"It's safe enough to go downstairs." His breath was warm against my skin.

"Downstairs?" I wanted to turn to question him but his light kisses across any skin that he could reach were too delectable to stop.

"I've got an appointment in twenty. At the rate I'm moving, we may be late. Help me?"

I nodded and he let his hand fall away. I slid out of bed and circled over to help him. Just like last night, I bent down to grip his shoulders. He leaned up with my assistance but then shot the last few inches, crashing into my lips.

Like last night, he moaned loudly from the sudden jerky movements but it didn't stop him from devouring me. I wove my hands around his back and supported him, letting my fingertips skate ever so gently across his back. His tongue pushed in between my lips and claimed ownership of every single inch of me. I lived to be kissed like that.

"I don't think this is helping," I said softly when I pulled back.

"Not in the least." He smirked before he reached up and kissed the tip of my nose. His smirk fell as he shifted his legs off the bed. Once or twice he flexed in a funny way and a look of pain shot across his face. When he finally got to a sitting position, he looked up at me. "Will you grab under my arms this time?"

I nodded as I straddled him and hooked in against his body. I was bracing myself to lift him when his breathy, pained laugh tickled the curve of my neck.

"This was a fantastic idea." He puffed out his chest and shimmied a little against mine, my nipples reacting, sending shockwaves down my body.

"At this rate, we're never getting downstairs." I rolled my eyes as I started pulling on him.

He finally worked with me and rose to stand, dropping the sheet from his body. My mouth dropped open. Sure he was the same perfectly ripped and artistically designed man he'd been yesterday but the bruises were so much angrier today. They competed with the black of his panther and the red of his roses, desperate to outshine them.

"For now, let's keep eyes up here." He pointed to his face. "Or down here." He pointed at his perfect cock and let his dimple hollow out his cheek.

"Up here isn't much better." My fingers hovered over the bruises that his jaw and cheek wore.

"Dick it is." He pressed his bruises into my hesitant fingers. "I don't mind one bit."

"You're terrible." I laughed but made sure it didn't shake my fingertips.

"I'm a monster," he growled before bending down to kiss me again, chastely this time.

"Not even remotely." I pulled away then kissed a spot on his chest before I walked over to the dresser.

I'd folded his t-shirts from the busted drawer and left them on top yesterday. Then I'd snooped enough to find the tight boxer briefs he wore. Luckily, his dimple made a guest appearance when I walked around like I owned the place. As I circled back I snatched the jeans Horse had discarded last night before kneeling at Cole's feet. He watched me closely as I held his clothes out for him. He used my shoulder when he needed to balance himself with only minimal grunts.

I held his shirt open for him and he slid in. As soon as I pulled it over his head, something delicious flashed in his eyes.

170

"I think we should make this a daily ritual." The way hunger and gratitude mingled in his voice had me contemplating a yes. "That's your bag over on the couch, yeah?"

I turned to find the familiar leather bag resting in the spot I'd occupied last night.

"Where did that come from?"

"The car." Cole breathed out roughly. "Thank fucking God Horse found it."

His eyes went dark and he wasn't with me anymore. The ghosts haunting him were almost as obvious as the bruises he wore. His fists balled at his side and his shoulders started to rise and fall too quickly.

"Are we going to talk about what happened last night?" My voice brought him back to me but he was still bathed in darkness.

"I don't ever want to say those words to you." His voice was a mix of fury and desolation.

We stood silent, staring at each other for a few moments. I narrowed my eyes the slightest bit and clenched my jaw. He drank in every inch of me before blowing out a heavy breath.

"He wanted proof I hadn't contacted you. He went through my phone." His voice was ominous but I didn't see why.

"Cole, you never called. You never texted. Didn't that just help us?"

"*That* did." Cole emphasized the word so there was no question that something else had worked decidedly against us. His shoulders started their haggard roll again. "But the video."

For a second I could only remember the sweet one I'd sent. It seemed like I'd sent it years ago, so much had happened since then. I was going to question him but then I reached back further. Back to the reason we were both standing here together in the first place.

"Of me? Of you covering me?" I couldn't bring myself to say masturbating.

He nodded once.

"Mr. Maloney saw that?" The embarrassment bloomed up along my collarbone.

171

"I couldn't stop him, Elle. Even if he hadn't already worked me over." He seethed as he spoke. "He would have known that there was something more between us. He would have dug."

My heart was alternating between a jackhammer and a flat line but it wasn't beating with anger, just fear.

"I understand." My voice was equally small. "I was going to tell you that yesterday but got distracted. It hurts, but I get why you've done...what you've done."

"It's more this time," he snarled lowly. "He wants you. He wants to watch you." His voice broke. "He wants to feel inside of you."

I couldn't breathe. It was a little bit because of Mr. Maloney but he was still an abstract villain in my story. It was mostly because I couldn't be with someone else. Any little space I had in my heart, or in my bed, were currently occupied by Horse. Cole was actually *my* everything.

"You won't let him." I meant it to be a question but it came out as a decisive statement.

Cole started to speak, his voice a stark reprimand, but I cut him off.

"No. That trudge through hell you told me about, well this is it. It's not pretty and it's not easy, but we *will* find something on the other side." I let conviction color my voice and whether I was delusional or not, believing in him, and in us, felt right in my very soul.

He moved faster than I'd seen in twenty-four hours, his hand came to my throat and he pulled me to his body. His fingers curled into my neck, crushing harder as his lips threatened to devour me. I matched him move for move until that hazy feeling started to filter into my face. The buzz that rang in my ears and the way my vision tunneled was almost as delicious as the taste of Cole against me.

"Everything," he growled when he pulled away but he didn't let go. "You're fucking everything."

I didn't fight him. I stayed limp in his grip as I started to gasp for air. He squeezed tighter. My eyelids fluttered shut as my head rolled back. The heat and throb that came with his brand of

172

ownership was taking over. I was happy to surrender to it, murmuring just one word before I was sure I'd pass out.

Everything.

He let go and it was the rush of air pummeling my limbs, not the disappearance of his hand, that had me stumbling. Cole tried to chase after me but he still couldn't quite move without crying out in pain. I caught myself against the arm of the couch and sucked in deep breaths.

We shared a look again, this one speaking volumes about everything between us. About how we understood each other on a level so basic it was like oxygen itself.

"Get dressed or I'll end up ruining you." He adjusted his stance a little so he could watch me, once again pain snapped across his face.

"I'm already ruined." I held his gaze for a split second before I reached into my bag and pulled out the cotton dress on top. I didn't need a bra so I pulled the black t-shirt fabric on and let it dance across my upper thighs. I reached down into my bag to grab socks and underwear.

"Don't you dare put on panties." Cole's voice was a different kind of rough when he commanded me.

I held up my knee-high socks with a smirk and let them unwind from my hand like some big reveal. I wiggled my eyebrows at him then twisted to sit as I rolled them on. I knew he could see straight between my thighs but then again, I wasn't really trying to hide from him. He was the one that wanted me bare anyway. I even threw my leg up on the armrest when I slipped on my hightops that matched his a little too well.

"Maybe you aren't an angel after all." A big smile split across his face and he reached his hand out for me.

I took it for just a second then slid in under his shoulder. I lifted up the best way I knew how and we finally made it out of the apartment. We even managed the stairs pretty well. He grabbed keys from somewhere and opened the shop.

A small bell rang when we opened the door but otherwise the studio was silent. He didn't have other artists buzzing away or a front desk person ready to take calls.

173

"Is it just you?" I asked when he stepped away from me and gingerly sat down on the rolling stool behind the computer.

"Yeah. I rent space out to a lot of my friends when they come into town and need a place to set up shop for a little while. It's pretty common to have visiting artists in the tattoo world." He smiled wistfully like it was a world a million miles away. "Take a look around, Ladyface. There's a bathroom and a closet in the back. A space for when I have company or need to tattoo something delicate, then there's all this..." He waved around a workspace full of drawing tables and tracing paper and I smiled. "I'd show you around but..." He pointed toward his side.

I shot him a look then started meandering around. My fingers traced over the surfaces that screamed Cole. A white wall was covered in frames, each holding colored tattoo drawings or photos of exceptional work. All of it arced with lines that reminded me of Cole's grip, bold and unrelenting but beautiful, each one held his signature without being signed.

The back had a rich, luxurious and dark wallpaper with velvet fleur-de-lis across it. A massage table was laid out with lighting above. The bathroom was tucked behind and the closet was even further away. As I walked back out, I found small figures and random collectibles on every single shelf.

There were army guys and a mini Dodge Charger, sketches, pin-up girls and a sheriff star but it was the random horses everywhere that caught my eye. Some of them were bigger, some teeny-tiny. Some were brand new, and even more seemed liked they'd been picked up off the street, dirt and scuff still covering them.

The shop was eclectic but artsy and utterly Cole. Manly beyond a doubt but sentimental and a haven for creativity. I loved it more than words could say. It reminded me of my workshop at home. Of Conrad.

"Shit," I swore at the very idea of how angry he had to be with me. "Can I use your phone?"

"No. No one can know, Elle. Absolutely no one." His brow creased and darkness filled his features again.

174

"But Conrad will be worried. He'll be freaking the fuck out." True panic at how far Conrad would speed off the rails was welling up in my chest. "He's my best friend. I left without telling him anything. I mean anything besides I was going stupid for you despite the Maloney stuff."

"Shhhhh, Ladyface," he soothed me, his voice wrapping around me like his hands would if he wasn't awkwardly frozen across the room. "Wanna draw? That always calms me down?"

The tightness in my chest unwound and I couldn't help but smile. Conrad would have worked himself into a fine lather, and he was likely ready to murder me, but I was happy here. Blissfully happy, actually. I couldn't regret my decision, even if I had to keep it quiet. I followed Cole's pointed hand to the workstation behind him.

"Don't touch the sketches, they're for clients, but help yourself to absolutely anything else." He busied himself on the computer as I settled in.

There was only one pile of papers in my way. I carefully lifted them and slid them over to the desk between us. One piece of paper slid out and fell to the floor. I bent to pick it up and put it back on the pile but my hand hesitated on it.

The image was unmistakable. It was me with my finger pointing in the direction of the artist. My hair snaked wildly and seemed to dance even on paper. My eyes twinkled on the page and I remembered how it felt to send him *that* video. That he'd watched it, drawn from it, thought about me in some small way, pushed worry so far from my mind, I couldn't remember what it was.

Yes. I would trudge through hell with Cole—for Cole— even if it was a death march that could cost me everything.

Cole

Elle had settled into a sketching station like she belonged there. She fit in my shop the way she fit underneath my shoulder.

Before my client came in, I watched her out of the corner of my eye. She evaluated every pencil I had, each stack of paper as if they meant something to her. She'd said she was an artist but now, watching her, I wondered about Elle's life before me, or outside of me.

Her hand against paper seemed so natural, the curves or her strokes so easy, she was almost entrancing. I checked emails, updated my books and printed off stencils but my eyes never really strayed far from her. Once or twice I caught her watching me right back.

The familiar bell clanged and pulled my attention from her.

"Hey man," I said as I nodded at the guy walking in.

"What up, Cole." He reached his hand over and I had to suck in a deep breath before I could reach my hand out to greet him, I managed to shake it without balling into a sandy sack. Maybe this wouldn't be so bad after all.

I managed to get my client set up without asking Elle for help. It wasn't that it didn't ache through my side but more that I didn't want to bother her. She was so intent on the page below her fingertips I felt awful interrupting.

When the buzz of my gun ramped up against the skin, I blew out a deep breath I didn't know I was holding. Doing what I loved with Elle by my side felt *right*. Mick wasn't lurking in the background, worry wasn't worming its way through my veins. Instead there was warmth and ease radiating from a few feet to my left.

For a few minutes—well, because of the size of the piece, a few hours—life was good. Better than good. It was perfect. There was quiet and calm. Not just around me, but within me. The last time I'd been able to lull myself into this sense of security was...*never*.

The artwork on the skin in front of me reflected the feeling taking root inside me. The curves matched the body just a little bit better, the shading was the slightest bit more refined, and there was a lightness I didn't expect. To say I was proud of the piece taking shape beneath my hand was an understatement. I just hoped it didn't stray too far from expectations.

I winced the slightest bit when I sat up straight and wiped the last little bit of ink away from the guy's side.

"Take a look," I said as I set the gun down.

My eyes went to Elle rather than the ink just as they had off and on throughout the session. Her head bobbed in time with the music and she seemed completely oblivious to the fact that I was still in the room.

"Holy shit, Cole!"

I looked over to where my artwork was highlighted in a mirror by overhead spotlights.

"That a good or a bad holy shit?"

"It's amazing." It was Elle's quiet voice that answered just before her hand came to rest on my shoulder.

"Fuck yeah it is. I mean, I knew you were good but this..." He whistled lowly, but it was Elle squeezing ever so slightly on me that made me proud.

"Glad you like it." I smiled and leaned back into Elle even though my kidneys told me to knock that shit off.

"Like it? Jesus. You're an artist." He was still looking down at his side in disbelief.

"You are, Cole," Elle agreed as her fingertips tickled along my shirt collar.

177

"Let me clean you up, take a pic and wrap it." I felt the dimple hollow out the side of my cheek as my chest puffed up under the touch of my Ladyface.

He sidled back over and held his arm above his head as I wiped him down then snapped a pic. Even on camera, the art made me proud. I couldn't help but smile as I covered him with the usual pads and neon tape. Elle's gently massaging fingertips at the nape of my neck didn't hurt.

The moment we were alone, I spun my stool toward Elle. She stood waiting for me and didn't seem the least bit surprised when I nuzzled against her stomach, her hands simply folded around the back of my head and massaged my scalp then down toward my neck.

"God, this feels good," I purred.

I moved my hands up to her hips and forced my mouth to stay shut. I was going to have this moment without a yelp if it killed me. Her hips bucked the slightest bit against me and I simply pressed my lips to where I knew her cute little belly button sat.

"It really was exceptional art, Cole." Her voice was low and warm like mine.

"And just what do you know about ink? You work in metal," I asked, barely able to contain the tease in my voice.

"Hey!" she shrieked and stepped away.

I gasped when I had to catch myself on the stool.

"Cole, shit." She rushed back and managed to catch me then steady my wobbling.

I clung to her hips like she was a life raft keeping me afloat. Her tiny hands clasped around mine and just like that, I could swim, I could breathe. And in the air hung the faint scent of cherry between her thighs.

"Speaking of art..." I had to change the subject or surrender to the cherries. "Show me what you were working on."

I looked up at her face and to my surprise, she didn't even hesitate. No blush, no fish mouthed excuses, no waver whatsoever. She just pressed me back and walked over to her little workspace.

178

She grabbed the piece of paper she'd been drawing on and held it out for me. I took it, expecting something simple, maybe high school level shading, but once again Elle floored me.

I was in front of me. Exactly. I could be looking in a mirror for how perfectly she'd captured me. The way I sat, the tattoos that poked out of my shirt when I bent over the desk in front of me. She'd drawn me with a slight scowl on my face as I turned a horse figurine over in my hands.

It was like she'd looked back in time to a month ago, like she knew why the small toys littered my shop without me ever having to say it. The picture proved just how deeply she understood me. Every inch of me.

Nothing would ever top looking at myself through her eyes. For a moment, I wasn't a monster, I was a man who'd been lost, riddled with sin but who'd kept faith and kept going. The fact that she stood so close was proof it had all been worth it.

"Come here." I could barely get the words out.

"It's not my best, I mean the shadow is a little warped and I don't think there's enough movement in the piece. I'm rusty because of the metalwork, sketches usually don't turn…"

She was rambling about art in the passionate and familiar way only a real artist could. Judging by the sketch in my hand, and the critique she had prepared, a far superior artist. I wanted to stop her and tell her how fucking fantastic she was. I wanted to stop her and ask a million questions; to geek out the way only two kindred spirits could. But I *needed* to stop her and kiss her.

I stood as swiftly as I could manage and tossed the piece of paper toward my desk. She stopped mid-sentence to scold me for getting up and her hands shot out to help me as the drawing fluttered to the floor. I cut her off with my mouth, swallowing her words and tasting them as much as I did her and her lips. Cherry filled my senses, and I let out a heavy sigh.

Elle groaned in response and the feel of that sound in my mouth was so delicious, I knew what I would wish for on death row.

Her hands wrapped around me, gently at first but the longer I kissed her, the more they begged to pull me closer. I let myself imagine that she would pull me right inside and let me live in her heart if she could.

But then her hands curled into my sides and pain ripped through my body like claws and fangs set on eviscerating my insides. I cried out in agony and my knees threatened to give way beneath me. Her lips stopped working against mine and her hands fell completely from me, and a whole new pain took over.

"Don't," I whispered.

"Don't touch you? I know. Oh, my God, do I know. I'm so sorry." She trembled in a way I'd never seen Elle do before. She was afraid.

"No," I said softly as I stepped back over to her. "I meant don't let go. Ever."

"But I hurt you." Her bottom lip quivered.

"I like to think you reminded me that this is real." I took her hands and placed them back on my hips before I reached up and locked onto her neck.

I yanked her roughly to me. My body could bitch and moan at the way I was making it work but I wouldn't stop. Not until I was buried deep inside her. I was fucking her here and now, on an art desk, with the hope that graphite and ink ended up on her skin. Maybe some lucky bastard would see us through the big storefront windows.

"Cole," she purred against my lips when I finally let her come up for air.

I wrapped around her, kissing down her neck as my hands slid up underneath the short dress she'd picked. I squeezed roughly on her ass then kneaded it in time with the flicks of my tongue across the seam of her mouth. My fingers wandered along the curve of her thigh and tucked in between her legs.

She was wet, so fucking wet. I knew why her legs brushed against each other, making for an irresistible little wiggle against me. It was a dance her body couldn't help but do for me.

"Fucking shit, Ladyface."

"I can't help it," she moaned almost in defense of herself.

"Thank God."

I cut my own words short as I latched back onto her lips and dug into her throat. As soon as she started moving her mouth against me, I slid my fingers up into her. I spun them around inside her. The tightness and little dips and waves against my fingers were starting to become familiar. With Elle that didn't make her boring, it didn't make me tired. I just wanted to explore every other inch of her so I could trace them in my sleep.

My fingers pushed deeper into her and she swore under her breath. There was the hint of something besides pleasure in her voice.

I pushed her back just far enough to study her face. She bit her lip and wouldn't meet my eye but her hips bucked against my hand all the same.

"Something not right, Ladyface?" I searched her face for an answer.

"This is honestly the least sexy thing I've ever said to you, but…" she hesitated long enough that I pulled my fingers from inside her and tugged her lip free from where her teeth held it.

She gasped when my shiny fingers touched her lip; her little tongue stuck out the slightest bit and tentatively tasted my coated fingers.

"Think you just made up for it with that little move." I sounded like a wild animal the way I snarled at her, and honestly, with her, I was.

"I have to pee," she whined and I couldn't help but burst out laughing.

"Not really my thing, but for you, I could maybe get down." I softened my grip on her neck and let my hand trail down her chest.

She found a smile before capturing my fingers. She brought them to her lips and started sucking. After just one spin of her tongue around my digits, I pulled it free.

"I'm gonna come without you. Again. And I'd really rather not." I turned her toward the back of the shop then swatted her ass to get her moving.

I watched her walk away, the black fabric of her dress hinted at the curve of her ass. The scandalously short length made

181

her legs appear longer and the naughty schoolgirl socks just gave me ideas that would make a porn star blush.

As soon as she came out, I was going to wreck her. I wouldn't stop until she couldn't walk upstairs. I didn't care if I had to call Horse to come over and haul us both up. I had to adjust my dick under the waistband of my jeans, the zipper getting too painful where I'd full-on tented into it.

The jingling of the bell above the door barely pulled me from the fantasy.

"You're looking better than I expected, all things considered."

That voice did though. It was a bucket of frigid ice water, not only because my fantasy washed away, but because of the very real shivers it sent up my spine. I turned as best I could, desperate to look like I wasn't wounded but failing miserably.

"There's the beating I heard you were handed." Siobhan leaned against my front desk with her arms crossed and her eyebrow arched. "What I wouldn't have given to watch you bleed."

"Why are you here, Siobhan? What the fuck does Mickey want?" I let my voice boom through the room, praying that Elle heard me and that she had the sense to stay hidden at the mention of Mick.

"I'm not here on official business." She lifted up from her perch and slithered over to me. I automatically took a step back. She followed me.

"Then get the ever loving fuck out." I shoved her as hard as I could but my side ripped and roared with pain, leaving it little more than a halfhearted push.

"That's not very nice." She lunged at me, clawing her talons into my wounded side.

I screamed and when her grip didn't lessen I collapsed to my knees in front of her. I couldn't even react before she had her nails digging into my scalp and yanking on my hair. She had me where she wanted me, beneath her and utterly vulnerable. I tried to fight back as much as my body would let me but she simply rested

182

her pointy-toed stiletto on my hip and pressed the wicked little tip into my side.

"Mick might believe you had nothing to do with our little toy disappearing from Seattle but I don't. Not for a second." She pressed harder into my side and yanked harder on my hair. "You're hiding something and I'm gonna find it."

She leaned down and the jostle on my side made me cry out again. Her devious smile spread across her lips, making them plump enough to brush against mine. I tried to jerk away from her touch but she folded neatly onto my lap. Her knee dug into my side keeping me at her mercy as she let her lips skate up my neck to the bruise on my chin. She bit down. Hard.

"Get the fuck off me, Siobhan!" My words boomed but they were riddled with pain and fear. What if Elle came out now? What if she saw?

"I'm gonna find her, Cole. I'm going to find her and I'm going to fuck you on her corpse."

With those disgustingly twisted words still hanging on her lips, she kissed me. I did everything in my power not to kiss her back but she shoved her tongue into my mouth and forced mine to dance.

Whether it was five seconds or five minutes, I couldn't tell. Siobhan's erotic moans as she rocked against me seemed to tick like the hands of a never-ending clock.

One of her hands found mine and tried to pull it between her thighs. I fought her until she twisted her grip and grabbed my balls and clawed into them. My utter agony echoed through the shop.

"Touch me." She bit down on the bruise on my chin again. "Stroke me until I come and we'll call it even. You got yours in my limp body and I'll get mine from yours."

Every inch of me revolted against the idea. Siobhan made my skin crawl. I hated her as much as I hated being inside her, that had always been the case. But now with my Ladyface...

If Elle was heaven, Siobhan was the fiery version of hell Dante wrote about. And it was heaven that stayed on my mind. Even here, even now.

Elle was feet away, and every second Siobhan was here was another second that she might find Elle. She could get up, she could need to piss, she could just be her fucking crazy self. The danger that Elle in was as real as the pain zigzagging through me and the demon sprawled over top of me.

I was no savior but it was the only play I had that might actually save her. Siobhan hadn't stopped biting into my sore spots or digging into the jagged bruise on my side. I didn't move as I started a prayer to God. He had no reason to listen to me, I was sin personified, and I was about to touch a filthy whore, but it didn't stop me. I could handle both his and Siobhan's wrath if Elle was safe.

The moment I whispered *amen* as quietly as I could manage, I stuck my hand between Siobhan's legs and started stroking.

Elle

The acid was coming up my throat in waves. Each time either of them cried out, Cole in pain and this random woman in pleasure, my insides knotted up and squeezed out more bile.

I'd heard Cole yell Mickey's name and the hair stood up on the back of the neck. It had to be a signal. I went silent and pressed myself up against the wall next to the door sure that with Mickey Maloney, safe was better than sorry. When the next few words they exchanged were harder to make out, I pressed my ear to the door. I couldn't make out every word but the ones I did catch were sharp, angry things. And after a few minutes, they were punctuated with Cole's horrific cries. They were going to decimate me. My feet shuffled against the tiled floor, a reflection of how desperate I was to rescue him.

Until another set of cries mingled in with his.

Those sounds I recognized too. They were the unmistakable sounds of some woman's orgasm. They were loud, exaggerated, gross porn-like cries.

Unless she'd come in with some silent third person, she was making those noises with Cole. Throwing up wouldn't be enough to make my insides clean. Ever.

He'd told me this was a part of his life. Part of the life he was risking to protect me. I was disgusted when it was an abstract act, but now it was real and pure hate boiled in my veins. And at least some of it was directed at Cole.

I couldn't help it.

His cries were obviously agonized but that didn't stop me from feeling like he should have done something to stop this. Unless she was the size of Horse or as deadly as Mickey, he could have done *something*.

They went on and on, for God knows how long, and I could only slide down the wall and into a small little ball to listen. Listen as she crescendoed. Listen as he whimpered. Listen as my heart creaked and cracked.

Finally it ended with a giant screeching bang. The room on the other side of the door went quiet but I could still hear those calls echoing through my brain. I probably would forever. The tiny jingle of the front door bell was the only thing that punctuated the silence until Cole let loose an absolutely unholy bellow.

That sound would haunt me too. Loud, guttural, harsh but broken too. The tortured cry made the hair on my body stand on end and sent shivers up my spine. It would have garnered all my sympathy if I didn't feel tormented and splintered.

When the room behind me stayed silent, I pushed up from the floor. I hesitated at the door handle. I didn't want to go out there. I didn't want to look at him. I didn't want to be in Chicago anymore. I wanted to open the door and go back in time to the moment I saw a hot dude in the SeaTac terminal. This time I'd arch my eyebrow, undress him with my eyes and return to my book.

But I'd made my bed that day and now I had to lie in it. Or however sex in an airplane bathroom made that saying go. I opened the door and rounded the corner back into the main room of the shop.

I had to hold myself back from running to Cole.

The figure slumped on its knees was hunched awkwardly. If Cole hadn't been breathing raggedly, I would have thought he was a corpse left to die as blood trickled from his chin. His hair was disheveled enough that I saw claw marks running down his scalp.

"Are you okay?" My voice shook all on its own.

"No," he answered bluntly in a low, rough voice.

186

I stepped toward him, now more worried about getting him to the hospital than dealing with the emotional shit we were going to have to wade through.

Harlot red lipstick colored his neck and his jaw. I swore I'd never wear the shade again as the bile rose in my throat all over again. I stepped in front of him to find his chin was split in the center of the bruise he'd already worn; that was where the drip of blood came from. I stood there, a step away from him, taking in the destroyed man before me, but I couldn't make myself reach for him.

"You heard?" His voice was a sharp but shattered piece of glass. I didn't bother answering, at least not in so many words.

"This is the life I've signed up for?" I asked, my voice still a reflection of my tumultuous insides.

"You didn't sign up for anything. But this is my life." He sagged further.

"So if I want you—"

"Why in the fuck would you? I was damaged goods long before this." He raised his hands up to cradle his face and cried out something jagged and awful in pain.

"I'm no prize either," I murmured. "I tried to run from my family but they're catching up to me regardless. If it weren't for you…" I couldn't bring myself to list the things I knew he'd saved me from. "Mickey Maloney would already have me."

I swallowed the lump of truth like a sour lemon. He'd done everything, including that woman minutes ago, in an effort to protect me.

"You're not a prize, Elle, you're the holy fucking grail." He finally looked up at me and something ghosted behind his gorgeous eyes.

He reached for me and I stepped back.

"I need you to not touch me for a little while." I tried to soften my rejection. "I might get it but I just can't right now." His hand fell limply to his side and he winced. My heart thudded against my ribs but the reality of it all still wore around my neck like the lipstick on his. "Can I just go upstairs, for a while? Is that safe?"

187

He nodded and I turned to leave only for his broken voice to stop me short. "I have to ask you one thing first." He was struggling to keep it together, compassion welled in my chest.

"Anything, Cole." I was as soft and gentle as I could manage.

"Can you help me off the floor?"

My heart broke and I turned back without hesitation. As swiftly as possible, I bent and notched my shoulder in. I wrapped both arms around him and prepared myself to lift. He nestled into the crook of my neck and breathed in audibly.

"Cole," I scolded then pulled as hard as I could.

His breath turned into a battered howl. My fingers curled into him as though I might lose him. He swayed before we got to a stool and even then I was worried it was going to shoot out from under him. I had to drop my grip to make sure the stool didn't disappear. My body missed him immediately despite everything.

The bell on the door jingled again behind me and panic welled in my chest.

"Lucy, you got some 'splaining to do."

The ridiculous faux-lisp coming from the doorframe was the most comforting sound I'd ever heard. I spun and my hightops squeaked on the tile floor. I ran straight for the sound and let myself crash into Conrad where he stood by the door.

His thick, muscular arms wrapped around me and he bent down to kiss the top of my head. I breathed him in, happy to be wrapped up in the faint coconut smell of his hair products and the fresh deodorant that gave him a deceptively manly scent. I squeezed all the tighter as tears welled up in the corner of my eyes and balled in my throat.

"Hey, Belles, are you okay?" he asked softly in my ear as he matched my squeeze.

"You're real, right?"

"Jennifer Grey's original nose, baby." He kissed me where his chin rested again.

"How'd you find me?" The tears were getting harder to hold back.

He pushed me back and quirked up his eyebrow. "We have a copper-haired minion of Satan to talk about."

"No we don't," Cole growled from behind me.

"This must be Prince Charming." Conrad's voice went flat and lifeless as he narrowed his gaze and tucked me underneath his shoulder.

"Let's not do this and say we did." I gave Conrad a gentle nudge.

"What?" He batted his eyelashes innocently at me.

"Conrad, this is Cole. Cole, this is Conrad."

"He looks worse for the wear, you guys been getting into kinkier shit than choking?" Conrad hadn't lightened up much and I knew he was testing Cole. I thought about punching him.

They stared at each other, a weird warped mirror of the other. Both were inked up, blonde gods with trendy haircuts and big beautiful lips. But Cole's were cracked and marked up and Conrad's were perfectly cleaned and coated in his usual chapstick. Rough green eyes challenged lit-up blue ones across the room.

"Why don't you tell me about this red-head." I pulled on Conrad, bringing him deeper into the shop and seating him on a stool across from Cole. I stood in between them.

"She needs a dye job." He rolled his eyes.

"Conrad," I scolded him despite cracking a smile.

"Well, she does." He crossed his arms and legs and pursed his lips. "And when a haggard red-head comes in demanding your bestie's whereabouts, after said bestie disappears in the middle of the night without so much as a word, you hate her hair regardless."

"You would have talked me out of it." I crossed my arms.

"Damn straight." He eyed me and then Cole. "I mean I'm sure you're lovely in a thuggish, giant dick sort of way, but she shouldn't be messed up in that organized crime shit."

"Agreed," Cole grunted.

They stared each other down again. Conrad kept glaring at Cole when he started explaining again.

"She was awful. Disgusting and foul and brutish. She went through your stuff, Belles. Destroyed a ton. I could have taken her but she pointed a gun in my face. I had to let her."

189

"Awful, disgusting, foul and brutish are the nicest things anyone's ever called Siobhan." Cole's lips thinned further and his shoulders started heaving.

The name rung a bell. Cole had said that name right before Mickey's, right before... I had to choke back something different than emotion this time. I probably would for the rest of my life.

"She was..." I tried to say it but my mouth still wouldn't form those words.

"Just here," Cole finished softly for me.

"Yeah, I know. When a tramp comes in like a whirlwind of vengeance the likes of which I haven't seen, pointing a gun all willy-nilly, I may not fuck with her but I'm sure as shit going to follow her." Conrad reached out and grabbed my hand. "I knew you needed me."

"She has me." Cole's eyes locked on to where our fingers were interlaced.

"And I'm sure her Pikachu is just pleased as punch, but there are so many things that you and your magical dick can't give her."

Cole snarled and then tried to shove up off his stool. He groaned and his whole face went from severe to syrup. I shot toward him, letting Conrad's fingers drop as I lunged to keep Cole from hitting the ground.

"Don't. Don't even think about it," I said as I settled him back to the stool.

He cupped his hand around the back of my thigh and I jerked back. His face crumpled in on itself.

"Now it's your turn." Conrad was as serious as I'd ever seen him. "Spill it, Elle. Now."

The door jangled again. Cole and I both went rigid but Conrad whistled lowly. "Well, well, well. Now that's better than a redheaded hellcat."

"Cupcake, Fucktart, what's going on?" Horse was taking up the doorframe as he took in the scene. He studied us for a split second then his eyes fixed on Conrad. Something twinkled in them as he swept over the man between him and us.

190

"Cupcake? Fucktart? Interesting… What kind of pastry do we have here?" Conrad asked as he blatantly undressed Horse with his eyes.

"Conrad, this is Horse," I introduced him with a genuine smile.

"Giddy up," Conrad's voice was laced with lust. "How does the saying go? Ride a horse, save a cowboy?"

"Are you telling me you've got a lasso and you'd like to tie me up?" Horse asked and I noticed that his eyes danced as he drank in Conrad's tight jeans and fitted shirt, both of which showed off his well-crafted muscles.

"Honey, I'd tie you up, tie you down and do anything else in between." Conrad shamelessly fanned himself.

Horse walked right up to him and lowered all six-foot, eight million inches over him. He let his hands come to rest on Conrad's upper thighs. They were nose to nose, two sets of eyes speaking to one another. Horse let his gaze slowly sweep over Conrad, stopping to stare unabashedly at his ink then down at his crotch. He licked his lips.

"Then saddle up sweetheart. It's gonna be a bumpy ride."

Conrad's jaw fell open and he swayed on his stool. Horse pushed himself closer, his lips brushing Conrad's.

"Or are you not man enough?" Horse challenged.

Conrad started, "Yeah…um…" he cleared his throat and lowered his voice. "Swear to God, I'll rise to the challenge."

Horse let his thumbs start stroking Conrad's thighs, maybe even catching a little bit of his dick as his focus followed his fingers.

"Seems like you already have." Horse cocked his eyebrow and licked his lips before looking back up at Conrad's contorted face. "If only I didn't have business to attend to."

Horse stood and turned his back on Conrad or he would have seen the furious scarlet he was turning or the way his breathing rattled his chest.

"Let's go. We've got info on Jimmy." Horse jerked his chin toward the door.

191

Cole tried to stand up off the stool but failed even worse than before. I tentatively stepped toward him but Horse beat me to it. His whole face crumpled when he took in the fresh blood coating Cole.

"What happened here today?" He looked over at me then Conrad.

"Siobhan happened." I choked on the words.

Horse's whole face fell and he turned without a word to pull me into a hug. I nuzzled into the valley between his pecs.

"Forgive him. Whatever happened, forgive him. You don't know what she's like." His tree trunk arms wormed in tighter.

"I think I get the drift." I shook in his arms for a moment. "That's why I already have."

"I'll take good care of him Fucktart, okay?" he whispered into my ear. "Maybe do the same for me?" I felt his smile turn up against my cheek.

He broke away and nodded toward Conrad, then turned for Cole. He effortlessly hauled him up to his feet.

"You got this?" he asked Cole gruffly.

Cole nodded and lifted his hand to scrape a little of the blood off his chin. His beautiful green eyes looked up at mine, every little fleck in them pleaded with me. Without thinking, I reached out and brushed my fingertips down along the back of his hand. He trembled at my touch but he didn't reach back, still adhering to the single request I'd made.

His face pinched in on itself but he turned to lead Horse out of the shop. At the last minute, he turned back. "Everything," he murmured then shoved out of the door, leaving nothing but the bell to cut the heavy silence.

Cole

"What she do?" Horse asked quietly from the driver's seat.

"Fucking made me get her off," I snarled.

"Oh I know what Siobhan did. What did Elle do? Do we still have a little Fucktart to share?"

"Didn't seem like you were interested in her anymore." I arched my eyebrow as I looked over at him.

"That man is hot. He can join all three of us for all I care if it gets his big pouty lips around my dick and his tattooed arms wound around me." He smiled the kind of smile that lit up his face and something relaxed inside me. For all today's shit, it had been a long time since I'd seen Horse give those smiles so freely. "Back to Elle, I mean she seemed like she was in one piece." He started chewing on his lips.

"She doesn't want me to touch her." I couldn't hide how badly it crushed me.

"She needs a minute. Can't say I blame her. You probably still smell like Siobhan."

I looked down at my hand. It was the one that had been all over her but it was also the one Elle had gently stroked to reassure me. I loved and hated that hand. I rolled it over, looking at it objectively as if it weren't my own. The creature before me had done horrible things. Honestly, being inside Siobhan was probably one of its lesser offenses except for how that gutted Elle. It had stolen, it had coveted, it had marked. It had murdered.

But somehow, she made all that disappear. It wasn't logic or science but it was as real as the oxygen filling my lungs and the blood thrumming through my veins.

"She's gonna come around." He reached over and threaded his hand into mine.

I didn't have a response. Mostly because I didn't believe him but I couldn't give that voice yet. I mean how could Ladyface ever forgive me of my sins? How she had so far was a mystery. I sighed heavily at the things I'd laid before her, the things she'd barely batted an eye at. Horse squeezed harder on my hand. He gave me strength, as weird as it may have looked from the outside.

"Well this is gay," I said flatly and lifted his hand a little.

He dropped it right away and grabbed at my dick. "No, this is gay." He stroked as he licked his lips. "Except with you that is, then it's just foreplay." His big laugh filled up the car the same way his big full smile took over his face.

"Okay dude. It's time to sack up." Horse finally pulled his hand away from my crotch only to shove it through his hair. "Partially because you're becoming a legit chick over this, and partially because I need a soldier next to me in there."

We pulled up to the curb as Horse pointed to a dilapidated building.

"You should have picked a different soldier. I can barely walk, let alone get your back," I grumbled.

"There's no one I'd rather have my back, wounded or not." Horse looked over and he was as deadly serious as I'd ever seen him.

It took a decent amount of effort but I clapped him on his shoulder.

"Under the seat," Horse said simply as he nestled into my hand.

His serious face remained but had an ease about it. This was right for us. I bent over and managed to grunt instead of cry out. My gun was hidden beneath the seat, as faithful a companion as Horse himself.

"So what's the deal here?" I asked as my hands automatically worked on my weapon, double checking every single inch of it and preparing for war.

"The Butcher has a new shop."

Horse might as well have dumped ice cold water on my head. The last time I'd met with the Butcher, I'd almost met with the Reaper too. To stay above dirt, I'd fought tooth and nail, I'd let blood run, and I'd thought I'd won.

"I thought he was dead?" My voice was as frosty as my insides.

"Found him so close, no one thought he'd make it. It was right around when you left."

It was exactly when I'd left. He was the reason I'd left. Or been allowed to.

"I thought he didn't pick sides?" I asked, my voice barely pushing past the lump in my throat.

"Technically he still doesn't but he's been leaning toward Mick as of late."

"That's terrifying." I shook in spite of myself.

His lust for death and chaos was as notorious as he was.

"Yeah, I know. That in and of itself says something's shifting, but damned if I know what it is. Mick's never trusted me like he trusted you." Horse sounded a little disappointed and that made my blood run colder.

"Count yourself lucky," I said softly as I did my best to push out of the car and up to standing.

Horse walked ahead and I noticed he'd shed his Adidas jacket to reveal holsters. More than anything I wished I had matching firepower. At least. Adrenaline started to pump through me and I managed to keep up without walking with too noticeable a limp.

I was a dead man walking.

As soon as we busted into the empty warehouse, the smell hit me like a ton of bricks. Rotting flesh. The rancid smell was salty, metallic, and mixed with warm shit. It was a violent siege on my nose and it wasn't just my stomach that heaved. Had I walked

195

in without details, all I would have needed was smell this and know who hid in the bowels of the building.

We turned the corner to find rows and rows of meat, butchered and hanging from hooks. Unlike regular butcher shops, this one didn't have any refrigeration, instead relishing in the smell of death. There was also no way to tell what cut of meat hung down the rows. Some were larger, some were smaller, some wore skin, some didn't. Some were bright red and fresh, others the greenish hue of something left to linger.

Horse and I were deep in the corpse landscape, him with his hand on his holster and me studying something that looked a lot like a human thigh, when crisp footsteps echoed on the concrete. Each one moved closer with the confidence of a man that didn't need to hide.

"Well, well, well. I expected Horse, but this is a pleasant surprise." The Butcher was close enough behind me to speak softly as he traced a metal hook across my throat. "How ya doing, Cole?"

Warm breath that smelled of the same putrid filth as the warehouse, filled my senses almost as brutally as the lingering stench itself.

"What can I do for you boys?" he asked as he slithered in front of me.

The Butcher had aged since I'd seen him last, crinkled to the point of being like leather and the slightest bit hunched. The scar from where I'd shot him still wore like mangled jewelry at his temple despite his skin hanging like wax paper from him. How he'd lived this long was still a mystery. How I was still breathing in front of him was too.

"Jimmy Ponies," Horse said flatly, oblivious to the history passing between us.

"Isn't he the popular man these days." The Butcher didn't take his partially bloodshot and cloudy eye off me. "Hear his stepdaughter is the only hotter commodity on the market."

My back bristled and my jaw clenched as my hand gripped tighter on the handle of my gun. I could vividly picture pressing it to his skin and pulling the trigger. It was already the video on loop in my memories.

196

"Sweet, blonde, young thing," he mused. "Tiny bones. Translucent skin." His hand holding the meat hook fell from my body as he stared fondly off into the distance.

It was instinct more than anything for my fists to fly to his chest. I went to swing but luckily my side stopped me cold before I'd really shifted. Horse eyed me, sensing how badly I wanted to lash out. Maybe even sensing some of the history unspoken.

"I haven't heard anything about her if that's why you're here. I'm not sure I'd tell Mickey if I did." The way the corners of his lips turned up ignited a bonfire inside of me that roared to burn anything threatening Elle to the ground.

Horse stepped closer and crunched his toes down on mine. "What about Jimmy? Why are the Italians hiding him?"

The Butcher's eyes softened and his smile spread. "Oh you know." He waved his hook aimlessly but his eyes narrowed on my face. "Wait, you don't know, do you?" he asked with amusement dripping from his lips.

"Territory, like always," Horse took a stab.

"Always was such a pretty dumb thing." The Butcher reached out and stroked his chest with the hook he held.

"They don't want Jimmy, they want whatever's gone missing." Suddenly it was clicking into place. Jimmy had Mick's missing personal effects since day one. It wasn't that he couldn't pay the debt, it was that he wouldn't. Not until the price was his own life. Now that he'd endangered Elle I was going to ensure he paid it personally. "What is it?" I snarled.

"A book." He shrugged.

"All this for a book?" Horse asked. "Not power, money, drugs, sex? None of Mickey's usual pursuits?"

"Books are powerful, Horse," I answered, knowing that if Mickey thought this one was, the things in those pages were as black as his soul.

"The Italians are playing a bigger game." The Butcher raised the meat hook to his tongue and licked then pressed the shiny steel to my chin and wiped against where I'd bled earlier. I made myself stay stock-still. "You boys should start too. I miss the days that blood ran in these streets."

197

"I miss the days your blood ran in the street." I ignored Horse's shocked face as I stepped forward to snarl in The Butcher's.

"I remember the way it poured down my face. The way it tasted as blood filled my mouth and I lost consciousness." He hummed in pure pleasure. "You haven't lived until you've died, Cole."

"I'll take your word for it."

His deranged laugh rang out, echoing off the carcasses around me.

"Life is always so much more entertaining with you around." He turned from me and planted his hook into the nearest hunk of muscle, laughing all the harder as he walked away. "Death too." His voice was fading.

"What kind of bigger game?" Horse called after him.

"You'll both look nice hanging in here." His voice was fading into the distance. "I might even wear Cole as pajamas," he added before his laugh carried him from the room.

A heavy door slammed in the distance, metal clanging against metal before it resonated all the way to my teeth. We were both left with only the sound of my labored breathing.

"I wish I'd fished the job," I said shakily.

"What?" Horse snapped. "What the fuck did you just say?"

"I wish my bullet had killed him."

"You did it? It was you? What the hell, Cole? Is that...?" The shock was as plain on Horse's face as his dark black scruff.

"How I got out? Yeah. Part of it anyway."

Horse looked over at me and I felt the weight of three years of unanswered questions hanging on the hooks between us every bit as heavy as the dead bodies.

"But why?"

"He's Mick's dad," I said simply. "And Mick hated living in his shadow. So when I found out, I struck a deal."

Horse's eyes bugged. "He didn't pull you back when they found him alive?"

198

"No," I said roughly. "We made a deal." The one that turned my blood to ice and my nightmares red. "And I traded his father's life for his son's."

"I can't believe it," Horse murmured for the tenth time as he drove back toward the apartment. "All these years, we blamed the Italians, and Mick let us."

"He was using it to his advantage. Fuel to blood war fire." Even now I could see red, so much deep, dark red.

"And he has a son?"

"Had," I corrected, barely able to swallow.

"No wonder he missed you so much," Horse's voice was laced with disgust. It was probably directed at Mickey but I let it weigh on me. I deserved it.

"See why I say she shouldn't forgive me? She should run far away." I turned to look out the windows as city blocks passed, buildings blurring together.

He let me sit in silence. Or he didn't really have anything to say. Either way, it made the shit I'd fallen in threaten to drown me. We pulled in front of my shop and he turned off my car, the rumble giving way to thick and stagnant air.

"You shouldn't forgive me, either."

"Too late," he grumbled. "See that's the thing about love, Cole. You don't really get a choice in the matter. I didn't, you didn't and she sure as hell didn't." He spat the words out. "We're all stuck, tied together all too tightly by a thread that should break, should snap. One you've personally tried to splice a million times. But the thing is, it's not that easy to unravel. It's easier to just forgive."

And with that he shoved out of the car and slammed the door, leaving me in the dark where I belonged.

Elle

"Fucking cats, Belles." Conrad punched his hand into the stone of Cole's island.

"Calm down," I said softly.

"How do you expect me to react to a story like that?" His voice became so sharp it grated on my nerves.

"Stop." I closed my eyes and pinched the bridge of my nose. "I really can't take it."

"Well you're going to bend over, spread those cheeks and let me press the cold hard truth up that sweet little ass of yours without lube. This is not okay, Elle. Like not even remotely."

I turned away from him and flopped down onto the mattress. Like a junkie, I sniffed in the smell of Cole, wanting that pure version of him back.

"This isn't some Hollywood adaptation where the killer has a heart of gold and despite all the odds you ride off into the sunset like some modern fairy tale. This is the fourth-page news story about how Chicago's murder rate is up seventy-six percent and still connected to organized crime."

"And if I refuse to believe that?"

"Then you're gonna confuse the angel of death with your fairy godmother."

A key scraped against the lock just a moment before two burly bodies squeezed through. That they were both back, and Cole looked unharmed—well, not more than he already was—made my heart pitter-patter.

"Conrad, I'll take my chances with either." I shot him a look as I pushed up from the bed and rocketed over to them.

Cole dropped his arm from Horse's shoulder and reached out just as I stopped short.

I couldn't help but picture red hair cascading over his body as a body ground against him. The sound effects started again too. I stepped back and his hand dropped to his side. My eyes closed as I sucked in a deep breath, they stayed tightly closed as I blew it out, feeling my whole chest deflate.

When I finally opened my eyes, Cole stood in front of me, his hands shoved into his pockets, making his muscles flex across his chest. But his eyes betrayed his fragile insides. We stared at each other for a few moments, watching the rise and fall of our breaths, our hearts synching again as if they'd always meant to beat together.

"You," Horse called to Conrad in a husky rasp, "grab your purse. We're going out."

Cole and I hadn't stopped looking at each other. Emotion was percolating in the room, bubbling up every bit as much as it floated through, connecting us in a way I'd never felt before.

"Oh hell no. I'm staying here. She can't be trusted," Conrad shot back, his voice getting squeaky sharp again.

Horse walked over and grabbed Conrad by the arm. His hand barely closed around the muscles Conrad took such pride in, but when it did, he pulled.

"I don't think you heard me correctly. You and I are going on a date." Horse's laugh colored his rich voice.

"I don't…" Conrad stuttered. "I mean…but Elle." His tanned skin had turned crimson red at Horse's touch.

"Despite what you may think, Elle's well taken care of. *Real* well. Aren't ya, Fucktart?" I nodded as Horse hunted Conrad like he was weak and withering prey. "I thought so." He arched his eyebrow. "The real question, is are you?"

Conrad's mouth dropped open and gaped around once or twice before he managed a, "I guess not," and let Horse pull him from the room.

The apartment door was heavy when it shut behind them, snapping into its frame with a deep boom. Or my nerves were so shot they amplified the sound.

I studied Cole as I had so many times since meeting him. He held himself gingerly and it was in such sharp contrast to the dips and grooves of his body, the savage brute I knew he could be. It was the man uncomfortable standing tall in front of me that was something to soften for.

"I don't know how to get her out of my head when I look at you." It wasn't a good place to start but it was all I could think of.

"I don't know how to get a future out of my head when I look at you," he answered then bit his lip.

I blew out a giant deep breath. It was a sucker punch I hadn't seen coming.

"How can you say that? It's like you want me gone. Want *this* gone." I gestured between us.

"I don't know how to make this better, Ladyface. This war doesn't just go away in a week or two. It doesn't end when Mick dies or even Siobhan. Otherwise, I'd kill them outright. So where does that leave us? We steal kisses between hellfire and brimstone?" His shoulders crept up to his ears and his eyes fell from me to the floor.

"Yeah. For eternity if it's an option." I sighed.

"You don't belong down here with me." His voice was shaky and unsure.

"You have to get over this fixation on heaven and hell, Cole." I took a step closer to him. "Maybe they're both real places. Maybe God exists, maybe Satan does too, but they're not your reality. Today, right here, right now, I'm real. *We're* real." I took another step toward him. "And real means you get everything. You let the light in with the dark."

His eyes traced my face, studying inch after inch. The green started to burn as he stepped closer.

This time I let him.

There was barely room to breathe between us. My skin vibrated with need this close to him. Copper hair picked that moment to flip in front of my face. I went to step back, but Cole reached out and caught my wrist.

I gasped.

"You're my light. I'll be your dark." His voice had gone husky.

"Doesn't change things. I still need time." I tried to break from his grasp.

"You asked me for a minute and I gave you about five hours longer than *I* needed." He yanked on his hold and I crashed back into his body.

The all too familiar cry of his pain split the quiet of the apartment. But he didn't let me go. He winced again when he wrapped around me.

"I can't." The sounds were too similar to this morning.

"You can." He buried his face in my neck.

"I can hear her. I can hear you two together," I whined.

"Let me erase it. Let me erase her," he begged right back.

"Give me time."

"No." He backed me up against the door. "Give me you. Give me everything."

"You already took it." My words were choppy at best.

"You said I could have it." He breathed the words against my lips.

"I didn't have a choice."

"Neither do I."

He crashed against me with the full weight of his body. I thumped against the door and it reverberated the same way the slam had. His lips found mine, pushing, pulling until he started biting. His cries punctuated each of our kisses but he didn't stop. It was like he couldn't.

Red hair was still a shroud behind my eyelids, her cries still echoed in my ears but my body couldn't slow down any more than his could.

His weight started to press against me, harder and harder until I thought we might splinter the door and fall into the hallway. I had the feeling he'd fuck me there too.

When he thumped me up against the door a second time, using just his mouth, I cried out a ragged sound. It mingled with his and a new sound filled my ears. He shoved his hands between my legs and started stroking.

"It's only you, Elle. Only ever fucking you," he growled as he crooked his finger up onto my G-spot.

"I know. Every fiber of your body tells every single inch of mine..." my words trailed off into a moan.

"Hear *that* play on repeat." He was stroking against me with strong, assertive strokes.

"I will."

"No. Now. Hear it now," he commanded. "Say it, scream it. So I can hear it too." He was working faster, flicking me faster.

"I. Don't. Know. What..." I couldn't finish my choppy sentence.

"You do." He bit down on my neck roughly and pulled. His cry tickled my skin where his teeth held me.

His hand was working so furiously inside me that my legs were going weak. It was a fast pump inside me and deep, wild strokes against the front wall of me. Something new, something insane was building inside of me. He bit harder on the skin between his teeth and I screamed.

For the first time in my life, a new and ridiculous orgasm consumed me. Heat pulled through my body and pure arousal splashed down onto his hand.

"Shit," I swore as wetness spread down my legs and trickled onto the shiny tips of his hightops. "Oh God. That's never happened before." Red flushed across my cheeks and chest.

"That's the fucking sexiest thing I've ever heard." Cole dropped to his knees with the most agonized cry I'd ever heard, but it was cut short when he shoved his face between my legs.

He rubbed his scruffy cheeks against my thighs almost as if he was soaking up the slickness. His tongue followed, licking every square inch of flesh before darting inside me. I screamed as my hands grabbed for his hair.

The second I grabbed it, I remembered how disheveled it had been, the claw marks there; she had to have done the same. I dropped my grip, plastering my palms to the door behind me.

"Grab me, Ladyface," he snarled, the sound muffled in my sex.

"No, she…"

He bit down on my clit mid-sentence and I screamed.

"You bring her up one more time and I'll ruin you. I'll make sure that you can't remember your name, let alone what happened this morning." He shoved his tongue into me again for a moment. "It's just you and me. Just. Fucking. You. And. Me." He roared each word up inside me.

His arm wormed his way up between my breasts and shoved me back against the door then balled in my dress. He used his fist to keep me pinned in place as he tongued me. His other hand crept up inside me.

"You're gonna give in to me again, Elle."

Cole rolled his face around on my skin then pointed his tongue to flick my clit in time with his destruction of my G-spot. My body started bucking against his face, my hands flew back to his hair.

"Grab it, Ladyface. Grab it and take it. Take me." His voice was a perfect mix of pleasure and pain.

I latched on and he went wild. My whole body shook as he worked me over. I was trembling again and worse than before. I didn't think that I could take another one of those orgasms.

"Stop," I begged quietly, not really wanting him to.

"No. Not until it's just you and me in here." His words puffed warm against my clit.

Copper was still there, the haggard cries of this hellcat Siobhan too, but there was no question in my mind that Cole would erase it. Someday I wouldn't remember anything but this, the way my body was about to go haywire all over again. The way I'd drip on his face this time instead of his shoes.

Shivers moved up my spine as he obliterated my G-spot. His hand shifted so he could fist my breast as he went wild. Then without warning his grip slipped and he yanked on my nipple.

205

"Fuck," I screamed as I fell off the edge of orgasm.

Cole's answering guttural cry was so beautifully turned on and tortured it coaxed the same absurd splash from me.

"You and me, Ladyface. Just us." His open mouth was everywhere between my thighs as my body trembled.

He kissed every inch of slick skin he could reach, up one thigh and then down the other. He lavished a few French kisses on my quivering sex and that did me in.

I crumpled. I couldn't have slowed myself if I tried as I crashed into his lap. He bellowed in agony but still collected me. We both breathed heavy and I let my head roll back to bang into the door behind me.

Cole bent in and kissed along my collarbone.

"For the record, Ladyface, heaven does exist," he purred.

I tilted my head the slightest bit to see his shiny cheeks smiling for the first time in days.

"And it's right fucking here."

He roughly pushed his fingers right back into me.

Cole

I couldn't believe she'd let me take her. Well take advantage of every inch of her was more like it. I didn't blame her for keeping her distance or for what she'd said, but I couldn't help myself. After the day I'd had, I needed her more than food, air or water combined.

I needed her to forget about everything but being mine.

And I needed to make being mine worth it.

"Grab your purse, Ladyface, we're going out." I used Horse's words, hoping for a laugh.

She was breathy but she fed me a giggle all the same. I ate it up like a dying man. And to some extent I was. My body was rotting away every single moment except for the ones she decided to breathe life into.

"Is it safe?" she asked as she tried to right herself. " I mean I thought we weren't supposed to leave the apartment?"

"I have something special in mind." I went to push her to standing but the hot poker in my back dug in and twisted.

"Don't hurt yourself." Elle's voice was soft and protective all at once. It was all the salve I'd ever need on my wounds.

I smiled as she carefully lifted off my lap and adjusted her dress. The fabric between her tits wouldn't lay flat after I'd handled it so roughly. My dimple hollowed out at the thought that someone might guess what I'd done to her. Or at least let their imagination roam.

She stood over me expectantly and gave me a look when she offered her hand. Normally, I'd push her away and stand up just to show that I could do it on my own but I didn't mind if she saw me vulnerable. Matter of fact, her seeing all of me, even my deeply hidden sides, was becoming more and more important. I gladly took her hand, as grateful for her help as I was to have her skin against mine and let her haul me up to standing. Only one pitiful moan dripped from my lips.

"Got your wallet?" I asked as I gingerly patted my pockets for my own and keys.

"I thought this was a date. Isn't the gentleman supposed to pay?" She scrunched her nose up into the most adorable button.

"You know damn well I'm no gentleman." I arched my eyebrow before I added, "And that I'll take damn good care of you." I wiggled my eyebrow as I reached toward her upper thigh.

She went to block me with both hands as her knees knocked together. I tried to bob and weave around her but I was just too damn slow. She batted at my hands then giggled loud enough to fill the loft.

It was the sound, not the sudden movement, that made me groan as my whole stomach clenched and my balls tightened. I leaned in to kiss her and she let me, finally opening up like the perfect little sunflower she was. She wandered around my mouth the same way I leisurely strolled through hers until her tongue went to trace my lips.

"You taste different," she said as she smiled against my lips.

"I taste like you," I purred.

"You gonna clean up?" she asked as she leaned back in, this time snatching my lip and nibbling.

I let her take her time, digging into my flesh while massaging my lip with the tip of her tongue. When she finally let me free, she arched her eyebrow expectantly.

"Nope," I popped my P.

She bit her lip almost as hard as she'd bit mine.

"Come on."

I grabbed her hand and swung open the door. Both made me wince, but I'd made the decision I was taking her out. For tonight, I was going to be nothing more than a man on a date with a bewitching little bird.

She was patient with me as I took the stairs slowly, her hand squeezed on mine each time I sucked in a deep breath. As soon as we got to the car she broke away from me to head to the passenger side. I caught her by the wrist and pulled her back into the side of my body. Together we rounded the hood of the Charger then I bent away from her to grab the door.

"Told you I'd take care of you." I bent to kiss the tip of her nose as she slid into the leather seat.

My eyes stayed fixed on her as I slowly moved back around the car. She watched me equally intent but a smile played on her lips. I blew out a deep breath and thanked my lucky stars she was back with me. That she was with me at all. When she reached for my hand across the stick shift, I had to keep from smiling like a giddy little kid.

Elle didn't hold her wide smile back. It lit up the darkest corners of my soul and threatened to liquefy my insides. I was addicted to that feeling.

"Where are we going?" she asked and the sunshine was obvious in her voice.

"Trust me?" I looked over at her unable to hold back my smile any longer.

"Way more than I should." She rolled her eyes but then her smile got even wider.

We snaked our way through the neighborhood, trendy shops giving way to dark warehouses and chained parking lots. The city lights got fewer and farther apart here, making it seem more like I was taking her to a back alley to die rather than a restaurant for dinner and drinks.

I'd pictured the way her eyes would light up at Fulton Market Kitchen the moment I saw her bent over the sketching table. The pop art canvasing the restaurant was a bigger draw than their food or drinks. Sculptures jumped out of the wall, sprang up from the floor and dripped down from the ceiling like live raindrops ricocheting in zero gravity. It was a visual playground second to only the dips and curves of Elle's body itself.

We pulled up and I tossed my keys to the valet before I collected her from shotgun. I pulled her to my side and, when the guy eyed her more than my car, I wrapped around her. She giggled as she nuzzled into my shoulder.

"My eyes only see you," she murmured against my skin then pressed her lips to the ink coating my neck.

"Liar," I barely breathed the word as shivers ran up and down my spine. "You saw him checking you out."

"Yeah and it made me even more sure."

I wanted to shove her up against the wall. There in the long, dark hallway where everyone and anyone could see as they walked in or out of the restaurant. I would shove her by the throat up against the velvety walls and take what was mine. I wanted to taste her as much as I wanted people to see what I got to feast on.

But I settled on kissing the top of her head where she was still tucked beneath my chin. Whether it killed me or not, whether my dick had other things to say, I was taking this girl on a date. She deserved that much.

I pulled her a little way up the hall before she swore under her breath. She broke away from my side and wandered wide-eyed into the room. The exhibit they were featuring was a delicate gauzy thing that reminded me of Elle and the way her white cotton dress would blow in the breeze on a hot summer day. Wood hung in various directions, some trapping the scraps of fabric while still others seemed to meld and flow to and from each other.

"It's a gallery?" she asked as her fingers skated over the patchwork and velvet furniture in front of us.

"It's a restaurant that features artists," I answered watching her, rather than look around.

"Cole, what's up man?" My friend Connor came over and reached out his hand, shaking it once before pulling me into a hug.

"Shit." My side burned where he clapped me.

"What's going on?" He pulled back as he questioned me.

"Hi." Elle interrupted with her sweet voice and held out her little bird bones for Connor. "I'm…"

"Elle Laroux. I know. Wow. What are you doing here?" His voice was a mix of interest and awe, I wasn't sure I liked it.

"I'm on a date," Elle answered seamlessly as she reached out for me.

I wove my fingers into hers and she smiled her sunflower smile again.

"I've wanted to meet you for the past year. Your pieces are amazing." At least Connor had the decency to only glance down at her tits once.

"How would you know anything about my pieces?" Elle's voice sounded shy but when I looked her over she met Connor's gaze just like she did everyone else: bright and unwavering.

"We have two. They're some of our favorites."

"I had no idea." Elle's excitement danced in her voice.

"Me neither." I wasn't quite as pleased. For some irrational reason, this bothered me more than Connor staring at her tits. This felt like he was peeking at her soul. "Why didn't you tell me, Elle?"

"I sell most of my stuff through dealers. I don't always know where it goes or who it ends up with." She started to look around, her attention now split between Connor, me and the room.

That didn't sit real well either.

"Here come this way."

Connor led the way through the bar and back into the dining room. I kept looking around, sure I'd know Elle's piece when I saw it, delicate and free just like her. Connor turned abruptly again and we were suddenly in a private dining room. The walls were dark and the furniture bright white. The slightest hint of wood in both the white furniture and dark siding on the walls gave it a warmth I didn't expect from such bright light next to all consuming dark.

But it wasn't the furniture or small art pieces that caught my eye. It was the giant sacred heart etched into the sheet of black metal that hung behind the table. It had been carved out tiny detail by tiny detail, intricacies obvious from far away that were likely amplified up close. The flames looked alive where they erupted from the misshapen heart.

I couldn't help but step closer. The details were entrancing. The smallest drops of blood dripped down the sides and pooled to form a landscape below. The heart itself wore a crown of dollars folded neatly into origami cranes before being lit on fire. Even in the black of the metal, they looked real enough to spend. The hint of white flecks danced everywhere the metal had been gouged. The piece was alive and it drew me to it.

Then I noticed something. A tiny E with scribbles behind it then an L with the same jerky scribbles.

"This is yours?"

She nodded then stepped up next to me and let her hands run down the piece like an old lover. She was distant but tender, tentative but familiar. It was bewitching.

"On Death and Destruction," she murmured.

"You named a beautiful heart *On Death and Destruction*?" I finally pulled my attention from the metal etching and looked over at her.

She met my gaze directly, wide blue eyes speaking volumes.

"It's about your mom?" I asked already knowing the answer.

"I haven't done an etched piece like this in ages." She turned back to the etching and I knew it was a silent yes.

"You said you were an artist, a sculptor..." I blew out a deep breath. "But I never imagined this."

Elle smiled, shrugged then slipped back to my side.

"Connor, what do I have to do to eat in here?" I asked as my arms wound around her.

"I'll fix it. Make yourself comfortable." He turned on his heel and left us alone in the shadow of Elle's bleeding heart.

"You don't just work in metal, you own it," I said, my lips so close to her ear, it rustled her hair.

"I don't own it." She laughed lightly. "I just understand being hard and soft and difficult to uncover all at once."

I held her as I pulled out the bench seat for her. The space across from her was wide open but I couldn't be that far. I sunk

212

into the bench right next to her, even going so far as to pull her knee up and over mine.

"Tell me all about it. The piece, the carving, your art." I sighed like a lovesick puppy. There was nothing she could say I didn't want to hear. "Tell me everything, Ladyface. Let me see your soul."

We talked for hours. Elle got chatty when she started drinking. Her cheeks flushed beautifully as she told me every single thought she'd ever had. Sometimes about the piece and then about herself.

She graduated with a BFA in print making. She'd sold her first piece at nineteen. Since she'd emancipated herself at sixteen, the money she pulled in had been a welcome success. It had driven her to do more, to learn more, and art had consumed her.

Conrad had come in to play early on too, seamlessly falling into the gaping hole her family's vacancy left. I wasn't quite sure how I felt about him. He was loud in the ways Elle was quiet, he was sharp in the ways she was soft. But he loved her and I couldn't be upset that she had someone to protect her in this crazy fucked up world before me.

Because that's what each word did to me. They fanned the flame burning within me to protect, to love. With small simple words, she was filling me up and taking over. With small simple words, she was lighting my soul on fire, my insides now a reflection of her sculpture, as she left me to live or breathe or die or God knows what.

Well, God knew what. He knew damn well what was up with me.

I was falling in love.

Elle

Cole had proven he could date almost as well as he fucked three weeks ago when he'd taken me to dinner. By some miracle, we sat underneath a piece of my artwork but he'd become the masterpiece that night. He'd been equal parts dark and light with his words but I saw through it and understood the brushstrokes of his canvas. If he were a sculpture he'd be made of pure casted gold.

Every moment I'd spent with him since was a moment that had my insides crumbling into perfect, Cole shaped dust. He owned all of me.

"One more client then the evening is ours." Cole wrapped around where I perched on my stool and grabbed my neck.

He squeezed as he brought my body back to his. The telltale buzz in my veins and thumping in my ears overtook my senses as his grip tightened. He was finally back to full strength and my body was being showered with the effects.

I surrendered to his grasp, letting my arms go limp at my sides then brush against his calves with my fingertips. He yanked me to the side and my hair fell away from where my shirt slid down my shoulder. Cole started kissing then nipping along my bare skin. He lifted me a little and I had to stand to keep from losing my breath. My fingertips slid up along his legs and dug in.

His lips came to my shoulder and he bit down. I moaned loudly, burying the sound of the shop bell tinkling.

"Am I interrupting?" The voice was vaguely familiar.

"Yes." Cole laughed against my skin then set me back down on my stool. "But you're on time, so I really can't bitch." Cole let his fingertips drag across my skin as he walked over. I turned to watch him go and recognized Connor from the restaurant lingering in the doorway.

"Come on in, take a look at the sketch. If you like it, we'll get going," Cole's voice was assertive when he dealt with other people but never cruel. It was one of the things that made my heart pitter-patter. How his voice changed completely when he spoke to me was another.

"Hi Elle, it's good to see you again." Connor watched me closely, almost too closely.

I just nodded at him and bent back over the table I'd adopted and slipped on my headphones. Beats started to play as easily as my hand flowed over the paper in front of me. I'd taken to drawing interpretations of the tattoos Cole was working on. I'd peek at his sketches each morning if we didn't lay tangled in bed while he showed me, sunbeams splitting through the tracing paper.

I'd attempted to capture the magic of those moments, limbs this way and that, covers in a weaving ribbon rather than flattened. Cole's heavily inked hand held a small anchor sketch as I burrowed into his body. My graphite drawing was pretty but it wasn't good enough. It didn't capture how my insides caught on fire in the morning sun. I gave up drawing him after that, none of the million sketches were perfect. I folded most of them into origami cranes.

But the abstract Celtic knot Connor was getting was easy enough to work with. It had shading but sharp edges. It played more with negative space than positive. It almost reminded me of my etchings.

When the buzz kicked on from Cole's gun, it was a sound that added to the soothing afternoon. This was home.

For the first time, I understood that home wasn't a place, it was a someone. A someone who let you burrow deep inside and rest in their heart. Despite Cole having to disappear to Mickey's at all hours, and doing God knows what there, I'd found a warm place to snuggle. The next time he told me he was an icy-hearted

215

monster, I'd tell him it wasn't true. I'd taken up residence and knew firsthand it roared with the most bewitching fire.

I was lost to my design when hands came around my hips and shoved me up onto the drafting desk in front of me. My chest flattened onto my designs from my day and pencils dug into my ribs.

Cole didn't bother pulling off my headphones, leaving sultry bass beats to thump in my ears while his finger crept into the wide-open legs of my short jean shorts. He rubbed the slickness and I rolled my head to the side so I could see my gorgeous man. Whether he meant to or not, he was moving in time with the slow burn playing in my headphones.

He leaned down and kissed the curve of my ass where it peeked out from under my shorts. Kiss after kiss peppered down my thigh as his finger explored inside of me. I closed my eyes when he nuzzled fully between my legs. He shoved the small scrap of denim to the side and started tonguing me.

I was so close to orgasm that all I needed to shatter around him was for him to change his tempo or switch one of his fingers clinging to my hips to my clit. Instead, a third hand lifted the big speaker from my ear and I jumped. Cole disappeared between my thighs only to capture me as I catapulted off the drafting table.

"So not fair when you guys do this without me." Horse smiled inches from my nose then leaned in to kiss me, soft and strong with his big lips devouring mine. He pulled my headphones down gently to rest around my neck and kissed my jaw. "We're all lucky Conrad stayed in the car." He winked as he pulled away.

"He's back?" I couldn't help but smile. Cole's grip curled into my midsection and pulled.

"Just got him from the airport." His eyes shifted to Cole behind me. "Let's all go out."

I felt the tension in Cole's body at the suggestion. My fingers automatically went to his forearms and skated back and forth.

"I don't know...Ladyface?" Cole burrowed into my hair.

"You know I'd love to, but it's your call." I twisted and kissed his cheek where I could reach.

216

"Come on, Cole, she never gets out." Horse leaned back against the table I'd been draped across.

"She's right here and she can speak for herself." I arched my eyebrow. "What if we do something shamelessly touristy? Conrad will eat it up and that doesn't seem like the type of place that…"

"Smart." Cole smiled against the back of my head. "Cheesy, but smart."

"We'll go flick The Bean and walk Navy Pier." Horse smiled and reached for me.

"I got this." Cole kept hold of me as he pushed Horse's hand aside.

"Possessive are we?" Horse cocked his head to the side.

"Yup." Cole rolled me into the crook of his shoulder and kissed my forehead.

"Bullshit." Horse threw up his arms.

"You do realize you have a date sitting in the car?" Cole started pulling me toward the door. "I sure hope you cracked the windows."

Horse didn't answer as he shoved out of the shop. Cole only broke away for a moment to lock the door then his hands came back to me and slid into my front pockets. He walked, wrapped around me, laughing as we went.

"Hey Belles," Conrad interrupted from where he leaned casually against the passenger door of Horse's Hemi-Cuda.

"Hi Conrad." I tried to break free to hug him but Cole shoved me up against the car and rested against me. He dug in my pockets to flick on my sensitive clit as he kissed along my neck. I rested my cheek against the metal and sighed.

"Well isn't this just the welcome wagon?" Conrad asked, sarcasm thick in his voice.

"You're just bitter that no one's deep inside your wagon," I smarted back, my body still pinned to the car.

"We'll see how the evening goes." He looked over toward where Horse had slid into the driver's seat.

"Are you two fucking finished?" Horse's irritation was thorough.

"More like finished fucking." Conrad arched his eyebrow.

217

"I'll never be done with this body." Cole's hands slid from my pockets up my front and grabbed my chest.

"Gross." Conrad opened the car door as he watched me get fondled.

I slid into the backseat while Cole stepped up, chest to chest to Conrad.

"You're just jealous." He reached up and patted Conrad on the cheek.

For a split second, I thought Conrad was going to take Cole. His fist flexed at his side and his chest started heaving. I was going to reach out and grab him when Horse beat me to it. His hand closed around Conrad's then rubbed up his arm.

"Get in the car. He's easier to ignore when he's out of sight."

Conrad did and I thought I caught Horse squeeze his thigh a little harder as he fired up the engine. We turned and snaked through the city streets, across a few bridges and darting in and out of traffic. The signs started to appear for Millennium Park and a champagne-like excitement bubbled up inside me.

We found street parking near the park, and when I got out of the car, Conrad reached his arm around me.

"Not even, Short Stack." Cole snuggled against my side, effectively dislodging Conrad.

"This is bullshit," Conrad exclaimed.

Horse seamlessly pressed his hand against Conrad's and wove his fingers into his. "We're on a double date. For tonight, you're mine." Horse pressed his body against Conrad's thick tattooed arm as he snarled in Conrad's ear.

My best friend shuddered. His bright blue eyes raked over Horse, and his mouth cracked open as he sucked in a deep breath. Horse's other hand moved to rest over Conrad's heart. I may have been mistaken but Conrad trembled beneath his hand.

"I'm nobody's," he finally managed.

"Liar," Horse challenged. "Surrender to it. To me. At least for tonight."

Conrad couldn't even answer. And I didn't blame him. I would have folded to Horse if he'd insisted like that. Eventually he

218

nodded and Horse seamlessly pulled him toward the sculpture garden.

Cole and I followed suit but at a much slower pace. He kept a hold of me by keeping one hand in one of my pockets the entire time. He guided me to this statue or that, we studied the LED displays and the bronze figures. He humored me every time I needed to touch one. I think he even smiled.

And when we made it to The Bean, Conrad and Horse were already there, taking pictures at every angle, of both reflections and selfies.

"Let's take one." I bit my lip as I folded into him.

"Can't, Ladyface. If they ever found one of us together..." He massaged his fingers along the nape of my neck. "But come here."

He pulled me underneath the statue to the warped underside. Just like he'd been doing all afternoon, he clung to me. But then he pointed up into the mirrored surface.

"What faces would you make if we were snapping selfies?"

I crinkled up my face and looked at him rather than up at our reflection. He was sticking out his tongue full and flat, making rocker horns with his free hand. I couldn't help but laugh. I kept watching him instead of our reflection and he folded his tongue into the insane clover he could make. I twisted to see the shape fully where he stared up at the mirrored statue. As soon as I was watching his face changed and he spun to kiss my cheek. My giggles were shaking me quite thoroughly against his lips.

"It's not a picture..." he leaned back to whisper in my ear. "But I'll remember this until the day I die."

It wasn't even a conscious choice to turn and snake my arms around him. I pulled Cole to my lips and he didn't try to resist. Instead he grabbed at my thighs and pulled me up around his hips. He lifted me high enough that I had to arc down to kiss him. Green eyes blazed into me when I finally opened my eyes and rested my forehead against his.

"Maybe he's not the worst thing to ever happen to you." Conrad had walked up with Horse in tow, still attached firmly to his hand.

219

"Just maybe." I smiled at Conrad then down at Cole, hoping that every ounce of feeling I had was somehow pouring out of my heart and into his hands. I needed him to feel it every bit as much as he felt my ass resting in his hands.

We circled back to the car and drove to the Navy Pier, I couldn't help but look up at the massive skyscrapers as we went. Cole's hand played at the frayed edges of my shorts then between my thighs and back again where we were hidden in the backseat.

On the pier, we rode the swings and for a moment I felt young and wild and free. My hair whipped behind me as Cole and I tried to keep hold of each other's hands. When we slipped apart, I shot further out to the side and laughed just as loudly as I had earlier. Cole's smile broke across his face like a wave upon the shore, washing every heavy weight and worry he'd ever had away.

It was one of those perfect evenings, where music drifted on the soft summer breeze and the sounds were straight from a movie edit. I would have given anything to capture it in a jar to open from time to time.

"Ferris Wheel?" Cole asked when we were back on the dock.

All of us agreed and Cole footed the bill for a fancier car, one with four plush seats instead of eight bench ones. The second they shut the door behind us Cole pulled me into his lap.

"Shhhhh," he whispered in my ear as his hand slid underneath me and flipped upwards.

Luckily Conrad and Horse were taking turns being fixated on the bright city lights or on each other, they didn't even see him slip up the seam of my denim. His fingers explored gently, teasing at first but then he slipped inside. I couldn't help but roll my hips. I felt his hand creep up toward my neck to still me then fell away. Horse would know what we were up to immediately if Cole started squeezing on me.

He kept stroking me, poking inside then falling out and flicking my clit. I did what I could to stay still but my body wanted to roll against his the way it always did. Need was building like the skyscrapers I'd stared at in the late daylight earlier today, fiery pillars piercing into the sky.

220

Across from our naughty antics, Horse leaned across and grabbed Conrad by the neck. He looked him full in the face for a minute then down at his lips. I felt the needy fireworks all the way in my bones just before he pulled Conrad the rest of the way to his lips.

At first Conrad was too shocked to do much of anything but to stare wide-eyed at the man kissing him. But after a few heartbeats, he melted and met him move for move. Big plump lips rolled over each other and teeth grazed across the dark or light scruff depending on who was more interested in biting or lapping.

Watching while Cole started spinning circles on my clit was going to make me rupture.

Conrad gave up his seat to straddle Horse after a few minutes and my view became big Horse hands roving sculpted Conrad muscles through a thin white t-shirt. Conrad's ink trembled beneath the fabric until his hips started a slow steady rock against Horse.

My hips started to do the same.

"You like watching as much as I do don't you, Ladyface?" Cole murmured in my ear as he sent more fingers between my legs to work.

Since they weren't paying attention to us, he wrenched my legs wide and gave himself free access to my sex. It wasn't long until I couldn't hold back. I cried out as I leaned back to stare up into the deep black night. It was even less time before I turned my face into Cole's neck and bit hard to muffle the cries that accompanied my orgasm.

"Without me?" Horse purred from across the car and I sat up to see where he'd twisted a shocked Conrad to watch.

"Sorry man. Some moments are too good to pass up." Cole stroked along my neck where I stayed turned into him now smiling instead of tearing at his flesh. "And if it's any consolation, she got really excited watching you two. Gives me ideas for next time." Cole's husky laugh told me just how much he liked his idea.

"Next time? Next time what? Next time you're left out? As in you've been in?" Conrad shoved off Horse's lap.

"I told you I was bi." Horse raised an eyebrow.

221

"You never told me you fucked my best friend." Conrad's voice was getting sharper.

"Your best friend. My best friend. A lot of other somebodies' best friends, too." Horse shrugged his shoulder. "I've never made out with them on a Ferris Wheel though."

The ride stopped as if on cue and Cole quickly folded my legs back together just before the door opened.

"Like fuck if that matters. You've been in her Dolly Parton signing Jolene." Disgust was thick in his voice as he pointed his finger at me. If we hadn't been over just how foul he found vaginas in general, I would have been insulted.

"Jolene, Nine to Five, and the rest of the Grand Ole Opry," Horse shot out after Conrad and they tore off down the pier.

"Was it something I said?" Cole asked, a mischievous smile played on his lips.

"You better start being nicer to Conrad," I scolded as best I could; it wasn't very harsh.

"Or you're going to punish me?" Cole's hand came to my throat and he used his grip to push me out of the bright carnival lights of the pier and into the dark recesses behind a building.

I crashed into a building between two A/C units just before he bent to kiss me every bit as unrelenting as my orgasm had been. His body pressed fully up against me, adding weight to my chest and making it even harder to breathe. I surrendered fully to the feeling.

Until a throat cleared behind us.

"What are you doing, Cole?" The voice was thick with an Italian accent and stopped Cole cold.

"This is neutral territory," he snarled as he turned away from me, one hand automatically shielded me while the other blindly patted around the small of his back only to come up empty.

"I mean what are you doing with Jimmy Ponies' stepdaughter?"

I peeked out to see the man that knew who I was. He was wearing nondescript jeans and a white t-shirt. He wore lace up boots but the way he'd tucked the cuffs around them, I could see a large knife tucked in the side. Automatically I scooted closer to

222

Cole and grabbed his t-shirt. His hand that hadn't been able to find a gun wrapped around me, pulling me in even tighter.

"How do you know her?" Cole's voice rumbled wildly in his chest.

"There might as well be a police APB out for her. Jimmy has us, Mickey has Siobhan. That might as well be a citywide mobilization." The guy stayed back, his stance casual. I could feel how nervous that made Cole beneath my fingers.

"Why do you want her?"

"To protect her," he said simply and Cole's whole stance changed.

"Why would you protect her?" Cole was honestly questioning now, his voice less menacing than it'd been a moment ago.

"Jimmy's helping us with a project, it's the least we can do." He shrugged.

"For as long as it's convenient," Cole sneered and I knew that voice was directed at Jimmy. I didn't blame him one bit.

"Not this time." The Italian man stepped closer and Cole stepped back. "Look, Cole, you and I don't have the best history, we're both bad men." He sighed. "But we're bad men that do bad things to other bad men. Even we have a bit of a code and when it's innocent girls getting hurt, you'd step in too."

"What do you mean?" Cole leaned toward him, now more curious.

"So it's true, Mickey took you back but it's not like the old days. You aren't the right hand of God." The man studied Cole and I prayed the look on his face meant he liked what he saw.

"I'm only in for her," Cole admitted as he squeezed on me. I nestled into the space between his shoulder blades. "I'm only for her, period."

"Good. Someone needs to be." The Italian stepped back and jostled his pant leg, seamlessly covering the blade that had been on display. "Something's coming, Cole."

A whistle broke the conversation. First one long then two short and loopy ones. The Italian swore under his breath and started slinking deeper into the darkness behind us.

"What's coming?" Cole asked, his voice lower as he started to shuffle me in the same general direction.

"Well at this exact moment, that whistle means Siobhan."

Cole

If Vinny's words had made my blood run cold than the fact that Siobhan was on the pier was my own personal ice bath to drown in.

I shoved Elle into the dark nook beside me and held my fingers to my lips to shush her. She nodded wildly but grabbed for my hand. I let her hold it while I patted my low back, desperate to magically find my gun back in place. We both stayed stock still as Vinny disappeared into the background.

Horse was still somewhere. And what was worse was he with Conrad. A Conrad that Siobhan knew. And more than that, knew was as intimately tied to Elle as I was.

We were fucked if she found them. Simple as that.

To me, wishing on a star was the same as praying to God, neither of them would do us any good. Neither of them would help us out. It didn't stop me from doing both. I would have done far more if it meant keeping Elle safe.

Over the past week, Mickey had been in El Paso of all places and Siobhan has been MIA, it was the only reason that I'd been able to choke back the anxiety about us going out. As always, the ginger siren picked a perfect moment to resurface. I squeezed on Elle's hand as she slunk by.

Elle craned her head from where she was plastered up against the wall and I knew the moment she laid eyes on Siobhan. Her fingernails dug into the back of my hand and a tiny little snarl rumbled in her chest. The sound was so adorable I had to hold back a laugh as warm as she made my insides.

"That's her?" she spat the words at me as she spun away from me.

I quickly stepped toward her and folded her arm and body into me. Only the sound of us breathing broke the silence.

"She's a red-headed harpy that might as well grow horns, so yeah, that's her."

We both watched as Siobhan slithered down the pier.

"I hate that I can picture her with you," Elle said loudly when she thought Siobhan had gotten far enough away and she shoved against my arms then against me.

Siobhan's head whipped in our direction and she stepped back. I automatically pulled Elle in and covered her mouth as I pressed our bodies flat against the wall behind us. My breath balled in my throat and stayed there as Siobhan peered into the darkness. My fingers curled into Elle's cheek as the first true fear I'd felt in years hammered inside me.

Elle struggled in my arms and grunted against my hand. Siobhan took one step down the dark passage and narrowed her gaze further. My heart jackknifed in my chest. I thumped Elle up against the wall to get her attention. It worked too well and she shot me a venomous look.

I did the only thing I could think of, I dropped my hand from her mouth and dropped my guard. The sheer panic inside me had to show as plainly as if *terrified* was scribbled on my face. She went to say something but I held my finger up to my lips then mouthed the most broken *please* I possibly could. Something about the combination soothed her, maybe even scared her as she slumped back against the wall.

Siobhan had frozen just around the corner, combing the darkness with her satanic glowing eyes. I flattened myself to Elle, partially to hide further from the demon, partially so that if this was the last moment I breathed on this earth, I breathed in warm cherries.

"Cole, where the fuck are you?" Horse's booming voice split the tension from somewhere.

226

"I knew it." Siobhan had crept so close I heard her murmur under her breath as she turned on her heel.

I leaned out far enough to watch as she all but careened into Horse. He grabbed her by her upper arms and held her in his vise grip. He shook her as he bent in close and though his mouth moved, I couldn't catch the words.

There was a chance he could talk our way out of this. He could deflect, he could come up with a reason we were on the Pier that didn't sound like bullshit. Words weren't his strong suit but I had to believe in him.

After a few ragged heartbeats Horse set Siobhan down and narrowed his eyes at her as he pointed back toward the parking lot. She was every bit as pinched and suspicious as he was but she started turning. For a moment, I believed miracles did exist and we'd be in the clear.

"Horse, what in the hell?" Conrad's voice was nails gouging out glass.

My eyes went wide as the loud, tattooed queen barreled down the sidewalk for what was the equivalent of a nuclear train collision. If Siobhan didn't murder him, I would.

"You," Siobhan's raspy, ragged snarl carried on the wind. "And with you." She shoved her finger into Horse's chest.

They barely exchanged words but the way Siobhan lit up as she challenged Horse said everything. This was confirming every suspicion she ever had and there was no way to hide anymore.

Elle's arms wove around me and she dug her nails in. When she bit into my pec, I squeezed her as tight as I could. Even she understood what very real and present danger we were all in.

"Where is she?" Siobhan's three words stopped my heart.

When she turned toward the dark cranny we'd been hiding in with a glint in her eye. I was ready to run or fight or die. It was only Elle burrowing further into my chest that kept me from choosing which.

"Tell me where, Horse. Tell me now!" Her voice was getting closer to where we hid. "If you don't, I'll take it out on your pretty little piece of ass right there." She laughed her evil laugh. "And then Cole, again, when I find him."

Horse's thundering footsteps plowed toward us and a second later a smash of a body right around the corner shook the metal we were flattened against. Siobhan yelled out and I couldn't tell if it was in pleasure or pain. Conrad swore loudly afterward.

"Not if I kill you first," Horse growled and I swore I felt his warm breath around the corner.

"Horse!" Conrad shrieked and it made Elle twitch.

"Do it. I dare you. See how long your precious Cole and his little whore last if I'm dead," Siobhan's voice was sharp and acidic.

"If you threaten her ever again…" Horse thumped her body up against the wall again.

"Next time you slam me into a wall, you better shove your dick in me. This whole Elle thing is rather frustrating."

My skin crawled when I thought about it. The vivid memory of her fucking someone as she slit his throat came to mind. Bile coated my tongue at the thought she might ever touch Elle.

I kept my grip on Elle and started to shuffle along the wall. We were tangled in each other the slightest bit and I had to catch us when we stumbled. My hand shot out and the metal beneath me made a far too loud creak as it flexed beneath our weight. We stopped cold, except Elle's breathing, which was ratcheting up to shallow little things.

When I didn't hear anything behind us, I pulled myself from her grip and turned. Neither Horse nor Siobhan had turned the corner at the crash.

"Ladyface, we need to run. Okay?" I cradled her little face between my hands. "I'm sorry it came to this and I hate what it means, but we have to, all right?"

"I'm not very fast," she whispered as her big eyes searched mine and her bottom lip trembled.

"Not that kind of run." Her innocence made me smile despite everything and I rubbed my thumbs along her cheekbones as I explained. "We aren't going back to my place. Not now, not ever, unless it's to burn it to the ground." I sighed at the memories that would smolder in those ashes.

228

"Horse? Conrad?" Her whole body shivered when she asked. Mine felt like someone had gutted me like a fish.

"There's a chance we won't see them again." My chest heaved.

Tears pooled immediately in the corners of her eyes but she nodded as they spilled down her rosy cheeks.

"I never meant for this to happen, Elle. I wanted to be your everything, your only thing, but because you picked it, not because it was forced on you." I wiped away a few of the tears then dropped my hands to reach for hers.

"Cole." Her little voice didn't tremble as I expected. It was a strong, certain tone instead. "I did pick you. And I'd do it all again." She pressed up on tiptoe and kissed the tip of my nose like I'd done so many times to her.

When she lowered back down and gracelessly wiped away her tears, she flashed a serious smile up at me. My heart almost split and I swore I might grow wings. But then Siobhan's guttural cry grounded me back in the moment. I peered back into the darkness to see what was happening. No one was in pursuit and I found myself sending up silent prayers that Horse had finally snapped her neck.

I couldn't wait to find out though so I threw my arm around Elle and started pulling.

"We have to get back onto the walkway to get off the Pier. When we do, we have to act completely natural, okay?"

She nodded wildly.

"Don't say anything unless you have to and then don't say my name. If I tell you to do something, just do it."

The look of determination on her face was reassuring. She wasn't lying in the least about sticking by me. The set of her jaw said as much.

We walked with the pace of traffic but my insides were jumbled, tripping over themselves, desperate to both go faster and go back for Horse all at the same time. Elle's grip kept tightening too like she was tempted to drag me in either direction herself. I swore I could feel the tension rolling off her, and my body matched. I managed to stroke small circles on the back of her hand as we faded into the crowd.

Finally the crowds and lights of the Pier dissipated. I hadn't seen any backup with Siobhan and for the first time, I thanked my lucky stars she was such a filthy hellcat.

I had seen a few Italian faces watching us from various posts and now that we were just two people walking down a normal Chicago street, my mind wandered over what Vinny had said and why the fuck they'd be looking out for Elle, let alone me.

Something was coming.

How could three-word sentences alter my life so frequently? So completely?

We had to run but I needed to buy us enough time to find some answers. It was the only way to know with any certainty what was actually chasing us. The Butcher was with Mickey. Mickey was disappearing to the south for God knows what reason.

"Elle, do you have cash?" I asked as my mind raced.

"I have a couple hundred bucks and then my cards."

"Can we use them?" Plastic would pinpoint her if Mickey still watched bank accounts but it was downtown Chicago. I had to take my chances that he couldn't find us that fast if we pulled out cash.

"Of course." She squeezed my hand again.

"Good." I wracked my brain for an ATM.

Since we couldn't pick up the car without Horse, I started to travel the streets nearby from memory. My mind gravitated toward Millennium Park, where we'd been just hours ago. I could picture Elle in the reflective metal of the Bean, I could feel the happiness. Even the desperate wish to have the same photo she'd wanted. If I'd known our little world would crumble hours later, I would have agreed. My fingers dug into hers this time, an automatic reaction to still having a hold on her hand.

And then I saw it. The faint reflection of a bank sign on the curved surface of the statue. I knew exactly where we could draw out money. The fact that it was smack in the middle of some thirty-odd hotels didn't hurt either. I picked up the pace even though Elle had to jog to keep up. We needed to get out of plain sight. Like now.

I blew out a deep breath when I saw it. I yanked open the glass doors and scanned the street around us as I shoved Elle into the entryway to use the fluorescent-lit ATM.

"Max it, Ladyface." I blew out a deep breath as I kept fixed on the street rather than on her.

Even if Mickey was watching her accounts, waiting to see, he couldn't get someone here fast enough. Or so I prayed. That didn't stop me from sweeping my gaze up and down the street then back again.

"It's only going to let me get a thousand bucks."

"That'll do. I'll max mine and that'll just have to work until we can get to my stash." I turned and shot her a brief smile before returning to the street.

The sounds of the machine behind me made me jump and Elle didn't miss my unease. Her shoulders started to inch up to her ears as she pulled the bills from the ATM.

"We're good," she said as she placed her hand on my shoulder.

I jumped and she tensed in response.

"We're the furthest thing from good." I shoved my hand into her hair and raked it down to cradle the back of her neck. My thumb pressed into her throat as I pulled her to me and kissed her. "But you trust me, right?"

She nodded just as wildly as before, as I stroked and down on her neck, pressing a little bit more firmly as I did.

"Give me your card." I let go of her and held out my palm.

She wordlessly gave it to me then watched wide-eyed as I bent it down the middle. The plastic bent and warped turning from red to distressed white. I bent it back the other way then dropped it to the floor before smashing it like a cockroach. It splintered down the center just like I hoped. I picked up the two halves and pocketed one, tossing the one that said *Elle La* into the trash.

"Watch the street. If anything suspicious happens you tell me right away," I commanded before I turned to pull out my thousand.

231

As soon as I had the money in hand, I did the same thing with my card, leaving *Cole Ry* in the bin next to hers.

Elle was gnawing on her lip when I turned and grabbed her hand and shoved out of the little glass box. I turned down the sidewalk, grateful that it wasn't as well lit as the ATM had been. The fact that we were skirting a big beige brick building didn't hurt either.

We rounded the corner all too quick, we were exposed to the traffic of the city and the lights of a far more populated street. My stomach jumped up into my throat as I scanned the faces passing us. When one was a hotel valet everything inside me unwound.

"In here, Ladyface. Follow my lead."

I took a few steadying breaths as we skirted the small circular drive.

"Welcome to the Fairmont Millennium Park sir, miss." A doorman in a lightweight, short-sleeved uniform greeted us with a nod as we slipped into the revolving door.

The inside was glammed out with lush fabrics and low sultry lighting. I imagined having drinks with Elle in the sunken bar under different circumstances. In my fantasy, we were here celebrating something besides living through the night. I couldn't get lost in it or jog down to shoot a little bit of whiskey. Instead, I pulled her toward the front desk.

The LED sculpture behind the front desk woman was hypnotic but I didn't let myself relax. I kept scanning the room even as she started speaking.

"Welcome sir, do you have a reservation?" She smiled brightly like the world wasn't falling to pieces outside.

"We don't actually. Do you have anything?" I did what I could to keep the edge out of my voice.

"And your check out date?" she asked smiling up at me, polite as could be.

"Not tomorrow but the next day." That would be enough time to figure out what Vinny meant but not lingering too long.

"For two nights, we have a park view, Signature Suite. It would be five hundred and twenty-nine dollars a night."

"Perfect. We have another joining us too. Can I leave a key for him?"

I was going to risk a coded text to Horse and I prayed he'd figure it out. Prayed he was alive to figure it out. Leaving him at the Pier was enough to make me feel like a small part of my heart had been left bloody on the concrete.

"Certainly. We just need a credit card to hold."

"I'd like to pay cash for the room," I inadvertently snarled this time as my insides started to knot again.

"We still need a card to hold for incidentals." Rather than cower, she got slightly more forceful.

It took everything I had not to reach across her modern mahogany desk and latch on to her throat. My fingers itched at the opportunity to make her bend to my will with a smash to the wood she stood behind. I was losing control of myself, morphing back into the savage Mickey had always wanted me to be.

That was what stilled me. That and the small little hand that curled around mine.

"I plan on putting that card to serious work tomorrow on Michigan Avenue," Elle's voice was perfectly calm, perfectly clear and oh-so-sweet when she interrupted. "If I give it to you, do you run it or do you just hold it in case? A girl's gotta know how many pairs of shoes she can buy."

"If you pay cash for the room upfront we don't have to run the card unless something goes awry in the room." The woman responded to Elle like the ray of sunshine she was and once again I found myself smiling despite it all.

"Well then here you are." Elle counted out the cash from our new pile then dug in my back pocket for my wallet.

She flipped through and found my business card as if she knew it was there. My dimple hollowed out at how well she played this game, after all it was least likely to be on Mickey's radar.

After a few plinks of the keys the front desk woman gave us the keys and courteous directions to the elevator. I yanked Elle into my side as I pulled out my phone.

remember that time we did coke off a
stripper's tits? good times one block up.

I hoped he remembered the party in the apartment building one block down. It had been a hot, sweaty mess of bodies and cocaine but it was the first time I let him touch me without Mick around so I figured the evening was a little more clear to him than me. I hope that he'd know to ask for me at the desk.

I hoped that he was still breathing to do both.

The elevator dinged in front of us and Elle had to urge me into the elevator. I'd gotten momentarily lost on the Pier with Horse.

"Hello?" she questioned softly. "Earth to Cole?" She twisted to look up at me from under her long Bambi lashes.

"What if...?" I couldn't formulate the rest of that sentence.

"What if tonight you forget about it?" she asked quietly as she wrapped herself around my front and rolled her hips suggestively against mine. "What if you forget about the outside world and just live and breathe me?"

I shuddered with need. If only she knew how I already did.

"Devour me," she whispered as she raised up on tiptoes to bite my earlobe. "Consume me." She drug her teeth down my neck then pressed her lips to the skin right above my collar. "Take my everything tonight. Until there's nothing left of me."

My body trembled beneath her again, and this time because I was worried that in the morning her words might actually prove true.

Elle

I needed him. I needed Cole touching me to take away the panic, and kissing me to know that love still existed in this world. I needed him choking me to feel like I was still alive. He was the only thing that could.

Him.

Maybe Horse or Conrad could have helped but right now they just made a knot rise in my throat that I couldn't swallow past. Cole would just have to swallow up the sadness and fear for me.

He was somewhere else even though I'd all but begged him in the elevator and I couldn't take it right now. He needed to be here with me. In me.

When our room number appeared, I shook my hand from his and whirled on him. He was so distracted I was able to shove him and actually get his muscled body to move. I used my full weight to slam him up against the door.

Cole was face first against the cream wood of the door, his hands splayed to catch himself from crashing into it. I let my hands skate up along his broad back and down his sculpted arms before I laced my fingers into his. I kissed his neck then down across his shoulders. The cotton of his shirt tickled my lips until they felt raw and on fire.

"What if they don't…"

He slumped beneath me, his head banging against the door.

"You wanna go back?" My voice wavered at the thought.

Siobhan was every bit as awful as I'd imagined. It wasn't her devil red hair, sharp pointy heels or sharper, cat shaped nails. It was the way hatred hung on her soulless features. If I hadn't already forgiven Cole, I would have at first sight. She oozed evil out of every pore.

"We can't." He turned in my arms, keeping ahold of my fingertips. One of his arms folded down between us while the other wrapped around the back of my neck. He pulled me in and kissed me hard before he leaned his forehead to mine. "I'd crack if I lost Horse. Nothing would fill that space. But if I lost you, I'd shatter with no hope of ever putting myself back together."

I shoved against him again, keeping our arms tangled up as they were. We crashed back against the door, this time so hard I thought it might splinter.

This time Cole was with me. He kissed me back, meeting my lips move for move, hungry to taste more. He took my tongue roughly and I moaned.

"Ladyface, you want it rough?" He breathed just before he bit down hard on my bottom lip.

Everything below my belly button clenched, desperate for the savage Cole could be. A ravaged body would match my ravaged soul.

"Yes." I did my best to answer as I pulled away, not giving a damn that he was scraping so hard he might draw blood.

"Good."

He broke away long enough to grab the key and unlock the door. He grabbed the handle and kicked the door open, propping it open with his toe as he turned back and grabbed me by the throat to yank me into the room. His hand clutched down on me and pulled.

I surrendered completely to him and he tossed me up against the wall like a little rag doll. I crashed into it the way he'd crashed into the door. The moment after, he was up against me as I'd been at him. His lips were a little more aggressive, mussing my hair before they found the curve of my neck. He kissed me then lapped at the spots before he bit down. I groaned and rolled against my spot on the wall.

He fisted his hand into my hair and yanked my head to the side. He bit down on the exposed part of my neck harder than he had before. His lips closed around his teeth and sucked, blood thundered in his mouth and it threatened to burst just like my soul.

Cole yanked harder on my hair and I thought he'd bring me to my knees. I started to fold but he shoved his hands between my thighs and kept me standing as he wormed his way between the tiny scrap of denim and up into me. He used his body to thud me up against the wall again as he started stroking me.

His hand shifted from my hair to my neck and he slowly drummed his fingers along my skin. The vibration made me tremble as it moved in time with the thrusts inside me.

"Squeeze," I begged.

"Don't you dare tell me what to do," Cole snarled as his hand moved back in my hair and used his grip to shove me down to the carpet.

I didn't even slow my body, I simply let him reign over me. He needed control as much as I needed to surrender it.

He shoved my face into the carpet then gently skated a single knuckle over my cheek and traced the spot he'd marked on my shoulder. I quivered beneath the tender touch and a slight ragged moan slipped from my lips.

"Until there's nothing left of you, right?" There was a soft thump as his knees hit the carpet behind me.

"Own me," I gasped. "Obliterate me. Make me feel like there's absolute nothing left but our bodies as they burn."

He didn't answer me. He didn't have to. His fingers shoved inside me and started to dance in the way only Cole's ever could.

The friction threatened to burn a hole straight through my shorts. Or maybe just my insides. Maybe both. He worked hard on me. His fingers flying in and out, working my G-spot over. Thank merciful God I was down on the floor or I would have collapsed. As it was, I screamed as I clawed into the carpet.

How he'd found this spot inside of me or pulled this reaction from me, I wasn't sure. But once again the outside world fell away. Nothing was left but the feeling of us together.

237

This orgasm wasn't the kind of honeyed wave crashing over me. It was a frantic wrecking ball to the pit of my stomach. The newly discovered splash that came with it soaked the denim and Cole's hand.

His hand fell away and my body stilled. Cole stood and left me in that pile on the floor. He plopped onto the couch in the small living room of the suite. His eyes narrowed as he stroked overtop of his fly.

My vision was hazy but the animalistic way he watched me wasn't lost in the fuzz. I knew we weren't remotely done. Limply, I moved to pull off my top. Cole watched intently and the more I trembled, the brighter his eyes flashed. I went to take my shorts off but he stopped me with a simple hand gesture. He crooked his finger, telling me to come over. I tried to stand but once again he stopped me.

"Crawl." His voice was gruff and thick with lust.

I managed to get up on all fours and do just that. My body was Jell-O and when I slid between his legs I collapsed against his thigh.

"I'd crawl across broken glass."

Cole collected me off the floor and draped me across the couch, one leg up and over his shoulder, the other hanging down to the floor. He bent between my knees and leaned right into the wet spot between my thighs. Just before he latched on to the fabric, he licked his lips. My body clenched and I thought about splashing all over him again.

"My little cherry," he said and bit into the denim, pulling my shorts off with his teeth. "I'd crawl across worse."

He ripped off his shirt and bent down to kiss between my breasts. His hand fumbled between my thighs as he twisted to flick my nipple with a pointed tongue. My body jerked wildly as his warm, wet tongue worked on me.

The clink of his belt made me jerk too.

A moment later it was doubled up across my throat. I stretched my neck out and a faint smile played on my lips as denim hit the ground. I caught a glimpse of a gloriously naked Cole and the deep, dark ink that wrapped his perfect thighs before my eyes fluttered shut.

Heaven. I was back in heaven.

He tightened the leather across my neck as my body bowed up to meet his. Cole drug his teeth up my body then bit down hard on the skin he'd kissed between my breasts. His perfect tip pressed teasingly into me, over and over. He hovered above me, one hand on either side of the belt, his grip growing stronger, my breathing going ragged.

Then he shoved into me, quick and hard and fast.

I tried to scream but it cut off when the haggard sound hit the belt. The breathy, trapped sound was becoming synonymous with pure pleasure. Being stuck inside myself was almost as delicious as Cole being stuck inside me. Over and over.

The pain I couldn't swallow around was gone, it was replaced by want and need and surrender and Cole. Always Cole. Forever Cole. With my heartbeats and my dying breaths.

Cole.

I brought my fingertips up to trace down his beautiful cheek. Air wouldn't seep into my lungs and the disconnected floating feeling was taking over, but the way everything inside me fluttered when I held his face in my hands made it all fall away.

"Cole." It was more a shaky sound than an actual word. "Cole." I tried again but it faded into darkness. "Everything," I said shakily.

His lips came down to mine but didn't press down to kiss me. Instead he whispered, "Everything," right back.

A wild crash rang through the room, followed by the reverberation of something that wasn't my bones. The door had smashed open, threatening to destroy the wall and echoing down the hallway.

"Thank fucking God," Horse bellowed. "You're both okay." He blew out a deep breath.

"Now that you're here." Cole's voice almost broke and it made my heart hammer for him all the more.

"It's gonna take more than Siobhan to keep me from you. From both of you." He strode right over and looked down at me.

239

His fingers skated along my cheek then down to trace the leather crossing my neck. Cole's strong, steady thrusts didn't waver. Not even as Horse palmed up along Cole's arm to the back of his neck. Horse's chocolate eyes locked on Cole's the same way they had on mine. But then he melted like the drizzle over some delicious treat.

He pulled Cole up to his lips and Horse's big pout caressed and consumed Cole right over top of me. They worked against each other but more frantic than usual. Cole wasn't humoring Horse, he wasn't just letting him participate either, he was celebrating being able to kiss him.

I wanted the same kiss and my hands did what they could to scramble up to his chest. He pulled away from Cole and smiled down at me.

"Oh my little Fucktart. I'm glad to see you too. Really glad."

He whipped off his shirt and fell to his knees. I was still gasping when he kissed me full on the mouth. When I couldn't really kiss him back, he showered smaller butterfly kisses around my face.

"I've got something else for you," he said as he uncurled and unzipped his pants.

Kneeling put him at mouth level and he pulled out his cock.

"He can fuck your mouth right, Ladyface?" Cole asked as he shoved into me and stayed there.

I couldn't answer. Hell, I could barely move, constricted by that amount of muscle. So I closed my eyes and nodded as best I could manage.

Horse pushed in unceremoniously. I felt his soft tip against my lips just seconds before the mouthful hit the back of my throat. Whether it was my imagination or reality, Horse seemed to hit the belt. I tried to moan again but this time the sound was even more trapped than before.

"For a second I thought this was gone. That you both were." Horse's words turned into moans.

He palmed my tit as he picked up to a punishing pace. Cole leaned in and kissed his shoulder then picked up speed to match.

240

My skin was on fire. It was a vague reflection of how my insides felt. The fabric of Horse's pants brushed against my skin as his hands kneaded on me. His finger pinched on my nipple and he started twisting. I jerked at the touch and Cole snarled at the way I went rigid against him.

"What in the fuck are you doing?" Conrad shrieked from the door and I froze again.

I'd been too far gone to realize he was missing.

"It's called fucking. You should try it sometime." Cole's voice was liquid sex and I trembled beneath him.

"You're tag teaming my best friend!" His voice was the obscenely high note that only dogs could hear. I wanted to smack him. "And I thought I wanted to kill you for almost murdering that insane chick."

The room went icy when Conrad brought up Siobhan. I was stuck with a mouthful but the tightness at my throat disappeared. A moment later Cole pulled out of me and leisurely strolled over to Conrad. His hand flew to his throat and he pinned him to the wall.

"We aren't tag-teaming her. We're *with* her."

Conrad ground his teeth where Cole held him. "You want this?" he spat at Horse.

"I want everything in this room. And each for a special, unique reason." Horse twisted and fell from my mouth.

"It's disgusting," Conrad shouted.

"It's us. It's all of us," Horse defended.

"I'm out." Conrad threw his hands up.

"If you walk out that door, you're walking out on all of us." I kept my voice quiet but put weight behind each word.

"You need to watch," Cole added.

"And if I refuse?" He leveled his gaze at Cole.

"You're gonna watch, and you're going to like it. Because I said so," Cole snarled at him just before he grabbed Conrad by the throat and thudded him against the wall.

"Yeah? And who died and made you king?"

"No one. Have you seen my dick? I *am* king."

"You're nice looking and all. I mean, I could definitely hang a load of clothes out to dry on your line, but I'll take Horse. Any

241

day. And seven times on Sunday." Conrad crossed his arms while Cole held him, managing to huff despite the circumstances. Horse moved closer to the both of them but didn't quite know what to do.

"No, I'll take Horse." Cole let go of Conrad and reached for Horse's shoulder, guiding him to the ground.

"Make it good. Make him fucking jealous," Cole whispered as he leaned in, never taking his eyes from Conrad.

He wove his hands into Horse's dark locks as his dick danced against Horse's full pout before he pulled him in. I could imagine the feel of Cole deep down my throat and my hand automatically went to my neck.

Horse's big hands wrapped around Cole's body to grasp onto his ass. For a few swallows Cole let him control the rhythm of their movements but then Cole took over. He slammed the pile of muscle that was Horse up against the wall, right next to Conrad who hadn't moved except to cover his shocked and wide open mouth. Otherwise, he watched unflinchingly.

My hand wandered down between my thighs, unable to stop itself. Cole in control was a beautifully terrifying thing to watch. Every inch of my being remembered what it was like to be tossed, every inch of me craved it. I groaned when I hit my mark.

"Told you I was king. Don't even have to be inside Elle to make her moan," Cole said as he thrust hard enough to jostle Horse into the wall.

"Good Christ what's wrong with you guys?" Conrad's voice had changed though. It wasn't horror or outrage coloring it this time, but a sense of wonder.

"Nothing," I cried out as I fondled myself.

"Yeah, there's something." Conrad didn't peel his eyes from the show in front of him to answer.

"You don't find his lips around my dick, swallowing over and over and over hot? I mean look at him..." Cole commanded and I did even though it wasn't me he was commanding.

Horse furiously worked his cock, cheeks hollowed where Cole's inked hips shoved in over and over. He couldn't break away because Cole had him in a vise grip up against the wallpaper. Every inch of Cole's perfectly defined ass and thick roped legs flexed as he thrust. Every tiny definition in Horse's forearms or chest did the same as he pulled him in relentlessly. Horse's thick cock bobbed and wove like a snake in front of a charmer where it stood tall out of his jeans.

And the noises Horse made, muffled as they were by Cole's cock were still as sinful as the scene itself.

My circles and dips got a little more furious on my clit.

"You like it." Cole leaned toward Conrad. "You like it so much, you want in. You want to touch me," he murmured. "You want to share what Horse has. You want to share in what's Elle's."

"I don't." It was a weak defense, and his voice wavered.

"You do. You crave it. You crave the intimacy after tonight. The connection that sharing would give you. You don't want to be alone in the cold." Cole's hand found its way back to Conrad's throat. "I know because I've been there."

My body twisted and writhed as I watched. Conrad couldn't answer and I didn't know if it was Cole squeezing or because he honestly couldn't this time.

"Touch it. Touch me." Cole was inches from Conrad's face, teeth bared.

Conrad's hand hesitated at his hip.

"Do it. We all know you want to."

This time he lifted it and hovered over top of where Cole rested in Horse's mouth.

"Do it!" he yelled and Conrad's hand fell into the fray.

He groaned as he grabbed the thick root of Cole. I couldn't help but follow suit with the sound and wishing my hand was in his place.

"You," Cole said, suddenly rounding on me, leaving both Conrad and Horse gasping against the wall. "You're mine. Your pleasure is mine. Your orgasms. Everything." He softened while he spoke and his last word as the usual soul-obliterating, tortured whisper.

He grabbed me from the couch and twisted me to perch on top of him. My knee slid off the slick upholstery once or twice as I straddled him and I felt off kilter completely but that didn't stop

243

Cole from taking my arms and pinning them behind me back as he laid back and smoothly lowered me down to his chest.

"Ladyface, everything," he almost breathed the words in and out as he thrust into me.

I screamed but then he slowed to a long, leisurely pace that had pure pleasured moans replacing my need to breathe.

After Cole set about splitting my being in two, Horse's familiar big hands wrapped into my hips. He pulled me down hard onto Cole then bent over so his warm breath puffed against my ass. His fingers curled into my cheeks then spread them a second before his nose touched my tailbone and his tongue sank into me. My sounds were more tears this time, tears from a body begging for release, tears over the emotional turmoil that still hung heavy on my skin, tears of pure pleasure that was actually unhinging my bones.

Maybe even tears from a heart so full it might burst.

Horse lapped at me, tongued inside of me, even nibbled a little while Cole kept up his perfect rhythm. Even if he hadn't held my arms behind me, I would have been powerless to stop it. It was too good.

We were too good.

So I surrendered to them completely, sure Cole was, in fact, my king. I turned my head to the side and let sensation wash over me. Right before everything went blurry I saw Conrad start to stroke himself.

Cole

Familiar groans and the new wails came from the living room. The furniture jostled and thumped outside, taking a beating just like someone's ass. Horse and Conrad sizzled together and I was glad I'd lit the fire under them. Conrad wasn't so bad when his mouth was full.

Matter of fact, if Elle hadn't been dead to the world, I would have used her body to get off listening alone. Instead I was up in more ways than one, watching the dark shadows shift across the ceiling.

Her breathing was soft and soothing but considering the evening, I needed more than soothing.

When I wasn't lost inside her, I was just lost. This situation was spinning wildly out of control. I'd never really had a plan outside of *hide her*, but the reality of how long that could ever last was washing over me. Well, more like slamming into me.

Siobhan knew. Even if she didn't have proof, she knew. And Mick would listen.

I was looking down the barrel of a loaded gun. This time someone was going to pull the trigger and I wasn't going to dodge the bullet. If it meant keeping Elle safe, I was okay with that. But something said she wouldn't be.

Well, Vinny said it.

His words turned over. How were they involved? *Why* were they? Could they help me keep her safe?

I slowly pulled myself from under Elle's fingertips and slid out of bed. Her hand clutched into the sheets when I was gone. I wanted to walk away from her like I wanted a hole in my head. That this was for her, for a hint at how to protect her, a way to maybe see the future, was the only thing that kept me moving.

At the door, I turned back and let my eyes sweep over her. In the moonlight, she was creamy pale against the soft gray sheets. They fell across her body in little waves. Her big, pouty lips were parted and her soft breaths and sweet sighs slipped between them. Her golden hair was a haphazard pile cascading around her face, tangled here and there from where I'd fisted into it. The hickey on her shoulder was bright even in the faded light.

I wanted to mark her permanently as mine. I didn't care how I did it, but I needed the world to know that she was meant to be with me and I was a lucky son of a bitch to find her. Maybe a tattoo. Something delicate and small, barely altering that perfect skin.

The idea made me smile as I slipped out the door.

A very different sight met me there. Horse was deep inside Conrad, one hand fisted in his Conrad's surfer blonde hair. The other was supporting himself where he was bent over the arm of the couch. Conrad was at his mercy, arched back up toward Horse's flexed chest. Conrad's toes were scrambling to stay grounded on the carpet.

Tanned skin was tangled up, all dewy with sweat. Ink poked out here and there where Conrad scrambled to keep their balance or reach back up to clutch on Horse. Like this, my best friend was a savage rather than the submissive he was with me. I couldn't stop watching as I grabbed jeans and slid them on.

"Someday," Horse purred. "Someday, I'll have you like this." He rammed into Conrad all the harder.

I walked right over and batted his hand from Conrad's hair. The big beautiful body fell limp beneath Horse. I leaned in, close to both of them.

"Dream on," I murmured before I planted my lips on Horse's.

He started thrusting again as his hand came to cup the back of my neck. Conrad started to protest beneath us and this time I didn't feel like forcing myself on him.

"Elle's the only one that gets me like that." I pulled back. "Conrad should get the same courtesy." I smacked Horse square on his ass as I walked over to my shirt, slid it on, then walked out the door.

It was a different world out here. Even with the faint sounds of Conrad back behind the door, there was no pleasure out here. Only pain. And it was made all the worse because I missed my blonde little puzzle piece like a lame man missed his cane.

I grabbed a cab downstairs and gave it an address that barely formed in my mouth.

"The Italian neighborhoods, eh?" my cab driver asked. "Don't take many visitors out that way."

"I have an old acquaintance there."

"Seeing him late tonight?" He was trying to make small talk but under the circumstances, it just felt like prying.

I decided not to answer, instead turning to watch the streetlamps and few headlights barrel past. Chicago was all I'd known, the grit and the grime tucked among the beacons of industry. The lake had always been the edge of the world, a sudden stop to all the city madness, a tumultuous sea replacing the clean, sharp glass. Spanish class mildly attended was as close as I got to a different world.

We pulled up to a dimly lit street, a few lamps flickered on and off. It was miles away but it reminded me of the street outside Mick's. Simple, plain, like any grid in the city, but it was covering a giant gaping entrance to Hades itself.

I waited for the cab to pull away before I walked under the streetlight and turned my pockets out. One by one, I pulled up the legs of my pants to show there was nothing shoved in my shoes. I held my hands out to the sides and turned in a slow circle. Then I waited.

The sounds of the city were vague in the distance as if I'd entered a bubble where the usual activity didn't wander. No sirens were nearby, nothing rustled in the garbage, no dog made a ruckus and no music played. It was how I knew they'd seen me coming.

Eventually, a lone figure started walking down the street, their footfalls echoing off the buildings.

There was a small chance that I was dead right now. If Vinny had lied or the Giancomos misunderstood. This was as good as a bullet walking into range. I held my chin high and thought of Elle. Her little body and its slight but beautiful curves. Her large eyes and big plump lips. And her laughter. Her beautiful, twinkling laughter.

"Cole," Vinny started when he was close enough to speak in an even tone. "Glad you came. Let's get inside." He jerked his chin and I couldn't help but blow out a deep breath as I followed him.

"You gotta start explaining. I can't be gone long." I shoved my hands into my pockets while I followed him into a small ranch style house nearby.

"I would but there's someone who I think'll do it better."

We stepped into a home that was nothing like Mickey's. It was actually a home with photos of generations on the walls and well-worn furniture. All of it looked like the original furniture off a 70s television show, shag and velvet in the most awful colors. There were a few plastic toys scattered in front of a TV, which seemed to be as old as the orange Formica countertop in the kitchen. Trippy flowers were interspersed here and there.

The space actually made me smile until I saw who was sitting at the vintage kitchen table.

I lunged at Jimmy, my hands finding his throat and squeezing before anyone could react.

"You did this to her!" I shouted as fury bubbled up in my throat and pulled my grip tighter.

He scrambled beneath my grasp, clawing at my hands until Vinny got his arms around me and pulled. I could take Vinny in a fight and I writhed against him until the click of a pistol stilled us both.

"We don't do business like that in this house." Nonno Giancomo was holding a pistol, silencer and all, against my head.

248

I looked up the barrel then swept my gaze along the patriarch of the Giancomo family. He was older and more wrinkled than the last time I saw him. His gold tooth still stood out of his thin-lipped smile and matched the golden chain he wore over his undershirt. Despite being in his eighties, he was strong beneath the thin cotton, even if he seemed leaner and more stringy than the last time we'd run into each other. The deadly glint in his eye was exactly the same.

My hands fell automatically from Jimmy's throat.

"Good bambino, good." His accent was thick but it wasn't patronizing. "The only person who sheds blood in this house is me and I'm not in the mood tonight."

"What's this all about? What's going on?" I tried to hold my temper back.

"Sit down. It's time for a story." Vinny gestured to the table as he turned a chair around to sit backward on.

I took a seat and the vinyl creaked beneath me, the thin metal frames of the furniture protested against my heavy body. I couldn't help but glare at Jimmy across the gold-flecked table.

"When it was the track it was kind of fun. We were like Sinatra in our fedoras, making money hand over fist and smoking good cigars. Elle's mom was this French goddess that liked long cigarettes, Baccarat and fast horses. I fell hard for Simone." Jimmy smiled wistfully and my heart softened a little bit. "Suppose the Laroux girls have a type too, bad boys suit them."

My eyes fell away from Jimmy and I swallowed down the self-loathing that statement welled.

"Elle didn't like the law breaking. There was no way of explaining that once you're in, you're in with the Maloneys. She definitely didn't understand Mickey's tastes..." We both shuddered thinking about exactly which tastes he was referring to. "It drove a wedge straight down the middle of the family but Simone stuck with me. The money let us fund a scholarship for art school for Elle. Let us buy her sculptures too, place 'em around town or hang 'em in the house. I can't regret those things, those years."

Jimmy looked up and his eyes begged me to understand. Vinny and Nonno hadn't said anything, letting us have a moment across the table instead.

"But then it changed. Mickey's business interests...diversified."

"Beyond gambling, laundering, loan sharking, arson, murder and rape? Into what?"

"Human trafficking," he said simply. "Mostly sex trade."

I was going to be sick. I had thought that Mickey had hit rock bottom years ago. He dealt in sin and shit for so long where was there to go?

"Simone couldn't watch that. He preyed on young girls, thirteen to twenty-something. He'd parade in his new crop and do any number of things to them. Then they were doped up, at the mercy of him and Siobhan's twisted desires. And that was the easiest part to stomach. If they lived, they were sold to any number of places for God only knows what reason. Based on the things I saw, I like to think it was an improvement."

The night I'd walked in to find two young girls attached to Siobhan's tits flashed in my mind. They hadn't been given the sick choice like the rest of us and that automatically made the scene all the more gruesome. I had to choke back the thick disgust.

"Simone stole the transit ledger. It has the details of where they were picked up, where they were sent, how... Apparently, it has the financials to go along with it."

"Apparently?"

"It disappeared before I saw. The day Simone was killed for taking it."

The room was thick with a pain and grief bigger than the death of Simone Laroux and the sick and twisted moves of Mickey Maloney. All four of us were hardened men but Vinny had been right, this was a deeper form of wrong. It didn't sit well. It flew in the face of monsters, hunting monsters.

"How are you all involved?" I asked as I looked from Vinny to Nonno and back.

"We heard the rumblings so we edged in but you know as well as we do what sticking your nose across the boundary lines will get you."

"Yeah, your head cut off." I looked down at my fingers and started picking at my nails.

"But then my sister went missing," Vinny snarled and I looked up. The fury in his eyes was a reflection of the torment inside me and I was glad to see him human rather than Italian. "A Giancomo doesn't go missing. *If* she couldn't fight her way out, she would have left a trail. No one in this family just disappears."

I knew exactly what he meant. They were just too high profile for things to slip through the cracks. Especially the dirty filthy cracks of the floorboards where things like murder and kidnapping laid thick.

"We started digging. Of course, it led to Mickey but we also found Simone. She had a plan to the tune of half a million to retrieve most of the girls that she'd been able to find. She had a journal entry, number 523476 that seemed like Giovanna."

"But then they killed her and the book disappeared." The odd puzzle was finally making sense. Jimmy nodded, his frown growing deeper as his brow furrowed.

"They want Elle because they assume she has the ledger." His voice was muffled in his hands but it was still a knife straight to my heart. The scenarios I'd been imagining were just based on Mickey's simple repayment plan.

"We want the ledger to get Giovanna back," Vinny added. "Are you gonna help us or help him?"

My head fell into my palms and I tried to catch my breath. I would do anything for Elle, that wasn't a question, but the weight of what that anything actually was, was daunting. I rubbed my face for a moment before I thought of a way to split the heavy silence.

"She doesn't have the ledger." I took a mental inventory of everything Elle had strewn about my apartment. The things that Siobhan had likely rooted through at this point. Nothing could be mistaken for a handwritten folio.

"Maybe she's hiding it from you?" Nonno asked. I had to keep from screaming at him.

"Not the way we work," I still snarled. "If she had it, I'd know."

"Then there are only two questions, Cole." Vinny took a deep breath. "Where is it and are you going to help us find it?"

Elle

Loneliness hit me like a sucker punch to the stomach when I woke up. Cole wasn't next to me, the soft indent of his body hadn't even lingered. Without even his scent hanging on the sheets, the events of the evening fell way too hard on me.

Sometimes this was still too much. The world had turned upside down and I didn't know how to right it. Ever since that damned funeral…

Just the thought made me realize. The world hadn't turned upside down, it had finally fallen back into the spot it was always meant to be, with me mixed up in the shit storm of the Maloney family.

"Goddamnit, Simone," I cursed my mother as I pounded my fists onto the mattress at my hips.

Conrad would understand this new wave of anger and commiserate with me until Cole reappeared and chased the demons away.

I wrapped the sheet around my body and left the bedroom in search of Horse and Conrad in the small living room. A t-shirt flew past my face almost smacking me when I stepped toward the couch.

"He kissed you. While you were inside of me," Conrad shrieked.

"You grabbed his dick while he was inside of me too," Horse countered.

"That was different." Conrad whipped on his shirt.

"How so?" Horse buttoned his jeans.

"The way he…" Conrad's cheeks were flushed even in the pale light. "I mean with a voice like that…"

I couldn't hold back my smile at the reference to Cole or what had happened hours ago.

"You wanted it. You wanted in with us. You wanted it exactly the way Cole said," Horse spat as he crossed his arms over his barrel chest.

"So what if I did? Apparently fucking anything that walks, *together*, is kind of a thing around here."

I pursed my lips at Conrad even though I doubted he'd noticed I'd appeared.

"How is that different than Cole kissing me on the way out the door."

"You used me!" Conrad threw his hands up. "You want to fuck *him*. You want to be dominating *him*. But he won't let you so I'm just a cum dumpster."

With a flick of imaginary long hair and a dramatic twirl, Conrad spun out of the room, the door slamming hard behind him.

"Fuck!" Horse roared.

"Well don't just stand there, go get him," I urged.

"I don't know where my shirt or my shoes are," he whined.

"So hurry." I shot him a wide-eyed look and pointed toward the door.

He hesitated a second then bolted, flipping the lock bar so the door crashed loudly into it without shutting.

I laughed a little at the reunion I pictured in my head, Horse riding in as a knight in shining armor, well, glowing tanned skin, to force Conrad back to the room. Conrad would probably swoon in his arms. I went to grab water in the bathroom so that I could have a front row seat for the Officer and a Gentleman-style carry.

The metal scraped against metal as I rounded back into the living room and I looked up expectantly.

"No," I murmured when an evil smile glinted in the moonlight rather than either of the big beaming ones I was expecting.

"My reputation precedes me?" Siobhan's voice was like the hiss of a snake. Probably exactly like the one that tempted Eve into original sin. "Yes?" she asked again when I stayed frozen. "Good, yours does too."

She walked in with swishy hips as she placed one sharply pointed toe directly in front of the other. Her long pointed nail dragged down the wallpaper as she slithered toward me. I automatically took a step back.

"Matter of fact, I'm quite interested in what the fuss is all about. I mean you've got a queen and an animal all worked up down the hall." She nodded her head toward the elevator. "And thank goodness for those two or I may never have found you." She took another few steps toward me and I thudded into the wall behind me.

"And then there's Cole," she pressed herself up again me. "Beautiful, tragic, savage *monster* that he is." She brought her lips together and hummed like she was eating a delicious dessert.

"Don't you dare talk about him," I growled through gritted teeth.

"You're not in a position to make requests." She drug her nail down my cheek and my hands flew to bat her away.

The sheet dropped from my body and her eyes glinted.

"Well, that's certainly got something to do with it." She reached out to cup my breasts.

"Don't touch me." I squirmed and shoved against her.

"Oh honey. I think I'm going to touch every inch before I take you to Mickey."

I turned to run but she shoved her hand out, clotheslining me and forcing me to stumble back. Before I even had a chance to steady myself one of those terrible heels crashed down on the back of my knee. I cried out and crumpled to the floor.

"I like it when you scream." Her voice was laced with lust as she fisted my hair and started pulling.

I screamed. I couldn't stop as she yanked me toward the bedroom, me scrambling both to keep up and get her off me.

"Yes!" she cried out. "That gets me so wet."

"You're disgusting," I shouted as I dug my fingers into hers and wildly kicked at her legs.

"Yes," she whispered as she leaned down and curled her nails into my head. My scream pierced the air the way she was piercing my skin. "I'm the spawn of Satan himself and you'd do well to remember it." Her tongue shot out and licked up my cheek. "MMMmmm, you taste like cherries."

She threw my body to the floor and almost instantly had her legs straddling my shoulders. I writhed and kicked and screamed beneath her but it didn't do me any good. Her satanic strength was so encompassing, she was able to wrangle my arms underneath her shins.

"Buck my little buttercup, buck." Her voice was a mix of encouragement and lust.

Siobhan's cat-like fingernails scraped down my cheeks before she brought them to her lips.

"Even cherry tears," she purred. "No wonder everyone's making idiotic decisions."

I hadn't even realized I was crying but I wasn't ashamed I was. She was unrelenting and the way her wicked smile hung on her lips or pure evil danced in her eyes, was bone-chilling.

Or so I thought until the cool barrel of a gun pressed to my forehead. That's when my insides turned to ice.

"Don't think I won't. With you out of the way, everything becomes so much easier. No one to chase around, no one to hide the ledger." She rolled her eyes as she spoke. "I imagine your corpse will put up less of a fight when Mickey fucks you too."

"No," I screamed an awful, blood-curdling scream. How no one had heard us I didn't know.

"No to death or no to Mickey?" She bent down. "Because both are inevitable for you, buttercup."

"Stop calling me buttercup!" My words were as violent as the way I fought against her.

She cocked the pistol. "I'll call you my bitch up until the moment I call you Mick'd. Do you understand?" She shoved the metal deeper into my skin.

The tears started to pour faster as she started to ruck up her skirt. Once the pencil skirt was up around her hips, her pussy was on display, every bit as wet as she'd claimed it to be. She shuffled against me, notching herself onto my face. I tried to twist away, side to side, anywhere.

"That feels nice but I want you to lick it."

I screamed but this time it was muffled by her thighs.

"Lick it!" she bellowed and shoved her hips down onto my mouth. "Tell me what I taste like."

"No," I cried out again and this time she shifted so that her clit brushed my lips.

"There you go, buttercup. Come on." She writhed her hips all the more wildly on me.

We'd found some sick and fucking twisted rhythm as I went insane beneath her and she humped my face. My cheeks were wet from the never-ending tears and her salty slickness.

She pitched forward, her legs still firmly trapping my arms as she lowered on her forearms to the floor above my head. Mercifully the gun wasn't against my skin anymore.

"You're going to tongue me until I come or I'm dragging your corpse out of here." She made eye contact with me as she spewed her venom.

Then she twisted so she could place the barrel at my temple and all but shoved her clit between my lips.

"Lick it," she commanded. "I said lick it you little bitch." She shoved both the gun and herself harder against me. "*LICK IT!*"

The tears kept pouring down my face, the panic welling in my throat was making it hard to breathe. Deep in my bones, I felt my death coming. Conrad had been right. This wasn't a fairytale where Cole charged in. This was a moment in time where I was forced to fuck a monster and then bleed out on the soft gray carpet.

I was operating on pure self-preservation as my tongue made a point and moved up toward Siobhan's skin. First I tentatively tapped her clit trying to get away with a barely there touch.

257

"Lick. Make me come or die." She made sure I could see her arched eyebrow and evil smirk. "I may come when I kill you anyway. If you lick it we may not find out."

This time she just shoved the barrel roughly into my head.

I surrendered and flattened my tongue to her. She let out a long low moan. The tears poured harder and harder down my cheeks but I didn't stop. She kept pushing the gun harder and harder into me like that was a natural response to an impending orgasm.

"Tell me how I taste. Do I taste like cherries?" She lifted her hips just the tiniest bit from me.

"You taste like fucking fish!" I screamed and jerked beneath her.

"For that, you're gonna tongue my ass or die trying." She swatted her claws across my face and I felt the warmth of blood trickle down my cheek the same way I had when she'd clawed into the back of my head. Tears mixed with the blood as she adjusted her hips so that her backside rested just above my lips.

"Tongue..." her screamed command was cut short by the wispy crinkle of a plastic trash bag.

She jerked above me and the gun slid from my temple. A moment later she bucked back up on top of me but this time it was her struggling on top of me rather than anything pleasure fueled. She screamed but it was cut off by the same crinkle of a bag.

A second later, she was almost levitating off of me. The moment I was free, I shot backward, desperate to get away from her. Her face was distorted behind a thin sheet of plastic and a big familiar hand covered her nose and mouth. She tried to scream again but the plastic was shrinking down and suctioning to her face. It was as tight to her neck as the belt had been on mine earlier.

My mouth fell open as I watched her struggle. Slowly but surely she moved from wildly twisting to desperate flop. When she went limp, the hands around her neck simply shifted to press into her flesh and check her pulse. The second he was satisfied, Horse tossed her to the floor and barreled at me.

"Fucktart? Elle? Are you okay?" He gathered me up and cradled me to his chest.

I was gasping for air, but I was fixated on her body. She'd had so much fight, so much spunk, but now she was nothing. She was just as inanimate as the coffee table.

The tears started all over again and I buried myself into Horse's warm beating heart.

"What just happened?" Conrad's voice was trembling behind us.

Horse reached back and squeezed his hand. I lifted up just desperate to see his face, leaving blood and glistening tears smeared across Horse's chest. The three of us shared a look that wasn't just heavy, it was terror. A very real, very life altering fear.

"Conrad, we just killed someone."

Cole

"Fairmont Millennium Park, right?" The cabby cleared his throat from the front seat, finally drawing me from my thoughts.

"Yeah. Sorry." I shook my head, trying to shake Elmwood Park from my brain.

The Giancomos could have blown my brains out and my thoughts would have been less scrambled. I mean, Jimmy was a good guy? The Giancomos wanted my help? Obviously this tornado had landed my house in fucking Oz.

I threw cash at the driver and stepped out into the silent late night. Even the city at four a.m. was quiet. Quiet enough that the buzz of my cell startled the valet dozing at the stand. I pulled it out to silence it as I smiled a thin smile in apology. The notifications caught my eye.

Fourteen missed calls. And all from Horse.

There was no real reason for Horse to call unless... Unless something had gone really fucking sideways.

I shoved on the revolving door and bolted down the hallway, whoever was around and whatever they thought be damned. I skidded on the freshly polished marble in front of the elevator getting stupidly annoyed at the floor guy the same way I had at the cabbie. My gaze pinched in his direction and I vividly pictured throttling him out of pure panic.

Instead I took my aggression out on the elevator up button, desperate to get back to them. To *her*. Because deep down I knew Elle was the only reason he'd call fourteen times.

When the elevator took forever, I turned and slammed into the stairwell door and started running. Flight after flight after flight. They seemed to be stretching out like that sketch study on perspective where you couldn't figure out where the stairs began or where they ended because it was just a fucked up loop.

I screamed when I reached yet another landing and the feral sound ping-ponged off the concrete of the stairwell.

I'd crawl across worse.

My words from earlier tonight came back to me and singlehandedly started shoving me up the stairs. Mercifully the door finally appeared to our floor and I busted out, barely breaking stride as I barreled toward her.

Well, the room. Automatically I tried the door and it was locked just as it should be but I shook it wildly anyway. When it didn't give my fists flew to the door and punched, bellowing again.

"Shut the fuck up and calm the fuck down," Horse growled as he whipped open the door.

"What happened, why did you call me a thousand times?" My shoulders were heaving up toward my ears with deep, heavy breaths.

"I said calm down." He grabbed me by the shirt and pulled me into the room.

When the door shut behind me, my eyes had to adjust to the dim lighting. Only the city beneath us cast shadows across the space. That didn't stop me from finding my Ladyface where she was cuddled on Conrad's lap. My heartbeat stopped and a searing pain shot through my side.

Elle was aimlessly gnawing on her thumb hard enough that blood was smeared on her lips as she stared vacantly into space. There were similarly bloodied gashes on her cheek and crimson colored her hair where Conrad tenderly stroked.

"What happened?" I asked again, this time my voice was broken, my question desperate.

I took a few steps toward her and she didn't even turn to look at me. I was ready to scoop her out of Conrad's arms when Horse put his hand around the back of my neck and gently guided

261

me toward the bedroom. He didn't say a word, he just pushed me in.

My eyes went to the one thing out of place in the room. The sheet covered lump at the foot of the bed. I shook my head as I studied the unmistakable outline of a body.

"You answer me, and you answer me now." I rounded on him and shoved him up against the doorframe.

I frantically searched his face and then Conrad's where he watched us. For the first time, not a single light danced on his sunny features.

"Who's under that fucking sheet and what did they do to Elle?" Terror became a softball in my throat that I could barely speak around.

"See for yourself," Horse's low, serious voice was almost as scared as mine.

Even though my feet weighed a million pounds, I managed the trudge over. I crouched down and pulled up the corner and recognized the pointy fucking shoe peeking out. Both bile and relief rose inside me as I uncovered Siobhan's broken and blue body.

"She…" I couldn't bring myself to ask.

"Got in the room when I went after Conrad. I found her on Elle doing what she does best."

"Did she…?" We both knew Siobhan well enough to know what I was asking.

"Yes," Horse whispered.

I dropped the sheet back over the body and stood, pushing past Horse and directly to Elle.

"Give her to me," I snarled at Conrad, he simply raised his hands in surrender and let me grab her.

As soon as I touched her, she came alive, struggling against me wildly, her eyes still vacant. I tried to wrangle her up to standing but her nails flew at me. My stomach rolled over, knowing this was what she'd had to do against the corpse in the other room.

"Elle, it's me," I cooed but she only fought harder as I tried to pull her to me. "Ladyface," I shouted a little harsher.

262

At first, she looked as though I'd smacked her, going stock still, but then she melted into me with big, wet, gasping sobs.

"Shhhhhh, Ladyface. Shhhhhh." My hand skated the back of her head trying to soothe her the way Conrad had been, only to find the sticky mat of blood that had trickled from her skull.

My fingers got tangled so I simply pulled her into me. I rubbed up and down her spine, breathing in the slight scent of her as it mixed with Horse's freshly laundered shirt.

"Where were you? Why weren't you here?" She sobbed into my chest, my heart wanted to shatter beneath her tears.

"It seemed more important," I whispered and started to pull her toward the bed without thinking of anything but winding my body around her.

Conrad and Horse waved wildly at me and tried to tell me to cut it out but it was Elle's broken, "*No!*" was what stopped me.

"Fuck," I swore under my breath. "Sorry, Ladyface."

I bent swiftly and picked her up to cradle her to my chest. She let me, nuzzling into my skin. I carried her to the bathroom and turned on the bathtub. As it filled I gently pulled her out of Horse's shirt and tossed it up onto the counter. When I turned back she was trembling but I was sure it wasn't from cold. I coaxed her into the warm water and her perfect pale skin blanched beet red in the water.

She collapsed into the bath, I had to slow her crash into the water. But then I helped her get comfortable. She balled up on her own knees then slumped toward me. I grabbed a mug from the vanity then I knelt down next to her. I poured a few waves of warm water over her head, hoping to help clean the blood from her hair. When it was more pink than red I reached around her with both arms and cupped her shoulder, pulling her in despite the edge so I could kiss the cap of her shoulder.

Her hands left her shins and wrapped up around my forearms. Warm tears started to spill down onto my skin again and all I could do was rest my forehead against her. We breathed in unison bent over the tub and wrapped up in each other as we were.

"Why weren't you here?" she asked, defeated when she finally broke the silence.

"I went to see Vinny. I needed to know what he was talking about before." I stayed as calm and quiet as I possibly could.

"Why didn't you take me?" Her voice crackled before tears took back over.

I blew out a deep breath. There was no way to soften this or make it pretty. At this moment, Elle wasn't dealing in pretty, she was dealing in truth. I hated myself for doing that to her.

"I killed his brother." I sucked in a deep breath. "Back in the day, I killed him with my bare hands for no other reason than he burned down Mickey's old house." She tensed beneath my hands. "I couldn't take you there any more than I could take you into the lion's den itself."

Her nails clutched into me.

"Forgive me." I lifted up and breathed the words into her hair. "Say you'll forgive me. Someday?" I added, scared that I'd finally broke us. "I never will. But if you do, we'll survive. I'll survive."

She rocked ever so slightly in my arms. "Ladyface," I breathed and tried to scoot closer to her.

"What did you find out?" she finally asked, her voice trembling as much as her tiny body.

"We don't need to talk about it right now."

"Oh yes, we do." She choked on her tears. "Whatever it was, it better be good, because you… It took you…" Her sobbed choked her off all over again.

"Shhhhh," I nestled into her.

"Tell. Me. Cole," she managed in between shotgun breaths.

I felt my eyes go wide and my frown play on the corner of my lips but I told her. I told her about her mom. And about Jimmy. About what they had done in the past and what Jimmy was really up to now. I iced that shit cake off with the real reason her mom died. If I hadn't had her to hold onto, I would have melted into the floor and died there.

Elle started crying big salty tears.

"I'm sorry, Ladyface. I know that wasn't what you wanted to hear." I stayed quiet in her ear.

264

"That there's a little bit of good left out there? That my mom had it and you're trying to find it?" She let out one huge sob but the end was laced with the slightest bit of laughter. "It's the only thing you could have told me, Cole. I've never been proud of my mom. I've never thought anything above worms about Jimmy. But now…" Her voice was gaining strength even as she trailed off. "You gave her back to me."

She turned and kissed my collarbone. My whole body shuddered.

"At what price?" I let go of her shoulder and gently traced her face.

She jerked away at first then stilled herself back into my palm. Her wide eyes found mine and her bottom lip quivered until I stilled it with my thumb.

"Look at what she did to you," I whispered and had to consciously keep myself from digging my hands into Elle to make sure she was still real. "I'd kill her if she wasn't dead already."

It was Elle's turn to shudder as her eyes left me and darted toward the bedroom.

"I just want her gone." Her voice shook a little. "And then I want you to make me forget she ever existed."

"With pleasure." I shot her a shy smile. "On both counts."

"They're building that parking garage over by the university." Horse cleared his throat behind us. "We've got about two hours of darkness left." He came over and crouched next to me. "How you doing, Fucktart?"

"Better now." Her hand skated along my arm then laced into my fingers and squeezed.

"I'll never forgive myself for running out, for leaving the door open."

For a second my temper raged inside me, an inferno at his words, but then I caught those big chocolate eyes dancing with tears. He cared for her as if she were a precious gem and he'd added the weight of protecting something so valuable to his shoulders without question.

I adjusted a little so I could lean on him. He sucked in a deep breath waiting for the sucker punch that would follow but I just turned and pressed my lips to the back of his shoulder. He blew that same breath out and shifted his weight to lean into me.

"Are we getting rid of the hellcat or are we all gonna sit around and sing *Kumbaya* or some shit? Personally, I don't think it's the most fitting song for this situation. Maybe *Move Bitch*?" Conrad spoke up from behind us and this time I really did think about throttling someone, using his snark as an excuse to let my fury free.

But then Elle giggled.

I managed a smile as I bent to kiss each of her knuckles one by one then reach to do the same with the tip of her nose.

"It seems we have a date with a construction site."

Cole

Conrad, Horse and I stood back and surveyed the site. Nothing seemed out of place, besides our footprints in the loose dust. Siobhan had fit too easily into the mold for the concrete pillars they'd be pouring soon. Horse had suffocated her and then carefully wrapped her in a sheet, making the only DNA she took with her into the parking garage Elle's.

That ate at me a little bit but aside from cutting off Siobhan's hands, I didn't really have a choice. And with dawn approaching there just wasn't time.

"So this is going to work?" Conrad asked as he pulled Horse back and wound around his body.

"In theory," I sighed.

"Has before," Horse echoed.

"The footprints?" he asked, his voice stronger than I would have guessed as he leaned his chin on Horse's shoulder.

"Compressed air." I grabbed the can I'd shoved in my waistband and started spraying, fading the footprints into nothing.

"Is it wrong that this kind of turned me on?" Conrad asked as we turned back toward the car.

I couldn't help but laugh. Slowly but surely he was winning me over.

"Making a body or hiding a body?" I asked as I slid into the driver's seat.

"I'm not gonna lie, I'm gonna do everything in my power to block out what she was doing to Elle Belle when we walked in, but the way Horse handled her…"

I gulped and I couldn't help but look over at Horse. There was a darkness to his eyes that hadn't been there the past few days which made me swallow hard.

"I mean, I feel safe." Conrad leaned forward from the backseat and wrapped his arms around Horse. Horse softened a little but there was still a vacant ghost hiding behind his eyes.

"It was that bad, huh?" I murmured as we backed out with my headlights off.

"Seeing her with Elle made me feel like the world was ending. Like there'd never be light again. I can't help but feel like I've made a lot of really bad choices." Horse settled into Conrad's grip but his face stayed crinkled.

"We *have* made a lot of really bad choices, Horse." I bit my lip and sucked in a deep breath. "But I think we finally have a chance to do something right."

"What?"

I'd piqued his curiosity but his face was still rough as he stared out at the dark street. The way he looked out and the way he worked on his big bottom lip was easy enough to read. He knew exactly which *something* I was referring to. I swerved off the road and slammed on the brakes.

"Tell me that you didn't know!" I looked over and in the faint pink of sunrise, watched as he shifted away, unable to meet my eyes.

"Didn't know what?" he grunted.

"Don't play me like that," I snarled.

He blew out a deep breath and shifted on his hip to turn away from me.

"You did? Really?" I banged the wheel and both the guys jumped. "Fuck, Horse! And you let him?"

"What was I supposed to do?" He spun back toward me and his hands curled into my t-shirt.

"What's going on?" Conrad scrambled to keep hold of Horse's heaving shoulders.

268

"They're kids, Horse." I knew deep down his hands had been tied unless he decided to wring Mickey's neck with them. That didn't stop me from wanting to wring his. "They're someone's daughter. Someone's sister. They're sweet, innocent and pure like Elle. That's why Jimmy did what he did. That's why Simone..."

"What do you mean? What in the hell is this about?" Conrad shot forward, jostling the seats. "Why are you talking about Elle's mom?"

"She was trying to save innocent girls. She was trying to keep families together. And she was doing it for Elle." I slumped back in my seat.

"And now we're going to do it," Conrad said matter of fact.

"Yeah, we are. And I need to know if you're in Horse. I need to feel in my bones that you're with me and with Elle..."

"And with me," Conrad interrupted.

"And Conrad," I picked up seamlessly, suddenly certain that he had a place in this life every bit as much as Elle. "And that when we go at Mickey and when things get dark that you're with us."

Horse lunged at me, his hand sliding behind my neck and he pulled me to his lips. His lips tangled with mine with an urgency I'd never felt before. He pushed and pulled on me but then abruptly pulled away, leaving his forehead to mine. He was breathing heavy and his eyes were squeezed tight.

"I'm always with you. Forever," he breathed the word. "No matter who I'm with or who you're with, I'm *always* with you." He sat back and dropped his head into his hands. "I'm sorry I didn't do right by you. I'm sorry that I fucked up while you were gone."

I reached over and rubbed along his spine.

"Help me understand, Horse?" I made sure to keep the bitter out of my voice.

"Me too," Conrad was less gracious in the backseat.

"I lost my way." His shoulders heaved and I wondered if he might actually cry. I swallowed hard, Horse's tears had a way of splitting my soul. "You were the compass, Cole. You know where north is. I just know how to stay alive."

I rubbed a little harder on his shoulders trying to keep them from shaking.

"It's okay." I patted his back. "We'll make it okay."

"Does this ever get easier?" Conrad grumbled in the backseat.

"I don't know, Conrad." I blew out a deep breath. "I sure as fuck know this isn't going to be the easy part."

"I was talking about seeing my main salami desperate for a different deli sandwich." Sarcasm was thick in his voice. "But the whole Mr. Fix-It thing is important too."

"It sounds like you have a plan." Horse perked up.

"Yeah. And buckle up, it's gonna be a bumpy ride." I turned on the car and flipped on the lights as I pulled back onto the road. "We've gotta go pick up Jimmy Ponies then we have a date with Mickey Maloney."

That was enough to silence the car. I knew the feeling. My insides alternated between frozen completely and bubbling like a cauldron. But this was the only play we had.

"I'm not letting him go in there." Horse shot a look back at Conrad.

"He's not going to. He's gonna take the train back to Elle."

"I like that." Horse hummed and I saw Conrad smirk in my rearview mirror. "But where does that leave us?"

"We're buying Elle time. We're giving Mickey the only thing that will distract him from her."

"Jimmy," Horse finished.

"But I thought he was a good guy in the end?" Conrad asked.

"Yeah." I found myself nodding. "I don't know that Elle means much to him, but her mom sure as hell did. It was his idea to do this for her because it was what Simone would want. It's what she did, after all."

"Mickey's gonna kill him," Horse's voice was low but steady.

"I think he knows that." I remembered the look in his eyes as he made the plan.

"But it's him or Elle isn't it?" Conrad was quiet too.

"If we get really fucking lucky," I answered past the lump in my throat.

The car was silent as we drove toward Elmwood Park. Siobhan's body was gone but her ghost would take a lot longer to fade. And the shadow of Mickey… Well it wasn't a shadow at all. He was looming just like the John Hancock building.

Horse was the first to break the silence when we pulled in and parked at the train station.

"For the record, I'm glad you're gonna go take care of our little Fucktart but I don't like letting you out of my sight right now." He reached back and grabbed Conrad's knee.

"You can say more things like that."

I could hear the smile in Conrad's voice.

"When I told Cole, no matter who I was with, I was with him, I was picturing our life. Together. And how Cole fit into it. How Elle and Cole fit into it. But it was us."

"Get out of the car," Conrad commanded with something carnal in his voice. "Get out!" He shouted when Horse didn't budge.

Finally, Horse slid out, leaving Conrad to shove the front seat out of his way. The second he was free of the car, he pushed Horse against the car shaking the whole damn thing. I clutched at the steering wheel as I rolled my eyes.

Conrad found Horse's lips and the set of his jaw while he kissed him was enough to say how much adoration was passing back and forth. When they kept at it, my stomach knotted with want for Elle. I wanted to kiss her. I wanted to breathe life into her, I wanted to live the future she'd magically made appear.

I got out of the car and went to sit on the hood. After they pulled apart breathless, I cleared my throat.

"This better be good, Cole," Conrad spoke against Horse's lips. "Like someone touching someone else's dick again good."

"I need you to tell Elle something." I looked off in the distance. I couldn't quite meet his eyes.

271

"What?"

"Tell her I love her, okay?" I looked down at the calluses on my hand.

"Oh hell no." He broke away from Horse and stood by my knees, shoving his hands on his hips as he flexed and puffed up in front of me.

"Thanks for nothing." I went to shove off the hood and circled away from him when he stopped me cold with a truly strong and sturdy stiff arm to the chest.

"The first time that girl hears *I love you* it's coming from your lips, not mine." He let his arm go a little limp. "I'll tell her that she's everything, though. I'll tell her that you're trying to prove it."

I couldn't help but smirk as I studied his shoes.

"That'll work," I added as I rubbed the back of my neck.

He grabbed my shoulder and pushed me back so that I could meet his eyes. "You get back and you tell her that. She needs to hear it." He smiled at me for the very first time and my heart thudded because of Conrad. Not because I wanted him but at the idea that both Horse and I had happy and it was worth fighting for. "Make sure you bring him with you." He jerked his chin toward Horse then seamlessly turned toward the station.

Horse slid next to me on the hood of the car and we watched Conrad buy a ticket then get on a train. He blew out a loud exaggerated breath as the train pulled away.

"Cole, you ever feel like you're saying goodbye for the last time?"

"Every time." Something pummeled at my insides.

It kept going crazy as we drove to Elmwood. Jimmy was sitting on Nonno's step watching the sunrise. The rumble of the engine told him we were there but he didn't flinch. I watched him closely from the car not wanting to interrupt.

The sky was turning into warm and liquid gold over the top of the neighborhood houses. There was a pair of shoes strung over the power lines in the middle of the street and, as we sat there, the pink faded around them so they could shimmer too.

272

"Should we do this?" Horse asked softly, noticing the moment enveloping us.

"Not yet." I leaned back and stayed fixated on the sky as blue filtered into the rays of gold.

I was taking a man to the slaughterhouse and unlike all the times before, it felt weird. Wrong even. Maybe I did have the moral compass Horse had accused me of earlier.

Right now, Jimmy was just a man. He played with a pen and a scrap of paper in between taking in the sunrise panoramas. The views were likely the last ones he'd have of any space that wasn't Mickey's horrific lair. For a split second, I thought about killing him myself. It would serve Mick's purposes but I'd make it quick and painless. And somewhere like this, filled with the simple beauty of a new day washing over the same old street.

But I couldn't do it and make the plan work. Bile rose in my throat.

Finally he stood and Horse wordlessly stepped out to make room for him in the backseat. The heaviness in the car was almost stifling when I pulled away from the curb and pointed towards Mickey's.

There was nothing left to say. No words fit the situation. None ever could. It was a vacant blackness that settled in and wrapped around my soul. When I parked, it threatened to consume me. We filed out, with me lording over Jimmy as we'd planned. Monster playing the executioner rather than man saving his world. The role made me choke back puke.

"Cole, you have to give this to her," Jimmy said urgently and under his breath as he shoved the paper he'd been toying with into my hand.

As discreetly as I could, I looked down to see lines and lines scribbled across a page but it wasn't the chicken scratch that caught my attention. It was a doodle on the flip side.

The Celtic cross was familiar, too familiar. I remembered inking it into Connor a few weeks ago. I still had Elle's intricate copy. One of the few drawings of hers I could keep without the fear of her identity being figured out.

"Jimmy, why did you draw this cross?"

273

"Drawing it helps me feel like I have some control over what he's gonna do to me." He jerked his chin at the front door.

"What do you mean? This symbol means something to Mickey?" I asked as dread settled in and tore at my stomach.

"Yeah, he chose this a few years ago, as *his* mark. He was on some cocaine bender and decided that he'd seen God. God told him the way to ascend and follow in his footsteps. It's when this whole madness started." He blew out a deep breath. "I feel like facing that symbol is a way of facing his madness within."

"It can't be a coincidence," I murmured to myself recalling each line as I carved it into skin.

"What can't?" Horse asked trying to pull me out of the haze that was settling in.

"It's too exact. Too perfect," I continued muttering.

"Cole, come on. Talk to me."

"Three weeks. He's known for at least three weeks." I could barely get the words out.

I remembered parading Elle into Fulton Market Kitchen. Introducing her to Connor. The whole evening was etched into my memory as the night I'd learned more, the night I tripped over myself and fell in love with her. But now it had a bitter rancid taste to match what was happening to my stomach.

"Who's known what?" Horse got loud and forceful.

"Looks like Judas finally came to his reckoning." A new voice was behind us, every bit as cold as my insides had gone.

"Yeah, we've got Jimmy." Horse puffed up at the kid that was standing behind us. The same one I'd threatened to kill weeks ago. Now I really thought about it.

He looked me over and when my shoulders slumped his wicked laughter pierced the early morning street.

"No, I'm talking about Cole."

274

Elle

The soft knock at the door startled me just as every sound outside had for the past three hours. They'd been gone so long it was easy to convince myself any number of things had happened. Horrible vicious things just like what had happened in here last night. If riding in the car with her corpse hadn't made me heave, I wouldn't be stuck here alone and with my whole world missing in action.

Whoever it was knocked again, still gently at the door.

"Elle? Elle, are you in there?" It was a vaguely familiar voice and I stood up from the couch and crept over to the door. "Elle, it's Connor. Cole needed to get a message to you and apparently, I'm the only one that knows you're in the city."

That was all it took for me to rush toward the door and whip it open.

"Oh, my God, is he okay?" Panic welled in my chest and I couldn't hide it in my voice.

"Yeah, everything's okay but Mickey knows where you are. You have to come with me."

"You know about all of that?" I blew out a deep breath of relief knowing I could speak freely.

"All of it. Every last detail." He smiled warmly at me, reassuring the knots that had bundled up inside me.

"Let me just make sure they didn't forget anything." I forced myself into the bedroom even though I had to steady myself at the door.

"You okay?" Connor had followed me like a ninja, I jumped when his voice was right behind me, his breath warm on my neck.

But it wasn't his closeness that made my skin goose bump or hair stand on end.

"I just need to check that nothing from the body…" I cut myself off short and snapped my hands back over my mouth to try and reel the words back in.

"A body? That's good to know." He chuckled huskily behind me.

The reaction was so wrong I spun to look at him. He had wild and dark eyes, just like the eyes that would be forever etched in my brain. *Her* eyes were soulless like that. I went to scream, hoping that this time someone would hear, someone would come help, but he shot behind me and covered my mouth and nose in a swift movement. His other hand came to my throat and squeezed.

My hands flew to his hand and clawed, my body knowing the difference between his and Cole's touch instinctually. But hard as I clawed, hard as I dug, or tried to bite at his palm, I couldn't get free.

"Shhhhh." He nuzzled against the back of my head. "It'll all be over soon."

My vision was edging in like it usually did, the buzzing in my ears was back. But unlike Cole, that wasn't the moment that Connor let me gulp for air. He kept squeezing and my body started to respond to the lack of oxygen. Or rather stopped responding at all. I still batted at him but they were sluggish half-hearted movements.

"Almost there." He squeezed a little harder and all I could do was go limp with little more than a heartbeat left to move my body.

"Perfect." Connor's hand left my throat to fondle in his pocket. I still couldn't breathe with his hand stopping my nose and mouth from sucking in air. In the picture frame above the bed, the

276

blurry image of a man with a syringe registered just a moment before he carefully inserted the needle in my neck.

I wanted to scream at the pinch, or worse, at what it meant for me, but I couldn't. I couldn't move or breathe, I could only think of Cole and pray.

"Sleep under a China White sky for a little while, Elle. I'll see you on the other side," he whispered in my ear before planting a tiny kiss on the side of my head.

Just as Connor pulled the needle from my neck, my world went dark.

I didn't remember getting here, wherever here was. I couldn't shake the fog from my brain to figure it out.

Slowly, I made myself take stock of the situation. Whatever I was sitting on was warm and it moved up and down in shallow little bursts like my breathing. The room around me was dark, almost pitch black except for a few blood red lamps and flickering candles that cast an eerie light on faces. Lots of faces. They were all watching something just in front of me, something highlighted in a blinding spotlight.

The bright white was disorienting and the figures bathed in light blurred when I looked at them. I lifted my hands to rub my eyes, hoping it would help me see clearer.

"She wakes." A voice was right behind my ear, and the hiss of the words vibrated against my back.

I was sitting on someone's lap.

"Finally, I get to meet the perfect Elle Laroux." The man behind me spoke again, this time letting his hand wander freely across my body, grabbing my breast then diving between my thighs and stroking me through my shorts.

I screamed.

The figure I hadn't been able to make out on the floor before snarled and tried to shoot toward me. My eyes focused this time.

On Cole.

He was shackled and chained to the floor in front of him. It didn't stop him from trying to snap the steel and get to me.

"Not a fan of my hands on her, Cole?" The man behind me laughed and it was the most purely evil sound I'd ever heard.

"Don't you fucking touch her, Mick."

"It's us you want." I would recognize Jimmy's slimy tone anywhere but I couldn't hate it today, not when it came to my defense so vehemently.

"It's all of you."

He seamlessly stood up from behind me, depositing me on a chair that felt more like a throne.

"I want the ledger from you." He walked right up to Jimmy and without hesitating, kicked him in the face. I gasped and my hands shot to my mouth as Jimmy's body wobbled. He only managed the most pitiful sound before he crashed to the floor. It wasn't until that moment that I noticed he was tethered like Cole.

"I want loyalty from you." He wheeled on Cole as fury peaked in his voice.

Micky crashed his elbow across Cole's jaw then his hands flashed to his throat and squeezed. His knuckles turned white as he squeezed and Cole turned a beet red. Once or twice Cole sputtered, a deathly sound mixed with little droplets of blood.

"Stop!" I screamed without even thinking.

Mickey didn't even waver, he just turned to me and smiled.

"You've bedded Judas, you know he likes this. He gets off on almost-killing you. Wanna know where he learned it?" He raised his eyebrows and smiled before turning back to Cole.

He turned darker, twisting and bucking against Mickey's grip, as Mickey slowly laid him down on the floor. When Cole was flat, Mickey straddled him with his back to me.

I shoved against the chair, desperate to spring to Cole's defense but big hands wrapped around me. Big hands that I recognized.

"Horse, let me go. He's going to kill Cole."

He said absolutely nothing in response, his grip simply got tighter.

"Oh sweet lass," Mickey said as he slammed Cole's head into the floor then let him go. "I would never kill him that quickly." He rose up from Cole and turned toward me, leaving Cole to roll to his side, gasping for air.

"You're going to kill him though, aren't you?" I asked, my voice less shaky than I would have guessed.

"Maybe." He shrugged then leaned over me where I was pinned to the chair. "Despite what people think about me, I'm not an unforgiving man. I'm willing to come to a compromise if I get what I want."

"And just what do you want?" I tried to shove my face into his but Horse still held me tight.

"Like I said, the ledger from Jimmy, unless of course you have it. Loyalty once and for all from Cole." His eyes glinted in the weird light cast from the mixture of the spotlight and the ambient red glow.

"And?" I could feel the weight of something more in the room.

"And you of course." His hand slipped up my leg, easily sliding up the leg of my cutoff shorts and a single finger flicked my clit.

"Don't touch me!" I screamed and kicked against him. Horse still held me but now I felt his fingers digging in. He was trying to diffuse the situation rather then run head on at Mickey.

"When you're mine, I'll touch you wherever I want, whenever I want to." He pushed his finger into me and despite Horse's unspoken warning, I went wild, writhing and flailing in the seat.

"I'll never be yours!"

Cole weakly fought against his bonds.

"We'll see about that." He pulled his finger from me and pushed it between his lips. "I think I can make you."

"You won't make me *anything*!" I spat in his face as soon as I screamed.

"Watch." He wiped my spit from his face and turned on Jimmy and Cole. "You say stop and I'm assuming it means you're willing to make a deal."

He started in on Jimmy, fists flying over and over to his abdomen like Jimmy was a punching bag in the gym. Then he moved higher and worked over on his jaw. When a few teeth scattered across the floor I almost screamed.

"Calm down, Fucktart, we have to let this play out."

I wanted to scream at Horse but then another wicked laugh caught my attention. I turned to the side to find Connor draped over a chair, casually kicking his foot where it was hung over the armrest.

"This is great." He smiled so wide it distorted his words. "I wish I had popcorn."

Jimmy screamed a blood-curdling sound and my eyes snapped back to the floodlit stage. Things had gotten much worse for my stepdad. An eye was swollen shut already as blood trailed down from his lips where he was crumpled on the floor. Mickey kicked him again in the back then looked up to meet my eyes overtop of the suffering body.

"No feelings for dear old dad?" He made a horrifying silly face as he let loose one more kick, this time into Jimmy's balls.

Jimmy vomited a mix of blood in response and I felt puke come up in my mouth.

"Fine. Have it your way, Elle."

He walked from Jimmy over to Cole and latched into his hair, yanking his head back. With Cole open and vulnerable to him, Horse's fingers dug into me again. I latched onto his hands and dug right back.

Mickey twisted Cole's face so that the already bruising spot was facing upwards. In an animalistic move full of twisting, writhing muscles, he crashed his elbow down on Cole's jaw three times in quick succession. Then he repeated it on his cheekbone. The entire room heard the answering crunch.

But Cole managed to stay quiet and his eyes focused on me until the moment he couldn't open his right eye anymore.

"Nothing?" Mickey looked over at me. "Not for the man who hid you? Who forfeited his life for you?" He cocked his head evaluating me. "Heartless." He purred with approval. "I like heartless. Siobhan does too."

I flinched when he said her name. I couldn't help it.

"That name means something to you?" He lifted his eyebrows up. "Interesting," he mused.

"She mentioned a body," Connor piped up from beside me.

"A body? Cole…" he turned back and had the audacity to chastise Cole like he'd spilled on the carpet.

Before any of us could respond, Mickey grabbed a knife from his boot, raised it high and plunged it into Cole's thigh. His answering scream made my blood run cold.

"No." Horse finally shot out from behind me. "He didn't kill her."

"What is this, Horse?" Mickey rounded on him.

The word *stop* was on the tip of my tongue but Jimmy silenced me from his pile of filth on the floor. "Don't Elle. Your mom fought for so much more."

I swallowed the words but I couldn't swallow the tears anymore.

"I killed her." Horse pushed himself in Mickey's face and tried to stand even taller in front of the devil himself.

Mickey looked over Horse but didn't say anything. Instead, he grabbed a gun he'd had hidden in the back waistband, pointed it at Horse and pulled the trigger.

My heart stopped. My breath was gone more now than it had been when I blacked out earlier. I couldn't hear Connor's laugh or Cole's screech from the floor until it was too late. It wasn't until the word *Stop!* flew from my lips that the world snapped to.

Horse had stumbled back and was holding his thigh, the matching spot to where a blade still stuck out of Cole's. He was alternating between grunts and cries of pain but he was alive and trying to stop the bleeding.

I bolted from the chair toward him but Mickey caught me before I could get to him. His arms wrapped around my midsection and towed me back against his body. A warm gun pressed against my arm and a stony erection against my ass. I scrambled wildly against his grip.

"I heard a stop, did I not?"

I audibly gulped but didn't answer him.

281

"That's what I thought." His words danced against my ear. "So here we are, making a deal." He nibbled on my earlobe. "I'll get Horse medical attention if you play ball." I stilled. "There's even a way Cole lives through this."

I turned in his arms and looked him dead in the face.

"Tell me. Now," I demanded despite all three wounded men yelling *No!* at me.

"Choose who dies and be mine, simple as that." He smiled like the Cheshire Cat. "I trade one of those worthless sacks for you. Eye for an eye has always been poignant if you ask me."

Cole screamed at me, weird distorted sounds, most likely butchered because of his mangled jaw.

"I won't be yours," I snarled back chancing a look over at both of my men.

"Then kill them both and let me taste you once." He shrugged still holding on to me.

"I kill them both and you let me go, simple as that?" I cocked my head back, sure there was some trick. I looked over to where Cole was still screaming, now maybe crying as he watched this unfold.

"Yes, my little murderer. I let you go, sure that my secrets will die with you some day, the way they'd die with these two." He shifted his grip on me, twisted my body so I was squarely between Cole and Jimmy then snaked his arms out along mine. He placed the gun in my hands then adjusted my fingers just so. "We'll just cock this like so..." He guided my hands. "We aim by lining this sight up with this sight." He adjusted the pistol so that it was aiming directly at the lamp in front of us. "Then you decide your future."

Cole

The pain that radiated from my cheek was consuming me, coming in waves as it throbbed like a goddamned marching band was playing on my face and stabbing me in time with their rhythm. The bone was broken. I knew it without checking. The crunch and the searing pain were familiar in that sickening way. It ping-ponged off the ache in the back of my skull from earlier.

There were no words for the spot that a knife still stuck in my thigh. It was torture. It was lightning. It was what I always expected hell to feel like. And I couldn't tell if taking the knife out would make it better or worse. I didn't have a choice anyway.

My wrists burned where they were bound. I'd been fighting so hard to get free I'd broken skin. Now the saltiness of the metal stung against my warm blood.

It all paled in comparison to seeing Elle with a gun.

Mickey wrapped around her like a snake begging for her to sin was stomach turning, but her, my sweet, innocent, perfect Ladyface, with her hands around a pistol was far worse. That she was bargaining with Mickey, that she'd said stop, was the torturous hot poker to my soul.

"Elle." My voice was rough, blood gurgled in my throat. "Take it back," I begged.

I needed her to. It couldn't all be in vain.

"I can't Cole." Her voice broke. "I can't see you or Horse in pain."

"This is just the beginning," Mickey murmured and rubbed his nose into her hair.

I jerked against the chains that held me despite the pain it shot through every inch of my body. The cry that came from my throat wasn't intentional. I didn't think any sounds I made anymore were. If only I were free, I'd fight my way out of here.

Mickey had been waiting. He'd known Elle was with me since that first date night. Connor was placed at the restaurant with the sole purpose of recognizing Elle if she came in to view her work. That I'd chosen that place freely was a really fucked up twist of fate.

We'd been some game that Mickey and Siobhan played. He sat back and waited for us while she went out and hunted us, knowing that soon enough we'd all collide in one hell of a nuclear explosion.

I just didn't expect that nuclear explosion to be Mickey waiting right inside the door with a single question for Horse—*are you with me or against me?*—and then a baseball bat to the back of my head.

I woke chained to the floor and brass knuckles to my stomach. Again. Horse was watching from behind Mickey and the fact that he couldn't sit in his normal chair to the side was enough for me. He was at war with himself; loyal soldier vs. loyal friend. I wanted to tell him that this was okay, he needed to live, he needed to take care of Elle if things went sideways. He needed to protect himself so we weren't two pillars in a parking garage. But then Mickey punched me full frontal and I swallowed a tooth as my lip split across the ones that stayed in place.

I'd been in pain when Connor had come in carrying a limp blonde body and everything in Satan's lair fell away. Mick sat down and Connor placed Elle on his lap then we waited. I couldn't feel anything after that.

Mickey helped himself to her drugged out body. He explored the dips and curves that were mine. He peeked at the flesh that should only be on display for me and palmed between my little cherry thighs.

284

When I finally roared out in fury, he simply twisted her face towards her and kissed her. Hard. His lips explored hers, his tongue lapped on her closed lips trying to coax them open, then they started down her neck as his hand slid up her shirt and he yanked on her nipple.

"I'll kill you, Mick," I shouted and he just laughed as his other hand wrapped around and moved similarly on her other breast.

"I have no doubt, Cole. That's why you've always been one of my most prized possessions." He laughed as his hands slid down her taut little tummy and beneath the waistband of her shorts. I fought wildly as her shorts started moving in time with his hands. "It's why you aren't dead yet."

"Kill me and let her go!" I demanded, blood spattering from my lips.

"Let this little cunny go?" He was still massaging against her, or in her, I couldn't tell. "Not without something in return."

"What do you want in return? I'll give it to you," I begged, broken on my knees.

"You'll see," he answered before he started kissing up along her neck.

If only I'd known how much worse it was going to get.

"Take a shot," Mickey whispered in her ear coaxing her to try the weapon out and pulling me back to the scene in front of me.

"I can't." Elle crumbled beneath his hands, hers falling away from the gun.

As bad as things were here in the den, of all things disgusting that happened, that pulled a tiny sliver of hope into my heart. Elle would always be Elle, perfect and pure, the reason for sacrificing everything.

"Elle," Mickey started as he roughly grabbed her hands and forced them back to the gun, "I know we just met but do you think you can toy with me? That I shouldn't be taken seriously?"

"No." Her voice was strong but I still wanted to reach out and lend her any ounce of strength I had left.

285

Hell, I just wanted to touch her one more time. I wanted to hold her while I told her that I loved her just like Conrad told me to.

"Good. So then you know you need to fucking choose," he hissed in her ear.

The room stood still, all eyes fixed on Elle as she took a million deep breaths with the gun outstretched.

I chanced a look over to Horse and his eyes were shifting from her to me and back again while he held the wound on his thigh. He jerked his chin toward Mickey and immediately I knew what he was asking.

Should I get the gun?

Part of me wanted to say yes. Horse could lunge at him and wrestle the gun free then he could start shooting. But even if he managed not to squish Elle, or shoot her in the process, and even if there were a full round of bullets in the gun, he wouldn't get far.

Watching Horse die with a bullet from Connor in his back would be the only way to make this whole debacle worse. Getting out was always what stopped me.

"Goddamnit, princess. Shoot someone!" Mickey roared behind Elle, shaking her violently.

When she didn't pull the trigger, he ripped the weapon from her hands to walk toward Jimmy. She fell to her knees without his support and for the first time, I saw Elle shake with fear. Every other time had been something else. Even Siobhan was more to shake the layer of ick off than terror. My scared Ladyface was a gut wrenching sight.

"It's this easy, Elle." Micky walked up to Jimmy and pointed the gun down at the distorted little ball of a body. "BOOM!" he yelled pretending to shoot him, then cocking back to soccer kick him in the ribs.

Tears started to fall down Elle's perfect little cheeks. Despite the pain I reached out for her, now so close, yet still so far away.

"Or this." Micky walked to me and kicked my hands back toward my body and held the gun at my temple. I couldn't fight

286

him, I just kept my eyes locked on Elle. "POW!" he shoved the gun into my head, jostling my whole body and making me cry out.

Mickey swiftly lunged down to where the blade stuck in my leg and twisted. I howled a sound that made me sick even though it was my own and the edge of my vision went white.

Bright white.

Like the dress Elle wore the day I met her. The dress I had fisted up around her hips while I fucked her in the airplane bathroom. The dress that had framed her perfect little pussy when she masturbated for me. The dress that had been faintly see-through when she agreed to come home with me.

Once upon a time, Elle had told me I needed to stop being hung up on heaven and hell. That they didn't exist. She was wrong. That dress was heaven. She was heaven.

And this is what I'd done to her.

I twisted enough that she filled my hazy line of sight. She sagged on her knees, with big, fat crocodile tears streaming haphazardly down her cheeks. Her hair was still tinged with pink and her cheek sported the angry gashes from Siobhan. The curves of her body had been assaulted by both her and Mickey.

Never had anything in my life been so clear. I'd dragged an angel down from heaven and forced her to burn in hell. I'd broken her wings without ever really seeing them unfurl. And for what? Love? Creatures like me didn't deserve it.

Mickey wrapped around her shoulders and violently hauled her back to standing. He yanked on her hair to level her gaze once she was standing. He slapped the gun back in her hands.

"Fucking pick now or it's you that's getting the bullet!" he screamed in her ear, spit splattering onto her delicate skin.

She jerked and cringed with every single word like they were the kill shots. This was causing her a deeper type of pain than I felt and I couldn't stand it anymore. There was only one thing to do. Only one way to fix it now.

"Elle," I breathed her name like it was the last bit of life in my lungs. And in some ways, it was. "I need you to do me a favor." I blew out a breath, still spattering a little bit of blood across my lips. "One last one, okay?"

287

Her eyes went wide and I saw her little chest expand as she held a breath.

"Ladyface, I need you to kill me."

Elle

"Ladyface, I need you to kill me." Cole's voice was soft and warm despite the horrific thing he said.

"Never!" I screeched, feeling tears dance on my lips.

"Ladyface, this is all my fault." He was having a hard time with words and I didn't know if it was his disfigured face or the emotion he had to be waging war against. "You shouldn't be here. You should be in a beautiful studio in Seattle, living a beautiful life with Conrad and some banker or shit. You should grow old and tell your grandkids how the worst thing that ever happened to you was some jerk never texted you back after joining the mile high club."

He was pleading with me. Begging for me to go free. Begging to die. My insides were going to explode and send shrapnel spray about the room. My whole body vibrated with terror.

"See? He's making it easy," Mickey whispered in my ear and the words were hot against my skin, almost burning, and his breath smelled like the almost dead bodies in front of me. "Kill him. Pull the trigger and watch the blood seep into the floor."

My stomach heaved.

"Kill Jimmy," Horse piped up from where he was still awkwardly propped up against a couch. "We can all go back home if you pull that trigger, Elle." His voice was ragged, desperate like my insides.

Cole looked over at him and sadness filled his eyes. I got the feeling he was saying *you know that's not true.* I knew I was right when Horse started bellowing.

"No! Cole, no!" Tears pooled almost instantly in his eyes. "We can." His voice broke. "All four of us," he whimpered.

"Take care of her, Horse." Cole tried to smile. "Fall in love with him. Let yourself, okay?"

He turned back to me.

"Jimmy doesn't deserve to die, Elle, but I do." His breathing was getting more labored, his eyes less vibrant. "I've always been a selfish monster but I really took the cake with you. I took you when I knew you weren't really supposed to be mine. I broke you when I knew I was supposed to be careful."

I thought I saw tears start to fall but his face was too distorted to tell. Or maybe it was just that my eyes were so blurry from the furious crying that I couldn't see straight.

"Ladyface, take that gun from Mickey."

Mickey was all too happy to shove it in my hand then push my wobbly body toward Cole.

"I'm gonna talk you through this." His voice was trying to stay smooth and soothing but he couldn't quite manage anymore.

I burst with one loud long rough sob before containing myself the tiniest bit.

"Both hands on it, okay?"

I didn't budge unless the wild tremors racking my body counted.

"Come closer."

That I could manage, so I stepped up to him. He lifted his bound hands to mine, blood tinged the skin beneath the cuffs marring the beautiful artwork up and down his forearms. The metal of his restraints clinked as he used what little mobility he had to wrap my hands around the gun. He continued to cradle them as he lifted the gun to point directly between his eyes.

His gorgeous green eyes that spoke poetry to my insides and forever would.

"Cole, no!" Horse howled. "Elle, please!" he begged but he also didn't move to stop me.

290

My head snapped toward Horse but all too quickly Cole was gently shaking my hands.

"Hey, there." He looked up at me and despite everything managed a smile. His dimple had disappeared and it felt like a hole in my heart.

"Cole, please," I cried then let the most painful, ragged sobs shake my body.

"Conrad made me promise to tell you myself," he started then tears interrupted him.

I couldn't help but fall to my knees in front of him. He held my hands fast to his forehead.

"Cole," I moaned.

"Ladyface, I love you. I love you so fucking much you split my heart in two. One half you take with you. Everywhere. And the other half just hangs around beating for you."

I hung my head, bawling, shoulders shaking as my fingers went numb where they wrapped around the gun.

"That'll never change," he whispered. "And that's why you have to do this."

"I love you, too." The words spewed out, a weird mixture of salvation and destruction. "That's why I can't."

"Look at me." I felt him bob and weave beneath the gun. I managed to lift my head enough to see him. "Let me die knowing that I did one thing right by the woman that meant everything to me. Please." His words were becoming harder to make out. It wasn't just the pain and the fear, or the fact that he was trying to be gentle with me even here, even now, it was that I was losing Cole. He was slipping away from me whether I liked it or not.

"Yes, please. I think I'd like to see this play out this way," Mickey purred, once again too close to my ear.

Horse was wailing in the background like he'd been shot all over again. He was the external soundtrack to my internal turmoil.

Jimmy hadn't been worth shit growing up but in the end, he lived and died for my mom. My mom that was a loving mother after all. A mother that Cole had given back to me. My perfect, precious Cole that really was offering to die for me.

"How do you kill someone, Cole?" My voice trembled every bit as badly as I did.

"You pull the trigger," he said softly. "And then you remind yourself you had no other choice."

"How do I kill you, Cole?" My voice was even more broken, just like my insides.

"You pull the trigger." He was still every bit as tender with me as he'd ever been. "And then you remind yourself that you did it to set us both free."

My giant, violent sobs took over again and I crumpled further in front of him. Only my arms were outstretched where he held them to his forehead. The only part of my body that wasn't going numb was the skin he still held. The only sound in my ears was Horse crying and the echo of the destruction of my soul.

I wanted to keep him. Forever. I wanted to go back and wear the white dress I'd worn the first day that I met him as I married him on the beach in some foreign country where Mickey and our pasts couldn't touch us. I wanted to feel him pressed against me again, his hands around my throat and my life his to take.

My life that he would always cherish.

The way he was doing right now.

Setting me free the only way he had left.

I wanted to keep him.

He was my happily ever after.

"You are my everything, Ladylove." His voice was so soft, so warm, so perfect. The new nickname was what I'd get tattooed on my skin to mark this day.

The day that I realized that *I* was the selfish monster as I sat up, gripped the gun with authority and lined up the sights just as Mickey had taught me then pulled the trigger.

Boom.

Fade to black.

Made in the USA
Columbia, SC
11 September 2020